A Season for
Living

A Season for
Living

A Novel by

Susan Willis Updegraff

iUniverse, Inc.
Bloomington

A Season for Living

iUniverse books may be ordered through booksellers or by contacting:

iUniverse
1663 Liberty Drive
Bloomington, IN 47403
www.iuniverse.com
1-800-Authors (1-800-288-4677)

ISBN: 978-1-4620-5173-1 (sc)
ISBN: 978-1-4620-5175-5 (hc)
ISBN: 978-1-4620-5174-8 (ebk)

Printed in the United States of America

iUniverse rev. date: 11/08/2011

This book is dedicated to my husband Don,
my daughters, Ashleigh Young Hynes, Paige Young Atchison
and Rebecca Young Parker
and to my beautiful granddaughters, Elizabeth Horne, Emily Horne,
Jessica Parker, Caden Updegraff and Matilda Updegraff.
Our first grandson is due to arrive in February 2011

Special thanks to my precious step-children,
Kristen, Miller and Heather Updegraff
for their encouragement and support.

You all light up my life.

Endless thanks to my life-long friend, Trudy Kitchin Woodard
who lovingly did the first edit of this book.
She is my prayer warrior and one of the finest
people I have ever known.

CHAPTER 1

*C*HARLOTTE SAT IN THE COMFORTABLE chair on the veranda of her Ansley Park home in Atlanta enjoying the early fall afternoon sun. The tall oak trees were beginning to turn shades of red and gold, and the formal gardens at the back of their home displayed the exquisite rhododendron and hibiscus blossoms. The scarlet crepe myrtles swayed in the gentle breeze. The smells in the back yard reminded her of her childhood in Roswell, a rural farm community north of Atlanta. She spent long summer days and fall afternoons after school outside romping through the woods, climbing trees, and having outdoor tea parties with her younger sisters, Anne and Nancy. Those days seemed two lifetimes away. She closed her eyes and took a deep breath, savoring the memories and the warmth that the sun so generously shared.

She had married John Wellington, the only son of Grant and Elizabeth Wellington, on October 30, 1945. Grant was the founder of Georgia Life Insurance Company in 1930. Their wealth and influence in Atlanta were well known, and the status had thrust Charlotte into unfamiliar territory when they were married three years earlier. Charlotte and John were both thirty-two years old when they married, and now at thirty-five she was expecting their first child. Grant and

Elizabeth were thrilled to be finally having a grandchild. For a long time, they did not believe that blessing would be theirs to enjoy.

Charlotte sipped her iced tea and thought about what Belle would make for dinner. Belle was her childhood nanny, and Charlotte had insisted that she move in with them when she and John married.

Belle ran the household with an iron hand, managing the butler and the gardener while taking perfect care of Charlotte, as she always had. Belle was in her late forties and had worked for the Reed family since she was eighteen. She was slightly built with dark skin and dark brown eyes. Charlotte rarely saw her when the nanny wasn't dressed in a flowered shirtwaist dress and a white apron. Belle and the butler, Robert, lived on the lower level of their home in simple but comfortable quarters. Robert was Belle's nephew, her brother's son. Belle kept him on the straight and narrow and reminded him often how fortunate he was to be working in such a wonderful home. Robert was a handsome young black man who needed guidance, and Belle was just the person for the job.

It was 1948, and blacks were not accepted into society except in some type of service role. Belle's brother, Tom, had been arrested more than once protesting the treatment he and his friends received while doing something as simple as getting in line at a lunch counter in downtown Atlanta. Belle knew that Robert would be in the same kind of trouble if she didn't keep him in line. Belle had long ago accepted her place and just worked to do the best job she could for the Wellingtons. She often told Robert that if he ever expected to get anywhere in his life, he needed to work hard and accept things the way they were. Robert never really did, but he knew that he had a good job in a good home, and he loved his aunt Belle and wanted to please her. He knew the sacrifices she had made for him and the sadness she had endured in her life.

Charlotte was feeling especially tired and achy today. The baby was due anytime, and it was getting more and more difficult to sleep. As she stood to go into the house to find Belle, the pain radiated from her back all the way around her body. She knew it was time.

"Belle, where are you?"

Belle appeared in the doorway from the kitchen where she had been preparing dinner. "What is it, baby? Are you all right?"

"Would you call John? It's time for the baby to come," Charlotte whispered.

"He's on his way home now, baby," Belle said as she comforted Charlotte. "Your bags are packed. I'll get them, and John will be here any minute. I'm calling Dr. Daniel to let him know you are coming."

"Belle, what would I ever do without you?" Charlotte said as she walked into the small den at the rear of the house. She sat in the Queen Anne chair facing the fireplace and looked around the room, thinking how different her life was now compared to her life in Roswell. She was so in love with John and felt lucky to be able to give her child all the things she never had when she was growing up.

As with everything in the Wellingtons' lives, John and Charlotte's home was grand and elegant, and they entertained clients and prospects who were wealthy business owners from New York to Miami. Their Georgian Revival home was on almost an acre and was the location of many of the business parties the young Wellingtons hosted. The portico was protected by a handmade iron gate that, when opened, led to the side entry into the kitchen. The front of their home welcomed guests with a driveway flanked by dogwood trees. The front yard boasted a hundred-year-old magnolia tree and azaleas of every color. Manicured boxwoods across the front of the house completed the stylish appeal.

Within ten minutes, John walked up the front steps through the Georgian column-covered entry. He entered the wide foyer with its high ceilings and black-and-white floor tiles that echoed the elegance found throughout the home. The curved staircase with mahogany stairs and handrails, white risers, and beautifully carved white balusters confirmed the affluence of its occupants.

Belle met John in the foyer. "Mr. Wellington, it's time for the baby to come. Miss Charlotte is in the den. I'm getting her bag now, and I called Dr. Daniel to let him know you're coming."

John dropped his briefcase and rushed into the den where Charlotte was sitting. "Darling, let me help you. *Oh my God*, our baby is coming!" John slid his right arm around Charlotte and lifted her. He guided her to the portico at the side entry into the kitchen and gently helped her into the Bentley's front seat.

Belle appeared at the door with Charlotte's bags. As she put them into the back seat, she said, "Miss Charlotte, everything's gonna be all right. You know Belle is going to take care of everything here."

"I know you are, Belle. You always do," Charlotte said with a loving note in her voice as she softly touched Belle's hand. She looked up at Belle and saw tears in her eyes.

When the car pulled out of the driveway, Belle walked back into the house to find Robert. She walked into the foyer and could not see him. She looked in the living room to the right. It had a beautiful hand-carved alabaster fireplace and mantle and was rather formal, with two antique Chippendale sofas and two cherry Louis XV armchairs on each side of the fireplace. An antique Chinese tea cabinet was on the wall to the right as you entered the room. Belle walked into the dining room that was to the left of the foyer. It comfortably sat twelve guests under a nineteenth-century Regency-style chandelier. Chippendale dining chairs with embroidered fabric complemented the large mahogany, double-pedestal dining table. Robert was in the dining room washing the windows, a task Belle had given him three days earlier.

"Robert," Belle began urgently, "Miss Charlotte and Mr. Wellington have gone to the hospital. She's having the baby. We need to get all these windows washed before she gets home. You know there will be lots of company when that baby gets home."

"I know, I know, Aunt Belle," Robert said, already tired of the job he had just begun.

"Now when you are finished in the living room and dining room, get the library windows washed." Belle continued her instructions.

"Yes, ma'am, Aunt Belle." He sighed and went back to his work.

The library was behind the living room and had mahogany judges paneling with built-in bookcases on each side of the marble fireplace and down the back wall. The coffered ceiling gave the room a warmth and elegance with the dark brown leather tufted-back sofa and leather chairs and ottomans that matched. An antique English secretary stood on the wall across from the marble fireplace, and a Louis XV desk was in front of the three palladium windows that brought the morning light into the room. With the exception of the library, Charlotte had decorated the entire house herself.

As they pulled out of the driveway, Charlotte's mind wandered back to when she met John. In 1935, after college, she took the only job she could find, assistant to the president of Georgia Life Insurance Company. Charlotte Reed was independent and resourceful and had a very nice life. She lived in a small house that she rented near Peachtree Street just off of Fourteenth Street and drove a 1929 Ford sedan that she bought for $900. It gave her a sense of satisfaction to be making her own money and her own choices. Charlotte had managed to save $10,000 and she had a feeling of security that she rarely had growing up.

Her father, Jack, worked odd jobs and was a very ill-tempered alcoholic. It was her mother, Irene, who gave Charlotte and her two younger sisters, Anne and Nancy, their values and work ethic. Irene worked at the Roswell Mill when the girls were very young. Later she was the assistant to the president of the Bank of Roswell. Irene was smart and resourceful, and Charlotte always gave her mother credit for those qualities in herself. After her father's death in 1930, Charlotte and her sisters seemed to blossom along with Irene. She set her sights on college and did not stop until she graduated and had a job in Atlanta.

The day she met John, she was at her desk outside of his father's office. It was January 15, 1945. She knew about his appointment with Mr. Wellington. John had attended Harvard for his undergraduate and law degrees. He had joined a large law firm in Boston after graduation and was very successful in corporate law for the firm, but Charlotte overheard his dad talking about wanting him to come home and work at Georgia Life. John was very handsome, with dark brown hair and striking green eyes. His chiseled features, six-foot, broad-shouldered frame, intellect, and confidence made him an asset to the law firm in Boston. Charlotte knew that Mr. Wellington talked often about how brilliant John was and how much he wanted him to join the firm.

Charlotte announced his arrival, and John walked into his dad's office, tripping on the door as he walked in looking back at Charlotte.

"My God, Dad, who is that beautiful woman?" John exclaimed as he closed the door and sat down in the chair in front of his father's desk in the mahogany-paneled office in the Candler Building in downtown Atlanta.

"Why, that's Charlotte Reed, Son, my secretary," Mr. Wellington replied matter-of-factly. "She's been my secretary for ten years."

"Where have I been?" John joked to his dad.

"You've been in Boston, John. You haven't made many trips home since you left," Grant replied with a smile.

"She is the most beautiful woman I have ever seen!" John continued in his astonished tone.

After the meeting, Charlotte learned that John would be joining their firm as "in-house counsel." It never crossed her mind that he was smitten with her. She never thought of herself that way, even though she had many male suitors who courted her frequently. Her slender 5'7" frame, fair Irish skin, walnut-brown shoulder-length hair, and large brown eyes did make heads turn. Charlotte had beautiful lips, and she wore just the right color of red lipstick to accentuate that attractive feature. Her choice of stylish suits always looked polished and professional with a generous splash of class. But she was not interested in marriage at this point in her life. She might never be interested. Charlotte was enjoying her life in Atlanta. Gentlemen offered to take her to parties in New York and Washington. But she chose her associations very carefully and was very private about her personal life, never discussing it at work.

John graduated from Harvard undergraduate magna cum laude and from Harvard Law with distinction. He made a name for himself quickly with the Rich May law firm in Boston. He was very valuable to clients in their corporate litigation group. By 1944, John was a partner in the firm and could write his own ticket. He was a master with relationships and commandeered at least a dozen large clients from other law firms during his time with the firm. He was the "fair-haired boy" in the truest sense. But his father's offer and his irresistible attraction to Charlotte caused him to agree to join his father's firm.

Three weeks later, John moved in to the office next to his father's and Charlotte became the firm's secretary to the president and in-house counsel. Charlotte was accustomed to Mr. Wellington; he seemed very pleased with her performance and told her so often. However, John was a different story. When he walked by her desk, he would stop to speak with her but rarely said a word. Most of her instructions from him came in the form of handwritten notes. She never understood why until later.

Charlotte became a very valuable employee to Mr. Wellington. She handled everything from his correspondence and appointments to travel arrangements and event planning for the firm. She rarely traveled with him, but occasionally he would ask that she accompany him to Sea Island to handle arrangements for meetings with important clients and salesmen for the company.

Three months after he arrived, John asked her to join him for dinner. She accepted, and they went to Aunt Fannie's Cabin in Smyrna, which was frequented by politicians, dignitaries, and movie stars. Over a dinner of fried chicken, mashed potatoes, and turnip greens, Charlotte fell hopelessly in love with John Wellington. She was very surprised by her reaction to him. Their wedding six months later was the social event of the season in Atlanta; guests included the mayor, the governor, and their state senator. The Robinson family hosted an engagement party for the couple, with several hundred people attending. It was truly a Cinderella story for Charlotte. After the wedding, John insisted that she give up her job at Georgia Life. Reluctantly, she did.

During the first year of their marriage, Charlotte found herself entertaining clients and prospects at their home regularly. She planned private dinners and large meetings for the firm. She and John often had garden parties during the spring and summer months. The formal gardens were always an elegant backdrop for these occasions. Charlotte was a meticulous planner, and no detail ever escaped her attention. She quickly became a valuable part of Georgia Life in a different role.

Charlotte's thoughts returned to the present when the next pain hit her as John was pulling into the emergency entrance to Crawford Long Hospital. She realized that she had not heard a word he said on their trip to the hospital. Dr. Daniel's medical staff was waiting to take Charlotte to the labor-and-delivery area of the hospital. John followed beside the wheelchair as the attendant parked their car. A soft-spoken nurse said, "This is as far as you can go, Mr. Wellington. We will take very good care of both of them."

John kissed Charlotte for a long time on the lips and whispered, "I love you, beautiful." Charlotte looked up at him, smiled lovingly, and then grimaced with the next pain.

John went to the father's waiting room and called his father to tell him the news. Grant was still in his office, but it was only four blocks from the hospital. Within fifteen minutes, John had his father and his best friend, Geoff Robinson, waiting with him.

Grant was very distinguished, with prematurely white hair. He had piercing green eyes and wore rimless glasses. His expensive custom-made suits, wing-tip shoes, and silk ties added to his commanding and often intimidating presence.

Geoff and John were best friends in high school and remained in touch while John was in Boston. Geoff's grandfather and father owned stakes in one of the largest railroads in the country, and Geoff enjoyed the wealth and privilege that went with their success. He had married Camilla Candler, the granddaughter of one the original Coca-Cola bottlers. Life was good.

The hours passed, and John began to count the minutes. He paced, sat, and paced again. "John," Geoff said to him at four o'clock the following morning, trying to distract him, "let's get some coffee."

"No thanks, buddy," John replied, not aware of Geoff's intentions. "I'm afraid to leave right now."

Geoff sat down, and John continued to pace. Grant was sitting on the sofa in the waiting room dozing off with the newspaper in his hand.

It was about a quarter after four when Dr. Daniel found John in the waiting room. "Mr. Wellington," Dr. Daniel beamed, "you have a beautiful baby girl. She and Mrs. Wellington are doing well. You can see your wife in an hour or so when she is fully awake." John could not help himself. He hugged the doctor, taking him rather by surprise.

Oddly, the first person that John called was Belle. "Belle, we have a baby girl, and Charlotte is fine. Call Richard Rich at Rich's Department Store and have him send over all of the girl furniture we chose. I want it all set up before Charlotte and Caroline get home." *Caroline*, John thought, *that's* my *daughter!*

John could hear the relief and joy in Belle's voice when she said, "Don't you worry about a thing, Mr. Wellington. It will be perfect when Miss Charlotte gets home. I know how she wants it. We talked about it over and over. Now you go on and take care of Miss Charlotte. I'll have something for you to eat when you get home, and then you got to get your rest, Mr. Wellington."

"Yes, Belle, you're right, as usual."

Belle's first phone call was to Irene. "Miss Irene," exclaimed Belle, "we have a little girl!!"

CHAPTER 2

*J*OHN FOUND HIMSELF ALONE AGAIN after his father and Geoff left the hospital to go home to rest. Emotion flooded over him while he sat in the waiting room, and he sobbed and cried with relief and joy. He went to the men's room to wash his face before he went up to the maternity ward.

He took the elevator to the neonatal floor, stepped off the elevator, and walked to the nursery window, where he saw her for the first time. She had beautiful creamy skin and thick dark brown hair like her mother. She was truly the most beautiful thing he had ever seen. He was, once again, *in love.* "Caroline Elizabeth Wellington," he said, as if he were addressing royalty. After he stood watching his new baby girl for more than thirty minutes, he went to find Charlotte before he went home. The nurse said, "Mrs. Wellington has just returned to her room." It was room number 317.

John turned and ran down the hall until he reached the private room where he found Charlotte still groggy from the anesthesia. He stood beside her bed, feeling the emotions overcoming him again. He took her hand, kissed her on the cheek, and cried. "She's beautiful, just like you. I love you, beautiful. Thank you for our perfect daughter," he whispered.

Charlotte opened her eyes and smiled. As she drifted back to sleep, John slipped out of the room to go home to rest.

The parking attendant had his car waiting when he exited the hospital. As he got behind the wheel, he realized how exhausted he was. *Thank God for Belle,* he thought.

Miss Caroline Elizabeth Wellington was born into wealth and privilege that neither of her parents or grandparents had when they were young.

Grant and Elizabeth were college sweethearts at the University of Georgia. Grant went to work for Brinson Railway in their business office in Atlanta shortly after their marriage in 1910. By 1929, the railway was bankrupt and Grant was looking for a new career. The Great Depression took its toll across the country.

The contacts he made during his time with the railroad put him in a good position to launch a new career. With little more than his wits, he opened Georgia Life, offering affordable insurance for working families. The business quickly grew into one of the area's largest companies.

Grant grew up in a farming community in Savannah. He was one of ten children and left home for college when he was seventeen years old. Although his family was far from wealthy, his father was a well-respected farmer and his mother took in ironing to keep a roof over their heads.

Elizabeth grew up in Tifton. She was the youngest of three children, and her mother died of polio when she was five. Her father was abusive, and after her older brother and sister left home when she was fourteen, she went to live with her mother's oldest sister in Athens. It was her aunt, Mittie Smith, who saw to it that she had a good education. She met Grant her freshman year at the University of Georgia. He was a senior, and after he graduated, he took a job at the post office in town until she graduated. Soon after they married, the couple moved to Atlanta for a better life and more opportunities. Elizabeth went to work for the telephone company as a long-distance operator. After John was born in 1913, Elizabeth began working at home sewing to bring in enough money to buy groceries for their small family. She never understood why she was not able to have another baby. John Andrew Wellington would be their only child.

In 1930, Atlanta was suffering from the stock market crash along with the rest of the country. The previous decades brought much change to the city, with the railroad being the centerpiece of that progress. But now there were more cars on the roads and the city began to grow in a different direction. An airfield and terminal were built, and Atlanta began airmail service. Soon after, the first passenger airline in Atlanta, Eastern Airlines, went into service. Grant's timing could not have been better. His associates were Coca-Cola executives, railroad tycoons, furniture retailers, and newspaper executives from competing Atlanta newspapers, the *Atlanta Journal* and the *Atlanta Constitution*. His associations were carefully and well chosen. Their employees were his first customers.

Irene Reed, Charlotte's mother, was her steady advisor and confidant. They had always been very close but had not spent much time together since Charlotte and John were married. Charlotte's involvement in Atlanta high society and business entertaining after her marriage to John left her little time to spend with her mother. Irene grew up in a family of mill workers. The Roswell Mill had provided jobs for the community since 1836. She was one of three children, and both her parents worked at the mill when she was a child. When Irene was fifteen, she went to work in the mill on weekends to help with living expenses for the family. In those days, everyone had to work to survive. Roswell was more than a half day's drive from downtown Atlanta. Many of the roads were dirt and much of the land farmland. The Civil War had devastated cotton production in the small Georgia city. In some ways, Roswell was still trying to recover. Roswell Mill provided employment to many of its citizens and helped the small city recover from the Depression.

For the five days following Caroline's birth, friends, family, and the aristocracy of Atlanta visited Charlotte's hospital room. Her room was filled with flowers. Irene was at the hospital every day to see Charlotte. This was her first grandchild too. Charlotte was comforted by her mother's presence and did not want to see her leave each afternoon for the long trip from Atlanta to Roswell. Irene was never totally at ease staying with Charlotte and John and certainly not with Grant and Elizabeth. But she returned every morning, and the nurses allowed her to stay with Charlotte, ignoring the strict rules about visiting hours. Irene and Charlotte never ran out of things to talk about. It was evident to anyone observing their conversations that they were very close and loved each other dearly. Irene was a striking woman with beautiful features. She was sixty, and the years of hard work showed on her face. Her arthritic hands and feet were evidence of the years she spent working in the Roswell Mill. But she was proud and strong and rarely gave in to the pain in her body.

Charlotte was amazed at the little creature who looked so much like a perfect combination of John and her. Over the next three days, she became accustomed to the baby's schedule. She preferred to feed her and do all the diaper changing rather than leaving it to the nursing staff. She loved touching her and holding her close. The day before she was to leave the hospital, the baby's nurse who would come to stay with the new Wellington family for three months came to introduce herself to Charlotte. She was a very kind woman in her late fifties whose posture showed that she had worked very hard during her life. Mrs. Strickland appeared very sturdily dressed in a perfectly starched nurse's uniform. It was easy to see that she was all business. She was thrilled to be chosen as the nurse for the new Wellington baby.

On the fifth day, Dr. Daniel declared that Charlotte and Caroline could go home. Dr. Scott Morgan, one of the finest pediatricians in the southeast, was Caroline's physician. She was deemed perfect in every way.

Charlotte wanted to name her Susan Elizabeth but deferred to John, not voicing any opposition when he came to bring them home. Belle was all smiles and standing in the portico when the Bentley pulled into the driveway. Mrs. Strickland came to take the baby into the house, and Belle could not wait to see Miss Caroline. "Miss Charlotte, I do declare. She is the most beautiful baby I believe I have ever seen," Belle exclaimed with tears in her eyes. She would take care of the third generation of Reed girls.

John helped Charlotte out of the car and into the house. They went straight to Caroline's room. Charlotte gasped when she saw the gorgeous pink-and-green room. She had loved Beatrix Potter as a little girl, and the room was decorated perfectly with all of her favorite characters. No detail had been omitted. Her grandmother's rocking chair was in the back corner of the room. Charlotte felt a lump in her throat when she saw it. "Thank you, John. The room is everything I wanted. I really love the rocking chair, sweetheart," she said.

"Nothing but the best for my girls," replied John boastfully. Charlotte put her arms around him and kissed him. She could not imagine life being better than it was that day.

Irene did not come to the hospital the day Charlotte and Caroline went home. She knew that Belle would take wonderful care of them. When she had arrived back at her house the previous afternoon, she found Mimosa Boulevard to be unusually quiet. She entered her small, immaculate house on the historical Roswell street and went straight to the kitchen for a glass of sweet iced tea. Strolling back to the front porch, she sat down to gather her thoughts. Irene had accepted her place in life and knew that she did not fit the Atlanta social scene. But she missed Charlotte and being able to help her oldest daughter with her first grandchild. She hoped that Charlotte would insist that she be there, but she hadn't. It was disappointing, but she understood her role very well. John's mother, Elizabeth, had a unique way of reminding Irene of her station in life. Irene typically steered clear of Elizabeth for that reason. Irene rose to go back into the house. She went straight to the sleeping porch. When she lay down, she could smell the crisp fall air as she fell asleep.

CHAPTER 3

*T*HE WEEKS AND MONTHS SEEMED to fly. Charlotte could
hardly believe it was Caroline's second birthday. She was
more beautiful than ever, and motherhood agreed with her
marvelously. Caroline was very active, and Charlotte was on the
move keeping up with her.

John insisted that she hire a nanny for Caroline to allow her to
travel with him when his business called for entertaining clients.
Charlotte was a very gracious host, and the parties at their home
were well attended and memorable. She became an important part
of John's business, and he knew that his clients looked forward to
an evening with her as much as, if not more than, with him. It was
no secret to John that Charlotte would prefer to stay home with
Caroline. Her protests were followed by acquiescing to his requests,
as she almost always did.

Katy Rucker came to live with the Wellingtons as Caroline's nanny.
She came very highly recommended from several Atlanta families.
Katy was a thirty-eight-year-old woman from Macon who had been
a teacher in Atlanta when she graduated from college. Richard Rich
noticed her when his son attended the Westminster School. He
offered her the job to nanny their four children, and Katy had found

17

the increase in pay irresistible. When the Rich's children were in high school, the Rhodes family hired her immediately. Since then, the affluent and wealthy families in Atlanta tried to hire Katy. She could pick and choose what family she worked for, and she jumped at the opportunity to work for John and Charlotte Wellington. Caroline took to her immediately, leaving Charlotte a little jealous from time to time. But Charlotte did have peace of mind that between Belle and Katy, Caroline would be in the best care possible when she was away.

"Miss Charlotte," Belle called from downstairs. "Miss Charlotte, are you up there?"

"Yes, Belle, what's the matter?" Charlotte appeared at the top of the stairs and answered in a very anxious tone.

"Miss Charlotte, there's a man at the door who says he has a gift for Miss Caroline's birthday party. Can you come down here and help me?"

Charlotte quickly ran down the stairs. She was wearing a pink silk shirt and trousers. She was stunning even when she was not leaving the house. When she got to the foyer, Robert opened the door.

"Good afternoon, Mrs. Wellington," said the casually dressed stranger. "I have come to deliver Caroline's birthday gift from Mr. Wellington." He presented a beautifully wrapped box that was clearly from Tiffany's. Charlotte took the box and thanked the man. Robert stepped outside the door, closing it behind him to be sure the man left the property.

"Sorry, Miss Charlotte," Belle said apologetically. "I am not used to strangers coming to the door, and you know you just can't be too careful. I read about all these terrible things that happen to children of wealthy people, and it scares me to death."

"You were right to be concerned, Belle," Charlotte replied in a comforting voice. "I prefer caution—you know that. Let's get everything set for Caroline's party tonight. Mr. and Mrs. Wellington will be here at five o'clock. My mother should be here by three thirty."

"I'll be looking for Miss Irene. You know I love that woman. She's not here enough, Miss Charlotte. I think she feels left out sometime," Belle continued.

Charlotte stiffened at the remark. "We see her as often as we can, Belle."

"I'm going to finish icing the cake," Belle said, scurrying off to the kitchen. She knew better than anyone how Charlotte's marriage to John had affected her family. The topic was seldom discussed, but Belle had overheard Charlotte and John arguing over her frequent trips to Roswell with Caroline in the last few months. The last time Charlotte took Caroline to see her mother, she told John that she was taking Caroline shopping for the afternoon. She felt caught between her love and commitment to her husband and the tug at her heart to see her mother. Anne and Nancy always tried to come to the small, neat house on Mimosa Boulevard when Charlotte and Caroline were there.

Charlotte returned to her bedroom by the back stairway. Caroline was napping, and she wanted everything to be perfect, as was always Elizabeth Wellington's expectation.

Elizabeth was a petite, blond-haired, blue-eyed beauty. She had settled very comfortably into her role as the wife of a wealthy business owner. She lunched at the Piedmont Driving Club, the oldest and most prestigious club in Atlanta, and she played bridge with high-society women, many of whom were wealthy in their own right. She traveled to New York twice a year to buy her clothes and went to the Cloister at Sea Island at least once a year. Although she grew up poor and in difficult circumstances, she was aloof and very focused on the appearance of perfection.

Charlotte slipped into a soft turquoise gabardine dress with black embroidered monogram on the hip and black saddle stitching. A jewel-like black glass button was at the back of the dress, with silver painted detail on the bodice. Her 5foot 7 inch 120-pound frame looked perfect in almost anything she wore.

She was coming down the back stairs to check on the status of the cake when she heard the doorbell. She diverted herself to the foyer, where Robert was opening the door for Irene. She ran to embrace her mother. Irene was typically stoic, but today she returned the affection. "Where is my beautiful little girl?" Irene asked playfully.

"She's still napping, Mother. Let's have tea on the back porch and catch up before she is awake. Katy is with her, and she'll bring her down. I can't wait for you to see her birthday dress. It is pink and white with Beatrix Potter characters embroidered on the front. She looks so precious," Charlotte said proudly.

Belle appeared from the kitchen to give Irene a hug. "Miss Irene," Belle exclaimed, "I'm so glad to see you. I have been looking for you all day!"

"Oh, Belle," Irene replied, "you are such a jewel. You look wonderful."

"Miss Charlotte and Miss Caroline make my life happy, Miss Irene," Belle said, chuckling.

"I know they keep you busy too, Belle," Irene said, smiling and hugging her old friend.

"Belle, we're going to sit on the back veranda and catch up until Caroline wakes up," Charlotte said as the mother-daughter duo walked out the back door.

Charlotte and Irene sipped iced tea talking about friends and relatives in Roswell. Charlotte always loved to hear the latest news. Irene knew most everybody in town, and during the time she worked for the president of the Bank of Roswell, she knew their business. She rarely talked about it, but Charlotte knew she would have the latest news.

It wasn't thirty minutes before Katy appeared at the door with a sleepy-eyed birthday girl. Irene stood to tell her happy birthday when Caroline squirmed down and ran to her grandmother. She held her arms out for Mama Rene to take her. It always made Irene feel so special. "MaWeen, MaWeen," exclaimed Caroline. She put her head on Irene's shoulder and said, "I wu u, MaWeen."

Irene melted and replied, "I love you too, precious girl. Happy birthday."

Once again, Caroline squirmed down and took Irene's hand. "See Belle," she urged. Irene followed her to the kitchen, where Belle was putting the finishing touches on the pink birthday cake. "Cake, MaWeen," exclaimed Caroline, pointing to the beautiful pink confection.

"We will have cake, precious girl. We just have to wait for the party," Irene said, coaxing Caroline out of the kitchen. Belle was laughing at the whole scene and was very glad to see Irene.

Within an hour, the Wellington house was filled with relatives coming for dinner and Caroline's birthday party. After dinner, when it came time to open gifts, John insisted that his gift to his daughter be opened first. The blue Tiffany's box was placed in front of Caroline. Charlotte helped her with the ribbon and the wrapping. Inside was a small, beautiful gold-and-diamond pendant with Caroline's initials in the center. On the back, the inscription was "Baby Girl. Love Daddy. 10/2/50" Caroline loved to play dress-up, so when the necklace was put around her neck, she went straight to her daddy and gave him a kiss. "I wu u, Da." She held out her arms for her daddy to pick her up. He did and walked over to the mirror in the hall. Caroline eyed herself and appeared very happy with what she saw. She wiggled down and went straight to Irene.

"Ma Ween," Caroline squealed. "Ma Ween, see!" She pointed to her necklace and then climbed up into Irene's lap. Elizabeth seemed a little jealous that Irene and Caroline seemed to have such a good relationship.

Katy came to take Caroline to bed about eight o'clock. After all of the good-night kisses, John and Grant began their ritual of scotch and cigars. Charlotte hated when John smoked cigars. Charlotte, Irene, and Elizabeth went to the living room, where Belle had tea waiting for them. Irene had decided to spend the night since it was such a long trip from Atlanta to Roswell and she did not like to drive the winding roads after dark. They chatted, mostly about Caroline.

At nine thirty, Grant appeared at the door and announced that it was time to leave. Elizabeth excused herself after the usual pleasant good-byes, and Robert escorted them to their car. Charlotte noticed that Grant seemed rather intoxicated, but she did not react. She and Irene exchanged knowing glances since they had both grown to hate alcohol when her father was alive.

Irene put her arms around Charlotte and said, "I'm tired, sweetheart. Do you mind if I go on to bed?"

"Of course not, Mother," replied Charlotte firmly. "I'll see you in the morning for breakfast, and we can spend some time with Caroline then."

"Oh, I would love that. Thank you, Charlotte. This has been such a nice evening," Irene gushed and disappeared upstairs.

Charlotte went to the library to look for John. When she entered the room, John was seated in the large leather chair beside the fireplace. He was holding a glass filled with what looked like straight scotch. His head was back, and his eyes were closed. "John!" Charlotte exclaimed. "Are you all right?"

John raised his head slightly, cut his eyes over to Charlotte, and in very slurred speech said, "Of course I'm all right. Just go to bed."

Charlotte left the room, not wishing for an argument. She had become concerned about John's drinking when they were entertaining but dismissed the dreadful thought that he could become an alcoholic. That could not possibly happen to her after the nightmares she endured as a child with her father's drinking and abusive behavior. She took the back stairs to their bedroom and changed quickly and got into the bed. She could not go to sleep and was still awake when John came to bed after midnight smelling of alcohol and cigars. She was disgusted. Finally, she slept.

Charlotte was up before John and in the kitchen with Belle when Irene appeared for breakfast. "Good morning, sunshine," she said, as she always had when Charlotte and her sisters were children.

"Good morning, Mother." Charlotte greeted her mother with a cup of coffee. Belle was just getting the biscuits out of the oven. She knew that Miss Irene loved homemade biscuits and fig preserves, and that was exactly what she would have this morning.

"Belle, you are just too good," exclaimed Irene. "Thank you so much. I don't know how you remember what everyone likes so well. You are a jewel."

Belle giggled and said, "Aw go on, Miss Irene, you know I have known you for a coon's age." Irene smiled and concentrated on enjoying her biscuits.

Just as Irene was finishing the last delicious bite, Katy appeared at the kitchen door with Caroline. As soon as she saw Irene, she wiggled down and ran across the kitchen. "MaWeen, MaWeen!!" She pointed outside. "Go side." Caroline loved to walk outside with Irene and discover the flowers and insects that were always there to bring wonder and joy to a two-year-old's curious senses.

"We will after you eat Belle's biscuits, okay?" said Irene softly. Caroline scurried to her high chair, and Irene lifted her into it. Belle brought a biscuit and Caroline's special formula.

Soon they were in the backyard going over every inch of it looking at every flower, every fallen leaf, and every tree. Charlotte thought her mother looked joyful as she held her granddaughter's hand. She walked back into the house where she saw John getting ready to leave for work. As she walked into the foyer she said, "Did you have one of Belle's biscuits, honey?"

"No, I'm running late. Have to go" came his hurried reply. He gave her a peck on the cheek, and out the door he went. Charlotte thought she could still smell alcohol on his breath. Her throat tightened, and she felt dizzy. She went into the library to sit down, and that is when she saw the empty bottles. There were two empty bottles of scotch sitting behind the chair that John had been sitting in the night before. *When did he drink this?* she thought, the panic getting worse. "God help me," she said out loud as tears fell. She knew that John's entertaining had increased over the past year, but could it be this bad? She gathered her thoughts and went to the powder room in the hall to dry her eyes. *I'll take the bottles to the kitchen and put them where he keeps extra bottles of scotch,* she thought. *He will know that I found them.* And that is what she did.

Irene and Caroline came through the back door to the den with Caroline holding a bouquet of leaves and flowers. Charlotte exclaimed how beautiful they were and went straight to the kitchen for a vase. Katy came to get Caroline to take her for her bath and to dress her for the day. Irene gathered her belongings and kissed everyone and headed back to Roswell.

Charlotte decided to give Katy the afternoon off. She took Caroline in her stroller and walked to Piedmont Park. The fresh fall air and the beautiful trees seemed to bring her some peace. She walked and strolled Caroline around the park for more than two hours. It was one o'clock in the afternoon before she realized how lost in her thoughts she was. She headed home.

When she arrived, Belle was wringing her hands. "Miss Charlotte, I was so worried about you and Miss Caroline. You just have to tell me where you are going. Your lunch has been ready for over an hour." Her exasperated tone was very evident.

"I am so sorry, Belle. I just enjoyed the park so much, and the fresh air was good for both of us," Charlotte said apologetically. They ate quietly, and then Charlotte took Caroline upstairs for her nap.

Charlotte went to the back veranda and sat staring at the trees for two hours. Her thoughts were interrupted when Belle came to the door saying, "Miss Charlotte, Mr. Wellington is on the telephone for you."

Charlotte rose from her chair and went to the library. "Hello," she said in a dismissive tone.

"Hi, sweetheart!" John said jovially. "A. G. and his wife want us to come to dinner at their home tonight. Can you be ready by six?"

"Sure, John—anything for you, dear," she said and hung up the phone.

CHAPTER 4

7HE STOCKTONS' HOME WAS ON West Paces Ferry Road north of the Wellingtons' Ansley Park home and was grander than John and Charlotte's house. It was called "The Pink Palace" and was designed by Phillip Schutze, who was a much sought after architect in Atlanta. When John arrived home at five thirty, Charlotte was dressed in a wonderfully elegant and flattering evening gown in black rayon crepe with an inset of black lace over beige organza lightly pleated at the hips.

As she descended the front staircase, her eyes met John's gaze and he did a "wolf whistle." "Charlotte, I believe you get more beautiful every day." When she reached the bottom of the stairs, she put her arms around John and kissed him on the mouth. Then she stepped back with her arms still around him and looked him squarely in the eye. "Maybe we should stay home tonight," he said slyly.

"Maybe we should," Charlotte replied with a sexy look that she rarely offered. But Robert was standing nearby with her mink jacket. She slipped it on, and out the door they went.

The evening at the Stocktons' home was wonderful. John was charming, as usual, and Charlotte enjoyed talking with their friends, whom she had not seen very much in the two years since Caroline was born.

As was their custom, the gentlemen retired to the library for whiskey and cigars after dinner. Charlotte, Miriam Stockton, Suzanne Regenstein, and Camilla Robinson went to have tea in the solarium. Charlotte loved this room in their home and wished she had one to bring the outdoors inside for Caroline to enjoy.

They were on their second cup of tea when A. G. appeared at the solarium door with a panicked look and said, "Charlotte, please come quickly, John is ill." Charlotte rose and ran to the library, where the other guests were picking John up and putting him in a chair. He was obviously unconscious.

"Oh my God, John!" exclaimed Charlotte. "Would someone please call Dr. Denmark and tell him we will be over to Crawford Long within a half hour?"

The butler retrieved Charlotte's jacket. "Please help me get him to the car," Charlotte pleaded, almost panicking. They complied, and as they were putting him in the front seat of the car, John raised his head and said in very slurred speech said, "Where are we going, Charlotte? I wasn't finished with my scotch." At that moment, Charlotte realized that John was dead drunk again.

"Don't worry about where we're going, John," Charlotte said in a very authoritative tone. "Just relax." Charlotte pulled the Bentley out of the driveway and headed up West Paces Ferry to Peachtree. She pressed the accelerator to the floor, and the car roared down Peachtree to the hospital. As she expected, Dr. Denmark was waiting at the emergency room entrance when they arrived. Charlotte exited the car and walked around to the passenger side where she opened the door and caught John before he fell out of the car. "Dr. Denmark, I think he is dead drunk. I need your help. Please admit him to the hospital so when he wakes up tomorrow he will realize what he has done."

"Fine, Mrs. Wellington," Dr. Denmark replied in his typical sterile tone.

"I'll be back in the morning to pick him up. May I ask you to keep this confidential?" Charlotte asked.

"Of course," Dr. Denmark replied, and they put John on a stretcher and took him into the emergency room.

Disgusted and embarrassed, Charlotte got back into the car and drove home.

After a very long night with little sleep, Charlotte drove back to the hospital as she promised Dr. Denmark. John was in room 110, and when she walked into the room, he barely acknowledged her.

"You can come home now, John," Charlotte said, disgusted with what she saw. "Please get dressed. I have taken care of checking you out. We can go straight home now." John complied, still not meeting her gaze or speaking to her. The silence continued all the way home.

When the car was in the portico, John turned to Charlotte and said, "I'm so sorry, Charlotte. I don't know what is happening to me lately."

"You are becoming an alcoholic, John. That is what is happening to you," Charlotte said furiously. "I'm horrified at your behavior. I found the empty scotch bottles in the library after Caroline's birthday party. Did you know that?" Charlotte broke down and cried. "Please don't ruin our lives, John," she pleaded.

"I love you and Caroline more than anything in the world, Charlotte. Don't you know that?" John sounded like a child asking a parent for forgiveness.

"Yes, John, but you have to love us more than you do scotch. You had better get yourself straightened out." Charlotte got out of the car, slammed the door, and walked into the side door of the house.

Belle knew everything that had happened, but no one else in the house knew. Katy was feeding Caroline breakfast, and the little girl squealed when she saw Charlotte at the door. "Good morning, sunshine," Charlotte said to Caroline. Caroline giggled and continued eating. "Belle, Mr. Wellington is ill and is not to be disturbed today. He will be in our room. Would you make some tea and toast for him? I will take it up," Charlotte ordered.

"Yes, Miss Charlotte," Belle replied. She did not remember Charlotte ever speaking to her that way. But she knew the trouble that was brewing and she understood.

John came in the house through the front door and went upstairs quickly so as to not be noticed by Robert or Belle. He had just closed the door to their room when Charlotte opened it. "Belle will have some tea and toast for you shortly. I will bring it to you. After you eat, you will go to bed for the day," Charlotte ordered in a tone John had never heard from her before.

"I have appointments this afternoon, Charlotte. I have to go to the office," he pleaded.

"I recommend that you call Sylvia and tell her to cancel your appointments. So that we all have the same story, let's say you had an allergic reaction to something you ate and the doctor recommended that you stay home. That is plausible, isn't it, John?" Charlotte quipped angrily.

"Yes, I guess it is," John said, resolved to comply.

Charlotte left the room and shortly brought the tea and toast to John. She did not attempt to see him for the remainder of the day.

About four thirty, Charlotte came into the kitchen where Belle was about to start dinner. "Belle, would you tell Mr. Wellington that Caroline and I have gone to Roswell for the night?"

"Yes, Miss Charlotte. Do you want me to go with you? 'Cause I will," Belle said, her voice breaking.

"No, Belle, you need to stay here and tend to Mr. Wellington. He will be having milk toast for dinner." Charlotte was obviously in charge, and Belle knew it.

"Yes, ma'am, Miss Charlotte," Belle said meekly. Charlotte walked over to her and put her arms around her and cried.

"I know, baby, I know," comforted Belle. "Now you go on and get to your mother's house before dark. You know the roads are winding up there."

Charlotte left with Caroline and began the trip to Roswell. Irene was waiting at the door with the front porch light on when the Bentley pulled into the unpaved driveway. Charlotte got out carrying Caroline and their bags. Irene met them on the porch to take Caroline. She reached back and kissed her oldest daughter on the cheek. "Come and rest, Charlotte. You must rest."

It was quiet in the house except for the occasional call of the whippoorwill and the chirping katydids. Charlotte was exhausted. She went to the front bedroom, leaving Caroline with Irene. She slept, but the nightmares were terrible and much too real.

Irene took Caroline to the sleeping porch where they curled up together for the night.

The next morning, she woke to the telephone in the hall ringing. Irene answered, "Hello. Yes, John, she and Caroline are here. They spent the night with me. Well, she isn't up yet. Can I have her call you when she is up? She was very tired last night," asked Irene with no intention of getting Charlotte to the telephone. She put the phone back on the cradle and peeped into Charlotte's room.

"I'm awake, Mother," Charlotte said. "Come on in." She could smell the fresh brewed coffee.

"What can I do to help you, Charlotte?" Irene said with a note of profound sadness in her voice.

"Just pray for us, mother. Just pray," Charlotte said distantly. The hall phone rang again. This time it was Grant Wellington. He had learned from John of the events of the previous evening and was furious with Charlotte. Irene handed Charlotte the telephone. "Hello," she said tentatively.

"Charlotte, I am so disappointed that you would treat John the way you did. How dare you take him to the hospital to teach him a lesson!" Grant shouted into the phone. Charlotte held the phone away from her ear.

"Mr. Wellington," she replied formally, "if you and Mrs. Wellington want to take care of him when he is drunk again, I will be glad to drop him off at your house."

Grant was fuming by now. "This could cost our company thousands of dollars if word gets out about this. The lifestyle you enjoy would end if that happened. Have you bothered to think about that?" he snorted.

"Of course I have," replied Charlotte. "You and Mrs. Wellington remind me of how lucky I am all the time. It's John you need to remind."

"I think—" Grant started to speak, but Charlotte interrupted him.

"Mr. Wellington, we will have this conversation later. The matter is between John and me, and the only way anyone else will know is if you tell them. Dr. Denmark put in his records that John had an allergic reaction to something he ate. Is that all?"

"I suppose it is, young lady," Grant said gruffly and hung up the phone.

By now, Charlotte was furious. She sat up on the side of the bed. "Dammit," she said out loud. She knew she had to compose herself and deal with this problem later.

After coffee for herself and breakfast for Caroline, Charlotte left her mother's house to return to her own. She hoped that her actions would allow John to see the destructive results of his drinking.

When she arrived home, John was waiting in the portico. He was not dressed for work but was in his flannel shirt and gabardine pants. "How are my best girls?" he exclaimed, taking Caroline out of the car. Caroline adored her father. She gladly went into the house with him. Robert came to get Charlotte's bags. Katy was in the kitchen with Belle, and she took Caroline from John when he brought her in the house.

Charlotte went straight to her room, closed the door, and slipped into the bathtub. She was trying to relax in the warm water when John knocked on the door. "May I come in?" he said meekly.

"Please allow me to finish. I'll see you in a few minutes," she replied dryly. John did not speak again. Fifteen minutes later, Charlotte emerged dressed in a lavender silk robe.

John spoke first. "Charlotte, I don't know how to tell you how sorry I am that I have hurt you and Caroline. I know I have, and for the last twenty-four hours, I have been going over all the things I have done and have promised myself, and now I am promising you, that I will not drink anymore. I love you and Caroline so much. You are my world." Charlotte walked over and put her arms around him. She kissed him. He embraced her, and they fell on the bed. They made love for two hours. *Thank God*, Charlotte thought. *Thank God I won't have to live with an alcoholic again.*

CHAPTER 5

*T*HE YEARS THAT FOLLOWED WERE good. John kept his promise and insisted that they move to West Paces Ferry to be near Westminster. He purchased the Peacock Mansion. Its proximity to Westminster School for Caroline was the main reason John wanted to move there and the main reason Charlotte agreed to move.

The Wellingtons had lived in the house for two years when Caroline began kindergarten. Charlotte could not believe that her baby was five years old. She and John took her to school together on her first day. The school was buzzing with the news that Caroline Wellington would be attending Westminster.

Caroline had been reading since she was three years old. Katy spent weeks and months with her and Charlotte read to her every night when she was at home. Caroline loved to read, and Katy boasted that she was already at a third-grade level. Charlotte and John were so proud of her and were both reluctant to leave her at school.

"Caroline, you know that Robert will be here to pick you up at two o'clock," Charlotte said as she prepared to leave.

"Yes, Mama. I'm fine. You and Daddy can leave now," Caroline said, sensing their hesitation to leave her. And she turned and went to talk with three little girls already engaged in getting to know one another. Charlotte and John looked at each other, shrugged their shoulders, and left.

Katy stayed as Caroline's nanny to help look after her when Charlotte and John were traveling, which they did very often and for several weeks at a time. Charlotte hired a housekeeper to help Belle because their new home was so large that she could not do the cooking and the cleaning. Charlotte placed Belle in charge of running the day-to-day operation of the house and the cooking. She supervised three people in service at the Wellington home; a duty she took very seriously and with a great deal of pride. Not much got by Belle, and Charlotte knew it.

Peacock House was a fourteen-thousand-square-foot English Regency-style house built in 1929. It was one of the finest mansions in Buckhead. The Wellingtons continued entertaining clients and the wealthy elite, but now it was on a much larger scale.

Charlotte and John began attending services every Sunday at Second Ponce de Leon Baptist Church in Buckhead. One Father's Day they were on their way to church. "Daddy," Caroline asked, "can I sit with you and Mama in big church today?" Caroline was eight years old now and considered herself to be pretty grown up.

"Sure, baby girl," John replied with the loving tone he always had when he talked with Caroline. Charlotte glanced over at him and smiled at him.

The sermon that day would have a profound impact in the life of the Wellingtons. "Good morning, and happy Father's Day to all of you lucky dads," Dr. Hansen began.

Susan Willis Updegraff

"We have eternity in our hearts, but only a few short years in our bodies."

All the health emphasis we hear today only makes the Bible speak with more power and relevance in this day in which we live. For it is shown in Ecclesiastes that our obsession with youth and muscles and perfect teeth and wrinkle-free skin is part of the sadness of our human condition. The author even suggests that God has played a trick on us (and here are his words) by placing "eternity in our hearts" but only a few short years in our bodies. What's more we don't know how long our ball of yarn is. Our end could come later today or next week or in sixty years. So the question becomes, how now shall I live?

Then, for you who have fathers, Ecclesiastes reminds us of the fleeting brevity of life and how short is the time we have with our dads. We need to show appreciation, love, and gratitude today while you still have him with you.

And Dad, you build self-confidence through play and adventure.

Not only should you seize the day, but take that life of yours and put it where it will make the most difference. Dads, that means spending time with your children. What's the old saying—no man ever said on his deathbed, "Gee, I wish I'd spent more time at the office." No, those regrets come from not having spent enough time with one's children. One of the things I think many of us dads are clueless of is how transformational our simple presence is in being with our children. More and more studies are showing the unique role of the dad in a child's development in their formative years. Mom's role tends to be that of caretaker and caregiver, while Dad builds self-confidence through play and adventure. Dad, you can have a magical impact just by showing up and paying attention. One of the great Baptist pastors of our time is Al Peterson who

36

serves in Dallas, Texas. Al recalls chaperoning his daughter's Girl Scout troop one weekend. He writes, "I remember a Saturday afternoon when our daughter, Elizabeth, and her Girl Scout friends were having an ice-skating troop event. We were at the public ice arena along with a large crowd of other youth. I was one of the adult come-alongs, and I stood at the edge and just watched our troop girls. One by one they would skate toward me and then, with theatrical skill, stop suddenly. Then they would say, 'Did you see that, Mr. Peterson?' I would always cheer them on with exclamations of encouragement: 'Mary, you look great!' 'Wow, Jane, you can skate backward as well as frontward!' Then a humorous thing happened. Totally random girls and boys would skate boldly toward my rink position and say, 'Hey Mister, did you see this?' I then realized that people need watchers who are like an encouraging anchor presence, especially if a few words of acknowledgement prove that you actually saw them at the most daring moment. That was what I was. I was just present in a friendly way. I was paying attention, and that in itself was important." Kids want their dad to see their daring moments. In the presence of his strength they grow in skill, daring, and confidence. As I read Al Peterson's story, it struck me that this is something that not only fathers but grandfathers can do.

Your role with your children is more important than you realize. In view of the brevity of life, don't let a single second slip through your fingers. There is something else that living with a view of death will do for you. It will awaken you to the supreme importance of this very moment. If you read these words and say, "Well, I need to lie low and play it as safe as I can for as long as I can," you have missed the message of Ecclesiastes. This is a carpe diem text. Seize the day. In view of the brevity of life, don't let a single second slip through your fingers. Live each moment adventurously for God.

Think how fast our children grow up.

"Fix it, Daddy," she lisps at two, showing him her scraped and bleeding knee.

"Fix it, Daddy," she says at four, tearfully producing her busted balloon purchased from the vendor at the parade.

"Fix it, Daddy," she says at six, struggling with her jacket zipper in her rush out the door to school.

"Fix it, Daddy," she says at eight, confidently wheeling her dented and lopsided bike toward him as he gets out of the car after work.

"Fix it, Daddy," she says righteously at ten, after coming out a loser in a knockdown drag-out battle with her impossible brother.

"Fix it, Daddy," she pleads at twelve, in the first of many struggles with her mother over whether she's old enough to wear eye shadow.

"Fix it, Daddy," she sobs at fourteen, when her image hits rock bottom because she didn't make cheerleader.

"Fix it, Daddy," she asks at sixteen, exposing her first broken heart over a lost love.

"Fix it, Daddy," she says at eighteen, when the college she wants does not want her.

"Fix it, Daddy," she implores at twenty-two, sending along her mangled checkbook and a 1040 IRS form.

"Fix it, Daddy," she prays at thirty, when her baby is in the hospital.

"Fix it, Grandpa," she insists at forty, as she turns her contrary twelve-year-old son over to you for the weekend.

"Fix it, Father," she prays at fifty-five, as she kneels at her dad's coffin, realizing that from now on he will be fixing things for her in a way he never could before.

You know, even Ecclesiastes gives a hint that death is not the end in verse 7: And the dust returns to the ground it came from, and the spirit returns to God who gave it. When God wanted the word that best described himself, he chose the word "father." Dad, this is your day. Let's live our lives with eternity's values in view.

When the sermon ended, there was a very long silence in the sanctuary. John looked at Caroline and saw tears running down her face. She looked up at him and said, "Daddy, please don't ever die."

"Don't you worry about that, baby girl," John whispered. And he took her hand.

Charlotte wiped tears and handed a tissue to Caroline. Then they all began to giggle. Thank goodness the service was over before they all got into trouble for being disruptive. After that, the young Wellington family attended church almost every Sunday. The impact this sermon had on them would be felt for years to come.

John and Charlotte grew closer and more in love than ever. They took weekend trips alone to the mountains of North Georgia during the summer months. Sometimes they would bring Caroline with them, and she loved hiking in the woods with her parents. John climbed trees with her, and they made bridges from fallen trees to cross streams. It was heaven on earth to Caroline hiking and enjoying being together in the beautiful North Georgia mountains with her parents.

Often, John and Charlotte would slip away alone on Friday evenings for dinner. When they returned home, the romantic evenings turned into passionate lovemaking that they both relished and enjoyed. Caroline loved that her parents had date nights. As far as she was concerned, life was perfect.

John loved teaching Caroline to waltz. He often took her to the ballroom in their home and played waltzes on the stereo. By the time she was eleven years old Caroline could waltz and foxtrot. She would rather jitterbug, and she did that when she went to school dances. Caroline didn't have a steady boyfriend, but she had many dates to dances. She was "that girl" that everyone wanted to dance with.

In July, when Caroline was twelve, the family went to Europe for a month. They enjoyed London, Paris, Rome, and Madrid. The trip would be a favorite memory for Caroline for the rest of her life. When they returned, she made a thirty-page photo album that the three of them enjoyed over and over.

One evening the following January, Charlotte and John were in the library talking when Caroline slipped out of bed and down the stairs. She heard John raise his voice to her mother, "Dammit, Charlotte, I haven't been drinking much at all in the past few years. Can't you just give me a break for one night?"

Caroline saw Charlotte put her hands on her hips and walk closer to John. She knew her mother was mad. "John, once an alcoholic, always an alcoholic. You know that!" Charlotte voice was loud, and she was obviously furious.

Just then, John raised his arm and hit Charlotte across the face with the back of his hand. She fell backward and her head hit the coffee table. She lay on the floor, stunned. When she sat up, blood ran down her face from the gash in her head. "Oh my God, Charlotte! What have I done? *Oh my God.*"

Caroline watched the entire scene in horror. She rushed into the library and screamed at her father, "Please don't hurt Mama. Daddy, why did you hit Mama?"

Just then, Belle came into the library and saw Charlotte bleeding. "Robert—Robert, get the car. We're going to the hospital," Belle shouted.

"I tripped over the coffee table and fell. That's all I remember, Belle."

"Okay, honey, let's get you to the hospital," Belle said. Robert was waiting with the car in the portico when John helped Charlotte to the back seat. He got in the back with her, and Robert sped down the driveway to the hospital.

Belle put her arms around Caroline. She was sobbing. "Your mama is gonna be fine, Miss Caroline. You know Dr. Denmark will take good care of her." Caroline could not be consoled.

"Why did my daddy do that?" She begged Belle for an answer. Belle did not speak, but she sat with her for more than an hour while she cried herself to sleep. Belle knew that Charlotte did not trip.

At the emergency room at Crawford Long Hospital, the doctors were evaluating the injury. It appeared that the gash was very deep and would require stitches. Charlotte had a very large bruise on her cheek. She explained that she hit her face on the sofa before hitting the coffee table. It was just a bruise, and it would heal just fine, but it would be black and blue for a while. The gash in Charlotte's head required twelve stitches, and she stayed in the hospital overnight. She was given antibiotics to prevent an infection. John slept on a cot next to her bed all night. The following morning, Dr. Denmark came into the room and sat in a chair next to Charlotte's bed. "Charlotte, John, I have known you both for a long time. Please tell me what happened," he requested.

Charlotte spoke and said, "I tripped in the library and hit my cheek on the sofa and my head on the coffee table."

"What did you trip on, Charlotte?" Dr. Denmark said, sensing that he was not getting the whole truth.

"My own feet, I think, Dr. Denmark," Charlotte replied.

"So that's it?" he replied sarcastically.

"Yes, Dr. Denmark," Charlotte said knowing that Dr. Denmark did not believe her. He noticed that John was looking down during their brief conversation.

"John, I would like you to bring Charlotte to my office in three days for a check of her bandage. Please allow at least a half hour for the visit," Dr. Denmark said, leaving John no choice but to agree.

"We'll be there, Dr. Denmark. Thank you," he said.

Charlotte rested for the next two days. Her head was very sore, and her face was black and blue under her right eye. She was a terrible sight. Every time John looked at her, he was horrified all over again.

As he promised, John took Charlotte to Dr. Denmark's office on the third day after the accident. The doctor asked them to join him in his office before he checked Charlotte's bandage. "John," he began, "I have been your doctor for more years than I care to say. I know your parents very well, and I have cared for Charlotte since you were married fifteen years ago. Let's say that I know you. Please tell me what happened," Dr. Denmark paused. Neither John nor Charlotte spoke. No more was said. Dr. Denmark checked the bandage and asked that Charlotte return in ten days to get the stitches removed. They agreed, and John and Charlotte left. Neither of them spoke on the way home. John denied repeatedly that he was an alcoholic, but he had come face to face with his disease and the destruction it caused.

When they arrived back home, John went straight to talk with Caroline. He made a promise that he would never hit Mama again. He would not keep that promise.

CHAPTER 6

*B*Y THE TIME CAROLINE REACHED high school, she had blossomed into a beautiful young lady with shoulder-length dark auburn hair and clear blue eyes. Like her mother, she was tall and slender. Her intelligence and confidence disguised her private nature. She never discussed her father's drinking or his abuse of her mother. As far as anyone knew, her life was perfect. She was involved in activities at school and with friends and spent very little time at home. French Club, International Club, and the debate team took her time most afternoons after school. On the weekends, she volunteered at Crawford Long Hospital in the gift shop. She was an honor student and a member of the Beta Club and National Honor Society. But heartbreak and sadness plagued her throughout her high school years.

During those years, Charlotte had a broken arm and stitches over her left eye, and Caroline did not know what else that her mother never told her. There was always a story, however implausible, and no one questioned it. Charlotte told Caroline that she was fine, but Caroline knew better.

During her times of solitude, Charlotte struggled to accept her life. She wanted to allow Caroline to graduate from high school and leave for college. She dreamed of divorcing John and moving away from the alcoholism, abuse, and nightmares that she endured. She never quite understood why she still loved him, but she did. There were aspects of their relationship that she could never explain to Caroline—or anyone, for that matter.

She knew how difficult it was for John to work for his father. Grant was demanding and unrelenting in his requirements for John to accomplish the things that he could not. John managed to perform admirably at work. He seldom had any energy or emotion left when he was home. Charlotte knew that he wanted to quit Georgia Life and open his own law firm in Atlanta. But she knew he could not maintain the lifestyle to which they had become accustomed if he did that. During their discussions, Charlotte truthfully told him she would rather live in a two-bedroom house than for him to be a slave to his father and have it ruin their lives. Nevertheless, he continued working for his father.

Charlotte knew the wonderful and loving man she married, and she knew how much he loved Caroline. Charlotte and Caroline seldom discussed anything to do with the drinking or abuse. In between the nightmares, they pretended nothing happened.

One summer evening in 1963, John and Charlotte were having dinner on the back veranda. It was Friday, and Caroline was in her room reading, Belle was resting in her room, and Robert was sitting on the front porch of the Peacock House watching cars go up and down West Paces Ferry Road. Charlotte knew that John was drinking. She rarely knew how much he had to drink before he got home, but today, she knew it must have been quite a bit. "I am so damn sick of working for my father," John said, as if his statement was something Charlotte had never heard. "He was so condescending to me today in front of clients that *I* brought into the company. It doesn't matter what I do, it's never good enough for him. I wish I had never come to Atlanta to work for him. I could be happy in Boston visiting once a year."

Charlotte could see the fury in his eyes. "You wouldn't want to miss all the good things in your life, like Caroline, would you, John?" Charlotte quizzed, mostly being conversational.

"*How many times do I have to tell you, Charlotte,*"—John was yelling at the top of his voice and slurring his words—"*that I hate working for my father; that's it!* Are you stupid?" he continued, gritting his teeth at her.

"I wasn't trying to make you mad, John," Charlotte said quietly, trying to avert a violent scene. "I was just trying—" Before Charlotte could finish her sentence, John stood up, grabbed her by her right arm, and pushed her over the railing of the porch. Charlotte fell into a large boxwood bush. Her head hit the sidewalk, and she was unconscious.

Caroline heard her father yelling and came out the back door in time to see her mother lying on the walkway below the porch. "Mama," she screamed, "are you okay?" Caroline bent over her mother and could see that she was unconscious but breathing.

Just then, Belle came out the back door. She surveyed the situation and rushed to get Robert from the front porch. "We gotta go to the hospital with Miss Charlotte again!" Belle said breathlessly. "Help me get Miss Charlotte into the car." Robert jumped up and ran to the back of the house where he saw Caroline holding her mother in her arms, crying. John stumbled backward and fell over the chair that Charlotte had been sitting in. No one bothered to see if he was okay, not even Caroline.

Belle ignored John and helped Robert get Charlotte into the car. For the first time, Belle looked at John picking himself up off of the porch and said, "Mr. Wellington, you are going to kill her if you don't stop." She had never spoken to him that way in her life, but she was tired of seeing him abuse Charlotte. Someone needed to stand up to him and, Lord knows Charlotte didn't anymore.

Charlotte had a slight concussion and a broken wrist. *It is a miracle it wasn't worse*, Belle thought after the doctor examined Charlotte in the emergency room. Charlotte would be in the hospital overnight so they could observe her to be certain the concussion was not worse than they thought. Her wrist was set in a cast almost up to her elbow. Caroline, Belle, and Robert stayed at the hospital with Charlotte until after midnight. When she was comfortably sleeping, they went home.

Caroline was crying because she was so mad with her father. "I'm done with this," Caroline declared in the car on the way home. "Either he's going to go or we are." When they arrived home, Caroline found her father in the library, still drinking. She stood in front of him and slapped the glass of scotch out of his hand, breaking the glass and spilling scotch all over her father and his leather chair.

"What in the hell did you do that for?" he asked, hardly able to form his words as he was so intoxicated.

"What are you going to do, Daddy?" Caroline screamed. "Hit me?"

"Shut up, Caroline, and go to bed," John said with his eyes closed.

"How about if you pack your shit and get out of my house, Father dear," Caroline continued screaming.

Just then, Belle walked in as John began to stand to face Caroline. Belle took her by the arm and led her out of the room and up the stairs. "Do you want to be in the hospital with your mother, Miss Caroline?" Belle scolded her.

"I'm so damn sick of the way he treats her I really don't care anymore, Belle. I can't stand to see my sweet mother suffer like this. It is tearing me apart inside," Caroline confessed. "My stomach hurts most of the time, especially when I'm at home at night. I never know what's going to happen. Daddy makes it so hard for me to love him. He's got to leave."

The following morning, Irene got word about what happened when Belle called her. At ten thirty, she walked in the front door of the Peacock House yelling, "John Wellington, get down here right now!" John appeared at the top of the stairs.

"Irene, please stop yelling," he said in a sober tone that let her know he had a bad hangover.

"I will stop yelling when you stop hitting my daughter, Mr. Big Stuff," she retorted sarcastically.

"Irene, I understand—" John began, but Irene interrupted.

"You don't understand anything, John. Everyone has begged you to stop drinking. You are a monster when you drink. You are killing my daughter. I have been silent as long as I intend to be," Irene said with a fury John had never seen. Just then, Belle appeared in the foyer where Irene was yelling at John. "John, if you hurt Charlotte ever again, I will kill you myself. Is there anything about that you don't understand?!" The fury and the sarcasm meshed, and John knew he was better off to keep quiet.

"I understand, Irene," he said quietly and walked back into their bedroom.

"Belle," Irene said, "I meant what I said."

"Miss Irene, I know you did. I have gotten to the point with this that I will help you," Belle said with her voice shaking.

"Wait a minute, Belle," Irene said. "John Wellington," Irene yelled up the stairs again. "John," she screamed. John appeared at the top of the stairs. "We are going to get Charlotte at the hospital now. You better be gone when we get back. I don't care where you go, just go," Irene ordered him.

"I'll be gone," John said sheepishly.

John packed and left for the North Georgia mountains where he would sequester himself until the following week. Neither Charlotte nor Caroline heard anything from him, and neither of them attempted to locate him. He was gone and they were glad. It would be peaceful at Peacock House.

That afternoon, Irene called Grant. "Grant, this is Irene Reed," she began, and not very cordially.

"Hello, Irene" came Grant's formal tone.

"Grant, your son has put *my* daughter in the hospital again. This time she has a concussion and a broken wrist. He's going to kill her if he keeps it up! He says his drinking is caused by hating to work for you. You are a tyrant, he says. Something has got to change, Grant." There was silence on the other end of the telephone. "Grant! Are you listening?" Irene screamed into the telephone.

"Yes, Irene," he replied dryly. "I heard everything you said."

"Well . . . What are you going to do?" Irene said furiously.

"I think John and I will have to discuss that, Irene. Is there anything else?" Grant said in a sarcastic and condescending tone.

"Yes, there is one more thing, Mr. Wellington," Irene began, returning the sarcastic tone. "If he hurts my daughter again, I will kill him. I have had enough, and she and Caroline have too. Is there anything about that you don't understand?"

Grant slammed the telephone down and did not reply to Irene. Irene's fury was beyond anything she ever felt before. She slammed the telephone back on the receiver and pounded her fist on the wall.

Then she composed herself and went to the hospital to get Charlotte.

When John arrived at the house they always rented in the mountains, he closed himself inside the house and cried for more than an hour. He was a broken man, and he knew it. *How did I get here?* he questioned, talking to himself. "The two people I love the most are paying for my drinking," he said out loud, convicting himself. He had made a deal with himself to stop drinking so many mornings that he could not count them. The deal always went out the window about five o'clock in the afternoon.

He unpacked his suitcase and drove to town to get something to eat. He hoped he would not see anyone he knew. So many of their friends had homes in Highlands. Main Street Inn was open for dinner, and he sat alone and ate beef pot roast and mashed potatoes. He wished he were at home eating Belle's pot roast and mashed potatoes with Charlotte and Caroline. When he returned to the house, he showered and went to bed.

The following morning he went to the small market in town to get some provisions. He got coffee, bread, milk, butter, and cold cuts. When he returned to the house, he made coffee and toast. The house had a deck that overlooked a creek. John sat in the one of the rocking chairs on the porch and drank coffee. It was peaceful with the sound of the creek and the birds. He stood to get another cup of coffee. The grief overwhelmed him again, and he cried. "God help me," he pleaded. He poured his coffee and came back to the porch and began to pray, "Lord, I can't do this without you. Please help me. Forgive me for all the pain I have caused my precious wife and daughter. You know my heart and you know I love them. If I need to quit my job, I am ready. Help me to know what is right. Give me the strength to stop drinking. I am not strong enough to do it by myself." John could hardly believe he was admitting that he was an alcoholic and could not stop drinking on his own. He always thought he could stop anytime he wanted to, but he knew now that he couldn't.

He felt as if a weight had been lifted off his shoulders for the first time in years. "Thank you, Lord," he whispered.

He walked down the steps from the deck leading to the back of the house. He decided to take a walk on the trail that Caroline and he always hiked on when they came to the mountains. His mind wandered back to all the conversations they had when she was in elementary school. *She was a very special girl even then. Those were very happy days,* he thought. His heart ached more realizing that he had missed so much of her adolescent years, partially because of his job and partially because he was drunk. Charlotte managed to hold their home together and provide Caroline with the stability she needed. He just didn't know if he could ever forgive himself.

For the next three days, he wrote letters to Charlotte and Caroline asking for forgiveness and promising to stop drinking. Before he went to bed each night, he got on his knees and prayed for help. He knew he had reached a turning point where he was going to lose his family if he didn't get himself together.

On Wednesday of the following week, Grant called to speak with John. "Mr. Wellington, he is not here," Belle said when she answered the telephone.

"Well, where is he?" Grand demanded.

"I'm sorry, Mr. Wellington. I don't know," she replied.

"Where is Charlotte?" came another demand from Grant.

"She is at Westminster with Miss Caroline today." Belle did not offer any more information, and Grant hung up the telephone without saying good-bye. For an instant, Belle felt sorry for John having to work for such an unkind man.

On Friday evening, John came back home. Charlotte and Caroline were out having dinner with Camilla Robinson and her daughter. Belle looked up from her baking when he came to the kitchen door. She did not speak to him but went back to her work. "Belle," John began sheepishly, "where are Charlotte and Caroline?"

"Out to dinner," Belle replied with as few words as possible. John turned and went upstairs.

The only reason Belle stayed in the kitchen until they got home was to tell them that he had come back.

Monday, John returned to work and walked into his father's office. Grant looked up from paperwork and stopped what he was doing when he saw John. "John, you just disappeared," Grant said inquisitively.

"Dad, I think you know what happened. I have been in Highlands for a few days to try to get myself together," John said in almost a whisper. "I'm here to resign. I can't work for you anymore."

"Now, John," Grant began, "Don't be so hasty."

"Hasty, Dad?" he asked sarcastically. "I am not being hasty. I am about fifteen years too late. I love and respect you as my father. But you are impossible to work for, and I won't do it anymore." John's tone was final, and Grant knew it.

"John, please give me a week and I'll work something out so we don't have to work so closely. You are so valuable to this company," Grant said, pleading with John.

"That's what I am to you, aren't I, Dad?" John said, disgusted. "Valuable to this company."

"John, that's not what I meant, and you know it." Grant's condescending tone was showing through. "I know you think I am a tyrant, and I have been very hard on you at times. But we have built a very valuable company here," he continued, softening his approach.

"Yes, we have, Dad," John said, "at my expense. I will give you a week to figure something out, and then I'm leaving," John said with a finality that Grant knew was not negotiable. John went to his office and closed the door. He intended to clear out his desk and prepare to find a job practicing law in Atlanta.

The following Monday morning, Grant called John to his office. "John, I have made the decision to sell Georgia Life. I am starting the process of having it valued and I will put on the market in January. If you will stay until it sells, you will have one-third of the proceeds of the sale and you can do whatever you want to do after that." Grant sat back in his chair waiting for John's reaction. John was stunned.

"Dad, I didn't expect this," he said, surprised.

"If the sale goes as I think it will, you will never have to work again in your life unless you want to," Grant offered. "I will give you the details of what I am thinking when I can complete my plan. I am ready to retire, and I can't run this company without you."

"Okay, Dad. I will stay and work through the sale of the company."

"Good, Son," Grant said. John had not heard him call him "Son" for a very long time. "I assume you know that your mother and I love you," Grant began, reticent to share his feelings. "But I do love you and I am proud that you are my son every day."

John broke down and sobbed. "I have waited a long time to hear you say that, Dad," he said, working to compose himself. "I love you and Mother, and I hate that our relationship has suffered so much for the sake of this company."

"It will be worth it when we are on the other side of the sale, John," Grant said. "I will keep you informed as we go along."

"Thanks, Dad," John said as he stood and walked around his father's desk to embrace him. Tears rolled down Grant's cheeks as they stood together in his office. John left the office, went to his office, and went back to work as usual.

For the next month, no one in the Wellington household had much, if anything, to say to John. Charlotte and Caroline were polite but mostly ignored him. Charlotte moved her clothes and personal things to a guest bedroom. Belle prepared meals for him and served him silently. John Wellington knew that he was losing his family.

John managed to stay sober for the entire month of July. He left the letters he wrote to Charlotte and Caroline in their rooms. He hoped and prayed they would give him another chance. If they read the letters, they did not tell him.

It was Sunday, August 2, and John had had enough of the silence and ostracizing. He decided to tell Charlotte about the sale of Georgia Life. He knocked on the guest bedroom door where she had been sleeping since June. "Come in," Charlotte said cordially. When John opened the door and stepped into the room, she stood up.

"Charlotte, I need to tell you what's going on at the company," John began, as if he were requesting permission to come into the room.

"Okay," Charlotte said dryly.

"I resigned from Georgia Life at the end of June," he said. "I told my father that I could not work for him anymore and I resigned. I planned to find a job in a law firm in Atlanta. I really didn't think it would be too hard. But my father surprised me and refused to accept my resignation."

Charlotte started to speak but did not. She sat back down and looked squarely at John.

John continued, "I gave my father one week to figure out what to do, and then I planned to clear out permanently. The following week he surprised me and told me that he planned to sell the company and retire. He will put the company on the market in January. I will have one-third of the proceeds of the sale, and then I can retire too. What I am getting to is that I am working to change the things in my life that cause me so much anxiety. I drink to stop the panicked feelings I seem to have almost every day. But I know I can't do that anymore. Losing you and Caroline is the worst thing I can think of in the world. I love you, and I'm so sorry I have hurt both of you. I hope you see that I am trying to get myself together."

"Yes, I have noticed that you have not been drinking lately," Charlotte offered, actually feeling sorry for him. "I would love for us to be a family again and enjoy being together, but we just don't know when you will get drunk and go into a rage. The concussion in June did it for me, John. I am done. When Caroline graduates from high school and leaves for college, I will be leaving too." She was glad to finally have her thoughts out in the open. She wanted to preserve whatever self-respect she had left and set an example for Caroline. It would be terrible, but it had to be done.

"Charlotte, please don't leave," John begged. His lips began to quiver, and Charlotte could see tears rolling down his cheeks. "Promise me you will give me another chance."

"John, I want to," Charlotte began, "but I have paid a terrible price for staying with you this long. Caroline is paying the price for your alcoholism too, and I refuse to allow her to think that it is okay to stay married to an abusive alcoholic." Charlotte had never been so direct and blunt with John. In her heart, she wanted to give him another chance, but her head was in charge now and she couldn't live this way anymore.

"Charlotte, the truth is, my life is not worth living without you and Caroline," John said, choking back the tears. "I will never hurt you again. I love you with all my heart, and I want take care of you for the rest of your life. I have so many regrets . . ." His voice trailed off.

"This has been the hardest decision I have ever made, John," Charlotte said. "Caroline loves you so much, but she doesn't trust you anymore. She wants to, but she can't. You have let her down so many times."

John put his face in his hands and sobbed. He knew he was emotionally fragile, and although he tried, he could not stop crying.

Charlotte had been through so much; she had no more emotion to spend on John.

"I want to be the person you married," John said, reflecting on their happiness for the first couple of years they were married. "You are the most beautiful woman I have ever seen, and I love you more now than the day I married you. You are the backbone of our family, and I know it. You will not be sorry if you give me another chance. I promise."

Charlotte's resolve was weakening. "John, the only way I can consider staying is if the drinking and the abuse stop completely. I will not put Caroline or myself through this anymore. I can't give you an answer today. You will have to allow me to think about it."

John saw a glimmer of hope. "Thank you, Charlotte," he said genuinely. "That's all I can ask for and more than I deserve." He turned and walked out of the room, closing the door quietly as he left.

CHAPTER 7

By September, life at the younger Wellingtons' home was back on a better track. John and Charlotte had talked through their many issues. They agreed to work together at least until Caroline graduated from high school. In her heart, Charlotte hoped they would work through all the difficulties and remain married. She knew that John loved her, and she loved him in spite of everything. She could see that John was truly trying to stop drinking. He did not stop completely, but he had not so much as spoken harshly to her, and he certainly had not hurt her again.

Caroline made him promise that he would not hurt her mother ever again. He did, and this time he kept the promise.

John was working very hard to restore the trust that was broken by his years of drinking and abuse.

Life at the Wellington home was, for the most part, peaceful. Belle and Robert were both glad to see everyone getting along and at least talking to one another.

Caroline learned the following March that her grandparents expected her to make her formal debut at the Phoenix Society Debutante Ball at the Piedmont Driving Club where they were members. Caroline did not like high-society events. She had endured formal parties at Peacock House almost all of her life. The orchestras, garden parties, and Christmas galas had left her with very little desire to make her debut. Grant and Elizabeth seldom acknowledged what was going on in their home even though they were aware of John's drinking and violent history toward Charlotte. It was swept under the rug to make the Wellington family look perfect.

Nevertheless, make her debut she did. In June, on her father's arm and dressed in a formal white gown with seed pearls on a silk bodice and a silk organza skirt with white gloves above her elbows, she made her debut to Atlanta society. She was almost sixteen, and it would have been embarrassing to her grandfather had she refused. Caroline was a vision, and John was very handsome in his tuxedo, beaming with pride and love for his only child. The crystal chandeliers cast a soft light as each girl walked the length of the ballroom on her father's arm. The room was filled with club members and other dignitaries invited for the occasion. Grant and Elizabeth were seated with Charlotte and Irene. As Caroline and John passed by their table, she winked at Irene and giggled, to Elizabeth's horror. After the presentations, the orchestra began to play. John took his daughter onto the dance floor, and that evening, one might have thought they were professional ballroom dancers. They glided to the orchestra's beautiful arrangement of the "Blue Danube Waltz." As they were leaving the ballroom floor, the orchestra struck up Frank Sinatra's rendition of "The Way You Look Tonight." The member of the orchestra who was singing sounded so much like "Old Blue Eyes" that people were straining to see if it was actually him. Before they reached the edge of the dance floor, John stopped Caroline and took her by the hand and back onto the dance floor. He said, "Baby girl, I am so proud of you. This is the song I will always sing to you." As they danced, John sang the song to Caroline.

Some day, when I'm awfully low,
When the world is cold,

I will feel a glow just thinking of you . . .
And the way you look tonight.

Caroline enjoyed every moment of the dance as tears streamed down her face. When it was over, she put both arms around her father and said, "I love you so much, Daddy."

"I love you so much too, baby girl," John said with the most tender and loving look.

Grant, Elizabeth, Charlotte, and Irene were so touched that there was not a dry eye among them when John and Caroline returned to the table after the song was over. That evening would be a very special memory for Caroline for the rest of her life.

She did not attend the traditional breakfast after the ball. Being in the spotlight was just not her cup of tea. Charlotte did not insist that she go. She felt that Caroline had honored Grant and Elizabeth's wishes, and most of the hobnobbing was over after dinner anyway. She would be in the *Atlanta Journal* and the *Atlanta Constitution*, satisfying Grant and Elizabeth's requirement for her to be in high society in Atlanta. Grant and Elizabeth could boast about it at the club for at least a year.

After they arrived home that evening, John found Charlotte in their bedroom. He took Charlotte's hands and again asked for her forgiveness. "Charlotte, I know I have been a monster. I love you and Caroline more than anything in the world. You have no reason to think that I will do better but I am trying. Please give me another chance."

Charlotte glimpsed the man she fell in love with, and her heart melted. She put her arms around him and cried.

"I am so sorry, Charlotte," John whispered as he held her and cried.

"You need to talk to Caroline, John," Charlotte said, trying to compose herself. "She loves you so much. I have never seen her so sad."

"I know I have a long way to go to regain your trust, but I really am trying," John said, still pleading. "I hope you can see that."

"I know that you haven't been drinking as much for a while," Charlotte said as she ran her fingers through his hair. "You'd better go and talk with Caroline." Charlotte stepped back from his embrace and looked him square in his eyes.

John did as she instructed. He knocked on her bedroom door. "Come in" came Caroline's sweet voice. John opened the door and stepped into her room. Caroline stood. "Daddy," she said, "are you all right?"

"Not really, baby girl," he replied quietly. "I want to tell you how beautiful you were tonight and how much I enjoyed the evening. I also want to you to know that I would like for you to forgive me for everything I have done to you and Mama. I am trying to do better. I told Mama and I am telling you that I know you have no reason to believe me, but I love you so much and I can't bear the thought of losing the two people that mean more to me than anything."

"Daddy, I love you and Mama more than anything," Caroline began as the tears fell again. "I am so scared that you are going to kill Mama." She sobbed, and John put his arms around her.

"I am so sorry, Caroline," John said softly. "You and Mama deserve nothing but good things. I have really let you both down, and I know it."

"Yes, you have let us down, Daddy," Caroline said, pulling out of his embrace. "I want to believe you, but I don't know how to trust you anymore."

"Caroline, I promise that I will never hurt Mama again," John said resolutely.

"Will you stop drinking too?" Caroline asked emphatically.

"I'm trying, Caroline," John said. "I am ashamed of myself, and I know I have a problem. I'm working on it. I promise I am."

John's pleading voice made Caroline feel so sorry and so sad for him that she put her arms around him and said, "Yes, Daddy. Mama and I want you to be okay, and we love you. Please stop drinking."

"I will, baby girl. I promise," John said as he broke down and cried. "Thank you for giving me another chance."

Caroline's heart broke as she hugged her father. She could not remember feeling so sorry for anyone in her life.

John returned to their bedroom. Charlotte looked at him expectantly. "I promised her that I would stop drinking and I would never hurt you again. She wants us to be a family again too. She deserves that," he said.

Charlotte walked over to him, put her arms around him and kissed him. That was all the invitation that John needed. They made love for the first time in months.

CHAPTER 8

*F*OR THE NEXT SIX MONTHS, John was sober more than he was drunk, but occasionally he drank until he could not walk upstairs to bed. Some of those mornings, Charlotte found him in the library asleep in his chair. Although he didn't keep his promise about not drinking, he did keep his promise to not hurt Charlotte anymore.

At the beginning of her senior year at Westminster, Caroline began worrying about leaving for college. She was afraid that her father would start being abusive to her mother again after she was gone. That concern brought her to the decision to ask her grandparents for help.

In February, Caroline visited Grant and Elizabeth. She drove a new 1965 Ford Thunderbird that John bought her for her seventeenth birthday to her grandparents' home. Elizabeth greeted her at the door, and the two of them walked toward the den where Grant was watching his favorite show, *What's My Line*.

"I need to talk to you, Grandmother. Would you get Granddaddy? I want to talk with him too," Caroline stated flatly.

"Well of course, dear. Come into the den, and Granddaddy and I will be glad to talk with you," she replied in an accommodating tone.

When the television had been turned off, Caroline began. "I have tried for years to reconcile the way my father has treated my mother. But I have concluded that there is no way I can do that. My father has been so abusive to my mother, and I believe both of you know that. He has been drunk at night so often that it would be easier for me to count the days when he has been sober. He is trying to stop drinking, and he has not hurt Mama in a while now. But this fall, I will leave for college. I have been the only thing standing between my mother and the abuse so many times. When I'm not there, I am afraid of what might happen to her. He has been a lot better in the last few months, but sometimes he still drinks too much. I love both of my parents very much. My father is a wonderful and loving man when he is sober, but he can be a monster when he drinks. I need your help to get my father sober. I have read about a twelve-step program that has worked for some people. It's called Alcoholics Anonymous. I can't convince Daddy to read the book and go to the program, but I think you can. Will you help me?" When Caroline finished her monologue, her grandparents sat silently staring at her. Caroline spoke again, "Well, will you help me?"

Elizabeth spoke first, "Caroline, truthfully, we believe your mother is part of the reason your father drinks. She has hounded him and hounded him to not drink for years. There are things that she has done that you don't know about that have humiliated him."

"You mean when she dropped him off at the hospital when he passed out at the Stocktons' house?" Caroline retorted.

"Well, yes, that and other things," Elizabeth said.

"That was a very long time ago, Grandmother. What about what he has done to my mother? She is not the reason that he drinks,

Grandmother," Caroline screamed. "Granddaddy, will you help me?" Caroline begged.

"Sweetheart, all this is going to be resolved when we sell Georgia Life. We're selling the company in June. Your daddy knows that. The day-to-day stress that he faces will be over. Your daddy, and you, of course, will have all the money you will need for the rest of your lives."

"What about my mother?" Caroline shouted. "What about her? She is partially responsible for daddy's success, and you know that. So what about her, Granddaddy?"

"Honey, she will be fine too. There are provisions for her—nothing for you to worry about. You just concentrate on college. We'll take care of things here."

Caroline rose stiffly, "I understand perfectly. I certainly do." And she left.

Caroline knew that she and she alone would have to be sure that her mother was safe when she went to college. She wanted so much for her father to be sober. Belle couldn't do it because she was getting older and was beginning to have difficulty keeping up with her daily cooking. Robert couldn't do it. Katy had long been gone to nanny for another family. So who would watch over her mother?

When Caroline arrived home about six o'clock, the house was very quiet. She walked into the kitchen where Belle was preparing dinner. "Where's Mama?" she asked.

"She's in her room resting, sugar. Your daddy is in the library, but you may not want to go in there right now. He is in his usual state, Caroline."

Caroline ignored the advice and walked straight to the library. "Daddy, I have to talk to you," she blurted out. "I have to talk to you now." She sat down on the ottoman in front of the leather chair where he was sitting. He was obviously drinking but was still pretty coherent. "Daddy, I'm so worried about leaving for college. I am worried about Mama and the way you treat her when you are drinking. I don't want her to be hurt after I leave, Daddy."

"Don't you think I know that every day of my life, Caroline?" he replied in a low and raspy voice. "I know I need help. I pray about it every day." His voice trailed off. "I'm not feeling very well today, Caroline. Could we have this conversation later, maybe tomorrow morning?" he said with a note of sadness Caroline had never heard.

Caroline stood up, kissed him on his cheek, and said, "Yes, Daddy, we can talk tomorrow. I love you very much."

"I love you too, baby girl," he said lovingly.

Their eyes met briefly, and Caroline saw his love for her. Caroline turned to walk back to the kitchen when she heard her father cry out. When she turned, she saw him sit straight up in the chair and fall back with his eyes and mouth wide open.

"Daddy, Daddy!" Caroline screamed. "Daddy, are you all right? Please don't die. Daddy, we can fix everything. Daddy, Daddy, can you hear me?" she said, still screaming. "Belle, call an ambulance, quick. *Belle, Belle, help me, Belle!*" She was still screaming but now crying.

Charlotte came into the library to find out what all the yelling was about. *"Oh my God, John,"* Charlotte shouted. "I knew this was going to happen. I knew it. Oh my God, John." Charlotte sank to her knees in front of the chair, sobbing. She took his hand and gently stroked it. She touched his face and closed his eyes. She kissed his cheek. "My precious love," she said quietly. "John, I know you loved me. I forgive you for all the bad times. John, John, John, please don't leave me."

Caroline was standing behind her mother sobbing inconsolably. Belle was holding Charlotte's hand. "It's gonna be all right, Miss Charlotte. I don't know how, but I know it's gonna be all right," Belle said, comforting Charlotte.

When the ambulance arrived the paramedics determined that there was no respiration or heartbeat.

John Wellington was dead at the age of fifty-three. Charlotte went to the telephone to call Grant and Elizabeth. "I'll do that, Mama," Caroline said, putting her arms around her and working to compose herself. "Let me do that." And she did.

Elizabeth and Grant rang the doorbell about a half hour after the ambulance had taken John's body to the hospital. Elizabeth was pale and trembling. Grant walked straight into the library, sat in John's chair, and cried. Elizabeth sat on the sofa with Charlotte and Caroline, and everyone cried. There was nothing else left to do. John was gone. Dr. Denmark confirmed later that evening that it was a massive heart attack.

Charlotte's memories of John flooded in. It was as if every minute of her life with him was in review in her mind. The special moments in their life together were in her thoughts almost like a movie. She wished she had sought help for him more urgently than she did. She wondered if help for him would have changed anything. The only thing she could do now is bury him. *God help me!* Charlotte thought. *I have lost my true love.* The shock was overwhelming, but she had to take care of all the arrangements. She would do that and put her feelings aside until it was done. Then she would have the emotional breakdown she had earned.

Elizabeth and Grant sensed that they needed to allow Charlotte to handle the funeral arrangements, and so with very little advice, Charlotte handled everything. She called Patterson's Funeral Home at Spring Hill, and the arrangements were made. Patterson's was a very beautiful old Atlanta funeral home. The formal gardens were immaculate, complemented by the granite exterior. The service would be at the Second Ponce de Leon Baptist Church, and John would be laid to rest in Arlington Cemetery in Sandy Springs.

The next two days were a blur for Caroline. There were flowers all over the house and at the funeral home. The night of the visitation at Patterson's, Caroline never met so many Atlanta dignitaries in her life. It seemed that Atlanta's most influential people came to offer their sympathy and pay their respects. Cards came from heads of corporations that worked with Georgia Life from New York to Miami. Irene was with Charlotte constantly and stayed with them at the Peacock House. Charlotte handled everything with grace and class.

The day after the funeral, Charlotte was sitting in the solarium with Caroline. Belle was close by, providing tea and sandwiches. The grief was palpable. The telephone rang. Belle answered, "Wellington residence." It was Grant. He asked to speak with Charlotte.

"Hello," Charlotte said weakly.

"Charlotte, this is Grant. I know this is an awful time for everyone, but I need to talk with you about John's will," Grant said.

Charlotte thought he was far too businesslike for a man who just lost his only child. "Mr. Wellington, could you give me a week or so? I am very tired—exhausted would be a better description," Charlotte replied politely.

"I suppose so, but we need to talk next week," Grant said, once again sounding very businesslike.

"Okay," Charlotte said and hung up the telephone.

What else can happen, she thought. *What the hell else can happen?*

Caroline returned to school the beginning of the following week. It was as if her world had stopped but everyone else's just kept on moving. Her friends were very kind, and most of them conveyed their own and their parents' sympathy. *They could not possibly know how I feel,* Caroline thought. *How could they?* No one really knew that her father was an alcoholic. Those things were not discussed. Caroline was glad that no one knew. She loved her father even with his problems. He was a brilliant lawyer who subjected himself to his father's tyranny in exchange for wealth and prestige. Caroline envied families with normal lifestyles. Why couldn't her father have left Georgia Life? He would have been successful on his own. That question would never be answered.

Over the next weeks and months, Caroline placed her father's memory on a pedestal and remembered the wonderful and loving man that he was when he was sober. She could hardly believe it was June and it was almost time for her to leave for the University of Virginia. She loved Virginia and Charlottesville especially. Her interest in political science led her to choose UVA. Charlotte was so proud of her daughter. She had received the only merit scholarship to UVA awarded that year at Westminster.

Two months before Caroline was scheduled to leave, Charlotte came to her room and said, "Caroline, honey, I need to talk with you."

Caroline looked up from her organizer and said, "Sure, Mama, have a seat," patting the bed next to where she was sitting.

"Caroline, Peacock House will be sold. There is a buyer, and if all goes well, the house will be sold in late July," Charlotte said, waiting for the news to settle in.

"Mama, I expected that you would. I have been saying 'good-bye' to these walls all summer. This house is just too big. What will you do with the money?" Caroline asked.

"Honey, I'm afraid there is no money for me from the sale of the house—only in trust for you," Charlotte replied with acceptance. "Daddy left me enough money to be okay, but I am going to move back to Roswell near Mama Rene. She needs me now anyway."

"What do you mean there is no money for you, Mother?" Caroline put her organizer down and looked directly at her mother.

"Your granddaddy talked your father into changing his will about six months before he died. My guess is that he caught him when he was drinking, and you know how Daddy was with Granddaddy," Charlotte said with more kindness than Caroline thought he deserved.

"What about Belle and Robert?" Caroline asked.

"Robert has a job in Roswell working for Mr. Mansard. He will treat him fairly. Belle will go with me. I am going to buy the old Seymour place on Mimosa Boulevard. I can walk to Mama Rene's house."

"I know where it is, Mama. Mama Rene used to let me climb a tree in the front yard of that house." She put her arms around her mother and hugged her so tight. "Mama, I'm so proud of you. You have taught me so much. I love you with all my heart." Charlotte cried, but this time the tears were joyful.

Caroline refused to allow her mother to see the fury she felt toward her grandfather. *How dare he kick my mother out of her own house*, she thought. But there was nothing she could do, at least not now.

Just like Irene and Charlotte, Caroline was extremely resourceful. She contacted her father's attorney and requested a meeting. He reluctantly agreed, and the appointment was on Tuesday of the following week. As Caroline was announced into Mr. Bernstein's office, he took in a breath and said, "My God, you look just like your mother."

"Why, thank you, Mr. Bernstein," Caroline replied as she sat in the Queen Anne chair in the formally decorated office. "Let me get straight to the point. I have a will here that my father signed two years before his death. I know there is another will that was signed six months before he died. I believe that my grandfather strong-armed him into signing the new will against his own better judgment."

Harvey Bernstein thought that Caroline was extraordinarily articulate for her age. He sat back in his chair and studied her face for a long time. "Caroline, I am in a very precarious position here. You know that I represent your grandparents, and it is unethical for me to discuss their business with you without their permission," he offered finally.

"Okay, then," Caroline said. "Refer me to the best attorney you know who can contest the will for me."

"Caroline, in my opinion that would be a waste of time and money. Your father's will has been probated and executed. Your mother has the details of her inheritance as well as yours. Your inheritance, although it is in trust, should make you a very happy young lady." His tone was condescending, and it made Caroline mad.

"Mr. Bernstein, I am well aware of the details of our inheritance. My mother's portion is far below the provisions in the original will. My grandparents are not open to discussing this with me. Well, hell, they are the culprits for God's sake," she said emphatically.

"Miss Wellington, I am very sorry, but I am unable to help you today. I wish you the best." He rose, dismissing her from his office.

This was Caroline's first real lesson in politics. Money and power—that is what it is all about—money and power.

Caroline dropped the notion of contesting her father's will on her mother's behalf. He had left her $12 million that she would receive on her twenty-first birthday. The funds were already in a trust handled by the court-appointed trustee, so her grandfather could not change that. She would receive $20,000 a year, and that was more than she needed. She would just take care of her mother herself. Caroline later learned that Georgia Life Insurance Company owned their home, and that is why it had to be sold when the company was sold. John had left Charlotte $1 million and all the furnishings and jewelry, so she would be okay for now.

On the day before the sale of the house, the doorbell rang at Peacock Mansion. There were boxes everywhere, but Robert hurried to the door. Grant and Elizabeth Wellington stepped through the door unannounced. Grant began walking through the house, and Elizabeth went to the kitchen to see if Belle was there.

Caroline came to the top of the stairs from her room. "Robert, who was at the door?" she asked.

"Miss Caroline, it's Mr. and Mrs. Wellington," replied Robert hesitantly.

"Well, where are they?"

"Why, they both just started walking through the house."

"What?" Caroline screamed. She flew down the stairs and into the library, where she found Grant looking at books that were not yet been packed. "What are you doing, Granddaddy?" asked Caroline.

"I'm just here to get some of the books I loaned to your father," he replied.

"Could you not have called to say that you wanted to stop by for that purpose?" she scolded him.

"Young lady, I do not need for you to correct me today. This is my house, and these are my books," he replied in a sarcastic tone.

Caroline walked over to her grandfather and said, "Get out of *my* house—get out now. I will let you know when it is *convenient* for my mother and me to see you here. Understand? First, you talk Daddy into changing his will and almost leaving Mama out of it, and now you have no regard for what we are going through just showing up and acting like we don't belong here. Why are you treating us so badly?"

Grant's eyes flashed at her, but he knew she meant what she said. He had never seen her act that way before. Caroline stepped into the hall and shouted, "Robert, Mr. and Mrs. Wellington are leaving now."

Grant found Elizabeth in the kitchen and said, "We will have to come back at a better time, Elizabeth. Let's go."

"But Grant," Elizabeth resisted.

"Elizabeth, we are leaving *now*," Grant said emphatically. And they left.

Caroline hoped that her mother had not heard the exchange. She was in her room packing. She called Robert and Belle and said, "Not a word to Mama. Do you understand? Not a word. She has been through enough."

"She sure has, honey," Belle replied sadly. "She sure has."

Charlotte did not attend the closing on the sale of the house, but she insisted that Grant allow her thirty days after closing to get everything moved. He honored that request, so the closing was actually a nonevent to Charlotte and Caroline.

On the morning of the closing, Charlotte called Caroline, Belle, and Robert and said, "Let's go to Roswell. We can take some of our stuff to our new house." They loaded as many boxes as they could into their new 1966 Chevrolet station wagon and off they went. When they arrived in Roswell, Charlotte decided to surprise her mother. When they pulled into the driveway, the house was dark and quiet. *Well, I wonder where she is,* thought Charlotte. Just then, Irene pulled into the driveway behind them. She jumped out of the car, seeing Belle, Robert, Charlotte, and Caroline.

"Is everything okay?" she asked in a frightened voice.

"Everything is fine, Mother. We just came by here before we went to our new house. We have some stuff to drop off."

"Lord, child. You scared the daylights out of me. With everything that's happened, I just don't know what to expect," said Irene, chuckling and seeming thrilled to see them as she hugged everyone.

"Mother, come on down to the house with us," Charlotte requested.

"As long as I don't have to walk. It's hotter than a June bride in a feather bed out here," Irene said in her typical southern drawl. The whole group howled with laughter. Irene hopped in the car with them, and down the street they went to the new house.

It was a beautiful, well-maintained old home on Mimosa. The house was built in 1898 and was a colonial-style with four large Georgian columns across the ten-foot wide front porch that went across the entire front of the house and wrapped halfway around both sides. The original leaded-glass windows allowed generous light into the dining room and the living room. Charlotte had purchased the house three weeks earlier, and the contractors had begun construction on the guesthouse for Belle behind the main house and the renovations in the main house. Charlotte allowed Belle to choose everything from her kitchen appliances to the wall colors. Belle had a twinkle in her eye that Charlotte had not seen for a long time. The guesthouse had two bedrooms, and Robert decided to accept the invitation to share the guesthouse with Belle. The only thing Charlotte asked is that he help her keep the yard. He agreed, and that was that.

After they had unloaded the boxes and walked through every room planning furniture placement, Charlotte said, "Let's go to the Public House for dinner."

"Great idea, Mama," exclaimed Caroline.

And off they went, the five of them walking the short two blocks across the square to the Public House. Charlotte had long ago stopped caring what people thought of her. It was unusual in the 1960s for white people and black people to dine together in a nice restaurant. She was fifty-three years old now, still beautiful, and absolutely her own woman.

The Public House was a quaint restaurant on the Square in Roswell that served upscale southern cuisine. The building that housed the Public House was built in the early 1800s. It originally served as a general store for the mill workers at Roswell Mill. Caroline loved the stories that Irene had told her all of her life about her family in Roswell and the many generations of her kin folks who lived and worked in the community in the eighteenth and nineteenth centuries. Caroline always felt a connection in Roswell that she felt nowhere else.

The group was seated cordially with only a few raised eyebrows, and they all enjoyed a dinner of wonderful southern food.

CHAPTER 9

A MONTH LATER, WHEN THE MOVERS had emptied the Peacock House, Charlotte walked through the empty house alone. She went into each room, remembering. When she came to John's library, she sat on the floor where his chair had been and cried and cried and cried. She lay on the floor and cried. Her heart was broken, and she missed John so much. In spite of the abuse and the difficulties, somehow Charlotte had always been able to see past that with John. She knew that Grant was demanding and difficult. He expected John to make up for all of his deficiencies. John tried, and it killed him in the process. That is what Charlotte would believe for the rest of her life. He was her one true love. She missed him more than she could or would ever tell anyone.

She visited Arlington Cemetery at least once a week and sat and talked with John as if he were sitting in front of her.

Three days later, Charlotte was living in Roswell again. When she was unpacking at her new home, she found a journal that she had not paid any attention to before. When she opened the journal, she saw that it was in John's beautiful handwriting. The page she opened was dated October 2, 1958. "Today is Caroline's tenth birthday. She looks more like her mother every day. Today is the

second game of the World Series, and the Braves kicked the Yankees
butts. I wish Atlanta had a major league baseball team. The Braves
would be great in Atlanta. Dad wants Livingston Industrial to
accept our proposal of insuring their manufacturing operation and
providing insurance for their officers and employees. The 'key man'
insurance idea is not working with them yet. Dad told me not to
bother showing up on Monday if I had not landed that deal and
worked out all the legalities. I have become my father's lap dog.
It was my greatest fear. Every day is another mountain to climb
with him. I just can't face working with him anymore. How can
I tell Charlotte and Caroline that we have to move and be regular
folks instead of the Atlanta elite? I never thought of myself that
way anyway. My father and mother did, though. My education and
experience seem to be something for them to exploit. I am so tired.
I love my wife and daughter so much, but I don't know how to go
on. I have to go on for their sake. I know that. Caroline is the most
beautiful child I have ever seen. As it turns out, she is also quite
intelligent. Wonder where she gets that? Probably from her mother.
Charlotte, Charlotte, Charlotte, I love you more than I could ever
tell you. I am sorry for my shortcomings. I am working on it. I hope
you know that."

Charlotte wept for so long that she lost track of the time.

When she was able to recover, she stood up and said, "John
Wellington, your daughter is an incredible young woman. I hope
you can see that, wherever you are. Can you hear me, John?" And
she collapsed in the middle of the room, sobbing again.

The weeks that followed found Charlotte immersed in the total
renovation of her new home on Mimosa Boulevard. She restored
the front porch to its original beauty. The porch covered the entire
front of the house and was ten feet wide. It had a bead board ceiling
and a beautiful gray painted floor. She chose a white wood porch
swing that she had installed on the far right end of the porch. The
red and yellow cushions made the porch look almost like an indoor

room. There were two comfortable white rocking chairs on the same side of the porch with the same beautiful cushions. On the far left side of the porch was a white outdoor dining table and four chairs with cushions that matched the others. Two more rocking chairs with matching cushions finished that side. Ten people could sit comfortably out there. The clapboard two-story house was painted white with dark green shutters. The red front door complemented the cushions on the chairs. On each side of the front door were large brass gas lanterns.

Charlotte stood on the front porch taking another critical look at the placement of the furniture and the plants in the large clay pots. She opened the front door and stepped into the newly renovated foyer.

The foyer was wide, with the living room on the left and the dining room on the right. The stairs were the centerpiece of the foyer, and Charlotte had put a large table with a Tiffany blue lamp to the right of the stairs. The fireplaces in the living room and dining room were original to the house. Charlotte had them restored and repaired. She chose brown and white marble with a white mantle for the living room. For the dining room she chose a green marble that had a lot of brown, rust, and white. The mantle was white. The dining room had judges paneling painted white below the chair rail and beautiful Schumacher green-and-white wallpaper that looked like panels in light green and gold. Charlotte strolled through each room making sure every detail was covered. She had brought her dining room furniture with her, and the dining room was expanded to accommodate it. The green-and-white striped silk damask covered the two ceiling-to-floor windows. Behind the dining room was a butler's pantry that led into the kitchen. She was very pleased with the addition of the butler's pantry. Her hopes of entertaining in their new home allowed her to agree to that suggestion from the contractor.

She walked into the living room and sat on the red Chippendale sofa with the two Queen Anne chairs that had been in the den at Peacock House. The chairs were covered in a stripe with red, royal blue, yellow, and green. The drapes were a small repeating pattern of yellow silk with red fleur-de-lis. The room was inviting and interesting with light sage green walls that were the same color as the wallpaper in the dining room. She looked around the room, wishing that John could see it.

Charlotte love impressionist art and had several beautiful original artworks framed for the living room. It was comfortably elegant, as was the entire house.

She walked to the kitchen to get a glass of sweet iced tea. It had the latest appliances, beautiful granite counters, and white cabinets. Belle loved cooking in the new kitchen. The walls were painted a very light yellow, and the room was very cheerful. In the breakfast area was a light blue washed country French dining table with six matching chairs. She knew that she and Caroline would spend a lot of time in the kitchen with Belle, and she wanted it to be comfortable and cheerful.

The family room had John's leather sofa, but she had sold the chairs. She couldn't bear to look at the chair John was sitting in when he died. It was a comfortable room with cherry paneling and a beautiful stacked stone fireplace. There were two dark red club chairs with ottomans in front of the three windows, which were covered with dark wood blinds. The room was very warm. The house was not as elegant as Peacock House. It was smaller and very welcoming, and it felt like home to Charlotte.

CHAPTER 10

*C*AROLINE WAS DOING WELL AT the University of Virginia. Her looks and personality opened doors for her with very little effort on her part. She pledged the Chi Omega Sorority and was easily accepted. She hoped that her double major in political science and French would secure her a position at law school at Emory University in Atlanta. But she was enjoying her life at UVA. Caroline had many friends, but there was one in particular with whom she spent hours talking. He was a handsome young man from Charleston. Garrett Winthrop was a history buff, and Caroline loved his version of the Great War of Northern Aggression. He was the oldest of three children and had two younger sisters who were still in high school. His mother's family was from Charleston. His father was from Boston. They met at Washington and Lee and married the month they graduated. His father was a chemical engineer and worked in a civilian job for the military. Most of what he did was top secret, so Garrett could not really tell Caroline much about his job. His mother, although she graduated with a degree in nursing, worked only briefly, until Garrett was born. Garrett was very sympathetic when he learned of her father's death. "It's hard for me to imagine life without my father," he offered gently.

"It's very difficult for me to realize that he is gone," Caroline said quietly, choking back tears. "Let's talk about something happy, shall we?" she said as she stood to walk back to her dormitory.

"I'll walk with you, Caroline," Garrett said.

"Thanks, Garrett," Caroline said as she studied his face. She was beginning to wonder if she wanted him to be more than a friend. *Nope,* she thought. *Not now. I have too much to do. And she dismissed the notion all together.*

They strolled back to her dormitory. Caroline lived in Hereford Residential College in Malone House. It was one of the oldest buildings on campus, and she loved the diversity of the student population. The afternoon sun was warm, but Caroline could feel fall in the air. "Garrett," she quizzed, "do you know what you want to do after college?"

"Not really," he offered honestly. "One of my goals before the end of my freshman year is to have a better idea of what I want to do. I would love to live in Washington, DC, for a while and work at the Capitol. I love the energy there. My dad knows a couple of our senators pretty well, and he believes that he could get me an appointment into one of their offices after graduation. I probably will go to graduate school, but I haven't found the 'thing' that interests me enough to plant my feet. Do you know what you want to do?"

"Yes," Caroline answered without hesitation. "I want to go to Emory Law School in Atlanta and practice law there."

"Wow!" exclaimed Garrett. "That was very definite!"

"My father was a lawyer. I don't know if I ever mentioned that to you before," Caroline explained.

"We haven't talked much about your father. I think you lost him too recently to talk about him with someone you only just met," Garrett said softly.

"You're right. We were going to talk about something happy," Caroline said as she changed the subject. "Garrett, my sorority is having an informal tea on Sunday afternoon. Would you join me as my guest?" Caroline asked.

"I think so. I'm sorry to not give you a definite answer. I may have an event myself at the Sigma Chi house. Can I call you later?" Garrett said apologetically.

"Sure," Caroline said, dismissing the subject all together. They arrived at her dormitory and exchanged their good-byes.

Caroline had turned to go in when Garrett touched her arm. "Thank you very much for the invitation, Caroline," he said timidly. "I'll call you within the hour."

"Thanks, Garrett," Caroline said and walked into the dorm.

Garrett walked the short distance to Dillard Dorm. As he entered the front door, his fraternity brother, Scott Mason, stopped him to ask if he was going to the party after the game on Saturday night. "I have been so busy, truthfully, that I had not thought about it until you mentioned it," Garrett said. "What's the deal?"

"Boy, you need to get a social life, buddy," Scott said.

"What's that?" replied Garrett as he turned and went into the building.

"Well, are you coming or not?" Scott yelled after him.

"You'll be the first to know when I decide," Garrett retorted.

"Just trying to help you out," Scott said as he walked toward the stadium.

When Caroline got to her room, she found a message taped to her door. It said, "Call your mother." Caroline felt instant panic, and she ran to the telephone and called her mother. "Hello," said Charlotte in a carefree voice.

"Mama, is everything all right?" Caroline asked. Charlotte could hear the panic in her voice.

"Yes, of course everything is all right, sweetheart. I just needed to hear your sweet voice and catch up with you. I miss you, you know. I haven't seen you for six weeks," Charlotte said lovingly.

"I know, Mama. I miss you so much too," Caroline replied sadly.

"But," Charlotte began again, "I do have a question to ask you."

"Okay, go for it," Caroline said playfully. Charlotte could hear the relief in her voice. She worried about how severely her father's death had affected her. Caroline had terrible nightmares in the months after John's death. Even with counseling, they did not go away until she left for college.

"Mama Rene and I would like to come up to see you next weekend, if you are available. We want to see Monticello and go to Williamsburg, so we thought we would spend either Saturday or Sunday or both with you. We're flexible," Charlotte said.

"Mama, that would be fabulous," Caroline said, more excited than Charlotte had heard her in months.

"We will be staying at the Clifton Inn. Mama Rene and I would like for you to spend Saturday night with us if you can."

"That's *next* weekend, right?" asked Caroline.

"That's right, sweetheart," replied Charlotte.

"It's perfect, Mother. I can't wait to see you," squealed Caroline.

"Okay then, Sugar Plum. I'll call you when we get there on Saturday. I love you," said Charlotte.

"Y'all be careful driving up here," cautioned Caroline.

"Don't you worry about a thing, honey; we will," Charlotte said sweetly.

It was Thursday, and Caroline had a French exam on Friday. She had just sat down at her desk, opened her books, and began studying when the telephone rang again. "Hello," said Caroline.

"Hi, this is Garrett."

"Hi, Garrett," replied Caroline.

"I wanted to let you know that I will be able to attend the sorority tea with you," he said in a rather matter-of-fact tone.

"That's great, Garrett," Caroline said pleasantly. "Why don't you come to my dorm about two thirty and I'll drive us over to the sorority house. It's across the campus and pretty far to walk."

"I'll be there," said Garrett. "Gotta go study, myself."

"See you then. Bye," Caroline said and put the telephone back on the receiver. She went back to her books.

Charlotte had insisted that Caroline have a private room. Caroline required her "private time," as she called it. It was one of the things that Caroline agreed to that might have revealed her family's wealth. No one would believe that she herself was independently wealthy, and she wanted to keep that fact completely private.

Her room was bright and cheerful. She had brought an antique chest that had been in her room at the Peacock House. Above the chest was a large framed photograph of her mother, her father, and herself on their trip to London. She loved the photograph because it brought back such wonderful memories. Although Caroline grew up in a very lavish home, she preferred simple décor.

Most of her room was very practical, and the furniture and lamps were useful. Her closet was a different story. Caroline loved clothes and shoes. She didn't care much for jewelry, except the necklace her father gave her for her second birthday and the emerald ring her mother gave her for Christmas. The necklace had several new chains, but the pendant was still beautiful. It went with everything, and she wore it every day. As she stood at her closet looking for a sweater to wear to dinner, she wondered if her mother would bring some of her winter clothes when she came.

Caroline strolled to dinner at the dining hall at Hereford. She especially enjoyed meeting new people and getting to know them. She always felt that she had inherited her father's gift for engaging conversation, and she used that gift often. Jacquelyn Rhoades was a freshman from Kennebunkport, Maine. Her father owned land and was a timber broker. Jackie had a wicked sense of humor, and most of the time Caroline was totally entertained by her. Because of her comic nature, Jackie usually had a cast of characters that she associated with at school, and Caroline enjoyed meeting and getting to know all of them. They shared a desire to attend law school and often discussed the pros and cons of their choices.

Tonight, they would have a lively conversation about "men."

"I have decided that all men are pigs," Jackie said, disgusted.

"And, what, pray tell, made you come to that conclusion?" Caroline asked.

The other girls at the table chimed in, "Yes, do tell, Jackie!"

"Well, last weekend, I had a date with Scott Mason. You know him. He is the really good-looking Sigma Chi. He's a freshman and lives over at Dillard," Jackie began. "It was going great. We went into town and ate dinner at a cute little Italian restaurant. After dinner, he said he had a friend who was a junior and had an apartment near campus. He asked if I would like to go over and listen to music. 'Sure, I said. Sounds fun.' Needless to say, listening to music was not the only thing he had in mind."

"Oh my God, Jackie! What did you do?" exclaimed Jessica Lee, their friend from New York.

"When he tried to feel me up, I told him I wasn't that kind of girl and to take me home," replied Jackie. "It was the most uncomfortable ride home in my life. He did apologize, but the damage was done. So, men are pigs."

"I don't think they are *all* pigs," Caroline offered.

"And on what basis to you make that proclamation, Caroline?" asked Jackie.

"There is a really nice guy named Garrett who lives in the same dorm and is a Sigma Chi too. We're just friends, but I think he may be different than most guys," Caroline said somewhat hesitantly.

"He's really quiet and pretty shy," said Virginia Adams, their friend from Connecticut. "He is in two of my classes. Seems nice, and I think he is very smart."

"Well, there's hope for the world then, I guess," said Jackie.

Caroline stood up and said, "I guess there is hope. I have to go back to my books, girls. I would love to continue this enlightening conversation, but I have to study. Unless, of course, one of you has a good story like Jackie's. I am willing to stay a little longer if you do." All the girls laughed, and each one said they had to study too. Caroline walked alone back to her dorm.

CHAPTER 11

*I*T WAS SATURDAY MORNING, AND Caroline was fretting about what to wear to the sorority tea on Sunday. After what seemed like an hour, she settled on a beautiful navy A-line dress with a red jacket. Her red shoes were perfect. So that was that.

In Roswell, Charlotte and Irene were preparing for their drive to Virginia. They would be gone for a week, and the weather was changing, so they were having a terrible time deciding what to take. It had been a while since Charlotte had been out of town, and Irene had rarely traveled during her life. But they were actually having fun. Irene was at Charlotte's house where they were having dinner with Belle. Belle still insisted on cooking, and Charlotte loved it.

"I think we will need slacks and sweaters most of the time. We have to have a dress for when we visit Caroline at school, though," said Irene.

"Mother you are exactly right. On top of that, we have to have comfortable shoes. We will be walking a lot," said Charlotte.

"I'd better go a get a cortisone shot in my knee before we go," said Irene.

"Yes, you had, Miss Irene," instructed Belle. "You don't want to be caught in that cold weather with your arthritis acting up."

"So that's it then; we take slacks and sweaters and one dress, right Charlotte?" asked Irene.

"That's it, Mother," replied Charlotte with a smile. "Let's keep it simple."

Charlotte insisted on washing the dishes and sent Belle to her cottage about thirty steps from the back door of the house to rest. Belle gratefully accepted the offer. Irene drank coffee and talked with Charlotte while she cleaned the kitchen. Then Charlotte drove her mother the two blocks to her house. "I enjoyed the evening with you and Belle, Charlotte," Irene said sweetly.

"I enjoyed having you as much you enjoyed being there, Mother," replied Charlotte. "I'm glad we're taking a trip together."

"Me too, honey!" exclaimed Irene. "I can't wait! Goodnight, sweetheart."

"Goodnight, Mother," said Charlotte and she drove home.

Charlotte felt unusually tired. As she came back into the house, the only thought she had was to have a hot bath and go to bed. And that is what she did.

On Sunday morning, Caroline liked to attend chapel on campus. She had grown up attending church, and the week didn't seem right unless she went. She drove to the chapel on campus, which was a work of art, in her opinion. The peaceful time she spent there praying and enjoying the beautiful organ music was very special to her. After the worship service, she met up with Jackie and they had lunch in town at the Gaslight Restaurant, which was frequented by very interesting celebrities. "Are you okay after your horrible date?" asked Caroline in a genuinely concerned tone.

"I'm fine, Caroline. At least he didn't do any more than that. It could have been worse. I heard about a girl on campus that was raped by her date a couple of weeks ago," said Jackie with a fearful tone.

"Oh my gosh, Jackie! Who was it?" asked Caroline, concerned.

"Her name is Donna, but that's all I know," replied Jackie.

"I wish I could help her," said Caroline in a frustrated tone.

"You probably can't do anything now," replied Jackie. "She withdrew from school and went home."

"How sad," replied Caroline.

"I know," replied Jackie sadly.

"Dammit, that's not fair," exclaimed Caroline.

"So what is fair in the world today, Caroline?" Jackie retorted.

"I guess not much," replied Caroline. "Well, I hope the guy who raped her is gone too," Caroline said emphatically.

"I don't think he was a UVA student," Jackie said.

"How did she meet him then?" Caroline asked.

"Through a mutual friend, apparently," Jackie replied.

"I can't imagine such a horrible thing, can you?" Caroline asked off-handedly.

"Unfortunately, I can," Jackie replied.

Caroline turned to look at Jackie and saw a sadness that she had not observed before. "I'm really sorry, Jackie," Caroline said in a very concerned voice. "Do you want to talk about it?"

"Not today," replied Jackie. "I'll tell you about it sometime, just not today."

"Okay, Jackie," replied Caroline in a very loving tone. "You just let me know when you want to talk and I will be there for you. Okay?" Caroline said very sympathetically.

"I'll take you up on that," said Jackie, and she changed the subject. "Would you like to go to the library and study with me this afternoon?" Jackie asked.

"Ordinarily, I would love to, Jackie, but I have a sorority tea at three, and Garrett is attending with me," Caroline replied apologetically. "Rain check?"

"Absolutely," Jackie said without hesitation. She sensed that Caroline was an extraordinary person. She would learn that Caroline was, indeed, extraordinary.

Caroline arrived back at her dorm room about one thirty. She only had an hour to change and get ready for Garrett to arrive for the tea. *Thank heaven*, she thought, *that I chose my outfit yesterday*. She quickly changed and freshened her makeup.

At two thirty on the dot, her phone rang and the housemother announced Garrett's arrival. Caroline quickly grabbed her red jacket and went to the stairs that led to the living room. When she opened the door from the stairway, she saw Garrett standing beside the fireplace. She was struck by how truly handsome he looked in his blue oxford cloth shirt, gray trousers, and navy cashmere sweater. *Wow,* she thought. "Hi, Garrett," she said, trying to sound casual.

"Hi, Caroline," he replied. "You look beautiful."

"Why, thank you, Mr. Winthrop," she replied formally.

Caroline pointed him to the door and to the place where her car was parked, and they left for the sorority house. The drive was all of ten minutes, but they had time to talk. Caroline was rather shocked at her reaction to Garrett and did not start the conversation.

"How was your day, Caroline?" Garrett asked, obviously trying to break the silence.

"It was good. I went to church and then had lunch with my friend Jackie. She is a very interesting person," replied Caroline. "How about you?"

"I can't say that I attended church, but I did get up early and go to the library to get some studying done," Garrett said somewhat apologetically.

"We have to do what we have to do, Garrett," Caroline offered sympathetically.

When they arrived at the sorority house, it was buzzing with activity. Caroline was new to the place and was not totally comfortable with it. Sensing that, Garrett said, "Let's go in and see if we can help with anything."

"Great idea," Caroline said gratefully. Inside there were girls scurrying around obviously needing some help. "We're here to help, if we can," Caroline offered.

"Fabulous," replied Cathy. "If you would get the ice out of the fridge and put it in the cooler, that would be great."

"Easy enough," replied Garrett. He took charge as if he had been doing this for years. When the ice was in the cooler, he and Caroline took seats on the porch outside the living room.

"You don't seem very comfortable with your sorority. Why, Caroline?" asked Garrett.

"I have never been a person who felt as if my life were exclusive. I like a variety of people, some of whom are not sorority or fraternity people at all," Caroline confessed.

"I know what you mean," Garrett said to Caroline's surprise.

"Really?" Caroline questioned.

"Yes, really," Garrett said.

"I guess we have a lot in common, don't we, Garrett?" Caroline asked.

"We do," Garrett said definitely.

Caroline and Garrett participated in the tea for two hours with chitchat and small talk and then excused themselves, saying they had to study. "Do you really have to study, Garrett?" Caroline asked.

"Well, I could always study, but I have spent about as much time studying this week as I can stand. Let's take the rest of the evening off, shall we?" Garrett asked.

"We shall," replied Caroline.

They drove up to Monticello and enjoyed the view even though the home tour was closed. The sunset was magnificent, and Caroline drove to an overlook that showcased it. They both got out of the car and walked to the railing to get a better look. "I'm not sure if I have ever seen anything this beautiful," Caroline said quietly.

"Me either," Garrett said, staring at the beautiful scenery.

The leaves were starting to turn crimson, yellow, and orange. There was something magical about the evening, and Caroline wasn't sure it was totally due to the scenery. They enjoyed the view for almost an hour before Caroline said she had to get back to study.

Caroline dropped Garrett off at his dorm. He thanked her for a lovely evening and disappeared into the building. Caroline couldn't help but wonder what her father would have thought of Garrett.

CHAPTER 12

*I*T WAS THURSDAY OF THE following week, and Charlotte and Irene were preparing to leave for Charlottesville. "I can't remember if I packed all of my good underwear," Irene exclaimed. "What if I run out of underwear?"

"We will wash, Mother," replied Charlotte. "Quit worrying. If we have to, we'll buy new underwear."

"Okay, honey," said Irene apologetically. "I'm sorry. I just haven't done a lot of traveling, and I'm not sure what to expect."

"I do understand, Mother. I had to get used to traveling when John was alive. I learned to pack light and buy what I needed when I arrived at my destination," Charlotte said, trying to put her mother at ease.

"Okay, Charlotte. I trust you, and if we need something, we'll just buy it," Irene said, halfheartedly believing that was true.

"You got it, Mother," Charlotte said, reassuring her mother.

Early Friday morning, Charlotte and Irene were on Interstate 85 headed to Charlottesville. They would spend the night in Charlotte and then drive to Charlottesville early Saturday morning. Charlotte knew that her mother would have difficulty sitting in the car for more than four hours at a time. Irene was seventy-five, still active, and very engaged in life. But arthritis affected her entire body. Charlotte often marveled at her energy level.

Caroline was anticipating their arrival. It was Saturday morning and they were supposed to arrive by three o'clock. Caroline completed the studying she would have done on Saturday and Sunday. She was pacing in her room not daring to leave in case she might miss their telephone call. At a quarter to four, the telephone rang. "Hello," Caroline said, hoping it would be her mother's voice on the other end of the line.

"We're here, sweetheart," Charlotte said.

"I'll be right down, Mama!" Caroline exclaimed. When Caroline entered the living room of her dormitory, she did not know who to hug first. She went to her mother and embraced her for what seemed like several minutes.

Then she turned to Mama Rene, whose eyes were twinkling with love and pride for her only granddaughter. As Caroline gently hugged her grandmother, Irene whispered, "I don't know when I have ever been so proud of you, sweet girl." Caroline's eyes welled up with tears, realizing how much Mama Rene meant to her.

Caroline introduced her mother and grandmother to her housemother and to several of the girls who were talking in the living room. She then escorted them to her room. Charlotte was impressed with the relaxed style Caroline had created for herself. The room was bright with the afternoon sun. Mama Rene sat in the comfortable chair while Caroline scurried around gathering the rest of her things to spend the night at the Clifton Inn. Charlotte had reserved the Monticello Suite because they could all stay in the same room and spend time together.

95

The Clifton Inn looked like a stately southern mansion, and the hospitality was well known to be the best in the area. The Monticello Suite was a corner suite with views of the gardens, cascading waterfall pool, and surrounding mountains. It had terra cotta faux finish wall coverings and a separate sitting room with a full-size sofa bed, suede wingback chair, and game table. The bedroom was decorated exquisitely with a queen-size four-poster bed and antique armoire. The bathroom included an antique claw-foot tub and a separate shower. It was gorgeous and perfect. After the three women were settled in their room, Caroline suggested that they have dinner at the inn so they would not be in a hurry and could have more time to talk. Charlotte and Irene agreed, and they dined on shellfish bisque, roasted scallops, prime rib, and sticky toffee pudding watching the sunset in the solarium dining room.

Caroline told them about her many friends—especially Jackie and, more especially, Garrett.

"Garrett who?" Charlotte asked.

"Garrett Winthrop, Mother," Caroline replied, slightly irritated at the question.

"Well, where is he from, what does his father do, and what does he want to be when he grows up?" Charlotte retorted.

"Mother, really!" Caroline exclaimed. "He is a very nice boy from Charleston. We are actually just friends, if you must know."

"I must know," said Charlotte. "What about Jackie? Tell me about her."

"Jackie Rhoades is a wonderful girl from Kennebunkport. Her dad is a timber broker. She is smart and funny and is exactly the kind of friend I need to get me out more. I have a tendency to be quiet and private. I have to overcome that if I plan to be a successful lawyer," Caroline elaborated.

"It sounds as if you have your life planned out already, my dear," Irene said quietly.

"Not really, Mama Rene. I'm probably overplanning and just hoping my life will be good. I'm trying to make good decisions and be around people who are ambitious like I am," Caroline offered openly.

"Caroline, I have all the confidence in the world in you. You are the best of your mother and your father. You will succeed in whatever you choose, sweet girl," Irene said lovingly.

"Mama Rene, I wish I could bring you up here to live with me. I think I need a dose of Mama Rene every day," Caroline said, hugging her grandmother. Irene smiled and felt important for the first time in a very long time.

"I'm as close as your telephone all the time, Caroline. You call me anytime," Irene offered.

"You know, Mama Rene, I'm going to take you up on that," Caroline said.

"So what am I, chopped liver?" Charlotte said, trying to sound annoyed, but teasing.

"Yes, Mama, I have been trying to find a description of you, and I think it is 'chopped liver,'" Caroline said. And they all laughed hysterically. "This is our usual Sunday dinner conversation. We may be disturbing the other guests," Caroline said under her breath. "Let's go to our room and we can continue this conversation," Caroline said, still laughing. The three "Reed" girls went to their room and talked and laughed for another two hours until they were all exhausted.

The following morning, after a leisurely breakfast, Charlotte and Irene took Caroline back to her dormitory. Caroline had plenty of studying to do and planned to go to the library later that afternoon. "I am so proud of you, Caroline," Irene said.

"Thanks, Mama Rene," Caroline said with a note of sadness in her voice. "With the two of you as my examples, how can I possibly go wrong? I think of both of you every day, and it gives me courage and strength to know that my mother and my grandmother are two incredibly strong women. I will be fine. Y'all have a great time and just be careful. Remember to call me," Caroline said as she fought back tears.

"We will, sweetheart," Charlotte said as she stood up out of the car to hug Caroline. "I love you so much I don't know how to tell you, Caroline," Charlotte said with a tearful voice. "Just take care of yourself and enjoy college, sweetheart. Life starts soon enough," Charlotte coached her daughter. "We're headed to Monticello," Charlotte said excitedly.

"Bye, my sweet, beautiful girl," Irene shouted as the car was pulling out of the parking lot. Caroline waved and disappeared into the dormitory.

CHAPTER 13

*C*HARLOTTE AND IRENE WOUND THEIR way up to Monticello. It was late morning, and the house was magnificent, bathed in sunlight on a pinnacle. Irene thought how God had created such beauty for them to enjoy with the scarlet, yellow, and orange trees surrounding the home and in the valley. It was truly breathtaking. Charlotte's heart was aching because the last time she was here was with John before Caroline was born. She decided to enjoy the moment and not dwell on sadness. Not today. "Mother, have you ever seen anything so beautiful?" Charlotte exclaimed.

"My goodness, Charlotte. We have to take pictures to help us remember it and share it when we get home," Irene said, focused on the panorama.

They toured the house and the grounds for about three hours. There was so much to learn about Thomas Jefferson. Seeing his home made him seem like an old friend. "Mr. Jefferson was an amazing man, wasn't he?" Irene queried.

"Yes, Mother. He certainly was. Not only was he the author of the Declaration of Independence, but he was the founder of the University of Virginia. He conceived it, planned it, supervised the construction of it, and hired the first faculty. This was all after he served as governor of Virginia, secretary of state under George Washington, vice president, and then president. It was forty years from the time the land was cleared to the time the home was completed and remodeled. The bricks and the nails were made on the plantation, and most of the timber came from the five-thousand-acre estate."

"Good heavens, Charlotte! You sound like a history teacher!" exclaimed Irene.

"When John and I came here about a year after we were married, I got interested in Mr. Jefferson and the history of his plantation and the University of Virginia. I have talked to Caroline about it so much that when she was growing up I was not surprised when she chose UVA," Charlotte said. "The founders of our country were selfless men who had more backbone than anyone alive today in my opinion," she continued. Charlotte went to the gift shop on the grounds and bought her mother a book about Thomas Jefferson and the history of Monticello. Irene was thrilled with the gift, and they continued on their journey toward Williamsburg.

"Let's get going to Williamsburg," Charlotte said. It was about three o'clock in the afternoon, and they had a two hundred mile drive to Williamsburg. "We'll stop for dinner in about an hour, if that's okay with you, Mother," Charlotte said thoughtfully.

"That's great, sweetheart. On we go!" Irene exclaimed giddily. Charlotte giggled at her at her mother as they headed down the mountain toward Williamsburg.

Caroline stayed in her room until about two o'clock. She then decided to take a break from studying and walk to the dining hall. As she entered, Jackie, Jessica, and Virginia were walking out with a girl Caroline barely knew, Susan Spencer. "Well, Caroline, where have you been? We missed you last night," Jackie said.

"My mother and grandmother were in town, and I spent the night with them at the Clifton Inn. I've been studying all afternoon, and I had to have a break," Caroline offered somewhat tentatively.

"Well, if you're hungry, get a sandwich and a drink and come on with us. We're going into town to Main Street to window shop. We'll probably have dinner there. Come on, it'll be fun," Jackie coaxed.

"My car holds five people," Virginia said. "I'll be glad to drive."

"Okay, girls, but I have to be back by seven to finish studying," Caroline relented.

"Promise," Jackie said as the five girls walked to Virginia's 1965 Chevrolet convertible. Caroline sat in the back seat with Susan and Jessica. All the girls were chattering away when Caroline said, "Susan, I'm very glad to finally meet you. I know we live in the same dorm, but we barely see each other."

"I know. I have studied so much this weekend that my eyes won't focus anymore. I just had to get out," Susan said, seeming very glad to talk with Caroline.

"Me too, Susan. Where are you from?" Caroline asked, genuinely interested.

"I grew up in Charlotte. UVA was always the place my parents wanted me to go to college," Susan offered. "What about you?"

"I grew up in Atlanta. My dad went to Harvard and my mother went to the Women's College in Milledgeville. I think UVA is a fabulous university if you want to be a lawyer, and I do," Caroline said decisively.

"I wish I had my life figured out, but I'm still working on it," Susan replied.

"I think most people are still working on it when they are freshmen, don't you?" asked Caroline, fearing she sounded too snobby.

"Okay, girls, here we are on Main Street in beautiful downtown Charlottesville. Let's have a blast!" said Virginia as she got out of the car. The five girls walked up and down Main Street window shopping and commenting on just about everything they saw.

At five thirty, Jackie announced, "Let's go get pizza over there at that cute little restaurant. Caroline's got to be back by seven," Jackie said, leading the group to the restaurant. When they walked into the restaurant, Caroline immediately spotted Garrett with a girl she had never seen before double dating with one of his fraternity brothers, Mike Fisher. Caroline half smiled and walked to a table across the restaurant from the couples. "Isn't that Garrett Winthrop?" Jackie asked.

"Yes," Caroline replied stiffly.

"Who is he with?" Jackie continued questioning.

"I haven't the foggiest," Caroline said and quickly changed the subject. "Have any of you eaten here before?" Caroline asked.

"I have," replied Virginia. "A couple of times. Everything is pretty good." The server appeared, took their drink orders, and scurried off to get the drinks.

"My favorite is pepperoni," Jessica said as she opened the menu. Caroline opened her menu and halfheartedly glanced at it. The server reappeared with their drinks and was ready to take their orders. The girls ordered, and once again the server scurried off to get the pizzas.

"Okay, Caroline," Jackie said in a deliberate tone. "Garrett is the pink elephant in the room over there with another girl that none of us knows. What gives? I thought you two were dating."

"We're friends, Jackie," Caroline said, sounding a little irritated with the questions. "We have studied together, talked between classes, and been to a sorority tea. I hardly think that qualifies as 'dating,'" Caroline said flippantly.

"Okay, okay," Jackie surrendered. "I'm not trying to make you mad."

"I know. I'm sorry, Jackie," Caroline said apologetically. "I do like him a lot, but we've never really had a date exactly."

Susan interrupted, "Now that we have established that, let's eat our pizza and get back to campus."

"Sounds good to me," interjected Virginia. And that is what they did.

The two couples left the restaurant before the girls were finished with their pizza. Caroline was relieved that she didn't have to walk past them again.

When she arrived at her dorm, there was a note taped to her door. It said, "Call Garrett Winthrop 721-3555." Caroline walked into her room and over to the telephone. She reached for it and then decided not to return his call. Not now, anyway. She distracted herself with her books. At ten o'clock, she showered and went to bed.

Charlotte and Irene arrived in Williamsburg at eight o'clock on Sunday evening and checked in at the Williamsburg Inn. It was decorated in an English Regency style and was considered one of the world's greatest hotels. The hotel was built by John D. Rockefeller Jr. in 1937 and was a charming country inn with unparalleled service. "Wow!" was all Irene could say.

"Mother, close your mouth, honey," Charlotte said, laughing at her mother.

"Gosh, Charlotte, you didn't tell me we were staying in a hotel that looked like royalty should be here," Irene gushed.

"Mother, the service is even better than the hotel looks," Charlotte said. "We'll have fun here."

"Yes-sir-ree, we certainly will," Irene said, sounding like a country bumpkin.

Charlotte laughed out loud and led her mother to check in. Their room was a large suite with a sofa and two chairs, a writing desk, and a large bed. They unpacked and then went to dinner in the restaurant at the inn. Charlotte and Irene were exhausted and decided to go to bed early. Charlotte had lots for them to do tomorrow. Irene gladly put on her nightgown and got into the bed.

Charlotte decided to stay up to read for a while. When she finally got into the bed and fell asleep, John appeared in their room. He sat on the side of the bed and touched Charlotte's face gently. "I love you, beautiful," he said. He disappeared as quickly as he had appeared.

The following morning, Charlotte sat up on the side of the bed trying to decide if the visit was real or a dream. *It was so real. John, you are still with me, aren't you?* she thought. She hurried off to the bathroom so her mother would not see her cry.

Irene was chipper and ready to go. After breakfast, the mother-and-daughter duo went to Williamsburg. And what a day it was for the two of them! They loved the governor's mansion and having dinner at Christiana Campbell's Tavern. The bread pudding was second to none!

Caroline gathered her books and left the dormitory for the dining hall. She was unusually hungry and needed breakfast today. She was glad that her mother had brought some of her winter clothes. The air was chilly, and she needed a jacket. She quickly ate some toast and eggs and hurried to her first class. It was an easy walk, and the morning was beautiful. She had to pass Garrett's dorm to get to the building where her class was held. Walking as fast as she could past the building, she got to her class about five minutes early. Standing at the door when she arrived was Garrett.

"Hi, Caroline," he said casually.

"Garrett, why are you in the political science building?" Caroline asked, trying to seem nonchalant.

"I left you a message to call me last night," he said, seeming somewhat surprised that he had not heard from her.

"By the time we got back from downtown, I had so much left to do to get ready for today, I just couldn't call you. Why did you call me?" Caroline asked.

"I wanted to tell you that I tried to call you to go with Mike and his date and me to have pizza, but your housemother said you were with your mother and grandmother," he explained. "Mike wanted to take Melissa out, and he was nervous to go alone. He asked if I would go along and be her sister's date. I agreed, and that's what happened," he continued.

"Garrett, you don't owe me an explanation," Caroline said, feeling the butterflies in her stomach.

"I wanted to explain it to you, and there is a good reason. Would you go with me on Saturday night to the football game and to the Sigma Chi party?" he asked earnestly.

"Yes, I can go," Caroline replied, wanting to jump up and down. She was afraid she sounded too anxious.

"Okay, good," he said, sounding relieved. "I hope to see you before then, but if not, I'll pick you up about six o'clock," he said.

"Sounds good to me," Caroline said, trying not to sound too excited.

She had difficulty focusing in her classes the rest of the day. *What is the matter with me?* she thought. It took her until the next morning to truly focus on school. She was determined to stop this silly infatuation.

It was Friday morning, and the two Reed girls from Roswell were checking out of the Williamsburg Inn and heading back to Atlanta. "Charlotte, this has been the most wonderful vacation of my life. Thank you so much for taking me with you," Irene said sincerely.

"Mother, it has been wonderful to be with you this week. I have enjoyed sharing it with you. Memories must be made one day at a time," Charlotte said with her voice trailing off.

Irene sensed that her daughter was still grieving over John's death. It was just over a year since he died, and Irene knew that it would take a long time for Charlotte to heal. "Yes, they must. And you have given me a week of special memories that I will never forget," Irene said lovingly.

"Thanks, Mother," Charlotte replied, still seeming to be somewhat distracted with her own thoughts.

Charlotte planned to drive about four hundred miles to Charlotte, North Carolina, where they would spend the night and continue then on into Atlanta. She stopped to call Belle before they left. "Hello, Wellington residence," Belle answered the telephone as she had for so many years.

"Good morning, Belle," Charlotte said, sounding happy to hear her voice.

"Good morning to you, Miss Charlotte. I'm so glad to hear from you. Is Miss Irene okay?" Belle asked with genuine concern.

"Belle, I think she could run circles around me today!" Charlotte said laughing out loud.

"Lawzy, Miss Charlotte, I never would have believed that she would outlast you!" Belle said, laughing with Charlotte.

"Is everything all right at home, Belle?" Charlotte asked.

"Everything is fine here, Miss Charlotte. Y'all just be careful coming home now," Belle said.

"We will, Belle," Charlotte replied. "We should be home by Saturday evening."

"I can't wait to hear all about it!" Belle exclaimed. Charlotte had a tug of remorse in her heart for not having taken Belle with them. *Why didn't I take her with us?* Charlotte asked herself. "Okay, my sweet, Belle," Charlotte said. "Thank you for looking after everything while we were gone."

"Now you know, Miss Charlotte, I rested nearly the whole time. It was a vacation for me too. I went to see my brother down in South Atlanta, and we had a wonderful visit on Wednesday. So you don't worry about old Belle. I'm just so happy that Miss Irene got to have a good vacation!" Belle exclaimed.

"Me too, Belle," Charlotte said. "Me too."

"See you on Saturday," Charlotte said, and she hung up the phone. "Come on, Mother. We have lots of ground to cover today," Charlotte instructed Irene.

On Saturday morning, Caroline slept unusually late in anticipation of her Saturday-evening date. She got up about ten o'clock, put on jeans and a sweater, and headed to the dining hall. She hoped most everyone would be either still sleeping or already gone. She was right. The dining hall was empty except for a couple of people whom she really did not know. She quickly ate her usual toast and eggs and headed back to her room. When Caroline arrived at her dorm room, outside the door were a dozen roses. Caroline bent down to pick up the vase and opened her door. She sat the vase on her desk and opened the card. "Can't wait to see you tonight. Love, Garrett." Caroline was so surprised, that she sat on the floor. "Holy cow!" she said out loud. "What is going on? I'm only nineteen years old. I can't be falling in love with this man now, can I?" she said, still talking to herself out loud. Caroline had never experienced such feelings for a boy like the feelings she had for Garrett Winthrop.

At six o'clock sharp, her telephone rang. It was her housemother. "Caroline, Mr. Garrett Winthrop is here to see you," she said.

"Thank you," Caroline said and hung up the telephone, grabbed her purse, and went downstairs to the living room. As soon as she saw him, her heart melted. It was confirmed. She was officially "in love" with Garrett Winthrop. "The roses are beautiful, Garrett," Caroline said, trying to sound unruffled.

"I'm glad you like them, Caroline," Garrett said, saying her name as if he had been saying it for years. The curfew was midnight, and Caroline was one who always tried to obey the rules. "We'll be in by midnight, Mrs. Hastings," Caroline said as they went out the front door.

The short walk to the stadium gave them a chance to talk, but neither of them seemed to be able to start a conversation. "I think we have a shot at winning the game tonight," Garrett said, breaking the silence.

"I really haven't followed the team like I should have," Caroline confessed.

"Well, that's why you need me, Miss Caroline Wellington," Garrett said playfully.

"I must need you for more than a college football game, Garrett," Caroline said more seriously than she meant to sound.

"That's what I am hoping, Caroline," Garrett replied softly and turned to look directly at her.

Caroline's heart was pounding again. She wasn't sure if she liked this or not. Being out of control of her feelings was very uncomfortable and very unusual for Caroline Wellington. "What do you mean, Garrett?" Caroline asked tentatively.

"Caroline, I have never met a girl quite like you. You're smart, interesting, thoughtful, sincere, and easy to talk with. In the last few weeks, I have to confess that I have tried to get you off my mind, and I just can't. So here it is. I hope I am not being too forward in asking you if you will accept my pin. I realize that we have not really had a date exactly, but I don't need to have a real date with you to know that I would like you to be my girl," Garrett said openly.

"Garrett, I was not expecting to have the feelings for you that I have either, but I do," Caroline replied in a soft voice. "I would be happy to accept your pin,'" Caroline said.

They were standing under one of the very old oak trees on the campus. Garrett put his arms around her and kissed her as she had never been kissed before. Caroline felt like electricity went through her body. Her knees were weak, and she thought she might lose her balance. But she wanted this moment to last forever.

Garrett took her hand as if he had been taking care of her forever and led her into the stadium. They had a ball at the game, and the University of Virginia Cavaliers won! All was right with the world.

Garrett was very proud to introduce Caroline to his fraternity brothers at the party at the Sigma Chi house after the game. Caroline was very much her mother's daughter, elegant class. She was truly a southern beauty. They danced, talked, and had a fabulous time at the party. The one thing that Garrett noticed is that Caroline only drank Coca-Cola. She refused alcoholic beverages anytime they were offered. Because of that, Garrett only drank Coca-Cola too. Garrett usually would have a few beers with is fraternity brothers, but not tonight. At the end of the evening, Garrett drove Caroline back to her dormitory. In the car, he turned to her, put his arms around her, and kissed her again. Caroline believed she could stay here forever—in this moment, in this kiss, with this man.

CHAPTER 14

*I*N THE WEEKS THAT FOLLOWED, Caroline struggled to concentrate on her classes. She and Garrett were together almost every day. They studied together, ate together, and walked to classes together. They became almost inseparable. Caroline really was not comfortable with this new relationship because she expected her focus to be entirely on college. There was no room in her plans for a relationship. But an amazing relationship is what she had.

It was mid-November, and the Thanksgiving holiday was around the corner. Caroline and Garrett were at her dining hall. Garrett looked at Caroline and said, "Would you come home with me for Thanksgiving?"

Caroline was stunned. "Garrett!" she exclaimed. "I can't do that," she said, almost gasping. "I have to go home for Thanksgiving. This is the first Thanksgiving we will spend without my father. I have to be with my mother."

"I'm sorry, Caroline. I wasn't thinking. I was being selfish in not wanting to be away from you for the holiday," Garrett offered apologetically.

Caroline was so touched by his sincerity that she said, "I'll tell you what—why don't you come to Atlanta on Friday? We can hang around my house, you can meet my family, and we can head back to Charlottesville together on Sunday morning. Would that work?"

Garrett sat back in his chair and put his hand on his chin. "Hmmm," he said. "That just might work. Let me call my mother, and I'll let you know tomorrow. Okay?"

"Okay," Caroline replied. "I know my mother and my grandmother would love to meet you. I can show you all around Atlanta. It's really beautiful there." Garrett walked Caroline to her dorm and kissed her at the door. Every kiss from him was like the first kiss. She just never wanted it to end.

The following evening after Caroline returned from her classes and dinner, she was in her room changing into comfortable clothes to study for the night. The telephone rang. "Hello," Caroline answered.

"Hi, Caroline, it's Garrett. My mom said she is okay with that plan as long as she gets to meet you during the Christmas holiday," Garrett offered, anticipating her reply. "So do you think that will work?"

"Well, I will say it seems quite fair and reasonable. Let me talk with my mother, and I'll let you know as soon as I can. Okay?" Caroline replied, thinking that she would find a way for this to work.

"Okay, beautiful," Garrett replied. Caroline wished he were there so she could kiss him for being so precious and thoughtful.

It was too late for Caroline to call her mother, so she continued her studying until she fell asleep. The following morning, she called her mother as soon as she woke up. "Mother, good morning. It's me," Caroline said casually.

"Well, good morning, sunshine," Charlotte replied happily. "To what do I owe this honor?"

"Oh Mama, you know I call you all the time. I have to get to class, so I have to get right to the point. Garrett would like to come to our house on Friday after Thanksgiving to visit us and meet you and Mama Rene, and he would like for me to go to his home in Charleston after Christmas to meet his family. Are you okay with that?" Caroline blurted out.

"Caroline, are you really this serious about Garrett?" Charlotte asked in a very surprised tone.

"Serious, Mama? I don't think I would say that I am exactly serious about Garrett, but I can tell you that I really, really like him a lot," Caroline replied decisively.

"Well, my dear, if this is what you want to do, I'm all for it. I trust you and believe that you have very good judgment," Charlotte said pragmatically. "I will be delighted to meet Garrett."

"Thank you, Mama," Caroline said sincerely. "You are amazing, and I love you so much," Caroline gushed.

"I love you too, my sweet girl. Just be happy and be true to yourself," Charlotte counseled.

"You taught me very well, Mama. No need to be concerned," Caroline replied.

But Charlotte wondered what she had taught her by staying with an abusive, alcoholic husband. She hoped she had taught her about love and commitment, but she wasn't sure sometimes. If John were still alive, it would be a different subject altogether. But he wasn't.

Caroline found Garrett between classes and told him that all family members approved the plan. "That's great, Caroline!" Garrett said, relieved. "If it's okay with you, I'll fly down to Atlanta and drive back to Charlottesville with you on Sunday," he continued.

"Fine with me," Caroline replied. "It will be nice to have company on the trip back."

Garrett hitched a ride home on Monday before Thanksgiving with his buddy Rob Houston. They both lived in Charleston but did not know one another before they met at UVA.

Caroline headed out early Sunday morning. In spite of her distraction, she was on the dean's list, and she was happy about that. Charlotte expected nothing less from her only child.

Irene and Charlotte were waiting on the front porch when Caroline's Thunderbird pulled into the driveway. Charlotte always worried when she drove home alone. It was a nine-hour drive and over five hundred miles. But Caroline was stubborn and managed to make her mother feel somewhat at ease about the trip.

"Caroline, I thought you would never get here!" Charlotte exclaimed.

Irene walked to her only granddaughter and put her arms around her. She whispered, "I love you, sunshine. I have a surprise for you."

"Well, when do I get my surprise, Mama Rene?" Caroline asked, stepping back to take a good look at her grandmother.

"Let's get in the house. I'll show you," Irene said with a twinkle in her eyes. Charlotte thought her mother looked joyful once again. Caroline had had that effect on her since she was a baby. Caroline unloaded the car and brought her suitcase and, of course, a week's worth of laundry with her.

When they walked into the living room, there was the book that Irene made for Caroline. It was her life in pictures—pictures of her parents' marriage, of their first home, of Charlotte when she was expecting her, of Belle in the kitchen making her famous biscuits, moving to their home on West Paces Ferry, Caroline's first day of school, all the way through to her graduation. Caroline stopped when she saw the photographs of her mother, father, and her in Paris, London, Rome, and Madrid. Those were some of the most wonderful and cherished memories she had of her father. Tears were rolling down her face. She was so touched by Mama Rene's love and by the memories of her father that she could not speak. She put the book down and put her arms around her mother and grandmother, and they all wept.

"Mama, I want to go to the cemetery tomorrow," Caroline said, still wiping her tears.

"We'll go tomorrow, honey. But you must remember that your father is not there. He is with you every day," Charlotte said softly as she brushed another tear from her daughter's face.

"I know, Mama, but it's the only connection I really have to him now," Caroline said sadly. "Have you heard from Granddad and Grandmother?" Caroline asked.

"Yes, I have, dear. They would love to see you while you are home. I haven't mentioned this, but your grandmother is not doing well. She has a heart condition and doesn't get out of the house much except for doctor's appointments," Charlotte replied, waiting to see Caroline's reaction to that news.

"I love both of them, Mama, but they are the ones who decided that we could not have a relationship without Daddy. They are the ones who acted like they hardly knew us after he died. I will never understand that," Caroline said, looking at her mother and pleading for an explanation.

Elizabeth was seventy-eight years old, and Grant was eighty-two. Caroline wondered what would happen to their estate when they both died. It was a morbid thought, but she was their only heir except for her grandfather's younger brother, who was worthless and a leech. Elizabeth's father and two older sisters had been dead for many years.

"Caroline, it was all about money," Charlotte said dryly. "Your grandparents have about $50 million, and they are the unhappiest people I have ever known," she continued. "Money does not make you happy. It just gives you choices. Always remember that, sweetheart," Charlotte said softly as she turned to lead her tired child to the kitchen for something to eat.

"Where's Belle?" Caroline asked.

"She's in her cottage resting, honey," Charlotte said. "We'll see her tomorrow. She just can't do the things she used to do. She's almost seventy-three years old."

"I don't want to think about that right now, Mama. I have you and Mama Rene, I will see Belle tomorrow, and by Friday you will meet Garrett," Caroline said, trying to change the somber mood.

"Yes, we will, sunshine. I am so glad you are home. Mother, why don't you spend the night with us tonight?" Charlotte said to Irene.

"You won't have to ask me twice. I'll be up early for biscuits and fig preserves," Irene said as she did a little jig in the kitchen. Charlotte, Irene, and Caroline howled with laughter.

Caroline ate a pimento cheese sandwich and drank a glass of sweet tea. Then they all went upstairs to bed.

CHAPTER 15

THE FOLLOWING MORNING CAROLINE WOKE to the smell of fresh brewed coffee and biscuits. She knew Belle was in the kitchen. She jumped out of bed and ran down the stairs to see her. As she walked into the kitchen, Belle turned to see who was there. The biggest, sweetest smile appeared on Belle's face, and she rushed to give Caroline a hug. "I have missed you so much, sweet baby!" Belle exclaimed with tears in her eyes.

"I missed you too, Belle," Caroline replied as she hugged her for the third time. "I think I will just take you back to school with me after Thanksgiving."

"Reckon I better stay here with your mama, sugar," Belle said, chuckling and wiping her eyes.

"I guess so, Belle," Caroline relented. "But I'm here now, and I can't wait for your biscuits!"

"You just sit down right here and talk to me while I get these biscuits done for you," Belle said as she patted Caroline on her shoulder. Belle turned around and looked at Caroline, studying her face.

"Lord, child, I do believe you get more beautiful every time I see you!" Belle exclaimed.

"Belle, I just rolled out of the bed. I do not know how you could say that. I'm a mess," Caroline replied, smiling at the compliment.

"Well, sugar, you are a beautiful mess," Belle said, laughing out loud.

Charlotte and Irene appeared at the door. "I didn't think you would be up this early, my dear," Charlotte said.

"Are you kidding, Mama? And miss Belle's biscuits? No way!" Caroline exclaimed, giving Belle another hug. "I love this woman." They all laughed and enjoyed breakfast together for the first time in three months.

"Okay, family," Caroline said as she looked around at all three women in the kitchen. "I have to tell you about Garrett Winthrop. He will be here Friday."

"Yes, sweetheart, we are aware that we will have a man in our house on Friday," Charlotte said playfully.

"Mama, he is wonderful!" Caroline exclaimed, her eyes lighting up. "He is from Charleston, and he is the oldest of three children. He has two younger sisters who are still in high school. His father is an engineer and works with a private company that has government contracts. Garrett says his dad can't talk very much about what he does. His mother was a nurse, but she didn't work after Garrett was born. He is a gentleman, very nice, and extremely bright. He is funny, and he loves history," Caroline sat back to look at her mother, Mama Rene, and Belle.

"Well, Caroline, he sounds like a very nice guy. We won't embarrass you when he is here. Don't worry," Irene said, winking at Charlotte.

"Mama Rene, I didn't think you would embarrass me, for heaven's sake," Caroline said sarcastically. "Okay, then. You will just have to find out for yourselves about him," Caroline said, acting slightly irritated.

"We're just teasing you, sweetheart," Charlotte said, kissing Caroline on her cheek.

"I know you are, Mama. I just really like him a lot," Caroline replied, and the tears came in buckets. Caroline sobbed and sobbed with Charlotte, Irene, and Belle comforting her.

"Oh, sweet baby girl," Charlotte said as she tried to soothe her.

"It's okay, y'all," Caroline said as she tried to compose herself. "I'm really still crying because I miss Daddy so much," she confessed. "I wish he were here to meet Garrett. I have wondered what he would think of him."

"I know you do, honey," Charlotte said, feeling her heart breaking for her daughter. "It's so hard to realize he is gone, even now."

"I know, Mama," Caroline said, regaining her composure. "I think about him all the time and just wish I could talk with him just one more time."

"He is close by, Caroline. I feel him near all the time. He loved you so much, and that doesn't change even when someone dies." Charlotte reassured her daughter. "Daddy wants us to be a happy family. He wants us to remember the good times we had together. Caroline, I'm convinced that love is the most powerful thing in the universe. It does not disappear when someone dies. We are always connected by love," Charlotte continued.

"You're right, Mama," Caroline said. "I feel him sometimes too."

"Oh, he's there, sweetheart," Charlotte said emphatically.

Irene and Belle were looking at Charlotte with admiration. Belle spoke first. "Miss Charlotte, that is so true, and you are so wise to know that. We are connected by love forever."

"Okay. Now then, girls," Irene started, "let's get dressed and go shopping. Nothing like a little retail therapy to heal your soul." They all laughed and went to do just that.

The foursome went to Buckhead to shop at Lenox Square. Caroline ran into many of her former classmates, most of whom were attending the University of Georgia. They exchanged pleasant greetings, and the four continued shopping. "I'm starved," Caroline said about one o'clock in the afternoon.

"Okay, let's run to grab a bite at the Tea Room and then we can head back," Charlotte offered. They all agreed and had lunch at the Magnolia Tea Room at Rich's Department Store.

When they arrived back at the car, Irene exclaimed, "I'm pooped."

"Mother, we'll get you home as soon as possible," Charlotte said as she laughed at her mother.

"I've got to get home too, Miss Charlotte," Belle said. "I've got to get to the grocery store and get our Thanksgiving dinner together." Charlotte had taught Belle to drive several years earlier and bought her a new, red Chevy Nova. To Belle, it was the best car in the world.

"We'll be back in time for you to get to the store, Belle," Charlotte said as she pulled onto Peachtree Street heading north to Roswell.

Charlotte took her mother to her own house and dropped Belle off at home. Then she and Caroline headed for Sandy Springs to Arlington Cemetery. On the way, Caroline turned to her mother and said, "I know Daddy is not there, but could we stop and get flowers to put on his grave? It's the only place I have right now."

"Of course, sweetheart," Charlotte said, patting Caroline's hand. "We will get flowers." They stopped at a florist in Sandy Springs that usually had nice silk flowers. After making their purchase of a colorful fall bouquet, they headed on to the cemetery. Charlotte turned into the beautiful iron gates and headed down the road that led to the Garden of Roses, where John was buried. When they arrived, Caroline got out of the car with the flowers. She hated to see her father's name on a headstone with his date of birth and date of death on it. Caroline dropped to her knees. "Daddy, I miss you so much. I love you with all my heart. Daddy, I will always be your baby girl. Can you hear me?" Caroline said sounding as if she were expecting a reply. Tears were streaming down her face.

Charlotte stood back to allow her daughter that moment of grief. She struggled with her own feelings as she watched her daughter come to terms with her father's death. Caroline arranged the flowers in the vase and then stood and walked to her mother. She put her arms around her, and they stood together embracing for a long time. The afternoon was beautiful, the sun was setting, and the wind was blowing quietly through the trees. As they embraced, each of them felt a peace and strength they hadn't felt before today. The Wellington women were strong and independent. They had each other, and everything would be all right.

Charlotte took Caroline's hand and said, "Okay, let's go home and see what we bought today."

"Works for me," Caroline replied with a smile.

When they arrived at home, Belle was in the kitchen still putting groceries away. She had a big pot of homemade vegetable soup on the stove. With her black skillet out on the counter, Caroline knew there would be buttermilk cornbread too. "Yum, yum!" Caroline exclaimed as she walked into the kitchen. "Okay, that's it. I'm taking you back to school with me, Belle."

Belle chuckled, and her eyes lit up. "Sugar, I am gonna get up there to see you, but you know I can't stay," she said, wiping her hands on her apron so she could give Caroline a hug.

"All right, then you just come up there and show the people in my dining hall how to cook," Caroline said emphatically and laughing at the same time.

"Lord, child, it would take me too long to show those people all the stuff I know," Belle replied shaking her head.

"Well, you're right about that. I will just have to come home more often," Caroline said.

"Now that's a great idea," Charlotte said as she walked into the kitchen. "Belle, I'll help you put things away, and after dinner Caroline and I will clean the kitchen. After we eat, you go to your cottage to rest."

"Miss Charlotte," Belle said, turning to look at her, "I do appreciate that."

Charlotte, Caroline, and Belle enjoyed a wonderful dinner together. As promised, the Wellington women cleaned the kitchen. Then Charlotte and Caroline went upstairs to look at everything they had bought.

It was the Tuesday morning before Thanksgiving. Caroline decided to sleep later than usual. When she came downstairs, she heard Belle in the kitchen talking with Robert. "Good morning, y'all," Caroline said, still sleepy.

"Well, good morning to you, sleepyhead," Belle replied, laughing.

"Robert, I'm so glad to see you!" Caroline exclaimed sincerely. "How are you?"

"I'm great, Miss Caroline," Robert replied.

"Do you like working for Mr. Mansard?" Caroline asked, genuinely interested. "Yes, I do," Robert said. "He has been very nice to me, and I love the work I'm doing. Never the same thing, always something different, and I like being outside too."

"Robert, that is so good," Caroline said. "I'm very glad that worked out so well for you. You know we love you and Belle very much. You are family to us," Caroline said as she gave Robert a hug.

Belle piped up and said, "Robert has some very good news for us."

"Oh, yea?" Caroline replied turning to Robert with an inquisitive look. "So share."

"Robert, you tell her," Belle urged.

"Miss Caroline, I am engaged to Karen Collins," Robert said, smiling from ear to ear. "I met her when I went to work for Mr. Mansard. I can't wait for you to meet her," he continued excitedly.

"Well, what are you waiting for, Robert?" Caroline said, returning the smile. "Let's get this girl in here. We need to approve of your choice, you know," Caroline said jokingly.

"I figured I would have to get permission from at least one of you women," Robert said, laughing. "I would like to bring her to meet you on Wednesday. Is that okay?"

"Works for me. How about you, Belle?" Caroline asked.

"Robert, you need to bring her around for lunch on Wednesday. We can meet her and visit for a while. Then I have to get busy with Thanksgiving dinner," Belle instructed.

"Okay, I'm going to tell her that she will be meeting my family on Wednesday," Robert said proudly. "You are going to like her, Aunt Belle.

"I'm sure I will Robert. I'm very proud of you," Belle replied, putting her arms around her nephew.

"Gotta get back to work," Robert said as he went out the back door.

"Does Mother know about this yet?" Caroline asked Belle.

"I told her this morning before she left to go shopping," Belle said.

"Oh, where did she go?" Caroline asked.

"She had some last-minute things to get for the table for Thanksgiving. You know Anne and Nancy and their husbands will be here too," Belle said.

"That's right," Caroline said. "It will be very nice to see everyone together again."

After breakfast, Caroline went upstairs to get dressed. For some reason, she had her grandparents, Grant and Elizabeth, on her mind today. She decided to call them and go for a visit. It occurred to her that it would be better if she did not include her mother in the visit or any knowledge of it.

"Hello," Grant's answered, his voice sounding older than Caroline remembered.

"Granddaddy," Caroline started. "This is Caroline."

"Are you home from college for Thanksgiving?" Grant asked as if they had never stopped talking with each other.

"Yes, I am, and I would like to come to see you and Grandmother today for an hour or so if I can," Caroline requested tentatively.

"We would be very glad to see you. Please come anytime you like," Grant replied cordially.

"Okay, I'll see you about one o'clock. Is that okay?" Caroline asked.

"That's good, Caroline. Your grandmother will be very glad to see you, and I will too," Grant said kindly.

"Thank you, I'll see you then. Bye, bye," Caroline said as he hung up the telephone.

Grant walked slowly into the den where Elizabeth was dozing in her chair. "Elizabeth," Grant touched her arm, trying not to startle her. Elizabeth opened her eyes and looked at him. "Caroline is coming to see us today at one o'clock," he said gently.

Elizabeth's eyes brightened. She sat up in her chair. "I have to get myself presentable," Elizabeth said, standing and walking toward the bedroom. An hour later, she came back into the den looking better than Grant had seen her for months. "Elizabeth!" Grant exclaimed. "You look fabulous!"

"Oh, go on now. I don't want Caroline to know that I am not well." Elizabeth replied, smiling at Grant. "You tell all the girls that, anyway."

"Girls, what girls?" Grant asked.

"Grant, you never did have a sense of humor. Old age has not given you one either," Elizabeth said, slightly irritated.

"Well, it's good to see you chipper, my dear," Grant said sincerely.

"I accept that compliment, Mr. Wellington," Elizabeth said.

At one o'clock, the doorbell rang at the elder Wellingtons' home in Inman Park where they had lived since 1930 when Grant opened Georgia Life. They never saw the need to move since John left for college the following year. By the time the company had grown to the level it was when John became in-house counsel, Grant saw to it that Charlotte and he had the grand home for entertaining.

Elizabeth stood and started to the door. Grant decided to walk behind and allowed her to open the door for Caroline. When Elizabeth opened the door, Caroline stepped into the foyer and put her arms around her grandmother. "Grandmother, you look wonderful!" Caroline exclaimed as she turned to give her grandfather a hug. "Hi, Granddaddy," Caroline said, somewhat detached.

"My heavens, Caroline!" Elizabeth exclaimed. "You are more beautiful than ever, I think."

"Well, thank you, Grandmother," Caroline replied, smiling.

"Come on in, honey," Grant said as he ushered them into the den. "Would you like some iced tea, Caroline?" Grant offered.

"That would be great, Granddaddy," Caroline replied as she sat down on the sofa next to her grandmother.

"How is college, sweetheart?" Elizabeth asked.

"It's great, but a lot of studying. I'm busy almost every day, even on the weekends. I'm glad to have a break," Caroline said. "I've met lots of new friends from all around the country. That alone has been a good education for me."

"Your granddaddy and I went to the University of Georgia, so we weren't too far from home. But you are very far away," Elizabeth said, seeming very interested in what Caroline had to say.

"I know, Grandmother, but UVA is a wonderful place, and it will give me what I need to get into law school," Caroline said as she accepted the glass of iced tea.

"I didn't know you were planning to go to law school, Caroline!" Grant said, sounding very surprised.

"I want to come back to Atlanta and go to Emory when I graduate. That way I can be near Mama and Mama Rene. I could visit you more often too," Caroline said as she looked directly at her grandfather.

"That would be very nice, Caroline," Grant said, returning her gaze. Grant took a deep breath and sat forward in his chair. "Caroline, I'm so sorry that I behaved so badly after your father died. I have no excuse except that I was not thinking clearly and my priorities were in the wrong place."

Caroline sat silently, allowing Grant to continue. "The day your father died was the day you came to ask for our help. I just did not realize that it was as bad as it was until after he was gone. I'm sorry I didn't listen to you, although I doubt it would have changed anything at that point. I realize now that I wanted your father to make up for all of my inadequacies. It wasn't fair to him or to your mother." Grant paused. Caroline still did not speak. "I would give anything to be able to recall the last fifteen or more years and do things a lot differently. I realize that having all the money you or your family will ever need does not make you happy."

"Granddaddy," Caroline began. "I'm glad you know that now. It's better than your never knowing. We can't change the past, as sad as it is and as much as I miss Daddy. We can only do what we believe is right every day and try to make good decision for the future."

"You are wise far beyond your years, my dear," Elizabeth said. "And you are right. Most people spend a lifetime before they understand these things."

"That's right, Caroline," Grant continued. "I'm very glad you came to see us. Does your mother know you're here?"

"No, why?" Caroline asked.

"I did not treat her fairly or give her nearly the credit she deserved. You were right—she was, in large part, responsible for your father's success," Grant conceded.

"Yes, she was, Granddaddy. I was there every day, and I watched how she skillfully handled your clients and worked to support my daddy. She is an amazing person."

"A better example you could not have," Elizabeth said sweetly.

"That brings me to the next topic," Grant said. "Your grandmother and I want to leave our entire estate to you. You are our closest relative, and I believe you will do the greatest good with it. I don't think we have enough time to go over all the details right now, but the will is in place. You should know that." Caroline sat back on the sofa with her mouth open.

"Granddaddy!" she exclaimed. "I never expected this!"

"Well, who did you think I would leave it to, my worthless brother?" Grant replied, sounding funny.

"Well, I just haven't given it any thought. You were very generous to me, so I was thankful for that," Caroline said sincerely.

"I will do the right thing for my only granddaughter," Grant said with remorse in his tone. "My son would want it that way, and your grandmother and I want it that way too."

"Thank you very much, Granddaddy," Caroline said, still in shock. "How do you want me to handle this news with Mama?"

"I'll leave that up to you," Grant replied. "I want her to know that we love her and we really want the estate to go to both of you."

The tears came down Caroline's face, and she could not stop sobbing. "I know Daddy would be so happy about this, Granddaddy," Caroline said between sobs.

"We never stopped loving you, Caroline," Elizabeth said. "In fact, I have spent so many sleepless nights worried about this that your granddaddy and I finally understood what we needed to do. Ever since we made the changes, I have been able to sleep and am more peaceful than I have been for a long time. Your granddaddy and I realized that money doesn't make you happy if you don't have your family to enjoy it with you. Money can't buy good health or happiness."

Caroline sat quietly for almost a minute. She decided not to ask her grandmother about her health, and she was contemplating her next question. "I'm very glad I came to see you today. Are you having Thanksgiving with anyone?" Caroline asked.

"No, honey," Elizabeth said. "We'll just be here. But we are fine."

"Well, you need to come to Roswell to see our new house anyway. I will come to pick you up at ten thirty on Thursday morning. You will see Mama, Aunt Anne and Aunt Nancy, and Belle and Robert. And Robert is engaged, so we will be meeting his fiancée," Caroline said, leaving them no option but to agree. When she looked at Elizabeth, tears were running down her face. She reached for her granddaughter's hand.

"Caroline, you are an amazing young woman. I am so proud to be your grandmother," Elizabeth said softly.

As Caroline stood, Grant walked from his chair and put his arms around her. "I have dreamed of this day, Caroline. You truly are the best of your mother and your father. I am proud to be your grandfather," he said.

"It looks like we all have a lot to be thankful for this year," Caroline said.

"Indeed we do," Elizabeth said.

"I'll call you when I am leaving to pick you up, okay?" Caroline asked.

"That's wonderful, honey," Elizabeth said.

Caroline went to her car, waving as she pulled away. Her grandparents were standing in the door smiling and waving back. She wasn't sure how she felt. What a tragedy that she lost her father! *We have all been through so much pain,* Caroline thought. She was struggling to come to grips with the news of her inheritance and measuring that against losing her father. She would rather have her father any day. *But he worked for this money too,* she thought. *I will make him proud.*

When she got back home, she pulled the car to the back of the house and went in the back door. "Where did you go gallivanting off to today?" Charlotte asked.

"I went to see Grandmother and Granddaddy," Caroline replied, waiting for her mother's reaction.

"How are they doing, Caroline?" Charlotte asked, as if Caroline were talking about the weather.

"They're doing fine, Mama," Caroline said, somewhat surprised at her mother's response. "As a matter of fact, I invited them to Thanksgiving dinner with us."

"Caroline, that was so thoughtful of you," Charlotte said as she continued chopping squash.

"They would have been by themselves if I hadn't invited them for dinner, Mama," Caroline said defensively.

"I'm fine with that, Caroline," Charlotte replied, looking up, surprised at her daughter's statement.

"Thanks, Mama," Caroline said genuinely. "Let's talk later, okay?"

"Sure, sweetheart," Charlotte answered, looking quizzically at Caroline.

"It's all good, Mama; don't worry," Caroline said without hesitating.

"Okay," Charlotte replied quietly. And the subject was dropped.

"Did I get any telephone calls?" Caroline asked.

"Yes, honey," Belle replied. "Mr. Garrett Winthrop called to give you his flight information."

"Did he leave a telephone number, Belle?" Caroline asked.

"Yes, he did," Belle replied. "It's on your bed."

"Thanks, Belle!" Caroline said as she ran upstairs to her room.

Caroline dialed the telephone number as soon as she picked up the piece of paper with the message on it. "Hello" came the cordial answer on the other end of the telephone line.

"Mr. Winthrop, this is Caroline Wellington. I hope I'm not interrupting your dinner," Caroline said politely.

"Not at all, Caroline, you are not interrupting anything," Garrett's father replied. "He's expecting your call. Please wait just a minute and I'll get him to the telephone."

"Thank you," Caroline said.

"Caroline!" Garrett's voice sounded so wonderful to Caroline.

"Hi. Belle said that you called to give me your flight information," Caroline said, trying not to sound too thrilled to hear his voice, although she was.

"Yes, I did," Garrett said. "But I wanted to hear your voice too."

"Garrett, that is so sweet," Caroline said, sitting in the chair in her room.

"You didn't tell me about Belle," Garrett quizzed.

"Belle was my mother's nanny, and she has been with our family since 1916," Caroline replied matter-of-factly.

"You're kidding!" exclaimed Garrett.

"No, not at all," Caroline replied, somewhat surprised that he was surprised. "She is more a member of our family than anything else," Caroline said. "She always has been. I love her dearly."

"That is really nice, Caroline," Garrett said genuinely. "I will be glad to meet her and your mother and grandmother. Let me give you my flight information. I'll arrive on Friday at eleven o'clock in the morning on Delta flight 306. I think it comes in at Gate 18A," Garrett said, sounding very happy.

"I'll meet you at your gate, Garrett," Caroline said. "We'll have most of Friday and all day Saturday to meet my family and look around Atlanta."

"I can't wait to see you, Caroline," Garrett said sweetly.

"I can't wait to see you either, Garrett," Caroline replied with sincere affection evident in her voice. "Call me if anything changes, okay?"

"I will, but I don't think there is much chance of that," Garrett said.

"Okay, see you Friday," Caroline said, and Garrett understood that the conversation was over.

"Bye, Caroline," Garrett said.

"Bye, Garrett," Caroline replied.

Caroline danced around her room, smiling to herself. "Oh my gosh!" Caroline exclaimed out loud to herself. *What will I wear?* she thought. Charlotte had a large walk-in closet put into Caroline's room to accommodate her passion for clothes and shoes. Caroline spent twenty minutes planning everything she would wear while she and Garrett were together. Like her mother, Caroline's 5'8" 125-pound frame looked wonderful in almost anything she wore. With her walnut brown shoulder-length hair and crystal blue eyes, she was stunning no matter what she wore.

CHAPTER 16

*C*AROLINE WOKE ON WEDNESDAY TO a sunny, fall morning in Roswell. The oak tree outside her room turned a beautiful dark burgundy, and the maple tree was bright orange and yellow. It was cool outside, but the first frost had come and gone and it was very pleasant. That was typical of Atlanta weather at Thanksgiving.

Caroline heard her mother on the telephone in her room. She walked down the hall and overheard her saying, "Geoff, I am so sorry. I did not know that Camilla was ill. What can I do to help you?" After a short pause, she said, "I will be there by one o'clock. Be strong." And she put the phone back on its cradle.

"Mama, what was that all about?" Caroline asked as she walked into her mother's room.

"Camilla Robinson, Geoff's wife, is in Crawford Long. She has cancer and is not expected to live through the weekend," Charlotte replied as she sat down in one of the chairs in her room. Caroline sat down in the other chair in front of her fireplace.

"Mama, that is terrible!" Caroline exclaimed. "Do you want me to go with you?"

"Would you please stay here and help Belle with the preparation for dinner tomorrow?" Charlotte replied. "That would help me more than anything."

"Sure, Mama, I'll be glad to," Caroline said as she rose and put her arms around her mother. Charlotte wept quietly as her daughter comforted her.

"There is so much tragedy and sadness these days," Charlotte said, trying to compose herself.

"I know, Mama, but there's a lot of joy too," Caroline said, comforting her mother and trying to change the sad tone.

"You're right, sweetheart," Charlotte said.

"Mama, would you sit down for just a few more minutes?" Caroline asked in an almost instructive tone.

"Sure, honey," Charlotte replied looking directly at her daughter. "What's up?"

"You know I went to visit Grandmother and Granddaddy yesterday," Caroline started.

"Yes. Go on," Charlotte urged.

"Granddaddy told me that he and Grandmother decided to leave their entire estate to you and me," Caroline said as if she were talking about what to have for dinner.

"*What?*" Charlotte exclaimed, standing up.

"I was pretty shocked too, Mama," Caroline said, continuing her casual tone. "He even said that he would never leave the money to his worthless brother. On top of that, they both apologized to me for the way they treated you and me after Daddy died."

"Good Lord, Caroline!" Charlotte said, still completely surprised. "I have been in touch with them several times over the last year, but I never expected this. It doesn't sound as if Granddaddy told you about Grandmother's health."

"No, and I didn't mention that you'd told me," Caroline said.

"She has congestive heart failure, Caroline," Charlotte said as gently as she could. "Outside of medications to help with the symptoms, there's not much they can do for her. She may not be here next Thanksgiving according to what Granddaddy told me. It is good that they will be here tomorrow."

"I'm glad you told me," Caroline said, her tone changing. "I just want to be happy about something without being sad about something else."

"I know, honey," Charlotte said, touching Caroline's cheek. "You have had more than your share of sadness in nineteen years. You are so young to have dealt with the things you have during your life."

"I know, Mama," Caroline said in a comforting tone directed at her mother. "But it's not your fault, and we have each other now. You are so important to me, and I love you so much. You are strong, and I'm proud every day that you are my mother."

"Wow!" Charlotte exclaimed. "I needed that today."

"I'll get dressed and help Belle, and I'll tell her what is going on with Mrs. Robinson," Caroline offered.

"That's great, Caroline," Charlotte replied thankfully. "I'd better get going."

When Charlotte and Caroline walked into the kitchen, Robert was there with Karen. "Karen," Charlotte began, "we are so glad to meet you."

"Thank you, Mrs. Wellington," Karen replied timidly.

Charlotte looked at Robert and said, "You are a very lucky man, Robert. I know you two are going to be very happy." She turned to Karen, "Congratulations, my dear. Robert is a fine young man, and he will be a wonderful husband."

"Miss Charlotte," Robert began, "that is a very nice compliment. Thank you."

Caroline chimed in. "Robert, I am so excited for you. Karen, Robert really is a very lucky man. Robert, she is beautiful, and you look so happy together."

"We are, Miss Caroline," Robert replied. "I'm glad you got to meet her. I told her my family would have to approve." He chuckled.

"We definitely approve, Robert," Caroline said. She turned to Karen. "Karen, we will be very glad to have you in our family."

Karen smiled and said, "You told me they were great, and they really are."

Charlotte left, and Caroline filled Belle in on what was going on with the Robinsons.

The day went by so fast for Caroline. She and Belle worked in the kitchen nearly all day. The flowers for the dining table were delivered at three o'clock. Caroline and Belle set the table. It was an exquisite masterpiece. Everything looked beautiful. By five o'clock, all had been done that could be done before tomorrow morning.

Charlotte came home at five thirty looking very tired. As she came through the back door, Caroline and Belle greeted her. Her eyes brightened. "How did my family do today?" she said playfully.

"We did just fine, Miss Charlotte," Belle said, laughing. "Miss Caroline was a big help, and we have a surprise for you." Belle led Charlotte to the dining room where the chandelier was on along with the sconces on each side of the Carolina mirror.

"Oh my gosh!" Charlotte exclaimed. "That is the most beautiful table I think I have ever seen." The Royal Doulton china, Winfield Waterford crystal, and Wallace French Regency sterling flatware made a stunning impression in the dining room set for eight people. John had given Charlotte the Royal Doulton China for their fifteenth anniversary. It was appropriately named "Charlotte." It had floral green bands with a mustard-colored trim. Charlotte felt as if life had been breathed into their home, and she hugged Caroline and Belle and thanked them for making a very sad day joyful instead.

Charlotte went upstairs to change her clothes. When she came back downstairs, she said to Belle and Caroline, "Let's go to dinner at Lickskillet Farm."

"Fabulous idea, Mama," Caroline said. Belle took off her apron and got her sweater, and they all left together.

Early on Thanksgiving morning, Belle and Robert were in the kitchen getting the turkey ready for the oven. Charlotte was getting the serving bowls organized for the feast. The doorbell rang. It was Anne and Walter. Charlotte opened the door and welcomed her sister and her husband.

"Everything looks beautiful, Charlotte," Anne exclaimed.

"It's as we expected it would be," Walter chimed in as he gave his sister-in-law a hug.

"Come on in to the kitchen," Charlotte said as she led the way to the room where the wonderful smells were wafting out.

"Well, good morning, Miss Anne and Mr. Mitchell," Belle said as she looked up from the turkey.

"Belle, everything looks and smells wonderful," Anne said sincerely. Walter strolled over to the breakfast table where Belle poured him a cup of coffee. He sat contented to read the newspaper and drink coffee. Anne jumped in to help Charlotte with the serving pieces. Charlotte brought them up to date with who would be attending dinner today. "Any questions you have about Grant and Elizabeth will have to wait until another day," Charlotte explained. "We will enjoy the day, and they will be welcome in our home." That was all that was said about that.

Anne and Walter had married twenty-five years before. They never had any children and really never understood why. Walter's father owned 1,550 acres of farmland in Roswell that was being converted to subdivisions and shopping centers. Walter had inherited the land when his parents died, and he managed the sale of the land and the investments of the proceeds. Anne owned a gift shop in Roswell that sold beautiful linens, china, and elegant gifts.

Robert got fires going in the fireplaces in the living room, dining room, and den. The Wellington home on Mimosa Boulevard was glowing and warm with wonderful smells of cornbread dressing, sage, turkey, and banana pudding.

Caroline came downstairs about nine o'clock. She walked to the kitchen, where she gave her aunt Anne and her uncle Walter hugs. "Good morning, Caroline," Anne said as she hugged her niece. "It looks like college is agreeing with you. You look beautiful."

"Thank you, Aunt Anne," Caroline said as she walked to give Belle, Robert, and her mother a hug. "What can I do to help?" she continued.

"Looks like we are just about done, honey," Charlotte said. "Why don't you call Mama Rene and run down and pick her up?" Charlotte said.

"I think I will," Caroline said. And she grabbed her purse and keys and out the door she went. As she approached her car, she turned and decided to walk to Mama Rene's house. She thought it would do both of them good to walk this morning. It was only two blocks anyway. When she arrived, she saw Mama Rene sitting on her front porch. "Good morning, Mama Rene," Caroline said as she walked up the steps.

"What a lovely surprise, sweetheart," Irene said as she stood to give her granddaughter a hug.

"It's a beautiful day," Caroline said as she sat down next to her grandmother in the wrought iron chair on the porch. "Aunt Anne and Uncle Walter are there, and with Belle, Robert, and Mama in the kitchen, there's not much room for us right now." Irene nodded her head, laughing. "Mama Rene, I went to see Granddaddy and Grandmother on Tuesday. I invited them to Thanksgiving dinner with us," Caroline said, waiting for her grandmother's reaction.

Irene looked quizzically at Caroline. "Why?" was her only response.

"Because they would have been alone," Caroline replied somewhat defensively.

"So?" Irene continued.

"Well, it's like this, Mama Rene," Caroline began. Irene sat back in her chair, anticipating the story. "I went there just to be polite more than anything and because I thought it was the right thing to do.

140

Mama taught me that my actions should never be determined by someone else's actions."

"She's right, dear," Irene conceded.

"Anyway, Mama Rene," Caroline continued, "I had the surprise of my life when they both apologized for the way they treated Mama and me and when they told me they were leaving their entire estate to both Mama and me."

Irene turned and looked at her granddaughter with her mouth open. "I am shocked!" she exclaimed.

"Me too, Mama Rene," Caroline said genuinely.

"I'll believe it when I see it in writing," Irene said tentatively.

"Mama Rene, I don't blame you for being hesitant to believe them," Caroline said, trying to convince her grandmother that they were sincere. "They have no one, and grandmother is ill. She has congestive heart failure, and she will be lucky to live another year," Caroline continued in an attempt to convince Irene.

"Honey, I believe you. I just can't stand to see you and your mother hurt anymore," Irene said softly.

"I know, Mama Rene," Caroline said sweetly as she hugged her grandmother. "We've all been through too much."

"Let's stroll down to the square and enjoy the morning; want to?" Caroline said as she stood.

"Let me get my sweater, honey," Irene said as she stood to go into the house. And stroll and talk they did, down to the square in Roswell, down to the old Roswell Mill, and back up to Caroline's house. By the time Caroline and Irene walked through the back door it was ten thirty, and once again, hugs were all around. Caroline walked into the den and found Aunt Nancy chatting with Walter.

"Aunt Nancy!" Caroline exclaimed.

"Caroline, give your old aunt a hug," Nancy said.

"I will, but you're not old, Aunt Nancy," Caroline said as she hugged her aunt. "It looks like the single life is agreeing with you. You look wonderful," Caroline said, stepping back to get the whole picture of her aunt. "Why thank you, sugar," Nancy replied giggling.

Nancy had been married briefly to Allen Gentry. When they divorced, Nancy moved to Buckhead and went to work for Trust Company Bank. She was promoted in the trust department to manage a group of trust officers overseeing the Robert Woodruff Coca-Cola Foundation. She was well respected and independent, like her mother and sisters. She dropped her married name and took her maiden name back. Nancy Reed was seven years younger than Charlotte and was very attractive. She did not hide the fact that she enjoyed dating and partying with the wealthy and elite in Atlanta.

Caroline went into the kitchen. "Mama, I'm going to get Granddaddy and Grandmother now. I need to use your car, okay?"

"Okay, sweetheart," Charlotte replied. "We should be ready to eat about one thirty." Caroline walked to the telephone and called her grandfather to let him know she would be there in about an hour. While she was gone, Charlotte explained to her family that Mr. and Mrs. Wellington would be joining them for Thanksgiving dinner. She continued the explanation by telling them that Caroline needed to have some reconciliation with them to allow her the peace she needed. She did not share the information about the inheritance, nor would she.

When Caroline arrived at the elder Wellingtons' home, they were both dressed in their Sunday best and were ready to go. On the drive back to Roswell, they chatted about the University of Virginia and steered clear of any controversial subjects.

When they arrived, Caroline led them through the front door and into the living room. Charlotte greeted them and gave them both hugs. She invited them into the den with the rest of the family.

Grant and Elizabeth were very impressed with the beautiful home that Charlotte created for herself and Caroline. After greeting Belle and Robert, they complimented Charlotte and then went about chatting casually with the family.

When dinner was ready, Belle and Robert served and then excused themselves to Belle's cottage, where they would enjoy Thanksgiving dinner with Robert's fiancée.

It was a lovely day for everyone. After dinner, Robert and Karen cleared the table and washed dishes. Belle rested in her cottage.

At four o'clock, Grant said, "Caroline, I think I'd better take Grandmother home. She's pretty tired."

"Okay, Granddaddy," Caroline said, standing to get her purse and car keys. On the way back, they both thanked her for coming to see them and for including them in Thanksgiving. The compliments for her mother were lavished on her, and Caroline smiled with pride. "Thank you," Caroline said as she walked them to their door. "I'll call you and write to you after I get back to UVA."

"That would be wonderful, Caroline," Elizabeth said. "We want to know how you are doing." She hugged and kissed them both and got into her mother's car for the trip back to Roswell.

On the trip home, she turned her thoughts to Garrett. He would be in Atlanta tomorrow! She had butterflies just thinking about it. She began to plan the two short days they would have at her house. When she arrived home, her mother was at Mama Rene's house. She went in the back door and found Belle in the kitchen. "I'm glad you are here, Miss Caroline," Belle said as she looked up from writing her "to do" list. "What do you want for dinner tomorrow evening when Mr. Winthrop is here?"

"Belle, why don't we just do an old-fashioned pot roast with potatoes and carrots? That will be fairly easy. We can have leftover green beans and maybe pound cake. We can have dinner out on Saturday night. That way the only meals we will have here will be dinner tomorrow night and breakfast on Saturday and Sunday morning. Are you okay with that?" Caroline asked, sincerely concerned that Belle was too tired to do much of anything.

"Honey, are you sure? I can do most anything you want, and you know I will do that for you." Belle's reply seemed earnest.

"Yes, Belle," Caroline said decisively. "You're the best. I want you to give me your honest opinion about him. Will you?" Caroline appealed to Belle.

"Yes, I will, sweet girl. You know old Belle will tell you the whole truth."

"Good," Caroline said, taking her purse and walking toward the foyer to go upstairs. "Now then, you get some rest. You have done quite enough for one day. You know how much we appreciate and love you, don't you Belle?"

"Yes, I do, Miss Caroline," Belle said softly. "I am one of the luckiest people I know."

"We are the lucky ones, Belle," Caroline replied emphatically as she turned to look straight at Belle. She smiled at her and went upstairs.

Belle was very tired. After all, she was almost seventy-three years old. She wanted to keep working like she used to, but she just couldn't do as much as when she was young. Belle seldom gave in to her tired body, but tonight she would. She went to her cottage, took a hot bath, and went to bed.

Charlotte returned from her mother's house at nine. She saw all lights out in Belle's cottage and went upstairs to get ready for bed herself. *What a week!* she thought. She was exhausted.

CHAPTER 17

*A*T SEVEN O'CLOCK THE NEXT morning, Caroline came downstairs, dressed and ready to go to the airport. The evening before she had made sure the guest room and bathroom were ready for Garrett. "I'm too excited to eat, Belle," Caroline said as she walked into the kitchen. "I will have coffee, though." She poured herself a cup. "Where's Mama?" she asked.

"She's gone to the grocery store, honey," Belle said. "We're getting everything ready for Mr. Winthrop's dinner this evening."

"You are just too good, Belle," Caroline said as she took the last gulp. "Please tell Mama that I have gone to the bookstore and then I will go to the airport. I have two books I have to get before I go back to school on Sunday."

"I'll do that, honey. You be careful now," Belle replied instructively.

"I will, Belle," Caroline said as she walked out the back door.

Caroline headed for Border's Bookstore at Lenox Square. She could get the books she needed and walk around for a while until time to meet Garrett. At nine forty-five, she returned to her car and

146

headed to the airport. She double-checked his gate and then went to Terminal A, where most of the Delta flights arrived. She reached the gate at ten thirty. She couldn't sit and didn't want to walk, so she just stood and stared at the clock. Finally, she heard the announcement of the arrival of Flight 306 from Charleston. Garrett had been seated in the middle of the airplane, and Caroline thought he would never walk through the door. But there he was. He walked over to her, put his bags down, and kissed her on the mouth. "I missed you, Caroline," Garrett said as he took a step back to look at her.

"I missed you too, Garrett," Caroline replied softly, wondering if her knees were going to hold her up. "Do you have other bags?" Caroline asked, trying to regain her composure.

"No, this is it," Garrett said.

"Well, I have a lunch surprise for you," Caroline said, taking his arm and walking toward the escalator. When they were in her car, she exited the airport and headed straight to the Varsity. "I'm taking you to the Varsity for lunch. It is the world's largest drive-in restaurant. But we can go in to eat," Caroline said as she turned onto Peachtree Street. "It's pretty famous," she continued. "I think you'll like it."

And like it he did. They ate chili-cheese dogs with onion rings and a frosted orange to drink. "No wonder that place is famous!" Garrett exclaimed when they got back into her car. "That was the best hot dog I ever ate."

"It opened in 1928 right here. I used to come here when I was a little girl with my father," Caroline said. "I thought you would like it."

The pulled out of the parking lot onto North Avenue. "We'll drive down Peachtree Street so you can get an idea about the city. I will take you through Ansley Park and show you the house we lived in when I was born."

Garrett was looking at Caroline, watching her every move. When they drove by the Ansley Park house, Garrett said, "That is a beautiful house, Caroline. How long did you live there?"

"We moved when I was three."

"Where did you move to?" Garrett was more curious than ever about her.

"We moved to Buckhead. It's not far from here, but I'm not sure we'll have time to go by that house," Caroline said, not wanting to show Garrett the Peacock House.

"Will it take very long?" Garrett quizzed her.

"Not too long, I don't suppose," Caroline said tentatively.

Garrett sensed the hesitation. "If you would prefer not to drive by there, it's fine, Caroline," Garrett said.

"Let's go on to Roswell, if you don't mind," Caroline said. "I want you to meet my family."

"Oh boy!" Garrett said as he took a deep breath. "I hope they like me."

"Garrett," Caroline started. Then she hesitated. "Garrett, what's not to like?" He laughed, and Caroline sensed that her comment had put him at ease.

Caroline pulled into the driveway of the Mimosa Boulevard house. "Wow!" Garrett said. "This is a perfect southern home. It is gorgeous!"

"My mother has put a lot of work and time into restoring and remodeling the house. She really did a wonderful job. You'll see," Caroline said boastfully. Garrett and Caroline got out of the car. He retrieved his bag from the small trunk, and they walked up the steps to the front door. The afternoon sun gave the living room and dining room a beautiful glow.

As they walked in, Charlotte came from the kitchen into the foyer. "Garrett, it is so wonderful to meet you," Charlotte said.

"Garrett, I'd like you to meet my mother, Charlotte Wellington," Caroline said formally.

"Mrs. Wellington, it is a pleasure to meet you too," Garrett said sincerely. "Caroline talks about you and her grandmother quite a bit. I hope you had a nice Thanksgiving," he continued.

"We did, Garrett," Charlotte said politely. Just then, Robert walked into the foyer. "Garrett, this is Robert. He is Belle's nephew and has been with our family since before Caroline was born."

"Mr. Winthrop," Robert said, "we have been expecting you."

"Robert will show you to your room, and then let's talk in the den," Charlotte instructed. Robert picked up Garrett's bag and walked upstairs.

More surprises, Garrett thought. They have a butler. He followed Robert, and he showed him to the guest room. The room was beautiful, with a rice-carved four-poster bed with beautiful toile bedding, and he was amazed at how it seemed every detail had been considered. Robert escorted him into the den and then disappeared to the cottage. Belle had started dinner, and there was a wonderful smell coming from the oven. But she was in her cottage when Garrett arrived.

Garrett came into the den and sat in one of the club chairs near the fireplace. "Your home is beautiful, Mrs. Wellington," Garrett said somewhat nervously.

"Thank you," Charlotte replied. "It has been a labor of love."

"I see and feel that everywhere I look," Garrett said. Charlotte understood why her daughter liked him. He was very good looking, and he had perfect manners, at least so far.

"Garrett," Caroline said informally to change the tone, "Mama Rene will be here later for dinner. I want you to meet Belle too. She's the best."

"Tell me about your family, Garrett," Charlotte asked genuinely interested. Garrett told Charlotte most of what she already knew, and they all talked in the den for almost an hour. Charlotte was impressed, and Garrett was at ease within ten minutes of arriving. When Charlotte went to the kitchen to get everyone iced tea, Garrett looked at Caroline and said, "No wonder you are so beautiful. Your mother is beautiful too."

"She is, isn't she?" Caroline replied. "Thank you for the compliment. I always think she is, but she's my mother and I love her. It is nice to have support for my opinion." Caroline laughed as Charlotte brought iced tea for everyone.

After tea, Caroline took Garrett on the walking Roswell tour. It was chillier than it had been on Thanksgiving. He put his arm around her as they walked and talked. Charlotte looked out the living room window and smiled. *I'm so glad she's happy*, Charlotte thought.

They returned to the front porch and sat on the porch swing. Garrett kissed her longer than ever before. They embraced, and Caroline felt passion rising in her body. Garrett held her hand and gently touched her face. They were truly "in love."

Caroline and Garrett were in the den looking through the photo album that Mama Rene had made for her when she walked through the back door. "Something sure smells good in here!" she exclaimed. Caroline stood and walked to the kitchen.

"Mama Rene, come into the den. I want you to meet Garrett," she said, smiling from ear to ear.

Mama Rene extended her hand to Garrett. "Garrett, it's very nice to meet you," she said.

"Garrett, this is Mama Rene," Caroline introduced her grandmother proudly.

"Mrs. Reed, it is a pleasure to meet you too. Caroline has talked so much about you. You certainly have been an important part of her life," Garrett said as he took her hand gently.

Wow! Irene thought. *He's even better than Caroline told us.*

They sat and chatted in the den for about twenty minutes. At five thirty, Belle walked into the kitchen. "Belle," Caroline called from the den, "come and meet Garrett."

Belle smiled and walked into the den. "Mr. Winthrop, it's very nice to meet you," Belle said. Garrett extended his hand first, and Belle accepted his handshake.

"Belle, please call me Garrett. It's so nice to meet you too," he said. "Caroline wants you to come to UVA with her so she can have all the wonderful food she is accustomed to," he continued.

"Yes, she told me that. But I reckon I'll be staying here with Miss Charlotte," Belle said, laughing. "Please excuse me for now. I need to tend to dinner." And she disappeared into the kitchen.

They all enjoyed a dinner of roast with potatoes and carrots, green beans, and pound cake, just like Caroline requested. After dinner, Caroline said, "Mother, I would like to show Garrett around Roswell. We won't be gone too long."

"Sure, sweetheart," Charlotte said as she was clearing the table. "Have a nice time."

"Okay, Mama," Caroline said as she headed for the coat closet. It was in the low forties outside, and the wind was blowing. Garrett got his jacket, and they left in Caroline's car.

"It is so nice to see her happy," Charlotte said to Irene.

"It is nice, but I hope they don't rush things," Irene said with a look of concern.

"Caroline has a good head on her shoulders, Mother," Charlotte chided her mother. "She has her goals set, and she is focused on school. She made the dean's list."

"I know, but she has never really been in love before either," Irene said, continuing the concerned tone.

"I'll talk with her when it is appropriate, Mother, so don't you worry about it," Charlotte offered.

"I think that's a great idea," Irene said as she sat in a breakfast room chair while Charlotte cleaned the kitchen.

Caroline and Garrett returned home at ten thirty. They came in through the back door and each got a piece of pound cake and a glass of milk. As they were finishing, Garrett gave her a kiss on her cheek, took her hand, and said, "I love you, Caroline Wellington."

Caroline sat looking at his face and studying it to be sure he was genuine. "I love you too, Garrett Winthrop," she finally replied. They walked down the hall arm in arm and up the stairs. "See you in the morning," Caroline whispered.

"Yes, you will," Garrett whispered back.

The following morning, Garrett woke to the best smells coming from the kitchen. *More fabulous food,* he thought to himself. He put on his robe and slippers and went downstairs. Caroline and Charlotte were already there with Belle, and her famous biscuits were about to come out of the oven. "You have perfect timing, Garrett," Caroline said as she walked to give him a hug.

"Yes, you do, Garrett," Charlotte said. "You are about to experience the best biscuits and the best breakfast you have ever eaten."

"From the way it smells, I can believe it," Garrett said. "Belle, no wonder Caroline wants you to come to UVA with her." Belle chuckled and continued her cooking.

They enjoyed bacon and eggs with biscuits and homemade blackberry preserves. When they were finished and compliments were offered, Caroline announced, "Garrett and I are going to Buckhead today. I want to show him Westminster and around the area where I grew up,"

"Y'all have a great day," Charlotte said.

Within a half hour, both of them were dressed and ready to go. As they were driving down Roswell Road toward Sandy Springs, Garrett said, "Will you show me your house in Buckhead today?"

"Maybe, if we have time," Caroline replied and changed the subject.

Garrett was very impressed with the campus of the Westminster School where Caroline attended all thirteen years. She took him to Lenox Square, and they walked the entire mall twice. Caroline saw several of her classmates home for Thanksgiving, and she was very proud to introduce Garrett.

They continued the tour at the Regency Hotel downtown. It was the only round hotel in the Southeast. They were entertained going up in the indoor glass elevators. "We had our senior prom here,"

Caroline said, still giving Garrett the first class tour. As they were leaving the hotel, Caroline said, "I will take you to see the house I grew up in. I think we have enough time."

"Great," Garrett said. As they turned onto West Paces Ferry Road off Peachtree, Garrett saw the governor's mansion. Across the street was the Cox Mansion. Caroline turned onto Habersham Road and then into the driveway for the 320 West Paces Ferry Road home.

"This is the house I grew up in," she said casually.

Garrett did not speak. He turned and looked at Caroline. "Really?" he exclaimed.

"Yes, really," Caroline said, and she turned the car around and drove back up Habersham and onto West Paces Ferry toward Peachtree.

Neither of them said anything until they got to the Chattahoochee River Bridge going into Roswell. Caroline spoke first, "Garrett, I really did not want to show you the house. We lived there when my daddy was alive, and it really served a business purpose pretty often. My mother held large cocktail parties for clients and prospects and had formal and informal dinners all the time. It was just part of what we did for my daddy's company." Caroline said trying to diminish the surprise.

"Caroline, I'm sorry I acted so surprised. I should have realized as soon as I met you were from a really good background. I did realize it, but I just didn't know how good," Garrett, said trying not to sound distant. "My family is wonderful, but we are not in that league." Caroline turned and looked at Garrett.

"Garrett, we are not competing. I am not in one league and you are not in another league. In fact, I'm not in any league," Caroline said. Garrett could hear the defensive irritation in her voice. "Just like you had nothing to do with what family you were born into, I didn't either. And I am sure, just like your family, that there are some things that you don't typically share with anyone," she continued. Garrett picked up a pleading note in her voice.

"Caroline, I'm so sorry. I did not mean to be so surprised. I love you, and I don't care about how or where you grew up. Your family is wonderful, and I am enjoying being here with you more than anything I can think of," Garrett said.

Caroline reached to take his hand. He put both his hands around hers and again said, "I love you, Caroline."

"I love you, Garrett," she said softly. "Please," she continued, "don't talk about this back at school, okay?"

"Okay, I won't," Garrett said. "This is your story to tell, not mine."

They pulled into the driveway about five thirty. Belle surprised Caroline and was making fried chicken, mashed potatoes, and turnip greens. They enjoyed another wonderful dinner together.

The following morning after breakfast, Caroline and Garrett left for the long drive back to Charlottesville. Charlotte was fighting tears, but Irene just couldn't fight them. "You be careful, sweet girl," Irene said, wiping her eyes.

"Mama Rene, don't cry," Caroline pleaded. "You're going to make me cry."

Charlotte put her arms around Caroline and held her for a long time. "I love you so much, sweetheart," she said softly.

"I love you too, Mama," Caroline said with tears in her eyes.

"Garrett, it was wonderful to have you here. We are so glad you got to visit," Charlotte said cordially.

"It was wonderful for me too, Mrs. Wellington. Thank you so much for your hospitality. I enjoyed meeting everyone," Garrett said genuinely.

"Take care of my girl," Irene said.

"I will do that, Mrs. Reed," Garrett said and got into the passenger seat, and he and Caroline drove down Mimosa Boulevard toward the highway.

Most of the conversation on the way back was about school, friends, favorite restaurants, favorite foods, favorite books, and other "getting to know you" chat. They arrived in Charlottesville at six thirty.

"Let's go to the pizza restaurant downtown for dinner," Garrett said, wanting to extend the time they were together.

After they ordered, Caroline look at Garrett and said, "You know, we have to focus on school. We will have to wait until Saturday to really see each other."

"I know, Caroline," Garrett said. "I've already been thinking about that. I didn't expect this to happen to me in my freshman year either." After that, they enjoyed their pizza and talked about plans for Christmas break. Caroline dropped Garrett off at his dorm and drove to hers. After getting all of her things into her room, she just wanted to shower and sleep. She called her mother to let her know she arrived safely, and then, shower and sleep is just what she did.

CHAPTER 18

O N MONDAY MORNING AT SEVEN o'clock, Charlotte's telephone rang. She was in the kitchen making coffee. She had given Belle the week off because of all the work she had done for Thanksgiving.

"Hello," Charlotte said.

"Charlotte, this is Geoff" came the voice on the other end of the line. "Camilla died this morning at four o'clock."

"Oh, Geoff," Charlotte said, "I am so sorry. I will be to your house by noon."

"That would be great, Charlotte," Geoff said, sounding as if he was still in shock.

Camilla Candler Robinson was dead at the age of forty-nine. Their son and daughter, Candler and Cecile Robinson, were still in high school. Charlotte knew that it was devastating for all of them. She called the market and ordered a ham and potato salad. Afterward, she put on Belle's apron and made a pound cake. This was not how she intended to spend her day, but this is what she would do. As she was leaving the house for the trip to Geoff and Camilla's home, the grief washed over her and she went back into the house, sat down in the kitchen, and cried. John's death was such a short time ago, and now her precious friend Camilla was dead. Her heart broke for Geoff and their children. "Get yourself together," Charlotte said out loud as she wiped her tears. She opened her purse, took out her compact, powdered her nose, freshened her lipstick, and left to do what she could for the grieving Robinson family.

She arrived at their home in Buckhead, on Peachtree Battle Avenue, at noon. Lula, the Robinson's housekeeper, met her at the back door and took the food. "Mr. Robinson is in the den, Miss Charlotte," Lula said softly.

"Thank you, Lula," Charlotte replied as she touched her arm in a gesture of sympathy. "Will you let me know what else you need?"

"Yes, ma'am, Miss Charlotte," Lula replied gratefully.

Charlotte walked into the den where Geoff, Candler, and Cecile were sitting. Geoff looked up, walked to Charlotte, and broke down sobbing. She put her arms around him and said, "It is so hard to lose the love of your life." He stood back, wiping his tears. Charlotte walked over to each of the children and gave them a mother's hug. Candler was trying to be strong. He was seventeen and a senior at Westminster. But Cecile was almost inconsolable. She was fourteen and had just begun her freshman year. There was nothing Charlotte could do but just be there.

She took over organizing the house to receive friends and family. She and Lula prepared the dining room for a buffet. Flowers were being delivered to the house every hour. Neighbors were stopping by with casseroles, cakes, and salads. By five o'clock, the house was filled with family and friends all trying to help the Robinsons cope with this tragedy. It had only been three months between the time Camilla was diagnosed with uterine cancer and the time she died.

At six o'clock, Charlotte was tired. She believed that she had done everything she could do for the Robinsons that day. "Lula," Charlotte said, "I am going to leave you my telephone number. You call me if you need anything before I can get back tomorrow."

"Thank you, Miss Charlotte, I will," Lula replied. Charlotte could see that she was exhausted too.

"You try to get some rest yourself, Lula," Charlotte instructed her.

"Yes, ma'am, Miss Charlotte," Lula replied.

When Charlotte returned home, she ate a turkey sandwich, took a hot bath, and got into bed to read until she fell asleep. When she woke the next morning, the book was on the floor beside the bed. She did not remember falling asleep.

Over the next three days, Charlotte traveled between Roswell and Buckhead every day. The funeral was on Thursday at Peachtree Road United Methodist Church. She declined to be seated with the family, preferring to sit in the congregation. The church was packed. Charlotte saw many people whom she and John knew when he was alive. The funeral was one of the most difficult things she had been through since John died. After the graveside service, Charlotte got into her car. She could hardly wait to get home.

She parked in the driveway and walked the two blocks to her mother's house. They ate leftovers and talked for three hours.

It was just three weeks until Christmas break began. Caroline and Garrett were busy studying for semester finals. They had barely seen each other since they returned from Thanksgiving break. Garrett called her twice to meet him for dinner, but she did not feel that she had the time to be distracted. Caroline was very focused, and she intended to remain that way. He missed her, but he knew she was right.

On Saturday morning at ten fifteen, Caroline's telephone rang. "Hello," she said.

"Caroline, you just can't turn me down for dinner tonight," Garrett pleaded.

"Okay. I should be finished at the library about four o'clock. Do you want to go about five thirty?" Caroline replied, laughing at him.

"Perfect," Garrett said with a satisfied note in his voice. He hung up the telephone and did a little happy dance.

It was getting very cold in Charlottesville. The wind was howling, and the temperatures were dropping to near freezing. Garrett arrived promptly at five thirty to pick Caroline up. He drove her in his black 1964 Chevrolet Malibu. They went to the Michie Tavern on Thomas Jefferson Parkway. It was on the way to Monticello and was very historical, having served guests since 1784. They enjoyed hot mulled cider and a wonderful authentic colonial dinner in front of a roaring fire. It was the most romantic dinner Caroline ever had.

"Garrett, that was really nice," Caroline exclaimed as they got back into his car.

"I enjoyed it too, but mostly being with you," Garrett said sincerely. He drove back toward the campus. About a mile before they arrived, he turned down a dimly lit street and stopped the car. He put his arms around Caroline and pulled her close to him. As they kissed, Caroline felt the passion once again rising in her body. They had been in the car for twenty minutes when Garrett touched her breast and she gasped, trying to decide if she should tell him to stop. It felt like nothing she ever experienced before. The feeling went all the way down her stomach, and she felt aroused. She didn't stop him. Garrett started to put his hand between her legs.

Caroline said, "Garrett, we have to stop." As she brought her arm back across his lap, she brushed her hand against his hard penis bulging through his trousers.

"I know we do, Caroline," Garrett said, disgusted. "Dammit, I know we do." The windows were fogged up, and Garrett turned on the defroster to see how to drive the last mile to their dorms. When his car was parked in front of her dorm, Caroline turned to him and kissed him. Once again, they were in a passionate embrace. Finally, she pulled away from him and opened her door. Garrett got out and went to escort her to the door.

"I really enjoyed our evening, Garrett," Caroline said. She kissed him softly and then disappeared into her dormitory. Garrett returned to his car and sat there for five minutes before driving the short distance to his dorm.

The next two weeks went by quickly, with both of them totally focused on semester finals. Caroline refused to have dinner with Garrett anywhere but in her campus dining room. They ate and chatted about school, professors, and friends. They did not have any time alone, and for Caroline, that was by design. She made up her mind to not put herself in a situation like that again. Garrett spent his time trying to figure out how to repeat the evening that they had enjoyed in his parked car, but it never happened.

Caroline was packed and ready for her flight home. Since she would be visiting Garrett's family after Christmas, she decided to do what Garrett did when he came to her house for Thanksgiving. Garrett took her to the Charlottesville airport to fly to Atlanta. When they arrived at the airport, Caroline insisted that she would get out, check her own luggage, and go to her gate alone. "You've got a long drive to Charleston, Garrett," Caroline said. "You need to get on the road."

"I will miss you until I see you on the twenty-seventh," Garrett said sweetly.

"Me too, Garrett," said Caroline, and she got out of the car, retrieved her bags, and disappeared into the airport. As she suggested, he headed for Charleston.

The flight lasted an hour and forty-five minutes. Charlotte would meet Caroline at her gate. That would give Caroline enough time to put her feelings for Garrett in writing and work through where she wanted this relationship to go.

When Charlotte picked Caroline up, she learned that Robert and Karen would be getting married in their living room on December 23. It would be a small ceremony with only a few of their friends and family. Belle, Charlotte, Irene, and Caroline were working together to get everything decorated and ready for the wedding.

On the afternoon of December 23, Belle's brother and sister-in-law, Robert's parents, his brother and sister, and several friends gathered in Charlotte's living room. Karen's parents and her best friend were there also. Dr. Patterson, from the First Baptist Church of Roswell, agreed to officiate. Karen was beautiful, Robert was handsome, and Belle was smiling from ear to ear. She really felt as if Robert were her child.

The ceremony was very sweet, and it was evident that Robert and Karen loved each other. After the ceremony, they enjoyed punch and cake in the formal dining room. Charlotte had hired a photographer to capture the wedding ceremony and the party afterward for the couple.

For a wedding gift, she gave them a trip to San Francisco. She knew that Robert had always wanted to go to California. At the end of the evening, Robert's father and mother drove the newlyweds to the airport and they left for San Francisco where they would stay in the honeymoon suite at the St. Francis Hotel. Charlotte pulled some strings to persuade the hotel manager to allow them to stay in the honeymoon suite. The three hundred dollar tip went a long way in the persuasion.

Belle was a little teary-eyed for the rest of the day. Robert and Karen had decided to rent a small house on Frazier Street in Roswell. He would continue to take care of Charlotte's yard, but the couple needed a place of their own. Belle knew that it was the right thing to do, but she would miss him terribly. She could not have been prouder of him had he been her own child.

On Christmas Eve, Irene, Charlotte, Caroline, and Belle enjoyed a wonderful dinner of filet mignon, roasted rosemary potatoes, and asparagus. Charlotte had had John's wedding band made into a ring for Caroline. The beautiful wide gold band had a one-carat emerald in the center and two brilliant-cut one-half-carat diamonds mounted on each side of the emerald. "This means so much to me, Mama," Caroline said after she opened the gift and put it on. "You know I wear the locket every day that Daddy gave me when I was two years old."

"I know you do, honey," Charlotte said as she put her arms around her only child.

"I will wear this everyday too, Mama," Caroline said as she hugged her mother so tight. Love was all around in the small family.

Caroline woke up on Christmas morning to the smell of Belle's fabulous biscuits. The smell was indelibly imprinted in her memory. It was the smell of home, comfort, and love. The morning was cold, and it looked like it would rain. Caroline put on her fuzzy slippers and her quilted robe and went downstairs for some warm comfort and love biscuits. Mama Rene and her mother sat at the kitchen table talking about Christmas dinner. Anne, Walter, Nancy, and Nancy's boyfriend, Tom, would join them for Christmas afternoon dinner.

Despite the ugly weather, Caroline decided to go to Lenox Square for a couple of hours. She couldn't help in the kitchen, and she was bored, and besides, she had another gift to pick up. She took her mother's car and went to Buckhead. Lenox was decorated for Christmas, and it made Caroline feel happy and sad at the same time. She went to Rich's and bought small gifts for Aunt Anne and Uncle Walter and for Aunt Nancy. She bought a beautiful quilt for Mama Rene and a Sunday dress with shoes to match for Belle. After leaving Lenox, she went to the portrait studio where she ordered a 20" by 24" portrait of her father for her mother for Christmas. She arrived and went into the studio. It was the first thing she saw. "My God," Caroline exclaimed out loud, "It looks like he is standing there!" Just then, Rob, the portrait artist, appeared from the back of the studio.

"So you like it?" he asked.

"My gosh, Rob," she said, unable to take her eyes off of her father's image, "it's perfect! My mother will love it," she continued as she paid him.

Rob was considered the best portrait artist in Atlanta, and Caroline knew it. The portrait of her father confirmed his gift. "Thank you so much, Rob," Caroline said as she started to pick up the painting.

"I wanted you to see it before I wrapped it. If you can wait a couple of minutes, I will have it wrapped for you," Rob said as he retrieved the painting, believing that Caroline would, indeed, want it wrapped. Rob knew the Wellington family by reputation. Elizabeth had some work done there ten years earlier. The portrait of Grant and her hung in the lobby of the Georgia Life Corporate Office.

Rob returned to the front of the studio with the portrait wrapped in plastic and beautiful red Christmas paper. There was a large green ribbon and bow on the gift. Caroline loved it.

Belle was in on the surprise, and Caroline slipped the portrait into Belle's cottage when she got back home. Dinner was almost ready, and the family had gathered by the time she got back. It was a wonderful dinner, and Irene and Charlotte insisted that Belle join them. She changed into her Sunday dress and enjoyed Christmas dinner with the family.

Afterward, Anne and Nancy cleaned the kitchen and then came into the den to open gifts. Irene gave Charlotte a beautiful porcelain box for the dresser in her bedroom. Charlotte had paid to have Irene's house painted the previous September, and Irene insisted that would be her Christmas present. But Charlotte gave her a ruby bracelet anyway. Charlotte gave Belle a half-carat diamond necklace. After all the gifts were opened, Caroline stood and said, "There is one more gift to open. I'll be right back." She retrieved the portrait from Belle's cottage and came into the den. "Merry Christmas, Mama," she said as she sat the large gift in front of Charlotte.

"What on earth have you done, Caroline?" Charlotte asked, not expecting an answer. She pulled the wrapping off the portrait and sat staring at it, stunned. "My God, Caroline!" she exclaimed. "It looks just . . ." and she could not say another word. Caroline saw the tears and joined her mother. Charlotte propped the portrait up against the chair and stood to hug her daughter. "Thank you, sweetheart. This is the most perfect gift I have ever received except for you," Charlotte whispered to Caroline as they embraced. "Your father would be so proud of you."

"Thank you, Mama," Caroline said composing herself. "That means so much to me."

By nine o'clock, everyone was gone. Irene, Charlotte, Caroline, and Belle sat in the family room enjoying the lights of the Christmas tree. Charlotte insisted that Irene spend the night with them, and she relented willingly. By ten thirty, everyone was in bed. The first Christmas without John Wellington was finally over.

CHAPTER 19

THE FOLLOWING MORNING, EVERYONE SLEPT until after nine o'clock. Charlotte insisted that Belle take the next several days off. Belle accepted and decided to spend two days with her brother and sister-in-law. By the time Caroline got up at ten o'clock, Belle was already gone. Irene went home too, so it was just Charlotte and Caroline at home. When Caroline came into the kitchen, her mother was sitting at the breakfast table drinking coffee. "Good morning, sunshine." Charlotte greeted Caroline as she had so many times when she was a little girl.

"Good morning, Mama," Caroline replied as she bent to give her mother a hug.

"Have some coffee," Charlotte offered. Caroline poured herself a cup and joined her mother at the breakfast table.

"I'm glad it's just us at home today," Caroline said, looking at Charlotte and waiting for a reply. Charlotte sensed that she wanted to talk.

"Me too, honey," she replied casually. "What's on your mind?"

"I need to talk with you about Garrett," Caroline said as she sipped her coffee.

"Okay, let's talk," Charlotte said.

"I'm really afraid that I am getting too serious about him too soon, Mama," Caroline confessed.

"Do you want to give me some more specific information?" Charlotte asked.

"Not really, but I think I need to," Caroline said.

Charlotte looked up from the newspaper and closed it. Her full attention was on her daughter. "What do you mean?" Charlotte asked trying not to seem anxious about her answer.

"Every time he kisses me, it is like electricity runs through my body. We went to dinner the other night in Charlottesville and we parked and made out for twenty minutes. I didn't want to stop, but I knew I had to," Caroline continued her confession. Charlotte sat back in her chair studying Caroline's face and working to choose her words carefully.

"Caroline, he is a very nice young man. I understand why you like him. The timing of your relationship is not great since you have just finished the first semester of your freshman year. I can tell you that you are in total control of the relationship at this point. Men are made totally different that we are. Their hormones make decisions for them when we make our decisions with our hearts. Now, I realize that you are a young woman. You have the same issues at times, but you can control your actions more easily than he can." Charlotte stopped speaking. She hoped she didn't sound like she was preaching.

"Did you have the same feelings for Daddy?" Caroline asked, leaning forward for the answer.

"Absolutely I did," Charlotte replied. "Your father could walk in the room and I would melt."

"Really!" Caroline exclaimed.

"Yes, really," Charlotte said. "I can tell you where I was, what day it was, and most of the conversation the evening I fell in love with your father."

"But you were thirty-two years old, Mama," Caroline said.

"True, but the feelings are no different," Charlotte said. "What you are showing me today is a level of maturity that I always knew you had." Charlotte touched Caroline's arm lovingly. "I am very proud of you. You know what your goals are, Caroline. You and Garrett can be totally in love and have a wonderful relationship without it getting out of hand." She stopped, waiting to hear what Caroline had to say.

"But I'm afraid that it might get out of hand sometime," Caroline said, sounding as if she were pleading with her mother for an answer.

"Like I said, Caroline," Charlotte replied, "you are in total control of that. You do not want to wind up having sex with this young man and getting pregnant. That would totally derail all of your hopes and dreams. I will tell you this. If Garrett is really the man for you and if he really loves you, he will not insist that you compromise your values. If he does, then you will know all you need to know about him. It would be very sad and very hard for you, but in the long run, you will be a happier person. Just don't ever compromise your values. One evening of passion is not worth a lifetime of regret."

"I don't think I ever thought about it quite that way, Mama," Caroline said as if her mother had just shared an epiphany with her.

"You are strong, Caroline," Charlotte continued. "You are independent just like Mama Rene and me. You are your own person, and no man is going to make you change that about yourself."

"You're right, Mama," Caroline said, sounding as if she had been given a resolution to her problem. "Thank you very much. I knew I could count on you."

"I love you more than I could ever tell you, Caroline," Charlotte said softly. "I want you to be happy and achieve all of your dreams and ambitions. You have your whole life after college and law school to pursue a rich and rewarding relationship and marriage. Besides, you may be sitting at the breakfast table one day with your daughter, and you want to give her the right advice from your own experience and not from your mistakes."

"Wow!" Caroline exclaimed. "That is a great perspective. I think I can handle it now."

"That's my girl," Charlotte said, smiling.

"I need to go and pack for the trip tomorrow," Caroline said as she stood.

"Let me know if I can help," Charlotte said. Caroline went back upstairs while Charlotte sat quietly and prayed for her daughter.

CHAPTER 20

BELLE AND HER BROTHER, TOM, were born in Macon to Jim and Kibbie, a couple who worked for landowners in Monroe County. Mostly, they picked cotton and worked on a plantation. They were lucky. They worked for a very nice family, the Willis's, who took care of them. Belle was born in 1895, and Tom was born in 1897. When Jim died in 1905, Kibbie moved to Roswell to be near her sister, Maylene, who worked for a prominent Roswell family. Maylene got Kibbie a job with the Smith family.

The Smiths were a very wealthy Roswell family who owned and operated a large plantation. They knew that Maylene wanted her widowed sister and two children to come to live on the plantation. Mrs. Smith was kind and provided rooms for Kibbie, Belle, and Tom. Belle was ten years old and Tom was eight when they moved to Roswell.

Belle missed her father terribly but distracted herself with daily chores in the Smith house. She and Tom tried to help with the operation of the plantation as well as a ten—and eight-year-old could. The Smiths had four children. Mrs. Smith watched Belle and Tom and decided that they were good workers and deserved to have an opportunity for a better life. She had a tutor come to the plantation twice a week to give them lessons in reading, writing, and arithmetic. Later, Belle and Tom both graduated from high school.

Kibbie died in 1916, and Belle took her to the Willis plantation to be buried next to Jim. Before she died, Kibbie saw to it that both of her children were able to care for themselves. Belle went to work for the Reed family in Roswell; Tom went to work for the city of Atlanta.

Tom and his wife lived in College Park, a small suburb of Atlanta. Tom had worked for the city for forty-five years and was retired. He had been a mechanic and was a team leader for a group of workers who maintained all of the municipal buildings in the city. His wife, Mae, had worked at Grady Hospital in housekeeping for thirty years when she retired. Their children, Robert, William, and Sarah, grew up with parents who taught them a good work ethic, honesty, and integrity. Both William and Sarah graduated from a junior college in middle Georgia where most of the students were black children. There were both happily married, working and living near their parents.

Robert was the oldest child and was the "black sheep" of the family, getting into trouble with petty theft and other juvenile crimes. Robert's time with Belle changed all of that, and he was now a very trustworthy, productive young man.

Belle enjoyed the time she spent with Tom and Mae. They often talked about their parents and about the families they worked for. Tom and Mae had a very comfortable three-bedroom house on a street with similar homes. Tom maintained the house wonderfully over the twenty years that they had lived there. He was very proud to own his home without a mortgage. When Belle came to visit, they always made fried chicken, green beans, and mashed potatoes. Enough was cooked so they could eat leftovers without cooking for two days.

On this particular visit, Belle shared her final wishes with Tom and Mae. She had saved enough money to pay for her funeral, and she had purchased a cemetery lot within twenty feet of the lots owned by Charlotte. She wanted Tom to know that Charlotte and Caroline were her family as much as he and Robert were. "I've gone to a lot of trouble to be sure you and Mae do not have to worry about how to take care of my final arrangements," Belle said like she was talking about what to have for dessert.

"Now, Big Sis, you know we will take care of you. Besides, I don't want to be talking about that now," Tom said.

"Tom, I understand that, but I'm not getting one bit younger," Belle retorted. "You know I haven't asked you or Mae to do anything for me or for Robert while I was looking after him. I just want you to know this and do what I ask. It won't cost you a dime."

"Belle," Tom's tone softened, "I will never be able to repay you for what you did for Robert."

"He's a good boy, Tom," Belle said earnestly. "I could not love him more if he were my own boy."

"He knows that, Belle," Tom said. "He told me that a couple of weeks ago."

Belle looked over at Tom and was unable to speak. Tom saw the tears running down her face. She dried her eyes and the subject was changed.

Belle and Mae always enjoyed visiting with each other. Mae considered herself fortunate to have a good husband and good children. "You can't put a price on having a good family," Mae always remarked.

Tom and Mae would never allow Belle to lift a finger when she came to visit. Belle's protests were hollow, and she loved the time with her family. Belle said that Mae made the best banana pudding south of the Mason-Dixon Line. Mae knew she loved it, and that is what she made for dessert the first night of her visit. "You are going to spoil me, Mae," Belle said, chuckling and dishing out a heaping bowl of the pudding. "I may just stay a couple of weeks."

"Come on, Belle," Mae joked. "We got room."

"Maybe one of these days, but I got get back to Miss Charlotte," Belle said, leaving Mae thinking she had been serious.

"I know you do, Belle," Mae said. "Charlotte is a wonderful person, isn't she?"

"You just don't know half of what that lady has done for not just me but for so many people, especially her family," Belle shared. "I know she loves me and Robert too."

"It sure seemed like she did at the wedding," Mae said.

"That was mighty nice of her to do that wedding for Robert and Karen," Tom said as he entered the conversation. "I bet they're having the time of their lives in San Francisco. They haven't even called us," he continued.

"For heaven sake, Tom, they are on their honeymoon," Mae scolded.

"I know, I know," Tom said. "I just can't wait to hear about the trip. Did they take the Kodak?"

"Yes, I put it in his suitcase before we left to take them to the airport," Mae said. "Quit worrying. They'll be back in a few days."

Belle was laughing at the conversation, shaking her head and eating her banana pudding. The three of them enjoyed the evening and the next two days together. It was cold and rainy outside, so they stayed inside watching TV and looking at old photographs. Mostly they just talked.

Belle always made sure she didn't wear out her welcome. Three days after she arrived, she left to go back to Roswell.

CHAPTER 21

O N THE MORNING OF DECEMBER 29, Caroline was rushing around getting ready to leave for the airport. "Caroline," Charlotte said in a way that made Caroline know she meant business, "did you make a list of everything you needed to pack?"

"Well, I did make a list, but I am not sure I remembered to include everything," Caroline replied almost breathlessly.

"Okay, now," Charlotte continued, "stop making yourself a wreck. If you have forgotten something, just go and buy it while you are there. It's not worth having a nervous breakdown."

"Thanks, Mama," Caroline said. "I needed to hear that. You're right. I will just buy what I need there if I have forgotten something."

"Good girl," Charlotte said as she complimented Caroline.

Before boarding her flight, Caroline hugged her mother for a long time. "You are my rock, Mama," Caroline said, quietly feeling a tug at her heart because she was leaving her mother. "I love you very much. Don't worry about me, okay?" she looked directly into her mother's brown eyes.

"I know you, Caroline. I'm not worried except for the difficult message you must deliver to Garrett," Charlotte replied as she hugged her daughter tighter. "You will make the right decisions," Charlotte said emphatically.

"Thank you for your vote of confidence," Caroline said as she stood back to look at her mother again.

"Now, go," Charlotte said. "Have a wonderful time and call me if you need to."

"I will, Mama," Caroline replied. And she disappeared through the gate to board her flight to Charleston.

Charlotte returned to a very quiet house. Belle would not be back until tomorrow. Irene was visiting an old Roswell friend in Savannah. It was then that Charlotte realized that she must fill her life with a purpose. She would think about what she wanted to do. *It is really strange to have so many choices,* she thought. *The year 1967 will a better year for everyone. It has to be.*

The flight was uneventful, and before Caroline knew it, it was eleven o'clock and they were landing in Charleston. She took a deep breath and one more look in the mirror at her hair and lipstick. Everything should be perfect. Caroline was satisfied, although the anxiety she felt caused her to almost wish she were not going to Charleston at all. When she walked up the Jetway, there he was with the biggest smile she had ever seen.

"Caroline," Garrett exclaimed, "I'm so glad you finally got here! I have a surprise for you."

"Oh! You do, do you?!" Caroline exclaimed.

"Yes, ma'am, I do," Garrett said with more satisfaction than Caroline had ever heard.

He took her to the Battery in Charleston and drove her through the streets, pointing out the historical homes and landmarks. He drove her up Meeting Street, one of the most historical streets in the South. Caroline could tell he was very proud of his hometown. It was truly beautiful. "It is rare to see a city that has both colonial and Civil War history," Caroline commented as they headed toward his house.

When they arrived at his house in the West Ashley neighborhood of Charleston, Caroline was struck by the simple homes in the well-kept neighborhood. Garrett's family's house had four bedrooms and three and one-half bathrooms. Their home was nice, but simple. When they came through the front door, Caroline felt a sense of family that permeated the whole house. There was love in every corner of this home. Derek and Laura Winthrop greeted Caroline in the foyer.

"Caroline," Derek said as he extended his hand to her, "welcome. We're glad you're here," he continued genuinely.

"Caroline, come in, please." Laura said as she hugged Caroline. "Come on and let me show you to your room. I know you want to freshen up," she continued in her accommodating southern tone.

"Thank you very much, Mrs. Winthrop," Caroline said politely. "Mr. Winthrop, it is a pleasure to meet you," Caroline said as she was being ushered upstairs. Garrett was right behind them carrying her bag.

Caroline's room was bright and cheerful. It had a double bed with a dresser and mirror and a nightstand. She would have to go down the hall for a bathroom. She could deal with that.

"Please make yourself at home, Caroline," Laura said. "Come downstairs when you're ready. Everyone wants to meet you."

Everyone? Caroline thought. *Who is everyone?* Caroline hoped it was just Garrett's sisters. If they had invited grandparents, aunts, and uncles, she would be freaked out.

Thankfully, it was Garrett's two younger sisters. Emily and Allison were waiting in the family room to meet Caroline. Emily, fifteen, and Allison, seventeen, both stood as Caroline entered the family room. Caroline quickly surveyed the situation and made the determination of who was who. She extended her hand and said, "You must be Emily."

Emily shook her hand and said, "It's very nice to meet you, Caroline."

"And you are Allison," Caroline said as she smiled and shook Garrett's sisters' hand.

"Yes, I am," replied Allison. "It's very nice to meet you."

"Thank you," Caroline said politely. "It's very nice to meet you. Garrett talks about you quite a bit."

The girls exchanged glances as if they could not believe what they heard.

Laura said, "Caroline, we hope you will make yourself at home."

"Thank you, Mrs. Winthrop," Caroline replied graciously.

Caroline indeed felt at home. The atmosphere was relaxed and casual. Caroline had learned the art of making people feel important. She asked lots of questions and found ways to repeat some part of the answers she received back, allowing the person to know she was truly listening and interested. "Mrs. Winthrop, please tell me about the photographs on your bookcases," Caroline said, pointing to the array of photographs. There was everything from snapshots to professional portraits displayed. Laura went through each photograph explaining who, where, and when. Caroline listened intently and asked questions, especially about the photographs with Garrett in them.

After getting acquainted, the family had lunch together and Garrett said he wanted to take Caroline to one of the Ashley River

Plantations. "That's fine, Garrett," Laura said. "Remember to be home by five thirty. We are going to 82 Queen for dinner."

"Caroline," Garrett said as he helped her with her coat, "you are going to love 82 Queen. Wonderful low-country food."

"I can't wait," Caroline said. "He has told me so much about low-country food; I am excited to finally get to try it," she called back to Mrs. Winthrop as Garrett opened the front door for her.

"Y'all have fun!" Laura replied, waving to the couple as they left.

Garrett drove down Ashley River Road. The beautiful scenery on both sides of the road made Caroline wish she could see it in the spring and summer. The moss-draped two-hundred-year-old oak trees were majestic even in the winter. Garrett turned into Magnolia Plantation. Caroline just couldn't believe it had been there since 1676. Garrett told her that the Drayton family had built the house and that ownership of it had stayed in that family for over three hundred years. "The gardens are the oldest public gardens in the United States," he continued.

"You sound like a tour guide," Caroline quipped.

"Well, I did grow up here, and I actually forget that people do not know the importance of the history in this area during the Revolutionary War and the Civil War. There is so much to tell that I won't be able to tell you in just one trip. I would love for you to come back in spring. It is really pretty here then," he continued proudly.

"I was thinking as we drove here that it would really be gorgeous in the spring," Caroline replied.

They parked the car and began walking around the gardens. There was a very picturesque bridge that arched over a pond. The reflection of the bridge in the water made Caroline think of a Monet painting.

Caroline and Garrett strolled hand in hand over the bridge. He stopped under a moss-draped oak tree and pulled her close to him. "Caroline, you have my heart. I want you to know that. I look forward to seeing you, and when you are with me, I am so happy. No one has ever made me feel the way you do." Garrett spoke quietly, looking earnestly into Caroline's eyes. "I want you to know that I respect you and I respect your focus on school and law school after graduation. You are an amazing girl, and I have a feeling that there is a lot more that I don't know about you that would make me love you even more. I want to kiss you and hold you nearly every minute we are together. But I, like you, have to remain focused on my goals too. We are lucky and unlucky at the same time. Some people probably never find that one special person to share their lives. But we found each other too soon. Although the passion I feel for you is real and sometimes overwhelming, we have to maintain our self-control to the best of our abilities. I am not sure how good I will be at that all the time, but I am telling you today that I will always respect your wishes. I love and respect you more than having one evening of passion and then regret for the rest of our relationship."

Caroline took a step into Garrett's arms. He held her, and they stood on the bridge in a passionate kiss. "Garrett, I love you more every minute," Caroline said. "I have been worried about our passion getting out of control. Thank you very much for being so strong and for loving me more than your own feelings. How could I ask for more than that?" Caroline said, touching Garrett's face.

He put his arm around her, and they continued their stroll through the gardens. It was cold outside, so they decided to tour the house. Caroline had never seen such a huge porch that wrapped around a house. It was living area for the families who occupied the house, especially during the hot South Carolina summers without air conditioning or electricity. Caroline went to the gift shop and bought her mother and grandmother a book about the plantation. She knew they would love to see it too. She bought Belle a low-country cookbook with many very old recipes.

"We'd better head back home so we won't be late to go to dinner," Garrett said as they exited the gift shop.

"Sounds good to me," Caroline said as she turned and kissed Garrett on the cheek.

"What's that for?" he asked playfully.

"For being so perfect, Garrett. You are just perfect!" Caroline said as he opened the car door for her.

"Caroline," Garrett said as he got into the driver's seat, "I want to warn you that my dad can be very direct and pragmatic at times. He doesn't seem to filter much of what goes through his mind. So if he says something weird, just don't pay any attention to him."

"Thanks for the warning," Caroline said, feeling more puzzled than informed.

They arrived back at Garrett's house at four forty-five. After greetings and telling his family how wonderful Magnolia Plantation was, she went upstairs to change clothes for dinner.

At five fifteen, Caroline came downstairs wearing a black cashmere sweater and skirt. Her black suede boots completed her outfit perfectly. She was stunning with diamond-and-pearl earrings and, of course, the locket her father gave her when she was two. Caroline wore the emerald-and-diamond ring that her mother had given her for Christmas. She was the epitome of class and beauty.

Garrett stood when she came into the den. "Just when I thought you could not get more beautiful, there you are, more beautiful," he said as she sat down next to him on the sofa.

181

"Well, thank you very much," she said, blushing, and then she changed the subject. "Mrs. Winthrop, what is your favorite dish at 82 Queen restaurant?"

"I would have to say it is the she-crab soup and the shrimp and grits," Laura replied. "Those are their signature dishes, and I have never been disappointed. I hope you like seafood."

"Absolutely love it," Caroline replied. "I really don't get to eat seafood very much, so this is a big treat for me. Thank you so much for all your trouble and planning for me, Mrs. Winthrop. I know this is a very busy season, and I appreciate getting to meet all of you."

Laura thought what a wonderful girl Caroline was and found herself feeling proud that her son had made such a good choice. She had no idea how serious their relationship really was, but she liked what she saw.

"Okay, guys," Derek announced. "Let's get going. We have reservations." Everyone piled into the station wagon. Emily sat in the far-back jump seat so everyone could fit into one car.

During the short ride to the restaurant, Derek pointed out historical buildings and homes to Caroline. The city was still decorated for the holidays, and the cobblestone streets reminded her of Paris. The pre-Revolutionary homes were magnificent, and Caroline thought they looked like something out of a fairy tale decorated for the holidays.

They arrived at 82 Queen. The long narrow entryway, decorated with vintage chairs and beautiful plants, was typical of Charleston homes and gardens. The brick floors gave the restaurant the feeling of never having left the nineteenth century. The restaurant was dimly lit, giving the restaurant a warm ambience. The evening was wonderful, with Garrett's sisters chattering about school and friends. Derek and

Laura talked about their New Year's Eve plans, and Caroline and Garrett sat across from each other, oblivious to it all.

"Mrs. Winthrop," Caroline finally spoke, "you were right about the she-crab soup and shrimp and grits. I am not sure when I have ever enjoyed anything more. Thank you very much for recommending it."

"Caroline, I'm so glad you enjoyed it," Laura replied with a smile. "Garrett," Laura continued, "Dad and I have a surprise for you and Caroline."

"Oh, yea?" Garrett replied quizzically.

"We have arranged for you and Caroline to take a carriage ride around the historical part of the city. It will take about an hour. We will stay here and drink coffee and wait for you to get back. Do you want to go?" Laura said with a twinkle in her eye.

"Caroline, you have your coat, scarf, and gloves, and I do too. Do you want to go?" Garrett asked.

"What a lovely thing to do, Mrs. Winthrop. I would love to. Mr. Winthrop, thank you very much. That is so thoughtful!" Caroline exclaimed genuinely.

"Garrett, here is your ticket," Derek said. "Your carriage is waiting outside the front door."

"Thanks, Dad. Thanks, Mom," Garrett said as he gave each of them a hug.

He helped Caroline with her coat, and they went out the front door and stepped onto the waiting carriage. Caroline felt like Cinderella. "Good evening," said the carriage driver and tour guide. "You will see a magical city tonight." As the carriage pulled away from the restaurant, the horses' hooves were clicking on the cobblestone street. The lights made the city look like a fairyland. Garrett pulled Caroline close and kissed her for a long time. It was very cold outside, but neither of them felt it. It was truly a magical night that Caroline would never forget. The carriage driver narrated the tour in a perfect Charleston accent and sounded as if he had lived in the city for three hundred years. Once again, the beautiful architecture was amazing to Caroline.

When the carriage tour was almost over and they were heading back toward the restaurant, Garrett looked at Caroline and said, "I wish we could stay right here forever."

"I know; me too," she said, meeting his gentle gaze. He kissed her long and passionately again before the carriage stopped. "Thank you for one of the most memorable evenings of my life, Garrett," Caroline said as he took her hand to help her off the carriage.

Garrett tipped the carriage driver, and they returned to the warm restaurant where the family was waiting.

"This city is so beautiful. It's like a magical fairy tale with all of the Christmas lights. I enjoyed the carriage ride so much. It gave me a chance to see some of the architecture here that is so unique and beautiful," Caroline said, standing at the end of the table.

"Oh, Caroline, I am so glad you enjoyed it," Laura said sweetly.

"Let's head back home," Derek instructed.

"Thanks, again, Dad," Garrett said as he touched his dad's arm.

"You're welcome, Son," Derek replied. "I thought that would give you and Caroline some alone time." Garrett raised his eyebrows, and Derek knew the carriage ride was a big hit.

The following morning, Caroline learned that they would be attending a New Year's Eve party at the home of Derek's boss. He lived in one of the homes on the Battery. *Thank goodness*, Caroline thought, *I brought an evening dress.* Caroline had read about the Battery and Rainbow Row and had seen photographs, but that was the extent of her knowledge about the city, until yesterday.

When she came down for breakfast at eight o'clock, Garrett announced that they would be touring Boone Hall Plantation and having lunch down at the market in downtown Charleston. Caroline quickly drank coffee, ate eggs and toast, and went upstairs to get ready for the day Garrett had planned. While she was bathing, Caroline reflected on the previous evening with Garrett and his family. She couldn't imagine that anything could have been more perfect.

CHAPTER 22

*C*AROLINE DECIDED THAT WOOL SLACKS and a cashmere turtleneck sweater were the best choice of clothing for the day. With her long coat, scarf, and gloves, she was sure to be warm. As they arrived at Boone Hall Plantation, the Avenue of Oaks was majestic. Three-hundred-year-old live oaks lined each side of the dirt driveway for at least a quarter mile. The moss-draped oaks framed the iron gate and the house straight ahead. "My goodness!" Caroline exclaimed. "This is perfectly magnificent!"

"It is one of the most beautiful plantations in Charleston," Garrett replied proudly. "It is still a working plantation. See the slave quarters there on the left?"

"Yes. There are so many of them!" Caroline said, expecting more information.

"These are just the quarters for the slaves who worked in the main house," Garrett said. "Many more are behind the plantation. They were for the slaves who worked in the rice fields."

"*Wow!*" Caroline exclaimed again as she took in the beauty and history of the plantation. They toured the home, which was still decorated for Christmas. "This house is beautiful," Caroline said as they entered the gift area. Caroline bought three sweet grass baskets for her mother, Mama Rene, and Belle. The baskets were still made by the descendants of the slaves who worked on the plantation. "It is amazing that these people have been here for so many years," Caroline commented as they exited the house headed back to the car.

"It is a testament to how well they were treated on this plantation," Garrett offered as he opened the door for Caroline.

"I'm sure you're right," Caroline said.

They headed back to town where they went to the market in the middle of downtown Charleston. "This is where slaves were brought off boats coming from Africa and sold," Garrett continued his historical education for Caroline.

"Now it is a great place to shop!" Caroline said, laughing at how it had changed so dramatically.

Garrett took Caroline to lunch in a small restaurant downtown. They enjoyed crab cakes with low-country roulade. "I have never had so much delicious seafood in my life," Caroline said as they exited the restaurant.

"Stick around, sweetheart," Garrett said playfully. "There's more where that came from!" As they drove down East Bay Street and up Meeting Street, once again Caroline was astonished at the architecture and the well-preserved historical homes.

Garrett headed back to the simple West Ashley neighborhood where he had lived all of his life. It was remarkable how quickly the homes changed as they left the main part of the city. They arrived to enjoy a roaring fire in the family room and hot-spiced cider. Caroline welcomed the warm drink after being outside in thirty-degree weather all day.

"Mrs. Winthrop, Charleston is one of the most beautiful cities I have ever seen," Caroline exclaimed as she sat down with her hot tea.

"It is beautiful, isn't it?" Laura replied.

"You must have enjoyed growing up here," Caroline continued as she worked to get to know Garrett's family.

"I really did enjoy it, but, as you might imagine, I did not realize how unique Charleston was until I was almost grown," she replied. "You don't think about those things when you are growing up."

"I think that's true, Mrs. Winthrop," Caroline offered. "I see Atlanta that way too. I would love for all of you to visit us in Atlanta sometime when you can. Maybe when school is out there would be time for a trip."

"We would love that, Caroline," Laura said, patting Caroline's hand in a loving gesture.

Caroline finished her tea and was once again warm. "We have to be at the Sanders' home for cocktails at six o'clock," Laura instructed. "Emily and Allison will be staying home and having friends spend the night tonight. So the bathroom is all yours, Caroline."

"I'd better get moving, then," Caroline said. She wondered if she would be expected to have cocktails. She had always wanted to taste champagne but never had because of the stigma she attached to alcohol. *Nothing good has ever come from drinking it*, she thought as she drew her bathwater.

Caroline had a sense of style that was elegant and classic. This evening, she would navigate the political waters of the business New Year's Eve party with grace and ease that would astonish Garrett and his parents.

Caroline came downstairs at five thirty dressed in a black floor-length velvet evening gown. It had a sweetheart neckline and was sleeveless with an inset of black satin at the waist. It was straight with a slit in the back up to her calves. A beautiful ruby-and-diamond pin accented the front of the dress where the velvet and the satin came together. She wore simple ruby-and-diamond earrings and black velvet heels and carried a red evening purse. Her hair was pulled back on one side with a black barrette. She carried her black cashmere jacket trimmed in fox. As she entered the family room, everyone stood up and just looked at her. She stood in the door trying to decide why no one was speaking to her.

"Caroline, my goodness," Laura said astonished. "You are a vision!"

Caroline blushed. "Thank you, Mrs. Winthrop," she said as she walked to the chair beside the fireplace and sat down. Garrett was not ready yet.

"Garrett is still doing his hair," Laura joked.

"He is always the last one ready," Derek said. "We can count on him."

"I'm not sure I've seen that side of him yet," Caroline said, laughing.

Just then, Garrett walked into the family room. As Caroline stood up, he fixed his eyes on her and stopped. As he composed himself, he said, "Dad, do you mean I have to take her looking like that?" Everyone laughed, including Caroline. She knew she was not difficult to look at, but she was unaccustomed to being the center of attention. That quality in her would win people over for the rest of her life. She appreciated the humor and did not relish blushing at compliments.

The ride over to East Bay Street was, once again, beautiful. The lights of Charleston were magical, and Caroline could not get enough of them. The valet took the car, and the foursome ascended the stairs leading to the large porch. The gas lanterns that hung around the porch gave the house a nineteenth-century glow. As they entered the large foyer, they encountered two butlers taking coats. When the introductions began, Derek Winthrop was pleased to introduce Caroline Wellington as Garrett's girlfriend from the University of Virginia. Person after person complimented Caroline.

Garrett was very proud to introduce her to his father's boss. "Caroline, I would like for you to meet Mr. Sanders," Garrett said formally. "He is our host this evening. Mr. Sanders, please meet Caroline Wellington from Atlanta."

"Miss Wellington," George Sanders began, "I do not know when I have ever been so enchanted."

Blushing again, Caroline said, "You are so kind, Mr. Sanders. You have a magnificent home. Thank you for inviting us."

"Please, make yourself at home," George continued. "Cocktails are in the library." He offered cocktails as if it were a requirement to attend the party.

"Thank you, Mr. Sanders," Garrett said. Caroline smiled at him as they continued into the library.

"Garrett, I prefer soft drinks; you know that, right?" Caroline quizzed him.

"Well, I have never seen you drink any alcoholic beverage before, but I wasn't sure. That's no problem," he replied, taking her arm. Caroline felt relieved that she would not be pressured to drink.

She was quite surprised when he got her a Coca-Cola but himself a scotch and soda. "I didn't know you drank anything except beer!" Caroline exclaimed in a whisper.

"Usually I don't," he replied quietly, "but tonight is special." Caroline wondered what made the night special to warrant drinking scotch, but she did not make any more comments.

Caroline was introduced to the dean of the University of South Carolina. He was a handsome man in his mid-forties. Michael Satterfield was by all accounts, very successful at the university, but he also was from one of the oldest families in Charleston. Caroline suspected that he was wealthy. As their conversation turned to the University of Virginia and Thomas Jefferson, Caroline came alive. Michael Satterfield was very impressed with her knowledge of Mr. Jefferson and the history of the university and Monticello. After a twenty-minute conversation, Caroline said, "Mr. Satterfield, I have so enjoyed talking with you, but I'm afraid that I am monopolizing your time. There must be so many people who want to talk with you this evening."

"The pleasure has been all mine, Miss Wellington," Michael replied. "I'm delighted to meet you and invite you to monopolize my time whenever possible." They both laughed, and Caroline excused herself to join Garrett in conversation with one of his father's colleagues.

"Caroline, I would like for you to meet Mr. Scott. He and my dad work together. Mr. Scott, this is Caroline Wellington. She and I attend the University of Virginia."

"Caroline, it is truly a pleasure to meet you," Joe Scott said sincerely. "Garrett, I might have gone to UVA if the girls were as pretty as she is."

"Mr. Scott, she is as nice as she is beautiful," Garrett replied with a smile.

"Keep up the good work, Son," Joe said jokingly. Garrett gestured thumbs up, and they ended the conversation with Joe Scott, who seemed somewhat inebriated.

The chamber orchestra was playing a beautiful waltz. Garrett asked Caroline to dance. She knew how to waltz, tango, foxtrot, jitterbug, and twist, but she didn't know if Garrett knew how to dance.

Her question was answered when he took her in his arms and they began waltzing around the ballroom. She remembered her father teaching her to dance when she was a little girl and then insisting that she take ballroom dancing when she was thirteen. She used to dance with him in the ballroom of their home, and she could still remember how he smelled when he would hold her and waltz around the room. It was usually a mixture of alcohol and Old Spice. But it was his special smell, and it was a memory that she would treasure for all of her life.

When the dance ended, Garrett said, "Well, so you can dance too?"

"Well, yea. What did you think I was, a wallflower?" Caroline joked.

"I should have known. You know, you are just full of surprises," Garrett said as they walked off the dance floor with several couples applauding their performance.

Garrett steered Caroline toward Greg Baker. Greg was in-house counsel for his father's company. "Mr. Baker," Garrett said as he stepped into the group where Greg was engaged in conversation, "I would like you to meet Caroline Wellington. She and I are in our freshman year at UVA, and she wants to be a lawyer."

"Caroline," Garrett said as he turned to Caroline, taking her by the arm, "this is Greg Baker. He is in-house counsel for my father's company."

"Mr. Baker, it is a pleasure to meet you," Caroline said graciously as she took his hand.

"My pleasure, Miss Wellington," Greg replied with a slight bow. "Has no one tried to talk you out of being a lawyer?" Greg joked to Caroline as the other partygoers in the group laughed.

"Not yet, Mr. Baker," Caroline replied. "You have the honor of being the first."

"Ah ha!" Greg exclaimed. "I can see that I will enjoy having a conversation with you, Miss Wellington."

"Mr. Baker, pardon my impertinence," Caroline replied, slightly embarrassed at her remark. "My father was a lawyer, and I have always been interested in it."

"Where did he practice?" Greg's attention turned seriously to Caroline.

"Originally, after he graduated from Harvard Law, he was a partner in Boston at the Rich May law firm for about seven years. Then he joined Georgia Life in Atlanta as in-house counsel," Caroline replied, providing as little information as possible.

"Is that where you grew up?" Greg asked, genuinely interested.

"Yes, I did," Caroline replied, still not offering any details.

"Is your father John Wellington?" Greg asked. Caroline looked up at Greg, surprised that he knew her father's first name.

"Yes, he is," she replied not trying to hide her surprise. "How do you know my father?" she asked with full attention focused on Greg Baker.

"He and I attended Harvard Law," Greg said matter-of-factly. "I went up against him in court a number of times. He is a very formidable opponent. Is he still practicing in Atlanta?"

Caroline cleared her throat to be sure she would be able to speak. "Mr. Baker," she began carefully, "my father passed away last February."

Greg looked completely shocked. "You're kidding!" he said, not pretending to conceal his shock. "Of course you are not kidding. How could I ask such a question? I am so sorry to hear that, Caroline. Your father and I spent quite a bit of time together in Boston both during law school and after. I know his father wanted him to join his firm. I remember that he struggled with the decision but did decide to go back to Atlanta. Please, if you can, tell me what happened."

"He had a heart attack," Caroline said softly.

"Caroline, I would love to talk with you sometime," Greg said kindly. "Your father was a great lawyer and a very nice person. He really put Georgia Life on the map. He was not only a great lawyer, but one heck of a salesman."

"Thank you for your kind words, Mr. Baker," Caroline said, choking back tears. "I would love to talk with you about my father some time, but I don't think I can tonight."

"I am so sorry, Caroline," Greg said putting his arm around her and giving her a fatherly hug. "May I ask about your mother?" he said as he stepped away from the hug. "I met her when your father brought her to Boston shortly after they were married. It's no wonder you are so beautiful."

Caroline blushed again and replied, "My mother is doing well. She moved back to Roswell where she grew up to be near my grandmother."

"Please give her my best wishes, Caroline," Greg requested. "Would you do that for me?"

"I will, Mr. Baker," Caroline agreed. "I'm sure she will be pleased that you and I met tonight. Please let us know when you will be in Atlanta."

"I certainly will, Caroline," Greg said as he gave Caroline a full, face-to-face hug. Garrett could see tears on Caroline's cheeks as Greg released her from the hug.

"Mr. Baker," Garrett said, "it is amazing that you knew Caroline's father. We'll have to get together sometime." Garrett took Caroline by the arm and escorted her to the music room where there were very few people.

"Would you please show me where the ladies room is, Garrett?" Caroline requested. Without a word, he took her to the powder room and she entered and closed the door quickly. Within a couple of minutes, she emerged with fresh makeup and lipstick. "Thanks, Garrett," Caroline said, as she kissed him on the cheek.

"What's that for, beautiful?" Garrett said.

Caroline stopped and turned to face him. "Garrett, that is what my father always called my mother," she said looking very surprised.

"Well, it just fits both of you very well," Garrett replied laughing.

"You get more charming every time I see you, Garrett Winthrop," Caroline said, laughing with him.

It was near midnight, and the servers were passing champagne for the midnight toast. As the server approached Garrett and Caroline, Garrett took a glass. "Wouldn't you like to have some champagne for the New Year's toast?" Garrett asked playfully.

"Why not?" Caroline exclaimed and took the champagne flute filled with the sparkling bubbly treat.

"May I have your attention, please?" George Sanders spoke authoritatively as he attempted to get the attention of the group assembled to celebrate the New Year. "Ladies and gentlemen, I would like to propose a toast to each of you as we reflect on the blessings of 1966 and your hopes and expectations for 1967. May all of your hopes and dreams be realized, and may you join us next year as we celebrate another successful year of life and work." The guests raised their glasses and voices could be heard saying, "Here, here!" as each person enjoyed their champagne.

Caroline sipped the liquid of which she was so afraid and opposed. *Mmmmm, good,* she thought. And she drank the rest of the champagne. "I believe I may want another one of those, Mr. Winthrop," Caroline joked to Garrett.

"Coming right up, Miss Wellington," he said as he scooted off to get her another glass. At midnight, when the clock struck its first bong, Caroline and Garrett were locked in a passionate embrace and kiss. "Happy New Year, sweetheart," Garrett whispered.

"Happy New Year," Caroline whispered back. And they continued their kissing celebration.

Caroline realized that she and Garrett were being observed by several couples at the party. She became very self-conscious. "Garrett, I think we are being watched," she said as she pulled away from him. "You are wearing my lipstick, by the way," she said, laughing.

Garrett took a handkerchief out of his back pocket and wiped the lipstick off of his face. Caroline took the handkerchief to clean off the areas he missed. By now, they were both laughing hysterically. Garrett took her arm and steered her toward the back veranda. When they stepped out into the cold January air, they both shuddered but still could not stop laughing. Garrett took off his coat and put it around Caroline's shoulders. The moon was full, and the crisp night air with the smell of wood burning in fireplaces gave Caroline a sense of contentment. "This has been a very nice evening, Garrett," Caroline said as they kissed again.

Derek and Laura were looking for Garrett and Caroline. Laura caught a glimpse on them on the back veranda through the large French doors. She opened the door and said, "You two are going to catch pneumonia out here. It's time for us to go home."

"Okay, Mom," Garrett replied. We'll be right there."

Caroline insisted on finding George and Peggy Sanders to thank them for the evening. The couple was standing near the front door speaking to each of their guests as the left. "Mrs. Sanders," Caroline began, "I have not had the opportunity to tell you thank you for inviting me to your beautiful home this evening. I have enjoyed it very much. The evening was just perfect!"

"Caroline," Peggy Sanders took Caroline's hand, "it has been our pleasure to have you. Please have Garrett bring you back for tea sometime."

"That would be lovely," Caroline said as she exited their home onto the large front porch.

"Garrett," Peggy said as she patted him on the back, "you have quite a lovely young lady there."

"Yes, I do, Mrs. Sanders. Thank you so much for a wonderful evening."

"It's always a pleasure to have you and your family to our home, Garrett," she replied, smiling with her bright blue eyes sparkling.

Caroline looked out at the bay. The moon cast a beautiful light on the water, making it sparkle like a thousand diamonds. At that moment, Caroline fell in love with Charleston and decided that she could live in this beautiful city.

On the ride home, Garrett wanted nothing more than to kiss Caroline. But with respect for his parents, he decided to wait.

"Caroline," Derek began, "you made quite an impression on several of the guests this evening. Laura and I kept hearing compliments about Garrett's girlfriend."

"Thank you, Mr. Winthrop," Caroline replied. "I enjoyed the evening very much."

"We are very glad you were able to be with us tonight, Caroline," Laura picked up her husband's compliments.

"Thank you, Mrs. Winthrop," Caroline said gratefully. "You have made me feel at home, and I am very glad to spend time with all of you."

"Tomorrow we will have our traditional low-country New Year's dinner," Laura informed everyone in the car. "Y'all are gonna love it!"

CHAPTER 23

*A*FTER THEY WERE HOME AND everyone was in bed, Caroline found it difficult to sleep. She kept going over the conversation she had had with Greg Baker. She thought she knew most everything there was to know about her father, but she realized that she was hungry for every bit of information she could get to keep him alive in her memory. She had only had him for seventeen years of her life.

It was one fifteen a.m. when her bedroom door opened. "Caroline," Garrett whispered, "are you asleep?"

"No, not yet," she replied. Garrett walked over to her bed, pulled the covers back, and crawled into bed with her. "Garrett!" Caroline exclaimed, "What do you think you're doing?"

"We just haven't had any time alone since you're been here," he said earnestly. "I just want to hold you and kiss you, Caroline." He put his arms around her, pulled her in, and kissed her.

She could not resist. The passion was intoxicating, fueled by the champagne she had earlier. As their bodies came together, Caroline could feel Garrett's passion manifest in the evidence of his manhood.

She could hear her mother's voice: "You may be sitting at the breakfast table one day with your daughter, and you want to give her the right advice from your own experience and not from your mistakes."

Kissing Garrett was the most wonderful experience Caroline could remember. But she remained in control. As Garrett began touching her breasts, her resolve gave way to him. The passion in her body was complete. His hand moved down her stomach and to her panties. As he touched her inside her panties, Caroline lost all control of herself. Garrett removed her panties and his. As he climbed on top of her, he kissed her passionately again. She stopped him just before he entered her.

"Garrett, we have to stop. I want to make love with you so much, but we have to stop." He continued to kiss her, and he said, "I love you so much, Caroline."

"I love you, Garrett," she replied. As he sat up on the side of the bed, he found his underwear and put them back on. Caroline wished they were older and married and could just make love all night. "I'm sorry, Caroline. I did not mean to get that involved when I came in here. You just do that to me," Garrett said apologetically.

"It must be the champagne," Caroline said jokingly.

"We'll have champagne again very soon then," Garrett said. "I'd better get back to my room before Mom and Dad hear us."

"That would be very embarrassing," Caroline said, shuddering at the thought. *No wonder people like sex so much*, Caroline thought. She fell asleep thinking about how wonderful it was and how she should not have let him—or herself—go that far.

Caroline did not wake until eight thirty. As she lay in the bed, she tried to remember whether the previous night with Garrett was a dream. But she realized as she sat up on the side of the bed that it was, indeed, real. First she felt embarrassed. Then she was really mad—with both him and with herself. "What was I thinking?" she said out loud. As she gathered her clothes and toiletries to make the trip down the hall to the bathroom, she hoped that no one would see her and that she could bathe, dress, and emerge with her head back on her shoulders. But her hope was not fulfilled as she opened her door and saw Garrett standing in the hall. "Good morning," Garrett said timidly.

"Good morning," Caroline said as she continued down the hall to the bathroom. "I'll see you when I'm dressed." And she closed the bathroom door.

Garrett was stunned. After all their conversations and their commitments, he had screwed up, and he knew it. *What am I supposed to do?* he thought to himself. *I am a nineteen-year-old guy, and I get horny. But that's not how I feel about Caroline. I love her. Why did I do that? It was the scotch and the champagne. Guess I have to watch that and not drink around Caroline anymore.* As he was completing his self-imposed lecture, Emily walked down the hall.

"Is 'Sleeping Beauty' awake yet?" she asked, picking at Garrett as she usually did.

"She's in the bathroom, smarty," he replied.

"She'd better get a move on if she wants breakfast," Emily said, continuing her harassment.

"She is our guest, Emily," Garrett retorted. "She will have breakfast when she wants to have it. Any questions?"

"No, sir, drill sergeant," Emily bantered.

"I'm not in the mood for your attitude today, Emily," Garrett growled. "Got it?"

"Yea, yea yea," Emily said dismissively as she walked down the stairs.

Garrett followed her down the stairs and into the kitchen. Laura was making an egg-and-sausage casserole. "Is Caroline up yet, honey?" she asked Garrett.

"Yes, she is getting ready now," he replied casually as he poured himself a cup of coffee.

"You know she made quite an impression on several of the guests at the party last night, not the least of which was your father's boss," Laura said as if she were informing Garrett of something he had never heard.

"I know she did, Mother," Garrett said, smiling. "She is an amazing girl."

The telephone rang. Garrett heard his father answer, "Hello. Happy New Year, Greg. It was a great party last night." Garrett could hear his father's end of the conversation and thought it must be Greg Baker. *Why would he be calling Dad on New Year's Day?* Garrett thought as he moved closer to the family room to be able to hear better. "She's quite a girl, for sure, Greg," Derek said proudly. "No, I don't know very much about her family. I do know that her father died last February," the one-sided conversation continued. "Oh yea?" Derek said as he sat forward in his chair and listened to the caller for more than a minute. "Greg, could we talk next week in the office about this?" Derek said as more of a statement than a question. "Sure, I understand. Hey, thanks for calling. Sure, y'all have a nice day too."

"Dad, what was that about?" Garrett asked directly.

"It was Greg Baker. He was just calling because he was still surprised that he and Caroline's dad went to law school together," Derek replied, deliberately passive.

"What else did he say, Dad?" Garrett pressed.

"Not much, Son," Derek said, continuing his deliberate passiveness. Derek sat back and continued to read the newspaper and drink coffee. Garrett knew that Greg had said something that surprised his dad, but what? He obviously was not going to tell him. Garrett sat quietly drinking his coffee.

Caroline appeared in the kitchen. "Good morning, Mrs. Winthrop," she said jovially. "What can I do to help you with breakfast?"

"Not a thing, sweetie," Laura replied as she looked up at Caroline. "You look very lovely, as usual," she said genuinely.

"Thank you," Caroline replied and went into the family room. Garrett stood up as soon as he saw her.

"Can I get you a cup of coffee?" he asked as if reporting for duty.

"That would be great," she said as she sat down on the sofa.

Derek looked up from his newspaper. "Good morning, Caroline," Derek said kindly.

"Mr. Winthrop, how are you this morning?" Caroline said casually.

"Doing great," he said.

Caroline could feel his stare as if he were evaluating her entire life. *Why is he looking at me like that?* she thought.

Laura came to the door and announced that breakfast was ready. "Come and get it!" she said, sounding like she was on a farm instead of in a suburb.

Emily and Allison came strolling in to join the family for breakfast. They were chatting about the previous evenings' escapades with their girlfriends.

Garrett pulled the chair out for Caroline and then sat next to her at the table. Under the table, he touched her hand. She looked at him and then said, "Mrs. Winthrop, this looks wonderful! Would you mind if I got the recipe from you?"

"Of course not, Caroline," Laura replied in an accommodating tone. "I'll copy it down for you before you and Garrett leave tomorrow."

"Thank you very much," Caroline said sincerely.

There was small talk at the table consisting of when the Hoppin' John and ham would be served for New Year's dinner. Caroline learned that traditional New Year's dinner at the Winthrop house was ham, Hoppin' John, country apple slaw, frogmore stew, and for dessert, chocolate-espresso pots de crème with benne seed coins. Caroline had never tasted any of these dishes, except ham, in her nineteen years. But it all sounded very good, and she was always up for a new experience.

"Caroline," Derek asked her, "tell us more about your family. I know your father passed away less than a year ago and your mother moved back to the place where she grew up to be near your grandmother. I don't know a lot more than that."

"Mr. Winthrop," Caroline began, "I was born in Atlanta. My parents met at my grandfather's company, Georgia Life. My mother was my grandfather's secretary. My father took the position in the company as in-house counsel, and he and my mother fell in love and were married six months later. I went to the Westminster School from kindergarten through twelfth grade and then went to UVA. My father grew up in Atlanta, and my mother grew up in Roswell where she and my grandmother live now." Caroline was looking down at her plate of food, hoping he would not ask more questions. But he did.

"Didn't your family sell Georgia Life last year?" he asked, continuing to press her for information.

"Yes, they did," Caroline replied, not offering any more details.

"Was that before or after your father passed away?" Derek continued the interrogation.

"It was after," Caroline said, hoping someone would change the subject.

"Your grandparents are still alive, aren't they?" Derek's persistence was wearing thin on Caroline.

"Yes, they are," Caroline said, still offering no voluntary information.

"Garrett said that your home in Roswell is beautiful and you have a maid and a butler who live on your property in their own cottage," Derek pressed further.

"Belle is more like a member of our family than a maid. She has been with our family since my mother was three years old. Robert is not our butler any longer. He is Belle's nephew and just got married. He and his wife live and work in Roswell," Caroline replied defensively, hoping that would provide enough information to stop the questions.

"I imagine that your father owned part of Georgia Life," Derek said as more of a question than a statement.

"Yes he did," Caroline replied. She looked up from her breakfast that she had stopped eating and said, "Mr. Winthrop, if you don't mind, I would rather not talk about this now. I still have difficulty talking about my father." Caroline hoped that would be enough to stop his inquisition.

"I'm sorry, Caroline," Derek said thoughtfully. "Greg Harris called this morning and said that the Georgia Life sale was the largest business sale transaction in the history of the state. I suppose you and your mother will be taken care of for the rest of your lives."

"Would you excuse me, please?" She rose and left the room.

"Dad!" Garrett exclaimed, shouting at Derek. "What do you think you are doing? She told you she didn't like to talk about her father! You have upset her. Why did you keep asking those questions, which, by the way, are none of our business?"

"Greg Baker called this morning and said that he did some checking since meeting Caroline last night," Derek began. "She is an only child. She is, herself, independently wealthy, and when her grandparents die, she stands to inherit a huge fortune on top of what she already has." Derek blurted out the substance of his conversation. "Greg is friends with a lawyer in the firm that handled the sale transaction." Everyone sat silent staring at Derek as if he had warts all over his face.

"That was privileged information, Dad," Garrett said furiously.

"How could you interrogate her that way, Derek?" Laura entered the conversation. "I don't think I have ever seen you act the way you just did. If you felt that you needed to share the information, you should have done so with me privately. What were you thinking?" Derek stood up, threw his napkin on the table, and went upstairs to his bedroom. When he came back downstairs, he got his keys and his coat and left the house.

Pragmatic? Caroline thought as she finished packing. *That's not pragmatic; that's hateful!* she thought. *I need to get out of here for good.*

"Mom," Garrett began. "How am I going to make this all right with Caroline?"

"I'm not sure, honey," Laura replied. "There is a bigger issue here than your father's questioning Caroline. A privacy issue has been violated. I imagine that someone will lose their job over this," she continued. "Why don't you just go up and apologize for your father's behavior?"

"Okay, I'll try, but she is upset," Garrett responded warily.

Garrett went upstairs. No one finished breakfast except Emily and Allison. Even they could feel the terrible tension in the room. They quietly helped clear the table and began washing dishes for their mother.

Garrett knocked on Caroline's door. "Garrett," she said as she opened the door, "I'm almost packed. Would you take me to the airport? I'm going to go on and fly to Charlottesville this afternoon."

"Caroline, please don't do that," Garrett pleaded.

"If you can't take me, please call a taxi for me," Caroline said with absolutely no room for negotiation.

"Dammit!" Garrett exploded in the hallway. "My father was awful, and I am so sorry, Caroline," Garrett said earnestly. "Please don't leave."

"Garrett, I am not trying to create a problem for you or your family. I am not comfortable with questions about my family. That is not your fault. I just need to leave now," Caroline said with a finality that left Garrett no choice but to take her to the airport.

Garrett ran downstairs. "Mother, Caroline is leaving," he announced as he entered the kitchen.

"Leaving?" Laura turned to look at her son. "I am so sorry, honey," she replied and walked to give him a hug. "Your dad was out of line. I just don't know what got into him," Laura said, shaking her head.

"He should try not being himself once in a while," Garrett said sarcastically.

Garrett retrieved his coat from the downstairs closet and went back upstairs to get Caroline's suitcase for her.

"Garrett, please don't feel bad about your father's questions. I'm very sensitive about that subject," Caroline said, seeing the awful look on Garrett's face.

"I have nothing to say except that I am so sorry he upset you. He had no reason to question you that way. Mother can't figure out what got into him either," Garrett said, shaking his head.

"Doesn't matter now," Caroline said. "Thanks for taking me to the airport. I would like to tell your mother and sisters good-bye." Garrett lifted her suitcase and took it down to the foyer. Caroline walked behind him and around him to the kitchen. "Mrs. Winthrop," Caroline said, "thank you very much for your hospitality. I have enjoyed my visit. I really loved seeing Charleston. Please accept my apology for leaving early. I'm not feeling well."

Laura walked over to Caroline and put her arms around her. "It is I who should apologize for my husband's terrible behavior today," she said sweetly.

"No apology necessary," Caroline said and turned to leave for the airport. "Emily and Allison, I'm very glad to meet you. I hope you enjoy the rest of your Christmas vacation," Caroline said lightheartedly.

"You too," the girls said in unison and went back to their kitchen duties.

On the way to the airport, Caroline spoke first. "Garrett, this just isn't going to work for us. Last night was wonderful and terrible at the same time. You know how I feel about that, and you took advantage of the situation. I accept my part of the responsibility, so it is not entirely your fault. I need to return your pin." Caroline handed Garrett the Sigma Chi pin he gave her in November. "I hope that at some point we can be friends," Caroline continued with a distance in her voice that Garrett had never heard.

Garrett knew there would be no persuading her. He reached for the pin and put it in his coat pocket.

"Caroline, I loved you too much too quickly," he said with his voice shaking. "I'm so sorry our relationship is ending this way. I love you, and I will for a very long time," he said as tears rolled down his cheeks.

"Me too, Garrett," Caroline said quietly, choking back tears herself.

Caroline insisted that he let her out at the curb at the airport. He did as she asked and drove off, heading home for a confrontation with his father.

Caroline walked into the airport to the Delta Airlines counter. There was a flight to Charlottesville at five o'clock p.m. Caroline booked the flight and went to purchase a Coke and a book to read while she waited. After she arrived at her gate, she found a pay phone and called her mother.

"Hello," her mother answered happily.

"Mama," Caroline said, and she began sobbing.

"Caroline, what's the matter, honey?" Charlotte said sounding horrified.

"I'm okay, Mama, but I have to tell you what happened." Caroline relayed the story of meeting Greg Baker at the New Year's Eve party. Then she relayed the scene at the breakfast table earlier that day.

"Please tell me you are kidding, Caroline," Charlotte begged.

"I wish I could tell you that, but I can't," Caroline replied dryly. "I'm standing in the Charleston Airport now waiting to fly to Charlottesville at five o'clock. I will take a taxi back to campus."

"Oh, Caroline, honey, I am so sorry," Charlotte said. "I remember Greg. I imagine that Mr. Baker will not have a good week next week. I don't know who his contact is at the law firm, but that person will not have a good week either." Charlotte was fuming. "I will try to keep your grandparents out of this, but I have to contact Harvey; you know that," she continued.

"I know that," Caroline said. "I hope whoever the lawyer is who talked about this with Mr. Baker realizes what hurt he caused. I broke up with Garrett," she said more casually than Charlotte thought the situation deserved.

"You broke up with Garrett!" Charlotte exclaimed.

"Yes, Mama," Caroline said. "There are more reasons than this, but I will have to talk with you about that later. Until this morning, my visit was wonderful. His family is very nice, or I thought so anyway."

"Caroline, you just get back to your dormitory safely, sweetheart," Charlotte said lovingly. "We can take care of this later. I want you to be okay. I love you with all my heart, Caroline."

"I know you do. I love you with all my heart too," Caroline said sadly. "I am so thankful for you, Mama. You are my best friend. Thank you for always being there for me."

"That will never change, Caroline," Charlotte said sweetly. "Remember to call me when you get to your room, okay?"

"I will," Caroline said. And she hung up the telephone. She wanted to cry, but there were too many people around. She would have to wait to fall apart.

Garrett arrived back home to find his father's car in the driveway. He parked behind him and walked into the house. As he walked into the den, his father looked up from the newspaper. "Dad, why did you do what you did today?" Garrett asked angrily. "Caroline is a very private person. Couldn't you tell that she didn't want to talk about her family? Every question you asked her, she answered with as few words as possible. Most people would have picked up on that and stopped. Please tell me why," Garrett begged, still angry with his father.

"I wanted to find out if what Greg told me was true, Son," Derek replied, in his usual pragmatic fashion but embarrassed that he had caused such a problem. "Did you know that Caroline is independently wealthy and that she stands to inherit another fortune from her grandparents?" Derek continued, hoping the information would quell his son's anger.

"No, I did not know that, Dad. I didn't need to know that. But it doesn't matter now. Caroline broke up with me, thanks to you," Garrett said sarcastically. He turned and left the den and walked to his room and slammed the door. Derek got up to walk upstairs, mad that Garrett had slammed the door. Laura stopped him in the kitchen.

"I recommend that you go back to your newspaper, Derek," Laura said emphatically. "That is not a suggestion. You have done enough for one day, don't you think?" she continued sarcastically. Derek looked at her and started to speak. "No talking, Derek," Laura said. "Do you understand English?" He turned and walked back into the den and sat down.

Laura got her coat and her purse and drove to the Battery. She walked around Battery Park to clear her head and get out of the tense atmosphere.

Caroline's flight arrived in Charlottesville at seven o'clock p.m. She was glad to get a taxi and get back to her dormitory. After she unpacked and called her mother, she showered and went to bed.

CHAPTER 24

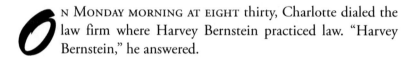N Monday morning at eight thirty, Charlotte dialed the law firm where Harvey Bernstein practiced law. "Harvey Bernstein," he answered.

"Harvey," Charlotte began, "this is Charlotte Wellington."

"Well, well, Happy New Year, Charlotte," Harvey replied jovially.

"Happy New Year, Harvey," she said. "Harvey, we have a problem."

"Oh?" Harvey said.

Charlotte relayed the information that Caroline had provided about meeting Greg Baker and about her boyfriend's father's inquisition.

"Charlotte, George Montgomery is the only other lawyer who worked on the Georgia Life sale with me. He was privy to the estate information since it was relevant to the sale," Harvey offered willingly. "Rest assured that before the end of this day, you will have an answer about this breach of confidence. I am so sorry this happened to Caroline. She is an amazing young woman, Charlotte."

"Yes, she is, Harvey," Charlotte agreed. "But she has been through so much in her life. She doesn't need this. She is very private, as am I. Neither of us wishes for anyone outside of our family knowing anything about the estate."

"I know, Charlotte," Harvey said sympathetically.

"Thanks for your help, Harvey," Charlotte said.

"It will be resolved to your satisfaction. That is a promise," Harvey replied.

Charlotte hung up the telephone and walked downstairs. Irene was walking in the front door as she got to the foyer. "Mother, you will not believe what happened," Charlotte said.

"Try me," Irene replied, intrigued.

When Charlotte finished the story, Irene was ready to fly to Charleston to kill Derek Winthrop and Greg Harris. "How dare he treat my granddaughter that way!" Irene exclaimed. "He wouldn't have any balls left if he were standing in front of me right now!"

"Maybe we should go to Charleston, Mother," Charlotte said. "I would like to see you remove his balls." They both laughed hysterically at the thought of Irene kicking Derek's balls off. "Well, I know Harvey Bernstein," Charlotte said. "Someone will be very unhappy by the end of this day,"

"I hope so!" Irene replied.

At two o'clock, Charlotte's telephone rang. "Hello," Charlotte said.

"Charlotte, this is Harvey," he said when she answered. "Sit down. I have a story for you."

"Okay, Harvey, I'm sitting," Charlotte replied.

"It seems that George Montgomery's secretary, Lisa Weeks, has been having an affair with Greg Baker for two years. She worked on the Georgia Life sale and of course had all the information about the estate. She apparently knew that Greg and John had attended Harvard at the same time, and she chose to share the information with him, I am sure during one of their so-called meetings."

"My God, Harvey," Charlotte said, surprised. "Does she not know that she isn't supposed to talk about the cases she works on?"

"Oh, she knows, Charlotte," Harvey continued. "She has been at this firm for twelve years. Her employment ended today. George is contacting Greg's employer to let them know that he is filing a grievance with the South Carolina state bar. It is likely that Greg with either be fired or fined for both."

"So how are we assured that this information will not be shared again?" Charlotte asked honestly.

"Charlotte, I wish I could assure you of that, but unfortunately, I do not have control over what everyone does in this firm."

"I know, Harvey," Charlotte said. "I appreciate your taking care of this for me."

"What we are doing, though," Harvey continued, "is beginning mandatory training for everyone in the firm regarding privacy issues. That training should start the week of January 16. Your phone call is the catalyst for it, but I suspect that it is long overdue. I have taken it a step further. Your files have been sealed, and I am the only person in the firm who will have access to them."

"That sounds like a good idea, Harvey," Charlotte said appreciatively. "Would you keep me informed about what happens in South Carolina too?" she asked.

"Of course I will, Charlotte," Harvey replied. "The privacy issue is extended to you and Caroline as well, though."

"We are already very private, Harvey. You know that," Charlotte said.

"I know," he replied. "Do me a favor," Harvey continued. "Please call me if you learn anything else or if there is any fallout on your end. Would you do that for me?"

"Of course I will," Charlotte said as if talking with an old friend.

"I'll call you later this week for an update," Harvey said.

"Thanks, Harvey," Charlotte said and she hung up the telephone.

Charlotte's next telephone call was to Caroline. "Hello" came Caroline's voice on the other end of the line.

"Hi, sweetheart," Charlotte said softly. "Are you feeling better today?"

"Not really, Mama," Caroline said honestly. "I just feel let down and sad, mostly."

"That's understandable, honey," Charlotte said, mothering Caroline the best she could from such a distance. "I spoke with Harvey Bernstein today. He has taken care of the situation. You can be sure that no more information about our family will be coming from their firm." Charlotte thought it best to keep Greg Baker's affair out of the conversation. "The person responsible has been identified and fired."

"I'm sorry someone lost their job, Mama," Caroline said sincerely.

"Not your fault, honey," Charlotte said. "Mama Rene wanted to go to Charleston and kick Derek Winthrop's balls off." Caroline laughed.

"Oh my gosh, Mama, I have a visual on that!" Caroline said and got hysterical. "I want a front-row seat and some popcorn for that one!" Caroline exclaimed, still laughing.

"Me too," Charlotte said between her gasps for air.

"Mama Rene could probably take care of him," Caroline said.

"She probably could, honey," Charlotte said, regaining control. "You put this out of your mind now. I am so sorry it happened, but it has been taken care of. You just take care of yourself and concern yourself with school," Charlotte instructed.

"I will, Mama," Caroline said. "You are the best!"

"Only because I have you, sweetheart," Charlotte said lovingly. "Call me later, okay?"

"Okay, I will," Caroline said, and she hung up the telephone.

CHAPTER 25

*D*EREK WALKED INTO HIS OFFICE on Monday morning and found a note directing him to report to the president's office immediately. He had an idea that his summons was related to Caroline Wellington. As he entered the office, George Sanders and Greg Baker were standing waiting for him. "Derek," Greg began, "you have created quite an uproar with your questions to Miss Wellington. When I shared the information with you, I asked that you keep it private. I take responsibility for my mistake in telling you what I learned. I was wrong, and you were even more wrong to press her for information about her family."

"Derek," George began, "one person has been fired at the law firm who handled the Georgia Life sale in Atlanta, and a grievance is being filed with the South Carolina state bar against Greg by that firm."

"Oh my God!" Derek exclaimed. "I had no idea that my questions would create such havoc!"

"It is a serious lapse in judgment, Derek," George said. "You disclosed information provided to you by our in-house counsel. Agreed, it was information he should never have shared, but this is one mistake after another. Pending what the bar association does, we may or may not be able to retain Greg as our in-house counsel. In fact, it is possible that he will not be able to practice law in South Carolina."

"Greg," Derek said, "I am so sorry. I am embarrassed and very upset. My wife and son are not speaking to me, and now I find out that I may have cost you your job. I am very sorry." Derek hung his head. "Caroline broke up with my son and left on Sunday to fly back to UVA. Our household has been in turmoil because of my mistake too."

"Derek," George said, "if Greg leaves our firm because of this, I will have no choice but to let you go too." Derek went pale and had to sit down.

"I am so sorry," Derek said. "I have no excuse except that I did the wrong thing."

"Let's see how it shakes out, Derek," Greg said kindly. "George has said that he doesn't want to lose either one of us. But if I come under the scrutiny of the state bar, he may have no choice. Derek, I am very sorry that I put you in this position too."

"Thanks, Greg," Derek said flatly. "But what I did was my fault, not yours."

George spoke. "Okay, I don't guess I have to say that none of this should be discussed outside this office or in the presence of anyone but the three of us. In fact, let's agree that we will not discuss this outside my office. Agreed?"

"Agreed," Derek said.

"Sure thing, George," Greg said. "I'm very sorry to put you in this position." The three men ended their conversation. Greg went to his office on the tenth floor, and Derek went to his on the third floor. Neither of them had any idea of the repercussions ahead.

When Greg returned to his office, there was a message from Lisa. Greg picked up the phone and dialed her office number. "Bernstein and Carter" came the receptionist's voice on the other end of the line. "Miss Weeks, please," Greg requested.

"I'm sorry, sir. Miss Weeks is no longer employed here. Can someone else assist you?" The receptionist's reply left Greg stunned.

"No, thank you," he said and hung up the telephone. He dialed her home number.

"Hello," Lisa Weeks said.

"Lisa, it's Greg."

"I figured you would get around to calling me sometime," Lisa said sarcastically. "Why did you tell your friend about Caroline Wellington? I told you it was to be kept in strictest confidence."

"That's a good question, Lisa," Greg replied. "My job is on the line too. Your former boss is filing a grievance with the South Carolina state bar. If they take it up, my job is gone along with Derek Winthrop's job. The fallout from this is pretty devastating."

"Greg, I told you that the Wellingtons were very wealthy and very influential. Their influence extends far beyond Atlanta. This is really bad!" Lisa exclaimed.

"I guess I didn't grasp exactly how wealthy and influential they are," Greg said, trying to excuse his mistake. "Lisa," Greg continued, "you know this means that we can't see each other anymore."

"I figured you would call to say that, Greg," Lisa said disgusted with what she heard. "There's just one problem," she paused. "I'm pregnant."

Greg could not speak and could not breathe. "That can't be, Lisa!" Greg screamed into the telephone.

"I'm not sure how you figure that, Greg. We've been having sex for two years," she blurted.

"Lisa, I care about you, but I can't leave my wife and children. You and I have talked about this before," he said distantly.

"I know we have, Greg," Lisa replied. "But you will do what's right, won't you? You will help me. I won't say that you are the baby's father. I will just need money to pay for my living until after the baby is born. I will need to pay the doctor and the hospital bill too."

"Of course, Lisa," Greg said. "I'll be in Atlanta in a couple of weeks. I'll call you and we can hammer out some plans then. Okay?"

"Okay, Greg," she replied halfheartedly. "I'm counting on you." They ended their conversation.

Lisa was a beautiful, blue-eyed blond from Savannah. She hated to go home pregnant and unwed. It would be a scandal in their small community in Savannah. As soon as their conversation ended, Lisa knew she would not be able to depend on Greg. He wanted her for one thing: sex. Now that she was an inconvenience, he was throwing her out with yesterday's garbage. Extortion was not in her nature, but at this point, she would have to do whatever she had to do for her child.

CHAPTER 26

*C*LASSES BEGAN AGAIN ON MONDAY, January 9. Caroline managed to avoid seeing Garrett since everyone was back from Christmas vacation. It was too cold to walk to class, so she drove to most of her classes and parked as close as possible to the buildings where her classes were held. It wasn't until the end of the following week that she saw Garrett.

"Caroline," Garrett called to her across the parking lot.

"Hi, Garrett," she replied casually. "I hope you are doing well."

"I'm fine," Garrett said. "Hey, I want to apologize to you again for my father's poor judgment."

"Garrett," Caroline said earnestly, "could we please forget it? That would be the biggest favor you could do for me."

"Sure, Caroline," Garrett said. Caroline turned and walked away. Garrett stood in the parking lot trying to figure out what just happened. Humiliated, he got into his car and drove to his next class, vowing to try to forget about her.

For the next five weeks, they did not see each other on campus. One day very cold in late February, Caroline was with Jackie at the pizza parlor in town on a Saturday afternoon when she ran into Garrett's friend, Scott. He walked over to their table. "Hi, Caroline. Hi, Jackie," he said cordially.

"Hi, Scott," Caroline replied. "Where's your buddy Garrett?"

"Oh, I thought you knew. He withdrew from school. I think his dad lost his job, and he couldn't afford to stay," Scott replied. "We miss him. I hope to get to Charleston sometime to see him."

Caroline's shock was apparent. "You obviously didn't know," Scott said.

"No, I didn't," Caroline revealed. "I'm really sorry about that," she said.

"My pizza's ready," Scott said. "See you girls later."

"Sure thing, Scott," Jackie said since she saw that Caroline could hardly speak. "What's up with that, Caroline?" Jackie asked.

Caroline lied, "I don't know."

When Caroline got back to her dorm room, she called her mother. "Hello," Charlotte answered.

"Mama!" Caroline exclaimed. "Garrett withdrew from school because his father lost his job. I have a feeling it's because of what happened at New Year's."

Charlotte hesitated and then replied, "Caroline, you're right. Both Greg Baker and Derek Winthrop lost their jobs. I'm very sorry that this has affected Garrett. He certainly did not deserve this."

"No, he didn't," Caroline said, still sounding shocked.

"Caroline, I have hesitated to tell you the rest of the story, but now I think you should know," Charlotte offered.

"Okay, what?" Caroline quipped. "How could it get worse?"

"Oh, it is worse, Caroline," Charlotte said. "Greg Baker apparently had a girlfriend at the Bernstein Law Firm in Atlanta," Charlotte began. "That's how he got the information about the Georgia Life sale. She worked for George Montgomery, who was the other attorney besides Harvey who worked on our case. Since Harvey drew the wills, George was familiar with the details of your father's estate. His secretary did a lot of the work on it. She also knew about Granddaddy and Grandmother changing their wills and leaving everything to you."

"You mean she told Mr. Baker all that?" Caroline asked, still shocked.

"I'm afraid so, honey," Charlotte said. "She was fired the day I called Harvey." Charlotte continued the story. "Harvey contacted the president of Derek's company to tell him that a grievance would be filed against Greg Harris with the state bar of South Carolina."

"That's very serious, Mama," Caroline said, remembering reading about ethics in one of her father's law books.

"Yes, it is, Caroline, very serious," Charlotte said. "Let me finish," she continued. "A month later, Greg learned that there would be an investigation and charges. Both he and Derek were fired on the same day."

"That's awful, Mama," Caroline said sadly.

"It is awful, Caroline," Charlotte said, "but I am not finished with the story."

"Good grief, Mama!" Caroline exclaimed. "How much worse could it get?"

"Plenty," Charlotte said. "Greg's girlfriend—" Charlotte began but Caroline interrupted her.

"Wait, Mama, I thought Greg Baker was married," Caroline said, questioning the story.

"Oh, he was married, Caroline," Charlotte said sarcastically.

"How terrible!" Caroline exclaimed.

"Yes, but worse than that, his girlfriend was pregnant when she was fired," Charlotte said casually.

"Pregnant!" Caroline exclaimed.

"Yes, Caroline," Charlotte said. "Let me get this out, okay?"

"Okay, Mama," Caroline relented. "I'm shocked, that's all."

"Greg flew to Atlanta a month after he found out she was pregnant and killed her." Charlotte blurted out the awful truth.

"Greg Baker killed someone?" Caroline's shock was overwhelming.

"Yes, Caroline, he did," Charlotte said quietly. "Then he flew back home and killed himself," she continued.

"Mama, are you sure?" Caroline asked, not wanting to believe what she heard.

"Yes, honey, I'm sure," Charlotte replied sadly. "Harvey told me everything about two weeks ago. I was hoping I would never have to tell you any of this, but since you asked about Derek, I thought you should know. I did not want someone else to tell you."

"Do you know if Mr. Winthrop found another job or not?" Caroline asked.

"I haven't heard one way or the other about that, sweetheart," Charlotte said, feeling her daughter's shock and sadness.

"I wish I had never called you about what happened up there. I feel like this is my fault," Caroline began crying.

"Caroline, none of this is your fault. Don't you think that for one minute," Charlotte instructed emphatically. "This is Greg Baker's and Derek Winthrop's faults. You were the victim of their poor judgment, Caroline," Charlotte continued in her forceful tone. "Unfortunately, you were only the first victim of their poor judgment. Garrett has been hurt pretty badly by his father's mistake."

"Yes, I can see that, Mama," Caroline said, trying to compose herself. "We can't do anything about their choices, and we can't get involved with them in any way. What has happened is a nightmare. I am so sorry to have to tell you this," Charlotte said sadly.

"I needed to know, Mama," Caroline said. "But I wish I didn't know."

"Spring break is in four weeks," Charlotte said. "Why don't you fly home and we'll go to the beach?"

"I would love to, Mama," Caroline said with a spark of enthusiasm in her voice.

"Would you like to invite a friend?" Charlotte asked.

"Not this time, Mama," Caroline said. "Let's take Mama Rene and Belle," she continued.

"We can do that," Charlotte said, excited that she had something good to look forward to. "I'll make reservations for us at Sea Island at the Cloister. You fly here on Friday after classes. We'll leave on Saturday and come home the following Saturday. That will give us plenty of time to rest and relax," Charlotte said.

Caroline could tell that her mother's planning skills were alive and well and that they would have a wonderful week. "Thanks, Mama," Caroline said sweetly.

"You don't worry about any of this, Caroline," Charlotte instructed her daughter. "Concentrate on school and looking forward to our trip."

"I'll try," Caroline said. "Call me later and give me the details, okay?"

"Okay, sweetheart, I will," Charlotte said. The conversation ended.

The next day, Charlotte made reservations at the Cloister at Sea Island. She reserved two suites at the Beach Club. Each suite had a living room and a bedroom with two bathrooms in each suite. The bedrooms each had two beds, so everyone would be comfortable. There was a small kitchen in each room. Charlotte did not intend to allow Belle to cook or clean while they were on vacation, though. Charlotte would have to inform the management that her maid would be traveling with them in order to allow Belle to stay with them. Race relations were changing, but in the South, there were some traditions that were still observed, especially at the Cloister.

Caroline arrived in Atlanta on Friday evening, March 26. Charlotte met her at the gate. "Mama, I am so glad to see you," Caroline said as she hugged her mother.

"I'm so glad to see you too, sweetheart," Charlotte said. "Let's get you home. Are you hungry?"

"Not really," Caroline said. "I'll get something at home."

"Belle made fresh pimento cheese for you," Charlotte announced.

"I've been thinking about her pimento cheese this week. That's perfect," Caroline said, realizing that she was very tired.

"We'll fly to Savannah tomorrow, and a car will pick us up and take us to Sea Island," Charlotte told Caroline. "I want all of us to just have a change of scenery and a break from school for you."

"Mama, I have been looking forward to this so much," Caroline gushed. "Some of my friends who are from north of the Mason-Dixon line have never heard of Sea Island."

"I'm not surprised, honey," Charlotte began to explain. "That is actually by design," she continued. "The developers of Sea Island and the Cloister do not want just anybody staying there. It's pretty exclusive. Your daddy and I stayed there a couple of times—once before you were born and a couple of times when you were really little when Katy was still with us."

"Why did you and Daddy go there?" Caroline asked.

"The first time was just a trip for the two of us. The other two trips were meetings to entertain Georgia Life clients. Daddy and Granddaddy went there more often than I did. They entertained clients there at least once a year," Charlotte explained. "It is still quite exclusive. You'll like our rooms. We will be next door to each other. You and I will stay in one room and Mama Rene and Belle in the other."

"It sounds like heaven," Caroline sighed.

Caroline slept in her own bed for the first time since Christmas. It was the best nights' sleep she had had in months. When she woke the next morning, she could smell fresh-brewed coffee and Belle's fabulous biscuits. *Home,* she thought. *I love home.*

After breakfast, she learned that her mother had packed her suitcase with appropriate clothes for cool and warm weather. It would not be warm enough to go in the ocean, but they would walk on the beach. Robert and Karen had agreed to stay at the house while the four of them were gone. Robert was glad that his aunt would have a nice vacation.

At ten o'clock, the limousine arrived to take them to the airport. As they were leaving the driveway, Caroline turned to Belle and said, "Belle, I don't think I have ever seen you wear slacks. You look wonderful in your slacks and sweater."

"Oh, go on, Miss Caroline," Belle said, laughing and pretending to be embarrassed. "I have to catch up to the times. I can't stay way back there in the thirties and forties."

"You sure can't, Belle," Caroline said, and they all laughed.

The flight from Atlanta to Savannah was uneventful. The limousine was waiting for them at the airport to take them to Sea Island. The ninety-minute ride was filled with chatting and planning their week at the beach. By the time they arrived, it was three o'clock. The butler at the Cloister opened the door of the limousine and said, "Mrs. Wellington, we are very pleased to have you visit again."

"Thank you," Charlotte said as she exited the car.

"Please follow me," he continued. "Your bags will be brought to your rooms immediately." He escorted them through the lobby to an area where an electric car was waiting to take them to their rooms. "Joseph will drive you to your rooms, Mrs. Wellington. Here is my card. Please contact me anytime you need something," the butler said as he assisted Irene onto the car. Another butler was unloading their bags as they arrived at their rooms.

Charlotte thanked Joseph as she gave him ten dollars. He tipped his hat and drove the electric car back to be prepared for the next guest. As the butler finished delivering all their bags, Charlotte gave him twenty dollars and thanked him. He, too, tipped his hat and disappeared.

"Let's get unpacked, and then we can go to dinner at the Georgian Club," Charlotte announced.

"I'm kinda tired, Miss Charlotte," Belle said. "I think I'll just stay in the room. I can run and get a sandwich."

"Belle," Charlotte put her hands on her hips and looked squarely at her, "you will be joining us for dinner at the club."

"Are you sure, Miss Charlotte?" Belle asked, still tentative about having dinner in such an exclusive place.

"I'm sure, Belle," Charlotte said. "Now scoot and get unpacked and change for dinner. We do have to wear nice clothes to the club. Belle, you have that pretty blue dress with the sweater. It will be perfect."

Belle giggled and went into her room with Irene. Charlotte could hear her say, "Lawzy, Miss Irene, I never thought I would be staying in such a fancy place as this."

"Me either, Belle," Irene replied, and they both giggled.

At seven o'clock, the four women dined in the Georgian Room. It had a stone-carved mantle and gold and crystal chandeliers. The food was exquisite, and the service was unmatched. There were a few surprised stares from some of the older guests, but Charlotte ignored them. After dinner, the four of them strolled back to their rooms. They had a wraparound balcony with tables and chairs. The four of them sat on the balcony and talked until it was too cold to stay outside. There were hugs and kisses all around, and then they all went to bed.

Caroline was awake first the next morning. She got up and put on her slacks with a sweater and a jacket and her tennis shoes. She wrote her mother a note and tiptoed out the door to take a walk on the beach.

It was early, but other guests were taking advantage of the beautiful sunrise too. The breezes were strong off the ocean, and Caroline took a deep breath, wanting to fill her lungs with the salt air. The ocean always put life into perspective for her. The sound of the waves lured her to understand how small we really are by comparison.

She knew that she was very fortunate in so many ways, but the last year had been very hard for her with her father's death. There had been so many changes in her life—moving from the home she grew up in and leaving for college. Even since she started college, so many things had happened. Garrett was almost always on her mind, even though she tried to focus on other things. Her love for him had not vanished the day he dropped her off at the airport in Charleston.

She had been walking for almost an hour lost in her thoughts when she saw her mother waving to her. She waved back and started jogging toward her. They embraced and began walking together.

"How long have you been out here, Caroline?" Charlotte asked.

"About an hour, I guess," Caroline replied. "Why?"

"Just wondered," Charlotte said. The two of them walked for almost another hour, enjoying each other's company.

"We'd better get back," Charlotte said reluctantly. "I want to stay here with you all day, Caroline."

"Me too, Mama," Caroline said, stopping and looking at her mother. The wind was swirling their hair into a wild style. "Mother, you are so beautiful," Caroline said lovingly.

"I don't always feel very beautiful, Caroline," Charlotte admitted. "I'm almost fifty-four, you know."

"Yes, I know," Caroline said. "But you are still the most beautiful woman I have ever seen."

"*Wow!*" Charlotte exclaimed. "Coming from a girl who looks like you do, that is quite a compliment. You, my dear, are exquisite."

"I see a contest brewing, Mama," Caroline said, laughing. "Exquisite, huh?" she said, still laughing. "You are magnificent."

"Okay, okay," Charlotte relented. "I give up. But even if you are my daughter, I think you are perfectly beautiful."

"Why, thank you, Mrs. Wellington," Caroline joked. The Wellington women walked arm in arm back to the Beach Club.

Every day of their spring vacation was wonderful. Charlotte and Caroline swam in the heated pool, had facials, and walked on the beach every morning and evening. They all enjoyed the wonderful food, and the service was without equal. Irene and Belle loved playing checkers and canasta. They sat for hours on the veranda during the day playing and talking. On the Friday before they were leaving to go back home, Charlotte ordered two bottles of champagne to their room after dinner. She invited Belle and Irene to join her and Caroline for a couple of glasses of champagne to celebrate their wonderful vacation together. They each had two glasses of the sparkling indulgence. Belle was giddy, Irene was silly, and Charlotte was totally entertained by them. Caroline watched them, amazed, having never seen them this way.

After Irene and Belle had retired to their room for the night, Charlotte and Caroline went to sit on the balcony and finish their glasses of champagne. "Mama, I had champagne on New Year's Eve at the party in Charleston at Mr. Winthrop's boss's house," Caroline confessed.

"You did?" Charlotte asked, not really expecting an answer.

"I liked it then and I like it now," she continued her confession.

"I like it too, Caroline. The key is moderation. Two glasses of champagne is plenty for one evening," Charlotte instructed.

"Yes, especially for me," Caroline said. Charlotte could tell there was a story coming.

Caroline told Charlotte about her experience in the bed with Garrett. "Mama, no wonder people like sex so much," she said in a whisper. "Good heavens! It was amazing."

"With the right person, for the right reasons, yes it is. Just for the heck of it, it just isn't right no matter how wonderful you think it is," Charlotte said.

"That was one of the reasons I broke up with Garrett, Mama," Caroline said. "I really do think I love him, but I can't get involved with anyone that way until I am older."

"Caroline, you are wise beyond your years, sweetheart. I told you I have confidence in you, and I still do. Even in a very difficult situation, you did what was right. I know your heart still hurts about everything that happened. But time will heal that even though it doesn't feel like it will ever heal."

"You're right, Mama," Caroline said, taking her mother's hand. "I love you so much."

"I love you more than I could ever explain to you, Caroline," Charlotte said tearfully. "C'mon. We're getting too serious out here. Let's get into bed. We have to leave by eleven o'clock tomorrow to catch our flight back to Atlanta."

CHAPTER 27

*A*FTER A FLIGHT HOME WITHOUT incident and a limousine ride back to Roswell, Robert stepped out of the front door to greet the four women. "Aunt Belle!" he exclaimed. "I'm so glad you're home."

"I think I need to go away more often with a greeting like that," Belle said giggling.

"Miss Charlotte, Miss Irene, Miss Caroline, Aunt Belle," Robert said, hardly catching his breath. "Karen and I are expecting a baby!" he said, stepping back to wait for their reactions. There were screams of joy and hugs from everyone.

"Well, where is Karen?" Belle asked.

"Oh, she's still at work." Robert replied. "I told her to stop by when she got off. I knew you would want to see her."

"We all want to see her, Robert!" Charlotte exclaimed. "Congratulations! I bet your mother and father are so thrilled!"

"Oh, they are. They can't wait for the baby to come," Robert said proudly.

Robert made sure all the bags were in the house before he gave his aunt a hug. "Aunt Belle, this will be like your grandchild too," he said sweetly. Belle was teary. She patted him while he hugged her.

"You are like my child, Robert. I am so proud of you. You have made me very happy," Belle said softly. "Your son or daughter will be very lucky to have Karen and you as parents."

"That is a big compliment coming from you, Aunt Belle," Robert said as he picked her bag to take it to her cottage. "Come on, I will get your bag for you and we can talk for a while before Karen gets here," he said, taking her by the arm with one hand and taking her bag with the other. They disappeared toward the cottage.

"Mother," Charlotte said to Irene, "let me take you home. I know you want to unpack and get settled."

"Thank you, honey," Irene replied. "I appreciate it. I will be glad to see my little house."

Caroline was upstairs in her room sorting laundry to wash and repacking for her trip back to college when the telephone rang. She walked to her mother's room. "Hello," she said.

"Caroline, this is Garrett" came the familiar voice.

"Garrett!" Caroline exclaimed. "How are you?"

"I'm fine," he said formally. "I wanted to let you know that I will be back at UVA after spring break."

"I'm very glad to hear that, Garrett. I didn't know about your father's job or any of the other awful things that happened until about two weeks ago. Mama finally told me. It was a terrible time for your family, I'm sure," Caroline said genuinely.

"Yes, I have to say that it was awful. But you must know that none of that was your fault, Caroline," Garrett said, sounding as if he were pleading with her.

"It has been hard for me to feel that it wasn't my fault in some way, Garrett," Caroline replied directly. "I'm working through it the best I can," she admitted.

"My father got his old job back about a month ago. The company really needed him, and they worked out a deal for him to come back," Garrett said, sounding as if he was trying to alleviate some of Caroline's guilt. "That is one reason I can get back to UVA. My dad was more upset about that than anything else, I think," he continued.

"Garrett, that is very good news. I hope he and your mother are doing well," Caroline said cordially.

"They're doing fine," Garrett said. "Thank you for asking. Listen," he continued, "I just wanted to hear your voice and tell you I would be back to school. I hope I'm not interrupting anything."

"You're interrupting me sorting laundry," Caroline laughed.

"Well, that's important," Garrett said, laughing with her. "I hope I see you on campus," Garrett said rather shyly.

"I'm sure we'll run into each other," Caroline said in an unfamiliar tone.

"I'm glad to talk with you, Caroline," Garrett said. "Hope to see you soon." And he hung up the telephone.

Caroline stood in her mother's room trying to sort out their short conversation. Charlotte walked into the room. "Were you on the telephone?" she asked.

"Yes, I was," Caroline replied, "and you won't believe who it was."

"I'll believe anything at this point," Charlotte joked. "So who was it?"

"Garrett," Caroline said flatly.

"Well, well," Charlotte said intrigued. "May I ask what Mr. Winthrop had to say?"

"He said his father got his old job back and he would be back at UVA next week," Caroline said, sounding puzzled. "I can't figure out why he called me."

"Caroline, honey," Charlotte began, "He was trying to see what kind of reception he would get from you. He's trying to win you back. It's as plain as the nose on your face." Charlotte put her hands on her hips. She did that when she was either mad or saying something she wanted understood by the person to whom she was directing her comments. "So what are you going to do, Caroline?" came the direct question.

"Mother, I don't honestly know at this moment," Caroline said, sitting down on her mother's bed. "I am caught between my head and my heart."

"Caroline, I don't want to tell you what to do about this. It's not my judgment call anyway. It's yours," Charlotte began her instruction. "If I were you, I would hold off on any decision one way or the other until after you have finished your freshman year. That's only about two months away. If he really loves you, he's not going to run off between now and then."

"You're right, Mama," Caroline said, hugging her mother. "That's very good advice." Caroline walked back to her room.

Charlotte hoped her decision would not derail her plans to graduate and go to law school. Charlotte felt as if she were walking a very fine line with her daughter. Typically, Charlotte waited until Caroline asked for advice before she offered. But she felt that Caroline was dealing with so much right now that a definitive suggestion might be right.

Later that evening, Caroline came into Charlotte's room. "I have made a decision," Caroline said emphatically. Charlotte looked up from her book. "I am not going back to UVA. I will transfer to Emory and live at home."

Charlotte stood up, unable to speak. "What?" she finally said, so surprised she couldn't comment.

"I'm not going back. I have made up my mind," Caroline said, and she turned and walked out of her mother's room.

Charlotte decided to allow Caroline to think about her decision before she tried to reason with her. But two hours later, she knocked on Caroline's door. "Caroline, I know you have been through a very difficult situation, but you need to think before you give up your dream of graduating from UVA. You love it there. In your life, there will be many times when you have to face difficult situations head on. You can't just walk away and pretend nothing happened. Why don't you think about this a little more before you decide what you want to do?"

"Mama, all that happened has been just about too much for me." Caroline's voice was shaky, and Charlotte could see tears in her eyes. "I just want something normal for a change."

"I understand that very well, Caroline," Charlotte replied. She turned and walked out of Caroline's room, closing the door behind her.

The following day, Caroline asked her mother to take her to the airport. Charlotte was glad that she made that decision, and she took Caroline to the airport to fly back to Charlottesville. "Remember to call me when you get to your room, okay?" Charlotte said, wiping her eyes.

Caroline was tearful too. "Mama, thank you for a wonderful week," she said, trying not to sob.

"We made a good memory, didn't we, honey?" Charlotte said.

"We sure did, Mama," Caroline said. "And thank you for helping me to see that I need to stay at UVA." She turned and walked down the Jetway.

Charlotte strolled solemnly back to her car and drove home.

CHAPTER 28

ON MONDAY MORNING, CHARLOTTE WAS in the kitchen with Belle having coffee and talking about the new baby that Robert and Karen were expecting when Irene walked in the back door. "Got any coffee left, girls?" Irene asked playfully.

"There's always coffee enough for you, Miss Irene," Belle said, getting up to get her a cup.

"Belle, I know where the cups are, honey," Irene said, holding her hand up to instruct Belle to sit down. Irene got her coffee and joined her daughter and Belle at the breakfast table. The three women sat talking about the wonderful week they had shared at Sea Island. Belle thanked Charlotte so many times. Charlotte knew that the week was special for her mother and for Belle, and it gave her a feeling of satisfaction that was difficult to explain. She was so happy to do something good for the two women who were so much a part of her life for all of her life. It seemed a small gift compared to what they had done for her.

Charlotte decided that the time was as good now as any to make her announcement. "Mother, Belle, I have hired a housekeeper to come twice a week to my house and once a week to your house, Mother.

Our housekeeper will take care of my home, your cottage, Belle, and your home, Mother," Charlotte said and waited for the reactions.

"Miss Charlotte," Belle spoke first. "I'm supposed to be taking care of you!"

"Belle," Charlotte said lovingly, "you have taken care of me for so many years I don't want to count them. You are the standard by which all others are measured. It is time for me to take care of you. You are as much my family as my mother, so just get used to it," Charlotte said as she touched Belle's hand. "You know, Belle," Charlotte continued, "I'm not sure I have ever told you that I love you, but you should know that I do."

"Miss Charlotte," Belle said softly as tears rolled down her cheeks, "I have loved you all of your life, and I have known that you loved me since we lived at the Ansley Park house."

Irene was wiping tears at this point. "Okay, you two," Irene joked, "that's enough blubbering for one day. We all love each other, and we have for a thousand years. Now that that is out of the way, why don't we go to the grocery store? I don't have a thing in my house to eat."

"Mother, you are so sentimental," Charlotte said as they all laughed hysterically. "Belle, you have spoiled me for so many years with your cooking, I must insist that you not stop now. Would you please just cook dinner for me in the evenings?" Charlotte asked.

"Miss Charlotte, I will cook breakfast, lunch, and dinner for you every day for the rest of my life," Belle said genuinely.

"Can't ask for more than that, can I?" Charlotte laughed. Irene and Belle left to go to the grocery store.

Charlotte walked upstairs to her room and sat down at her desk. She wanted to write Geoff Robinson a note. He had been on her mind for the last few weeks. Although she had spoken to him only once since Camilla's death, she felt that she should check on him. Instead, she dialed his number.

"Hello," Geoff answered the phone in his southern voice.

"Geoff, it's Charlotte."

"Charlotte, it's so good to hear from you." Geoff sounded genuinely happy to hear from her.

"How are you?" Charlotte asked.

"Coping, Charlotte. That's about it right now. I'm trying to make sure the children are okay. I think it would have been easier on them if I had died instead of Camilla."

The comment irritated Charlotte. "Well, Geoff," Charlotte said, "that's not what happened, and you have to stand up and be there for your children. I do not want to hear that note of 'poor pitiful me' in your voice. It is very difficult, no doubt. But your children must see a strong man supporting them. If I need to kick you, let me know. I can do it, you know."

"I have no doubt that you can, Charlotte," Geoff admitted. "You have been amazing with Caroline."

"You have to be, Geoff," Charlotte continued counseling him. "As much as the love you give your children, they also need an empowered parent, someone who can handle anything. Even if you can't, they need to think you can. It is their security."

"I know you're right, Charlotte," Geoff said timidly. "I am just tired right now, if you want to know the truth," he admitted.

"Very understandable, Geoff," Charlotte said. "Why don't you plan a special trip with your children when school is out?" Charlotte suggested. "We just got back from Sea Island for Caroline's spring break. It was fabulous."

"Great idea, Charlotte," Geoff said. "Would you like to have dinner with me next week sometime?" he asked.

Charlotte hesitated. "Geoff," she replied, "why don't you bring the children next Friday evening and have dinner here in Roswell?"

"It's a date," Geoff replied. "We'll be there."

"Belle will have something special for you," Charlotte teased him.

"I would drive farther than Roswell for Belle's cooking," Geoff said.

"Okay, then. I'll see you next Friday," Charlotte said, and she hung up the telephone. She wondered for a split second what the dinner invitation might mean and then dismissed the thought.

CHAPTER 29

*B*ELLE DID NOT TELL ANYONE that she had been to her doctor in February and learned that she had ovarian cancer. Her doctor wanted to do surgery the following week, but Belle refused. She went back to the doctor who had treated her for forty years instead. He told her the truth. The advanced stage of the cancer did not give her much of a chance for survival with or without surgery. Belle chose the latter. She was sixty-nine years old, and her fondest wish now was to see her grandniece or nephew before she died. Eventually, she would have to tell Charlotte and Irene. Although she had worked most of her life, she was far more fortunate than many of the people she had known in the past. She had been lucky to begin working for the Reed family when she was eighteen. She was grateful to her mother for seeing to it that she had a good family to work for before she died.

In her quite moments, Belle looked forward to seeing her parents again. There were so many questions she had wanted to ask them for most of her life that she never got to ask. Thoughts of her family reunion with her mother and father kept her happy most days.

Belle was very quietly religious. She believed in God and in Jesus as His Son. She believed in the resurrection and that His resurrection gave her the chance for eternal life and to see her parents again. It was her parents who taught her about Jesus when she was a little girl. Belle kept a Bible in her room and read it every night. She had bought spiritual books for fifteen years and pored through them during the times when she was not working. Belle never tried to impose her beliefs on anyone except Robert. She talked with him about her beliefs during the time they spent together serving the Wellingtons at the Ansley Park Home and at the Peacock House. She knew that Robert attended church with Karen, but she didn't know where. She would ask him to take her with him soon. Belle believed that you served God in more ways than just in the church. She thought you served by example and by showing other people how to be a servant.

It was Tuesday, June 6, when Belle decided that Charlotte and Irene should know about her condition. Caroline had finished her freshman year at UVA and was scheduled to come home the following Sunday. Charlotte and Irene were having coffee in the breakfast room when Belle sat down with them. "Miss Charlotte," Belle began, "Miss Irene, I have something to tell you."

"Belle," Charlotte said urgently, "what is it?"

"Well, I have ovarian cancer, and I probably will not be here this time next year." Charlotte and Irene were stunned. Neither of them could speak.

Charlotte stood and began to cry. "Belle, I realize that no one can live forever, but I really need for you to live a lot longer."

"Looks like that's not gonna happen, Miss Charlotte," Belle said casually. "Listen," Belle continued, "I will get to see my mother and my father. Just be happy for me."

"Well, Belle, I want to be happy for you," Charlotte said through her tears. "But I'm having a little trouble with that right now."

Irene looked at Belle and said, "Belle, I could not love you more if you were my sister. You are an example and an inspiration to all of us." Irene began to cry.

"Miss Irene, you are an amazing lady," Belle began. "You don't know how much I have watched you over the years and seen how strong you are. You are my example."

"Belle, it is you who is my example," Irene said sincerely.

"Belle," Charlotte began, "What can I do for your family?"

"Miss Charlotte," Belle replied, "I just want to see my grandniece or nephew when he or she is born. That is my biggest wish right now."

"And so you shall see that baby, no matter what I have to do, Belle," Charlotte promised.

"I have a small life insurance policy that should take care of my funeral and some money left for Robert's child's education. Would you be sure that Robert's child has a good education, Miss Charlotte?" Belle pleaded.

"Belle, your grandniece or nephew will have the best education available, guaranteed. Do you hear me, Belle?" Charlotte said, trying to regain control of her emotions.

"Yes, Miss Charlotte," Belle said, breaking down crying along with Charlotte and Irene. "We have been through so much together, haven't we?" Belle said softly.

"We sure have, Belle," Charlotte said. "It would not have been nearly so bearable without you."

"I don't know how to tell you how thankful I am that I have worked for you for these many years," Belle said. "Some of my friends have told me terrible stories about working for families that were very ugly to them. Some of them said they felt invisible except for the work they were required to do."

"Belle," Irene worked to compose herself, "our family was never wealthy until Charlotte married John. We know how it is to have to work every day to have a roof over your head and food to eat. We have respected you for your work ethic and for the time you spent being sure that Robert was a good boy."

"Thank you, Miss Irene," Belle said.

"Are you in pain, Belle?" Charlotte asked.

"Not really, yet," she replied honestly.

"You will let me know what you need, won't you, Belle?" Charlotte begged.

"Yes, Miss Charlotte, I will," she replied. "I have a very good doctor. I would like it if you would go to my next appointment with me."

"I will take you to your appointment, Belle," Charlotte said, standing up to put her arms around her precious Belle.

Belle stood and hugged Charlotte. "I had such a great time with you at Sea Island. Miss Irene and I played checkers and canasta so much that I think she knows I am the checkers and canasta champion of this family," Belle said, waiting for Irene's response.

"Champion?" Irene questioned. "I don't think that what you did to me at Sea Island qualifies you as champion," Irene replied, joking. "We'll have another match, Belle," Irene informed her.

"You'd better be ready, Miss Irene," Belle said, laughing.

"Oh, I'll be ready for you all right, Miss Smarty!" Irene said, trying to lighten the mood in the room.

"Okay, Miss Charlotte," Belle said, "you heard her. I think she has challenged me. I'll show you, Miss Irene," Belle said, still laughing at Irene.

Belle had managed to deliver very difficult news to the two women she loved the most in this world and keep the mood happy and positive. She was indeed an amazing woman.

Charlotte hated to tell Caroline the news about Belle. Caroline loved Belle the way Charlotte did, and she knew Caroline would be devastated. How much more could this family take in such a short period of time!

Charlotte decided not to tell Caroline about Belle's illness until she got home. She didn't want her to have to deal with that news alone.

Caroline drove home on Sunday and arrived about eight o'clock that evening. Her small car was packed with more than it should hold. Charlotte insisted that Caroline keep her dorm room and paid the university accordingly. The rest of her clothes Caroline mailed to Roswell. Consistency was always important for Charlotte where Caroline was concerned.

Charlotte was waiting for Caroline on the front porch. When she arrived, Charlotte was relieved that another long trip had ended safely. "I'm so glad you're home, sweetheart!" Charlotte exclaimed, not hiding her relief.

"I'm glad to be home, Mama," Caroline said, hugging her mother. "I'm going to sleep until noon tomorrow," she sighed.

The two women managed to get the car unpacked and Caroline's belongings into the house. Robert and Karen had taken Belle to

Sunday-night worship services at their church, and he was not there to help this time. "Where's Belle, Mama?" Caroline asked, walking into the kitchen.

"She's at church with Robert and Karen, honey," Charlotte said with a note of dread in her voice. "She should be home in about a half hour. I think Robert and Karen were taking her to dinner at the cafeteria after church."

"That's so sweet of them," Caroline said. Charlotte hated to tell Caroline the news about Belle, but she knew she would have to tell her. But not tonight.

Caroline had her favorite late-evening snack. She loved Belle's homemade pimento cheese. A pimento cheese sandwich and a glass of sweet iced tea meant home to Caroline.

Belle walked in the back door about eight forty-five. She walked over to Caroline and gave her a great big hug. "Lawzy, Miss Caroline, I am so glad you're home!" Belle exclaimed.

"I'm glad to be home, Belle," Caroline said, giving Belle a kiss on the cheek. "Thank you for making homemade pimento cheese for me."

"I always try to have that for you. I know how you love it," Belle said with a twinkle in her eye. She loved Caroline the way she loved Robert.

"Belle, I am going to sleep until noon tomorrow, so don't make biscuits in the morning. Wait until Tuesday when I get up early, okay?" Caroline asked.

"Okay, I'll wait," Belle said. "I'm tired, Miss Charlotte," Belle redirected her comments. "I would like to go to bed now if you don't mind."

"Belle, get some rest. I will make coffee for you in the morning. We have fresh blueberries that we can have with our cereal. That way you won't have to cook tomorrow," Charlotte said, instructing Belle to rest as long as she needed.

Charlotte and Caroline sat on the front porch talking until eleven o'clock. The gas lanterns gave the porch a beautiful glow. The warm spring night with the smell of honeysuckle and fresh mowed grass made them want to stay on the porch all night. "If I weren't so tired, I would sit out here another hour to talk with you, Mama," Caroline said as she stood to go in the house. "But I am pooped."

"Okay, sweetheart," Charlotte said as she followed Caroline into the house. "Sweet dreams."

"Sweet dreams, Mama," Caroline said, giving her mother a kiss on her cheek. Halfway up the stairs, Caroline stopped and looked back to her mother in the foyer. "I want to go to the cemetery tomorrow," she said.

"We can do that whenever you like," Charlotte said.

"Thanks, Mama," Caroline replied with profound sadness returning to her voice.

Caroline did sleep until noon. Charlotte had been up since six o'clock and was glad to see her sleepy-eyed daughter. Caroline quickly ate cereal, showered, and was ready to go to the cemetery. As was their custom, they stopped at the florist in Sandy Springs to buy summer silk flowers. As they walked to the gravesite for John, Caroline said, "It's hard to believe he has been gone for almost a year and a half."

"Sometimes it seems to me that he has been gone for years, and other times it seems like just the other day," Charlotte confessed.

"I just keep thinking he's going to be at home when I get there," Caroline said sadly.

"I wish he were here to see you now, Caroline," Charlotte said. "He would be so proud of you—like I am," she continued. "You finished your first year on the dean's list and qualifying for advanced classes in all of your subjects. You certainly have his intelligence, Caroline."

"I think so too, Mama, but how could I lose with two very bright parents," Caroline said, complimenting her mother. "You can do anything you decide to do, Mama," Caroline continued, affirming her mother. "I've watched you handle some of the most difficult situations anyone could face."

"We have had some difficult situations, haven't we?" Charlotte said as more of a statement than a question. "Let's sit here on the bench under this tree for a while, Caroline," Charlotte said, knowing that now was the time to tell Caroline about Belle. The two of them sat under the tree enjoying the warm June sun. "You know, Caroline," Charlotte began, "there will always be difficulties to face during our lives. We can't escape that."

"Yes, I have seen that, Mama," Caroline replied, sensing that her mother had something more to say. "What's going on, Mama?" Caroline asked directly.

Charlotte cleared her throat. "Belle is ill, Caroline," Charlotte tried to soften the news as much as possible. "She has ovarian cancer. It is late stage, and nothing can be done. Robert and Karen's baby is due in the middle of September. Belle wants to be able to see her grandniece or nephew before she leaves us."

Caroline could not speak. "What else can happen to us, Mama?" Caroline said, starting to cry. "I love Belle so much."

"We all do, honey. We have to be strong for her and make the rest of her life as happy as possible. She deserves that," Charlotte said pragmatically.

"We will do more than that, Mama," Caroline said. "Let's be sure Robert and Karen have a good home to raise their baby in. We can buy them a house, Mama. We can get furniture for the nursery and the rest of the house. Belle would be so happy to see them in their own home."

"Robert is a very proud man, Caroline," Charlotte said, expecting an argument. "He may not allow us to do that."

"Mama, you and I have more money than we will ever spend. We will do this for Belle. It will make her very happy. She is already proud of him, so this will be icing on the cake for her. I have to be able to do something for her. I can't just stand around and allow her to leave us without giving her something to enjoy before she dies!" Caroline said, pleading with her mother. "This would be the best gift we could give her."

"You're right, Caroline," Charlotte conceded. "Let's do it!"

The following week, Charlotte called a realtor whom she had known for thirty years. "Cathy, this is Charlotte Wellington," she said when Cathy answered her telephone.

"Charlotte, how are you?" Cathy Bishop asked.

"I'm doing well, Cathy. I need your help," Charlotte announced. She explained the situation and told her that she wanted Robert and Karen to pick their own home and Charlotte would purchase the home for them. Cathy was familiar with the Wellington family wealth, and she was only too happy to help her. There were only a couple of areas around Roswell where black families lived; those areas were not what Charlotte had in mind. After discussing the request with Cathy for several days, they decided that the only thing to do was to purchase acreage and build a house for them.

It was the following week when Charlotte called Robert and Karen to come to the house to discuss a proposition. She did not want Belle in on the initial discussion. Charlotte rolled out the plans to the young couple. Robert was stunned, and Karen was giddy. There was a tract of land about two miles from where Charlotte lived that she could buy from the Westbrook family. It was eight acres and had an old barn on the property. Charlotte engaged Charles Fowler, a builder in Roswell, to construct the house. He would work directly with Robert and Karen in choosing everything for the house. Charlotte would purchase the land and would have the house built by her for the records. She would give the house to Robert and Karen later when they were settled and had made the decision to stay in Roswell.

It was a beautiful, three-bedroom, two and one-half bathroom brick ranch house. It had a two-car garage and a screened porch on the back of the house. The basement had a large room and another bathroom that Charlotte had the builder finish as a playroom for the baby. Mr. Fowler finished the house in just over two months. On September 1, Robert and Karen moved into the house. Everything was perfect for them. Karen had stopped working the month before and looked like she could have the baby any minute. Robert's mother and father and Karen's mother were on hand for the move.

Belle was overwhelmed by the generous gift to her nephew. Charlotte knew it gave her some peace that she didn't have before.

All summer, Charlotte and Caroline worked on the project, insisting that Karen and Robert spend as much time as they could with Belle.

On September 14, Miss Samantha Belle Pritchett was born at Georgia Baptist Hospital in Atlanta. Although she was not feeling well most days, Belle was at the hospital with a smile from ear to ear. She got to hold Samantha first. Tom and Mae were right behind her in line to hold the beautiful little girl. Robert beamed, and Karen was happy but tired. On the fourth day, Robert and Karen took Samantha home to Roswell.

Belle's gift was a ten thousand dollar savings account for Samantha with instructions that it was to be used for her college education. Belle insisted that Robert and Karen see to it that she have a good education and a better life. Belle knew that Robert would do his best to honor her wishes. Although Belle tried to be strong, she was in pain more than ever. Her pain medication had been increased, and some days she barely got out of the bed. Charlotte and Irene saw to it that she had three meals and help with bathing and dressing and that she was taken to her doctor's appointments.

Caroline had to leave to go back to UVA to start her sophomore year on September 21. Two days before, she was packing and planning and dreading the drive. It was early in the morning when she heard her mother coming up the stairs. She stepped into the doorway of Caroline's room. "Caroline, Belle passed away during the night. I found her in her cottage this morning," Charlotte said, crying softly. "I have called the funeral home. They will be here to pick her up in a couple of hours. Robert and Karen are on their way over, and Tom and Mae are coming. You'd better get dressed."

Caroline sat down on the side her bed and cried. "Mama, how can I say good-bye to Belle? She has been with me every day of my life. I love her so dearly," she said as she cried. Caroline put shorts and a shirt on and ran downstairs and out to the cottage. Belle looked peaceful. She had a picture of Samantha in her hand. "Belle, please don't leave me yet!" Caroline begged. "I love you, Belle."

Charlotte walked up behind her and put her arms around her. "She is happy today, Caroline. She is with her mother and father. She told me she was looking forward to seeing them again," Charlotte said, struggling to keep her composure. Irene walked into the cottage with Caroline and Charlotte.

"Lord have mercy!" Irene said. "What are we going to do without her?" Irene stood beside Belle and touched her hand. "Belle, we all love you so much. Go on now. The angels have come for you. We will meet again, my precious Belle," Irene said tenderly as tears fell from her eyes.

Irene, Charlotte, and Caroline waited until Robert and Karen arrived before they left the cottage. Charlotte took Samantha from Karen and looked after her until Robert's parents arrived. Tom and Mae helped Robert with the funeral arrangements. Three days later, after a beautiful funeral at Robert's church, it was over. Belle was buried near John in Arlington Cemetery. Their church members brought food to their house, and Tom and Mae stayed with them for the next week. They were all thankful for Samantha, especially now.

The next day, when Charlotte was going through her cottage, she found three envelopes. One had her name, one had Caroline's name, and one had Irene's name on it.

Charlotte opened her letter.

> Dear Miss Charlotte, You have blessed my life since you were three years old. I have no words that will adequately tell you what you mean to me. I have watched you all of your life handle difficulties with grace. Thank you for everything you have done for me. Thank you even more for what you have done for Robert and Karen. I will be watching over Samantha. I hope she has a chance to learn how to be a graceful lady from you. I love you and I wish you peace and happiness.
>
> Love, Belle

Charlotte cried as she walked through Belle's cottage, where she had stored memories of her lifetime. She found old photographs of Jim and Kibbie. She knew that Robert would want the photographs. She took them to keep them safe until she could give them to him.

Charlotte took the other two letters into the house and put them on the kitchen table. She knew that Caroline and Irene would find them. Caroline delayed returning to UVA, but she had to leave tomorrow. She walked into the kitchen about an hour later and found the envelope with her name on it in Belle's handwriting. She opened it.

> Dear Miss Caroline, You have been a light in my life since the day you were born. I don't think I have ever seen a more beautiful baby than you. You are a shining star. Remember that difficulties in life make us stronger. You are a strong, beautiful young woman, just like your mother. Your father would be so proud of you. He loved you so dearly. I saw the love in his eyes every time he looked at you. Your mama was right when she said that love is the strongest thing in the universe. My love for you and your family will be forever. Take care of your mother. I want you to have my biscuits recipe and my pimento cheese recipe. So here they are. Don't share them with just anybody. You hear?
>
> I love you, Belle

Caroline laughed and cried at the same time. "Don't you worry, Belle. Your recipes are safe with me," Caroline said out loud.

Later that afternoon, Irene walked through the back door into the kitchen. "Lord have mercy!" she exclaimed. "It seems like Belle should be in here fixing dinner." Charlotte was in the living room and heard her mother.

"It sure does," she shouted so her mother could hear. "Come in here with me, Mother," Charlotte said to Irene. "I can't stand to be in the kitchen right now. I will get used to her being gone, but it hurts my heart so much right now," Charlotte said as Irene walked into the living room. It was a seldom-used room, but Charlotte was enjoying the beautiful day with the afternoon sun giving the room a warm glow as it came through the windows. Outside, the big oak tree was showing signs of yielding its green leaves to the crimson the fall air would bring.

Charlotte was sitting in one of the Queen Anne chairs. Irene sat on the sofa near her. Irene took Charlotte's hands. "Charlotte," she began, "You make me so proud every day."

"Mother, thank you for saying that. I love you very much. Right now, I am just plain tired," she confessed. "I hate to see Caroline leave for school. This house is going to feel so empty."

"You will find something to fill it up, Charlotte," Irene said convincingly.

"You're probably right," Charlotte said, patting her mother's hand and leaning forward to kiss her cheek. "I think I want to do some traveling now," she revealed. "The Woodruff Arts Center is going to open soon. I want to be an arts patron. You know that two of our close friends were killed in that Orly plane crash in 1962. Bill and Betty Bennett were very active in the arts in Atlanta. It has always interested me, but I haven't really had time until now to devote to it. Besides, I will meet some nice people and get reacquainted with some old friends. The opportunity to travel will be there, and I won't have to go alone."

"Charlotte, do you want to meet someone you can marry?" Irene asked directly.

"No, Mother," Charlotte retorted. "That is not the purpose. I'm not interested in marriage now, and I may never be again."

"Just asking," Irene said defensively.

"Sorry, Mother," Charlotte said apologetically. "Did you see the envelope that Belle left for you in the kitchen?" Charlotte said, changing the subject.

"No, not yet," Irene said as she rose to go to the kitchen. Charlotte walked up behind her as Irene opened the envelope.

> Miss Irene, my mother was so wise to be sure I was working for you before she died. You and all of your family have given me so much during my life. I am glad that we became friends too. Your strength runs through this family like a silver thread holding everyone together and in the right place. Thank you for your love and for allowing me to work for Miss Charlotte. As I leave this life, I am very blessed with love all around me. Please help me watch over Samantha. Robert will look to you and Miss Charlotte for guidance. I told him to do that. I know I will see you again. Until then, please keep my love in your heart.
>
> Love, Belle

Irene knew that she would, indeed, see Belle again soon.

CHAPTER 30

*C*AROLINE WAS BACK IN SCHOOL and working to catch up for the days she had missed. It was mid-October, and she was walking to the library to work on a project when she ran into Garrett. "Caroline!" Garrett stopped, looking happy to see her. "I haven't seen you at all this year. Where have you been hiding?"

"Not hiding, Garrett," Caroline replied, feeling somewhat disinterested. "I was late getting back to school, and I have been playing catch up. Belle passed away just before I was planning to leave. I stayed until after the funeral."

"Caroline, I'm so sorry. I know how much you and your family loved her," Garrett said, sounding genuinely sympathetic.

"Maybe I'll see you around campus soon," Caroline said as she turned and continued walking to the library.

Garrett made up his mind right then to forget about Caroline Wellington. They only saw one another in passing for the rest of their time at UVA.

———◦◦◦———

Caroline could hardly believe that her sophomore year was almost over. She decided to go to Kennebunkport with Jackie for spring break. She and Jackie had become very close friends and spent a lot of time together when their schedules allowed it. They arrived on Saturday afternoon, April 13. Jackie's mother greeted them at the Portland airport. Their home was twenty-five miles from Portland, and Caroline had time to get to know Jackie's mother on the trip to her home. It was about a mile from Drake Island, and there was a view of the estuary from the back of their home. Caroline felt the warmth and love that had been shared there. It was a New England-style house with five dormer windows in the roof. Jackie's room was over the attached garage. It was actually two rooms with a bathroom, giving her separate living and sleeping space. She had moved her room from the upstairs bedroom when she was a senior in high school. "It's like having my own apartment but still being home," Jackie said as she showed Caroline into the spacious apartment.

"Wow!" Caroline exclaimed. "This is really great, Jackie!" Caroline said, looking around the room and at the views outside her windows.

"Let's put our stuff away and then get something to eat. Mother always has something good for me," Jackie said as she offered Caroline space in her closet. When they were satisfied with unpacking for the week, the girls went down the back staircase and into the rear entrance of the house. The garage and apartment were attached to the house, and the girls did not have to go outside to get to the main house. Today they were thankful for that. It was cold and gray outside. There was a roaring fire in the great room's stone fireplace. Mrs. Lillian Rhoades had hot chocolate, coffee, and a delicious caramel cake waiting for the girls.

"Mrs. Rhoades, your home is beautiful. I love the views," Caroline said as she sat down with a cup of coffee.

"We love it here, Caroline," Lillian said. "Jackie's dad and I think we will just stay here when we retire."

"I can understand why you would want to do that," Caroline said, continuing the conversation as she sipped her coffee. "I hope you will show me around Kennebunkport while we are here."

"I already have our time planned," Jackie interjected. "I will take you to some of the neatest places. Can't wait for you to see the views from one of my favorite restaurants."

"*Ooooh!*" Caroline exclaimed. "Sounds fabulous!" The three women sat enjoying the warmth of the fire and coffee for the next two hours. Caroline really liked the comfortable house, and of course the porch was her favorite room.

Later that evening, after a dinner of lamb stew, the two girls were in Jackie's apartment room talking. "Jackie, I have been wanting to ask you something for a long time," Caroline said, hesitating somewhat.

"I know what it's about, Caroline," Jackie replied. "I should have talked with you about it before now. You want to know about the time I was raped."

"Yes, I do, Jackie," Caroline said with concern in her voice. "I actually hoped I could help you in some way."

"I'm really okay now," Jackie said honestly. "But it took a while and a lot of therapy for me to get there."

"What happened?" Caroline quizzed.

"I was fifteen years old and we had a guy who worked for my father's company who came and did work for us here at the house sometimes," Jackie began. "You know, handyman work and stuff like that. He was in his early thirties, and my father gave him a job and helped him get on his feet. He came from a very bad background and never really had parents. His father was killed in an automobile accident when he was very young, and his mother was an alcoholic who died when he was seventeen. He lived with families in Portland who would take him in for several months at a time. He managed to graduate from high school, but that was it for him.

"Anyway, he lived in a small garage apartment and worked for my dad's timber company. One Saturday, my parents went to have dinner with friends. I was here by myself, and Dan was working to repair some floor joists that were damaged by termites. We never locked the back door during the day because it is so safe here. No one did. I was in my room making a scrapbook of pictures of my friends. He walked into my room and asked when my parents would be back. It never occurred to me that he had anything like that on his mind. I told him they would probably be home in a couple of hours." Caroline was listening intently, not saying anything. "He walked over to where I was sitting on my bed and put his arm around me. He told me he always thought I was beautiful. I stood up to walk out of my room because I was feeling scared. He grabbed me by my arms, shoved me on the bed, and raped me for almost an hour. I was a virgin, so I was pretty messed up. I screamed so much I was hoarse, but my parents came home early and my father heard me and walked into my room just as he was getting off me. My mother called the police, and they came and got him. My father had beat him so badly he had to be hospitalized. I was taken to the emergency room, and I stayed in the hospital for two days. I was so torn up there I had to have stitches."

"Oh my God!" Caroline exclaimed horrified at the story her friend was telling her. "I can't imagine how horrible that must have been for you! Are you sure you are okay talking about it now?"

"I try not to think about it, but it has affected me, especially in my relationship with guys. I'm working on being able to allow someone to get close to me. I haven't been able to have a boyfriend since then. I have dates once in a while, but I just can't allow myself to get close to anyone in that way."

"I can understand that, Jackie. But you really have to work on not letting that monster take away a good part of your life. Someday, you will meet someone and fall in love and get married. You have to allow that person to love you in every way," Caroline counseled her friend.

"I know you're right," Jackie said. "I just have to work on it in my own time."

"If I can help you in any way, please let me know, okay?" Caroline said genuinely. She stood and walked over and gave Jackie a hug. "You are an amazing person, Jackie," Caroline said. "Look at you. You are smart, funny, thoughtful, and so much more. Everyone loves you. You will be just fine. The person who deserves a fabulous person like you just has not come along yet."

Jackie looked at Caroline and smiled. "I'm really glad we are friends, Caroline," Jackie said sweetly.

"Me too," Caroline said. "Okay," Caroline continued. "What happened to that monster?"

"He was convicted and put away for forty years. My father was not charged with beating him. I think everyone on the jury thought they would have done the same thing if it had been their child."

"Well, any decent human being would think that, Jackie!" Caroline exclaimed. "Thank you for sharing that with me. I know it was difficult. Anytime you need to talk, I'm as close as you need for me to be, okay?"

"Thanks, Caroline," Jackie said.

Caroline and Jackie enjoyed the spring break week, going to a different place every day. They visited Cape Porpoise and Goose Rocks Beach with its beautiful white sandy beaches. Caroline was struck by how different this part of the Atlantic Coast was from Sea Island. Jackie told Caroline about the history of the area, which went back to the 1600s when the original settlers were there with the Indians. They went antiquing at Arundel, and Caroline loved the beautiful, historical homes there. Most of the homes were on very large tracts of land. A peaceful feeling permeated the whole area, and Caroline wanted to tell her mother about it and bring her up here some time. She thought that Lillian and her mother would be good friends. When Caroline and Jackie returned to school at the end of that week, they both knew that their friendship would last a lifetime.

The years came and went so fast. Charlotte was traveling, Irene was volunteering at her church and playing canasta, and Caroline was working to finish her undergraduate degree. The following summer, Charlotte went to Kennebunkport with Caroline to meet Jackie and her parents. Charlotte fell in love with the New England coast and entertained the idea of buying a home there. She decided not to do that as long as her mother was alive.

Lillian and Charlotte became good friends and enjoyed talking about their daughters and their plans for the future. Although they did not have an opportunity to visit again, they wrote letters, and their friendship grew over the next two years while the girls were at UVA.

Caroline was easily accepted to Emory Law School and was looking forward to a change. She loved Charlottesville and UVA, but she was tired. She learned that she would graduate summa cum laude with a double major in political science and French. Charlotte and Irene flew to Charlottesville for Caroline's graduation. They were so proud of her, and she was recognized many times during the ceremony. She had distinguished herself admirably.

Caroline regretted that Belle never got to come to see her there. She still thought about her almost every day.

Following graduation, Charlotte had movers empty her dormitory room and move the furniture to Roswell. She would allow Caroline to decide what she wanted to keep when she moved into housing near the Emory Campus in the fall.

Caroline stayed home with her mother for the summer. They managed to get in a two-week vacation to Paris and London before she started her internship. Charlotte wanted Irene to go with them, but she declined the invitation, fearing she could not keep up with them.

They were both glad to make new memories there. They talked about John and the places they saw when they were there when Caroline was twelve. Caroline knew that Charlotte's life was pretty empty now. She was still very beautiful, and Caroline found herself hoping that her mother would find someone she could love and marry again.

Caroline had an internship lined up at the King and Spalding law firm in Atlanta for the summer. Many important connections were there that would be helpful to her later as she worked to choose the best law firm to join after graduation. The managing partner of the firm was a seasoned veteran at the firm in Atlanta. Lawrence Harris's area of practice was corporate contract law. Caroline knew him by reputation. She did not know that she would be recognized by her father's reputation until her first day at the firm.

"Miss Wellington," Mr. Harris said, welcoming her into his office. "I imagine that we can expect great things from you. I knew your father, and I must say I was glad that I did not have to face him in court. He was a brilliant lawyer."

"Thank you, Mr. Harris," Caroline said. "I know he certainly did a wonderful job at Georgia Life," she continued. The Wellingtons' wealth and power continued to be well known throughout Atlanta.

"May I say that I am very sorry that you lost him when you were so young," Lawrence Harris continued in a benevolent tone.

"Thank you, Mr. Harris," Caroline said. "Do you know where I will be assigned?" she said, hoping the subject would be changed for good.

"Yes," he replied. "I would like for you to work with George Hampton in our litigation group. I think that will be very good experience for you."

"Thank you, Mr. Harris," Caroline said. "Shall I meet him today?"

"You shall," Mr. Harris said. He pressed a button on his telephone. "Grace," he started speaking toward the phone. "Please have George Hampton come into my office to meet Caroline Wellington."

"Yes, sir, Mr. Harris" came the reply over the speaker.

In less than a minute, George Hampton walked into Lawrence Harris's office. "Good morning, Miss Wellington," he said, extending his hand. He was a very handsome man in his midforties.

"Mr. Hampton," Caroline replied. "It's a pleasure to meet you."

"George, I leave her in your capable hands. Miss Wellington, please let me know if I can do anything for you. My door is always open."

"Thank you, Mr. Harris," Caroline said. And she left with Mr. Hampton.

The summer seemed to fly. Caroline enjoyed her internship, but she was glad to have a break before starting law school. The time she spent in George Hampton's group made her think that litigation might be a good fit for her. George gave her high praise as a first-year intern and credited her with excellent contributions to his cases.

She rented a small house in Druid Hills near the Emory campus. It had three bedrooms, and she loved the small screened porch on the front of the house. Continuing to maintain a low profile was very important to

Caroline, and the house was close enough to campus to be convenient but far enough away that she could maintain her privacy.

She was very busy with her classes and getting settled. Her telephone rang one Thursday evening in late September. "Hello," Caroline said, expecting to hear her mother's voice.

"Caroline" came the familiar voice on the other end of the line. "This is Garrett."

"Garrett, how are you?" Caroline said cordially.

"I'm doing fine. I'm in Atlanta for an interview. I will be here for a couple of days. I was hoping I could talk you into having dinner with me tomorrow evening."

Caroline hesitated, trying to decide if she should or not and trying to decide if she had a good enough excuse to refuse. "Sure," she finally replied. "Why don't you meet me at the Abbey on Ponce de Leon at seven o'clock?"

"It's a date," Garrett said, sounding relieved and excited at the same time. "Hey, Caroline," he continued, "thanks." And he hung up.

Caroline was almost twenty-two years old, but she ran everything by her mother. The response she got was not what she expected. "Caroline," Charlotte said after Caroline explained Garrett's call, "I can't tell you what to do, nor will I. You and Garrett seem to have been connected off and on for about four years now. I hope the two of you have matured enough to determine whether your relationship is right. The only way you will know is to see him, talk with him, and decide if what you thought you had in your freshman year is worth continuing."

Caroline felt scolded. She was embarrassed and humiliated. "Mama, I can't talk with anyone else about this. I just wanted to run it by you. Isn't that okay?" Caroline said, sounding frustrated.

"Caroline, I love you more than anything on earth. My love for you is leading me to step away and allow you to make your own decisions without my input."

"You'll have to give me some time to get used to that idea, Mama," Caroline said with hurt feelings coming through the telephone.

"I'm sorry, sweetheart. What I really want to do is have you get out of law school and come home and live with me forever," Charlotte said softly. "But that is not right for either one of us, and I know it. Listen, Garrett is really a wonderful boy. He obviously cares for you or he wouldn't continue to set himself up for rejection. So go and see what he has to say. Enjoy your dinner and go from there."

"That's what I was going to do, but I just wanted to have your opinion," Caroline said timidly. "Mama, I really do think I still love him," she continued, confessing her feelings.

"Well, Caroline, there's only one way to find out, and you will start finding out tomorrow night."

"Yes, I will," Caroline said. Charlotte could hear happiness in her voice for the first time in a long time. The conversation ended.

Friday evening, Caroline arrived at the Abbey restaurant at about 7:10. Garrett was standing in the lobby of the restaurant with the biggest smile she ever saw. "Hello, beautiful," he said as he stepped to give her a hug.

"Garrett, it's very good to see you," Caroline gushed before she thought. It was almost as if their relationship had never ended.

"I can't wait to hear about your summer and law school," Garrett said as they were escorted to their table.

"What is your interview about?" Caroline asked as they were seated.

"Believe it or not, I may be working for a Georgia senator. I would be in Washington most of the time, but I would be connected to his office in Atlanta too," Garrett said, sounding as if the irony of his opportunity would not be lost on Caroline.

"That's amazing!" Caroline exclaimed. "Who is the senator you will be working for?"

"Richard Russell," Garrett said.

"Good heavens!" Caroline exclaimed again. "Why don't you just start at the top!" They laughed.

"It seems like a really good opportunity for me," Garrett said.

"I would say that it is, Mr. Winthrop," Caroline laughed.

They laughed and talked during dinner as if no time had passed. Caroline couldn't remember feeling this good for a long time. At the end of dinner, Garrett said, "Caroline, I never stopped loving you. I love you today. I don't want to spend my life without you. Please say you feel the same way," he pleaded.

Caroline sat back in her chair and studied his face for a long time. Finally she spoke. "Garrett, I never stopped loving you either."

Garrett took her hand and kissed it. "Could we go to your house and talk?" he asked.

"That's a good idea," she said. "You will love my screened porch."

When they arrived at Caroline's comfortable bungalow, Garrett walked in the door and told her how much he loved it. "This is really perfect for you, Caroline. It's private and very cozy. You've done a good job making it feel comfortable," Garrett said, complimenting her.

"I'll make coffee, and we can enjoy sitting on the porch," she said as she escorted him outside. She was turning to walk back to the kitchen when Garrett took her arm. He pulled her into his arms and kissed her. At that moment, Caroline knew she would marry Garrett Winthrop.

Caroline felt an emotion that she had not felt before with Garrett. All of her defenses fell down, and she cried. She put her arms around him, put her head on his shoulder, and cried. He held her tight. "Caroline, I love you so much," Garrett said softly as Caroline pulled away to look at him.

"I obviously love you too, Garrett," Caroline said. "I have tried to stay busy and not think about you for so long. Thank you for calling me. I'm sorry I left you, and I'm sorry I didn't talk with you at school. I was not in a good place then," Caroline said, confessing her feelings to Garrett in a way she never had before.

"Well, I have to tell you, I tried to forget about our relationship. I worked on it for a couple of years, but I just can't let you go," he said honestly. "Believe me, I tried, more for your sake than for mine, if I tell you the truth," he continued. "But Caroline, my feelings for you are so strong that I had to try one more time."

"I'm glad you did," Caroline said. "Let's make coffee," she said lightheartedly. They walked into her small 1930s kitchen. When the coffee was brewing, they walked back to the porch. They could hear the crickets and the katydids chirping. It was a peaceful sound to Caroline.

Garrett sat down next to her on the loveseat. "Caroline," he began. She saw him pause to take a deep breath. "Will you marry me?" he said earnestly.

"I will marry you, Garrett Winthrop," Caroline said and smiled from ear to ear. She saw a tear roll down his cheek as he kissed her.

Garrett reached into his pants pocket and pulled out a blue Tiffany's box. "Only the best for you, Caroline," Garrett said as he opened the beautiful box, revealing a two-carat solitaire diamond in a platinum setting. Caroline's mouth fell open.

"Garrett, how did you know I would say 'yes'?"

"I didn't, but just in case you did, I wanted to be ready," he replied boyishly.

"You are so precious, Garrett," Caroline said sweetly. "I know I will love you more and more, but right now I just don't know how that is possible."

"Caroline, you are the most beautiful, wonderful person I have ever known." His feelings gushed like a pent-up creek flowing for the first time in years.

They drank coffee and talked until three o'clock. Neither of them realized that it was so late. I'd better get back to my hotel. I have to meet with one of Mr. Russell's chief's tomorrow at eleven o'clock."

"You're going to be exhausted, Garrett," Caroline said instructively. "Just stay here. I have an extra bedroom."

Garrett agreed, and Caroline escorted him to the extra bedroom. It was a comfortable room with a double bed. Caroline kissed him good night and disappeared to her room. *It isn't the right time, not yet,* she thought.

Caroline was up at eight o'clock making Belle's biscuits for Garrett. When he appeared at the kitchen door, he said, "Is this what I can expect every morning?"

Caroline looked up from the bacon she was frying and said, "Well, that depends."

"Depends on what?" Garrett said as he walked toward her. He kissed her on the cheek and took her in his arms. "This is right, Caroline," Garrett said. "Our love is right."

"It feels right to me too, Garrett," Caroline said. "Let me get you fed and off to your meeting," she said, laughing.

"I didn't know you could cook," Garrett said playfully.

"Osmosis—I learned by osmosis," Caroline replied. "Belle was the best cook on earth," Caroline said. "I watched her for years when I was a little girl. My parents traveled sometimes, and I would be home with Belle and Katy, my nanny. I always wanted to be in the kitchen with Belle. So that is where I parked myself. She let me help her and she taught me how to cook. We had so many wonderful conversations." Caroline's thoughts seemed to wander off.

"I know you miss her," Garrett said sweetly.

"There will never be another Belle anywhere, anytime. I am sure of it," she said.

"So when I am finished with my meeting, can I come back to your house?" Garrett asked childishly.

"You certainly can," Caroline said, smiling. "What time shall I expect you?"

"How about two o'clock?"

"That works," Caroline said. "We have to tell our parents, you know," she said.

"My mother will be so glad," Garrett said. "She has worried about me."

"Mrs. Winthrop, worry no more!" Caroline said, lifting the biscuits out of the oven.

They enjoyed breakfast together. Caroline didn't tell him that was her first attempt to make Belle's biscuits. She was rather proud of herself. They tasted pretty good.

When Garrett left, Caroline wanted to call her mother. She resisted the temptation and decided to wait until he got back to her house that afternoon. They would tell her mother and his parents at the same time. She had to start thinking as a couple and not as an individual. That would be a challenge for her. She was independent and opinionated. She hoped Garrett could handle that. She busied herself with schoolwork and a few household chores. She had refused her mother's offer to have her housekeeper come to her house once a week. Her house was so small that she knew she could take care of it even with a full load in law school.

Garrett returned exactly at two o'clock. "I hope you don't mind that I checked out of my hotel. I would love to stay with you until I have to leave on Monday," he said confidently.

"You can stay here, Garrett. Let's try to keep you in the other bedroom, okay?" Caroline said, laughing as he was walking in the front door.

"No promises," he said, looking coyly at her. Garrett put his bags down in the guest bedroom. He walked back into the kitchen, and they went to sit on the porch, Caroline's favorite room. They sat for an hour and talked about their day before she finally said, "I am dying to tell my mother."

"Okay," he said. "Let's call her." Caroline dialed her mother's telephone number.

"Hello," Charlotte said cordially.

"Mama it's me," Caroline said.

"Well, hello, me," Charlotte said playfully. "How was your dinner?"

"Well, that's what I called you about." Charlotte detected a happy tone in Caroline's voice. "Garrett and I are engaged," she blurted. Silence followed on the other end of the line. "Mama, are you there?" Caroline said.

"I'm here, all right, Caroline," Charlotte said flatly. "Did you say, 'engaged'?"

"I did say that, Mama," Caroline said.

"Caroline, I knew it. You two were right for each other from the very beginning!" Charlotte laughed.

"Oh, Mama, is this how you loved Daddy?" Caroline asked.

"Yes, it is, sweetheart," Charlotte said.

"I understand so much now, Mama," Caroline said softly. "I love you."

"I love you too, sweetheart," Charlotte replied. "Is he there with you now?" she asked.

"Yes, he's right here," Caroline replied.

"Could I talk with him?" Charlotte asked genuinely.

Caroline handed the phone to Garrett. "She wants to talk with you," she whispered.

"Mrs. Wellington," Garrett said.

"Garrett, congratulations!" Charlotte said immediately. "Your tenacity has paid off." Garrett laughed.

"It did, didn't it, Mrs. Wellington?" Garrett said, laughing. "May I ask for your blessing?" Garrett said genuinely.

"You may, and you have it, Garrett," Charlotte said. "You must agree to take great care with my only child, Garrett," Charlotte instructed. "Any deviation will incur repercussions," she said laughing.

"I would expect no less, Mrs. Wellington," Garrett replied gallantly.

"May I speak with Caroline again, Garrett?" Charlotte asked.

"Of course," Garrett replied and handled the telephone to Caroline.

"Mama," Caroline said, "Are you really okay with this?"

"Caroline, I knew you were going to marry Garrett the first time I met him. I just had to let you figure that out," Charlotte said.

Caroline laughed hysterically. "Mama, I am done talking with you today!" Caroline said, and she hung up still laughing.

"Let's call your parents, Garrett," Caroline said. "Do you want to?"

"Of course," Garrett replied. He dialed his home telephone number in Charleston.

"Hello" came Laura's voice on the other end of the line.

"Hi, Mom," Garrett started.

"Garrett," Laura began the conversation, "how was your meeting today?"

"It was great," Garrett replied. "Looks like I will be working for Senator Russell."

"Son, that's great!" Laura said, sounding very proud of her oldest child. "Your dad will be very happy to hear that," she continued.

"Mom, I called you for another reason too," Garrett said, leading his mother to ask, "Okay, Garrett, what is it?"

"I called Caroline when I got to Atlanta. We had dinner last night," he said casually.

"How did that go?" Laura asked, bracing herself for another rejection story.

"Caroline and I are engaged!" Garrett said, sounding happier than she had heard him for a long time.

"Garrett!" Laura exclaimed. "Really?"

"Yes, really, Mom," he replied.

"I'm very happy for both of you, Garrett," Laura said genuinely. "I want nothing more than for you to be happy, Son," she continued. "Your dad will be home from the golf course in an hour or so. He will want to talk with you too, honey," Laura said, letting the news really sink in.

"Mom, Caroline wants to talk with you," Garrett said, listening to hear his mother's openness to that request.

"Well, of course, honey," Laura said.

"Mrs. Winthrop," Caroline began, "Garrett and I are so happy. You have a very determined son," she said, laughing.

"Apparently so," Laura said, laughing with Caroline. "Congratulations, Caroline!" Laura said genuinely. "I want the two of you to be happy and enjoy your lives together."

"We do too, Mrs. Winthrop," Caroline replied. "I think we just had to grow up to realize how much we mean to each other."

"I'm sure you're right, Caroline," Laura said, thinking what a mature, grounded girl Caroline was.

"I hope to see you and Mr. Winthrop and Emily and Allison soon," Caroline said, working to keep the conversation positive.

"We want to see you as soon as you can work it out, Caroline," Laura said sweetly.

"Thank you," Caroline said, and she handed the telephone back to Garrett.

"Mom, Caroline and I have some things to discuss, so I'm signing off for now," Garrett said. And he hung up the phone.

Laura stood in the kitchen looking at the telephone trying to believe what she had just heard. Could her son be getting married? She had a lot of questions. "I hope he's doing the right thing," Laura said out loud to herself. When Derek came in from Saturday golfing, Laura greeted him at the door. "Hi, sweetheart," she said, smiling. "How was your game?"

"Pretty good," Derek said, sounding tired. "Rick knocked me out of first place on the back nine."

"I guess that means you came in second, huh?" Laura asked.

"Yep, that's what it means," Derek said. He walked to the family room and poured a scotch and water and sat down to watch the baseball playoffs.

Laura sat on the sofa in the place nearest his chair. "Derek, Garrett called," she said casually.

"Really!" Derek replied, turning his full attention to Laura. "How did his meeting go?"

"He got the appointment to work with Senator Russell," she said proudly. "Aren't you proud of him?"

"I sure am, honey," Derek replied. "He is quite a boy, I have to say, even if he is my son," he continued as he sipped his scotch.

"Oh, by the way, he had other news," Laura said as if as an afterthought.

"What's that?" Derek asked, expecting her to continue the information about his job.

"Well, it seems that he called Caroline when he got to Atlanta," Laura began. Once again, Derek's full attention was on Laura.

"Oh yea?" he said sarcastically.

"They had dinner on Friday night. They're engaged," Laura just blurted the rest of the story.

Derek stood up. "What?" he shouted. "After all the rejection and all the trouble, he called her one more time and now they are engaged?"

"That's what he said," Laura replied. "Sit down, Derek," Laura instructed. "Garrett is twenty-two years old. He managed to get through UVA graduating with honors. He has landed a job with a senior senator and will be living in Washington and traveling

279

throughout the United States. Give the boy some credit, Derek," Laura pleaded. "He loves her, and apparently she loves him too."

"You believe what you want to believe, Laura," Derek said. "She caused a lot of trouble here, if you remember, Laura."

"Derek, she did not cause the trouble. You and Greg caused the trouble, as I recall," Laura stared at him pursing her lips angrily.

"Is he going to call us back?" Derek asked.

"I'm sure he will. And, I hope you will be supportive. They have a lot to talk about right now. He'll call us in the next day or so I am sure."

"I can't forget what happened, Laura," Derek raised his voice.

"I don't imagine she can either, Derek," Laura responded, raising her voice too.

Derek resumed drinking his scotch and watching baseball.

That didn't go very well, Laura thought to herself as she walked back into the kitchen.

CHAPTER 31

*I*T WAS SUNDAY MORNING, AND Caroline had managed to keep Garrett in the guest bedroom for the night. They shared passionate kisses for at least an hour, but they both remained in control. Caroline was thankful.

Garrett walked into the small kitchen just as Caroline was pouring a cup of coffee. "Your timing is perfect," she said, smiling and walking to give him a hug.

"Caroline, you are beautiful all the time," Garrett complimented her. "Maybe even more beautiful in your nightgown."

"Thank you," Caroline said, blushing. "I have a favor to ask of you today," Caroline said, changing the subject. "I would like to tell my grandparents about our engagement. They're pretty old now, and my grandmother is quite ill. If they agree to see me today, would you go with me and meet them?" Caroline asked anxiously, waiting for his reply.

"Sure, Caroline," Garrett said. "I would like to meet them anyway," he said, obviously very cooperative.

Caroline dialed the telephone to her grandparents' home. Grant answered, "Hello."

"Granddaddy," Caroline started. "It's Caroline."

"Yes, I could tell it was you, honey. And no one else calls me Granddaddy." Grant's wit made Caroline laugh.

"How is Grandmother feeling today?" Caroline asked.

"She's okay today, honey. She had a pretty good night," he replied. Grant would not let anyone take care of Elizabeth but him. They were both proud and very private. Caroline knew that is where her requirement for privacy came from.

"Would it be okay if I came over this afternoon for about an hour?" Caroline asked.

"Sure, honey," Grant said. "Do you need something, Caroline?" Grant asked.

"No, Granddaddy," she responded with a smile he could hear. "I want you to meet someone."

"Oh!" Grant exclaimed. "Is it a boy kind of someone?" he said playfully.

"Yes, it is," Caroline said, laughing at him. "Is two o'clock okay?"

"We'll be here waiting to meet this boy of yours," Grant said. "Grandmother will be very excited. I'd better go so we can get her primped up before you get here," Grant joked.

"I know she will insist, Granddaddy, so I guess you'd better get busy," Caroline said sweetly.

"See you at two o'clock, honey," Grant said and hung up the telephone.

"Garrett," Caroline began as she sat down to drink her coffee, "I need to fill you in on a few details. You will understand everything over time." Caroline told Garrett the story of Georgia Life and of her father meeting her mother, who was her grandfather's secretary at the time. Leaving out the details of her father's alcoholism and gliding over the problems they had after the sale of Georgia Life, Caroline told Garrett that she was now independently wealthy and that when her grandparents died she would inherit everything else. "I really can't give you a number, but neither you nor I nor our children or grandchildren will have to be concerned about money," Caroline finally offered a few of the details of her life that she so closely guarded. "You know I am very private about my life, Garrett," Caroline said.

"If I don't know anything else about you, Caroline, I do know that," Garrett said pragmatically. He was glad that Caroline was sharing this information with him, even though most of it he knew from the awful incident with his father.

"Then I don't need to tell you that none of what I tell you should be shared with anyone, not even your family. At least not now. Okay?" she continued. She stopped speaking to hear him answer.

"It will be between you and me, Caroline, I promise," Garrett said, and he meant it. He was not about to risk losing her again.

"I have a feeling that my grandfather is going to require that you sign a prenuptial agreement. It will legally affirm your understanding that you are not entitled to any portion of the estate. I have no idea what kind of time limits are involved, but we will cross that bridge later. I just want you to know, okay?" Caroline said, hoping that news would not put a damper on their happiness.

"Caroline, I don't care about the money. Sure, it's nice, but I love you, money or no money," Garrett said, and Caroline knew he was telling her the truth.

She kissed him and said, "I knew you were wonderful, but you just keep getting more wonderful every day!"

"Now I have to be nervous about meeting your grandparents," Garrett said. He stood and said, "I'd better shower and put my best clothes on."

"You are so silly," Caroline said laughing at him. "Let me warn you, if you are anything but yourself, my grandfather will know. I suggest that you cool it and just be who you are. That is what I want and what I need from you."

"Well, that's easy," he said, looking back over his shoulder at her as he disappeared into his room. Caroline looked down at her left hand at the beautiful diamond solitaire. She still could not believe she was engaged.

At two o'clock, Caroline rang the doorbell at her grandparents' home. Grant opened the door. Caroline thought he looked particularly handsome in his blue oxford cloth shirt and dark grey trousers. The alligator belt with the gold buckle with his initials on it let Garrett know that this man was still vital. Caroline walked in the door and hugged her grandfather. "Garrett, I would like for you to meet my grandfather, Mr. Wellington," Caroline began the introduction. "Granddaddy, this is Garrett Winthrop."

Grant shook Garrett's hand, evaluating him from top to bottom. "Garrett, please come in," Grant said as he showed them the way to the family room.

As they walked into the room, Elizabeth stood up. She was very unsteady, but she was dressed in a beautiful pink suit and her hair and makeup were perfect. "Grandmother," Caroline said as she put her arms around her. "You look positively gorgeous!"

"Granddaddy helps me to stay beautiful," Elizabeth said, laughing. "And who is this very handsome young man?"

"Garrett, I would like for you to meet my grandmother, Mrs. Wellington," Caroline said as she helped her grandmother to sit down again. "Grandmother, this is Garrett Winthrop." Elizabeth extended her hand daintily.

Garrett took her hand gently and said, "It is a pleasure to meet you, Mrs. Wellington."

Ida, the elder Wellingtons' housekeeper, appeared at the doorway. "Mr. Wellington," she said softly, "shall I serve tea now?"

"Yes, Ida," Grant replied, and she disappeared into the kitchen. Tea was served formally at the elder Wellingtons' home every day between two and three o'clock. Grant began the conversation. "Garrett, please tell us about yourself," he said, sipping his tea.

"Mr. Wellington, Caroline and I met at the University of Virginia in our freshman year. I was born and grew up in Charleston."

"Beautiful city," Grant interrupted.

"Yes, it is," Garrett continued. "My father is a chemical engineer with a defense contractor, and my mother was a nurse, but she did not work after I was born."

"What brings you to Atlanta?" Grant asked.

"On Friday, I interviewed with Senator Russell's chief of staff. I will be working for him in Washington and traveling throughout the country, but I will be in Atlanta quite a bit too."

"Congratulations on landing a great job," Grant said. "Senator Russell is one heck of a nice guy. If you do what he tells you to do and you are honest and work hard, he will be very good to you."

Garrett stuttered, "Does that mean that you know him, sir?"

"I've known Dick Russell for over thirty years, Garrett," he replied casually.

Of course you do, Garrett thought. "I came to Atlanta for another reason too, Mr. Wellington," Garrett said confidently. "If I may, in her father's absence, ask for her hand in marriage. Mr. Wellington," he continued, "I would like to ask for your blessing."

"Congratulations, you two!" Grant said, standing and patting Garrett on the back.

"Caroline, I am so thrilled for you, honey," Elizabeth said. "Does your mother know?"

"Yes, Grandmother," Caroline said. "Garrett and I called her together yesterday."

"Garrett," Grant began, "Caroline is our only granddaughter. We are so proud of her. Please make a commitment to me and to her that you will love her all of your life and you will care for her and honor the vows you take when you get married."

"Mr. Wellington," Garrett said as he sat forward on his seat, "I love Caroline with all of my heart. She is the most amazing and beautiful girl I have ever known. I want nothing more than to take care of her for the rest of her life and love her more every day." Garrett could see that Grant and Elizabeth were living what Grant was requesting of him. Caroline could see a tear in Grant's eye as it rolled down his cheek.

She stood up and walked over to put her arms around her grandfather. "I wish he were here too, Granddaddy," she said. She sat on the arm of his chair, and they both cried. Caroline walked over to her grandmother. "I love you, Grandmother," Caroline said. "You and Granddaddy are wonderful examples for me about commitment in marriage."

"Thank you, honey," Elizabeth said weakly. "Your granddaddy holds up his end of the bargain very well every day."

Grant stood up. "I am going to speak with Ida. We would like for you to stay for dinner, if you can," Grant offered hopefully.

"Granddaddy, we don't want you to go to any trouble for us," Caroline said.

"It will be no trouble," Elizabeth said. "It will be wonderful to have you two young people in our home for a couple of hours."

"Okay with you, Garrett?" Caroline asked.

"Good with me," he replied. Grant disappeared into the kitchen.

"Caroline," Elizabeth said, patting the seat next to her. "Please come and sit by me. Do you have a ring yet?" Caroline sat on the sofa next to her grandmother and held out her left hand. "My goodness, Garrett, you must really love our girl!" she exclaimed, laughing.

"I really do love her, Mrs. Wellington," Garrett said, beaming.

"She's one of a kind, Garrett," Elizabeth said. "You will never find a more wonderful person if you look the rest of your life."

"Oh, Grandmother," Caroline said slightly embarrassed. "Garrett's going to think I made you say that," she said, laughing.

Grant reappeared in the family room. "Dinner will be at five o'clock," he said. "I hope you don't mind that it is so early, honey. Grandmother and I have dinner at five every day."

"It's perfect, Granddaddy," Caroline said.

The dining room table was set formally. Garrett was unaccustomed to that type of formality. He thought he'd better get used to it. They enjoyed a nice dinner and chatted. Grant and Elizabeth asked Garrett a lot of questions, and he responded cordially and patiently to them all. Caroline knew that Grant would steer the conversation, and she remained quiet unless he asked her a question. At six o'clock, after coffee and dessert, Caroline gave her grandparents hugs and she and Garrett said their good-byes. She thought that her grandmother looked especially tired.

On the way back to her house, Garrett said, "Caroline, there is so much that I understand better about you now. You are just like your grandfather where your privacy is concerned. Your grandparents are amazing. I have to imagine that your father must have had a lot of class, and of course, your mother is the personification of class."

"Well thank you, Garrett," Caroline said, taking a good look at his profile as he drove her car. "They truly are unique. My father was very bright and very handsome. My grandfather's success story is inspirational. I will tell you about it sometime. They met during my grandmother's freshman year at college. He was a senior, and when he graduated, he got a job at the local post office so he could be close to her until she graduated."

"And they've been married for over five years," Garrett said.

"That's right, they have," Caroline said. She had not thought about how long her grandparents had been married. *They are an inspiration,* she thought. "Thank you for going with me to meet them, Garrett," Caroline said, touching his hand.

"Sounds like history is repeating in your family, Caroline," Garrett said.

"I never thought about that," Caroline said, "but you're right. We met in our freshman year at college too."

"Yes, we did," Garrett said smiling. "And I have waited for you too."

She looked at him and smiled. "Garrett, we have a lot of decisions to make," Caroline began.

Garrett could see her mind racing, and he knew she was working on organizing their lives. He knew she was very good at that, and he was satisfied to let her handle the organizing. "Caroline," Garrett said, "when would you like to get married?"

"How does the end of June next year work for you?" she replied, as if they were talking about making a dental appointment.

"Let me check my calendar, Miss Wellington," Garrett joked. "I'll have to get back to you on that."

"Smarty pants," she said.

"Next June is perfect," he said finally.

"I do not want a big wedding, Garrett," Caroline said, and Garrett understood that decision was made and the case was closed.

"Me either," he replied.

When they arrived back at her small house, it was almost dark. Caroline turned the lights on inside the house and went to the kitchen to make coffee. Garrett walked up behind her put his arms around her and just stood there holding her. "I still can't believe that we're engaged and I will have the privilege of sharing my life with you," he whispered in her ear. "I love you." Caroline turned around, they embraced, and he kissed her more passionately than ever before.

Caroline's resolve was quickly disappearing. "Garrett," she whispered, "you know I'm a virgin, don't you?"

"I could have guessed that pretty easily, sweetheart," he replied, smiling. He continued kissing her and began unbuttoning her blouse. After he removed it, he unhooked her bra. Her breasts were exposed. Caroline felt embarrassed and excited at the same time. He took her hand and led her into her bedroom. As he took off his shirt, unbuckled his belt, and removed his trousers, Caroline could see the bulge in his underwear. If she was going to stop this, it had to be now. He took her skirt off and pulled her panties down.

"Garrett, I'm scared," Caroline whispered.

"If you want to stop, I will, Caroline," he said. She pulled him on top of her. Garrett was very slow and gentle with her.

"Is it good for you, baby?" he said.

"It is better than good," she said. "I love you so much, Garrett."

They made love for almost thirty minutes before they were willing to stop.

"That was amazing," Caroline said.

Garrett kissed her and stroked her face. "I love you, Caroline," he said softly. "Thank you for trusting me."

"Thank you for waiting for me," she said.

"It was worth it, believe me!" Garrett said sweetly.

Caroline put on her robe and went to turn out the lights in the rest of the house. She came back into the bedroom and removed her robe and slipped back into bed with Garrett. They lay in the bed for three hours with their arms and legs wrapped around each other, talking about whatever came to their minds. "We need to get some sleep," Caroline said. When Caroline turned on the light in the bedroom, she saw blood on the sheets. She quickly removed the sheets and remade the bed. "I think I'll take a shower," she said. "I have a class at ten o'clock, and your flight back to Charleston is at eleven o'clock, isn't it?" she asked.

"You got it," Garrett said. "I'll shower too. It will save time tomorrow." He went into the tiny bathroom with a shower in the guest bedroom. When Caroline got out of the master shower and came back into the bedroom, Garrett was waiting for her. "I have wanted to sleep with you and wake up in the morning with you for so long," he said sweetly. She crawled into the bed with him and put her body next to his. They fell asleep in each other's arms.

In the morning, after Garrett left for the airport, Caroline telephoned her doctor to make an appointment to get birth control pills. She knew this was the beginning of wonderful sex with Garrett. She wondered what her father would think if he knew. *He probably does know*, she shuddered at the thought. *He and Mama probably did it before they got married too,* she mused, trying to justify her decision. "Well, it's done now," she said out loud, "and I am so happy!"

When Garrett's plane landed in Charleston, Derek was waiting to pick him up. "Hi, Dad!" Garrett said jovially when he spotted his father at the gate. "Thanks for picking me up."

"Sure, Son," Derek said dryly. They did not speak on the way to the car. When they were exiting the airport, Derek broke the silence. "You know your mother told me about your engagement to Caroline, don't you?" he began in a curt tone.

"I would assume that she told you, yes, Dad," Garrett replied. He was silent waiting for his father to speak again.

"You know I have a lot of bad feelings toward her because of what happened at New Year's," Derek said. "I have watched her reject you repeatedly. You have had a very hard time dealing with that. So what made you call her in Atlanta?"

"Dad, I love her. I have loved her ever since I laid eyes on her my freshman year. I had to try one more time," Garrett said, pleading for his father to understand.

"Son, you are smart and good looking, if I do say so myself. You are ambitious and so many things that any girl would want in a husband. You could have your pick of girls," Derek instructed him.

"Dad, at twenty-two years old, I have dated plenty of girls. I even dated other girls at UVA. No one has ever even come close to the way Caroline Wellington makes me feel. I love her very deeply," Garrett confessed, trying to allow his father to see his feelings for her.

"What about all the times she pushed you away?" Derek asked.

"Dad, she and I talked about it, and she was so focused on graduating and getting into law school that she refused to allow anything to distract her," Garrett offered. "I would think that you, of all people, would appreciate someone who is focused, mature, smart, and beautiful all at the same time."

"I guess if you put it that way, I could appreciate that," Derek said skeptically. "But I'm afraid that she will reject you again. I don't know how you can deal with that. My concern is for you," he continued.

"And I appreciate that, Dad," Garrett started, "but you have to know that I am a grown man. Within a year, I will be married and be setting up a home like you and Mom did. I want your support and your blessing. Caroline will be part of our family. It is very important to me that you care about her."

"What about what she did, Garrett?" Derek scoffed.

"Dad, what she did was get very upset that you were prying into her private life. She protects her privacy ferociously. All she did was call her mother when she got back to school. Her mother called their lawyer, who found out who had been talking to Greg Baker. It is not Caroline's fault that she was fired, and it certainly isn't her fault that the woman was pregnant with Greg's baby. What he did to her and to himself was horrible beyond my understanding. But none of that was Caroline's fault."

"Why is she like that, Garrett?" Derek asked.

"Well, Dad, I met her grandparents yesterday—her father's parents. We spent several hours with them. They guard their privacy the same way Caroline does. I think Greg shared some of the information about them with you along those lines, if I remember correctly," Garrett was baiting his father.

"I understand that, but—" Derek began but Garrett interrupted him.

"The only 'but' in this situation is the 'but' you had to press her for personal information that was none of your business."

"I was trying to get to know her," Derek said defensively.

"Bullshit, Dad!" Garrett exclaimed. "That's bullshit, and you know it."

"I'm still having a hard time liking her because of what happened," Derek said.

"That is about the most immature thing I think I have ever heard you say," Garrett shouted at Derek.

"Lower your voice when you are speaking to me, Garrett," Derek demanded.

"You are pissing me off, big time!" Garrett retorted. "Can you get that?" Garrett's temper was almost out of control.

"Yea, I get that, Garrett," Derek said sarcastically.

"The way I see it is right now you have two choices," Garrett said. "You can support Caroline and me in our engagement and marriage or you can decide that we won't have a relationship. It's up to you." Derek was silent the rest of the way home. When they pulled into the driveway, Derek stormed into the house, slammed the door, and went up to his room. Garrett took his suitcase upstairs and began unpacking and sorting laundry. He had to be in Washington on Wednesday. He did not have the time or the emotional energy to deal with his unreasonable father.

Laura came into Garrett's room. "What was that all about?" she asked.

"I think you know, Mom," Garrett said, disgusted with his father. He recounted their conversation on the way home.

"I can't understand why he is blaming Caroline for what happened. He and Greg Baker are the ones who screwed up," she said, sitting down in the chair in his room, visibly upset. She stood and walked over to Garrett and put her arms around him. "I love you, honey, and I am so happy for you and Caroline," she said sweetly.

Garrett kissed her on the cheek and gave her a hug. "Thanks, Mom," he said sadly. "I leave Wednesday for Washington, and I really don't know when I will be back. We'll have to talk about this later. Just so you know, Caroline and I are looking at late June next year to get married. Don't worry about a bunch of planning. She wants a very small wedding."

"It's about what the two of you want, Garrett. Not anyone else," Laura said as she patted his back. "I am very proud of you. You followed your heart until you wound up with the love of your life."

"That means so much to me," Garrett said, taking her hands. "You are so special and wonderful. I'm thankful for you and appreciate the way you have accepted this news."

A tear rolled down Laura's cheek. "No matter what, you are my son. I love you more than my life. Your happiness is very important to me," she said, choking back tears.

"This will pass, Mom," Garrett said as he hugged her. "Dad will have to dump his pride and admit that all of it was his fault. He'll get to that at some point. At least I hope so."

"I do too, honey," Laura said as she walked out of the room.

CHAPTER 32

O N MONDAY AFTERNOON, CHARLOTTE CALLED Caroline, whom she knew should be home by four o'clock. "Hello," Caroline answered.

"Hi, sweetheart," Charlotte said. "Mama Rene and I are dying to see your ring and hear all about how he asked you to marry him. You know we have to know everything!"

"Do you want to come to my house tomorrow afternoon? I should be finished with classes about three o'clock," Caroline replied, accommodating her mother's wishes. "Or I can come to Roswell on Friday afternoon if you want me to."

"We will come to see you tomorrow at three o'clock. I have a key to your house, and we can get in if you aren't there yet," Charlotte said, working to plan the visit. "Is that okay with you?"

"Sure, Mama," Caroline said. "I will see you tomorrow at three o'clock. There's a cool pizza restaurant near campus. We can eat dinner there."

"Sounds good to me," Charlotte said, and their conversation ended.

The following afternoon, Caroline arrived home at three thirty to find her mother and Mama Rene waiting for her. Caroline walked through the front door to find them sitting on her screened porch. "Don't you love the porch?" Caroline exclaimed as she walked over to hug Mama Rene and her mother.

"Caroline, this is just perfect for you, sweetheart," Mama Rene said as she kissed Caroline on the cheek.

"Okay, Caroline," Charlotte said. "Let's see this ring." Caroline held her left hand out for her mother and her grandmother to see. "Oh, my gosh!" Charlotte exclaimed. "It's gorgeous!"

"Caroline, that is a rock," Irene said. "Boy howdy," she continued, "that boy must love you."

"I think he probably does, Mama Rene," Caroline replied. "He has endured repeated rejection."

"Why did you reject him, Caroline?" Irene asked.

"Mama Rene, it's complicated, but the main reason is that I was focused on my goal of getting into law school. I just couldn't let anything or anyone stop me."

"Well, you certainly achieved that goal, my dear," Irene said.

"Caroline," Charlotte began, "what do Garrett's parents think of this engagement?"

"Well, I know his mother is okay with it. I don't know about his father yet," she replied tentatively.

"We'll invite them down for an engagement party," Charlotte said.

"I guess that would be okay," Caroline said. "Mama, I really don't want a big wedding."

"Well then, we'll have an engagement party at our house. We'll be sure everyone who is invited to that is invited to the wedding too," Charlotte said.

Caroline could see her mother's wheels turning as she began planning this party. "We'll keep it small, like fifty people or less. Does that work for you?" Charlotte asked Caroline.

"I think that's great, Mama," she replied. Caroline knew that whatever her mother did would be first class from start to finish, so she did not attempt to tell her anything. "I want to invite Jackie and her family to the party and the wedding."

"Absolutely," Charlotte replied.

"Okay then, now that that is settled, let's go for pizza," Irene said, laughing, and they left together for dinner.

Caroline found herself completely immersed in law school. She was almost too busy and involved with classes to talk to anyone. As it turned out, Garrett was equally busy in Washington. They talked on the telephone twice a week but little more. Each of them understood the other's commitments, and their relationship blossomed in spite of their schedules. Garrett knew that Caroline was very independent, and he gave her that latitude in their engagement. Caroline knew that Garrett needed affirmation from her regularly, and she provided that every time they talked.

In the middle of November, with the holidays closing in on them, Caroline was carrying a full load and needed as much time to study as possible. Garrett was working in Senator Russell's office, and he was trying to finish his work in Washington before leaving for home for the holidays. It really was a perfect situation for both of them.

Garrett called Caroline two weeks before Thanksgiving and invited her to come to his home for the holiday. Caroline was torn, because she knew of all the loss her family had suffered in the last few years. She didn't want to be absent and make it worse for them. It was almost a "no-win" situation.

Caroline asked Garrett for a few days to determine if that would work or not. She called him back on the weekend before Thanksgiving. "Garrett," she said on the telephone in his office in Washington. "Could you possibly persuade your family to come to Roswell for Thanksgiving this year? It would mean so much to me! You know we have lost Belle and my father. Holidays can be very difficult."

"I'll call them and see what they think, Caroline," Garrett said. "And I'll let you know as soon as I know what the deal is, okay?"

"Okay," Caroline said. "That's all you can do, sweetheart."

"I love you, Caroline," Garrett said.

"I love you too, Garrett, and I miss you so much," Caroline said genuinely.

"I hope we will be able to see each other one way or another," Garrett said.

"I hope so," Caroline said. "Call me when you know something."

"I will," Garrett replied, and their conversation ended.

Garrett called his home telephone number. Laura answered, "Hello."

"Mom," Garrett started.

"Hi, Son!" Laura said, excited to hear from him.

"Mom, I have a very special favor to ask you," Garrett said pragmatically.

"Okay, what is it?" Laura replied, waiting to hear the request.

"Caroline would like our family to come to Roswell for Thanksgiving. I invited her to our house, but because she lost her father and Belle so recently, she doesn't want to leave them this year. What do you say?" Garrett blurted out the situation.

"Garrett, I'll talk with your father. You know how he feels about this," Laura replied realistically.

"I know, but at some point he's going to have to accept the fact that I will be married to Caroline," Garrett said, pleading with his mother to make it work.

"Okay, Son," she said. "I'll talk with him."

"Thanks, Mom," Garrett said, relieved.

"Are your sisters invited too?" she asked.

"Well of course, Mom," Garrett said. "If you come to their home, everything will be taken care of, believe me," he replied.

"Okay, just being sure," Laura said.

"Call me after you talk with Dad, okay?" Garrett requested.

"I will, honey," Laura replied. And she hung up the telephone.

Caroline called her mother and told her that she had invited Garrett's family to Thanksgiving. "Caroline, that's a wonderful idea," Charlotte said. "I have a person who will be helping us with cooking for special occasions, so we will be okay," Charlotte said.

"Really?" Caroline asked.

"Yes, honey. No one will replace Belle. There is a very nice young woman who came highly recommended from the Robinsons," Charlotte replied with a note of sadness in her voice.

"I'm glad, Mama. You don't need to worry about all that. I'll call Grandmother and Granddaddy and invite them to come too. Garrett has met them. Did I tell you that?" Caroline said, realizing that she had not included that information in her reply.

"No, I didn't know you introduced them," Charlotte said, sounding somewhat irritated.

"The weekend we got engaged, I asked him if he would go with me to tell them. He graciously accepted, and we went," Caroline said. "Mother, I know that a prenuptial agreement will be required before we get married. I wanted to soften that to whatever extent I could before he knew the specifics of it," Caroline said, pleading with her mother to understand her position. "I have no idea at this point what Granddaddy will come up with, so I wanted to let Grandmother and him meet Garrett before he makes all those demands, which I know he will."

"You were right to expect that, Caroline," Charlotte said, her voice changing. "I understand, sweetheart," Charlotte continued. "Let's just try to make this a good Thanksgiving, okay?"

"I want nothing more than that, Mama," Caroline said earnestly.

"Let me know what you hear from Charleston," Charlotte requested.

"I'll call you as soon as he calls me," Caroline replied, and their conversation ended.

On Monday, Garrett called Caroline and said that his family would be driving on Wednesday from Charleston to Atlanta. "Garrett, that's great!" Caroline said, genuinely excited.

"I should be there no later than Tuesday afternoon. I'm trying to get a flight from DC now," Garrett said. "This place is a ghost town. I'll be glad to be with you."

"I'll be glad to see you too, Garrett," Caroline said. "I miss you terribly."

"I hope we can get away alone to your house while I'm there," Garrett said expectantly.

"I bet we can," Caroline replied.

Garrett felt himself getting aroused just thinking about it. "I'm counting on it," he said.

"Actually, I am too, Garrett," Caroline said.

"You've got to stop talking about that, Caroline. I can't stand up right now as it is," he said quietly.

"Well, Garrett, in that case, I wish you were here right now," Caroline said softly, making Garrett's situation worse.

"Okay, there are thirteen hours until we can be together. That's not fair," Garrett said playfully.

"You'll be here soon enough, Garrett,' Caroline said.

"Not soon enough for me," he said.

"Call me and let me know your flight information and I'll pick you up." Caroline asked.

"I'll call you as soon as I have it," he replied.

"Okay, see you tomorrow, sweetheart," Caroline said.

"That sounds good," Garrett said. "I love you." And he hung up the telephone.

The following morning, Caroline's telephone rang at seven o'clock. "Hello," she said sleepily.

"Hi, Caroline," Garrett said. "It's me."

"I recognize your voice, Garrett," Caroline said, trying to be funny.

"My flight leaves in two hours, and I should be in Atlanta by eleven o'clock. Can you pick me up?" he asked.

"I'll be there," Caroline said, sitting up in bed and trying to wake up. "I'll be the girl with the big engagement ring."

"I think I can find you," Garrett said, returning her wit.

After they hung up, Caroline called her mother to let her know the travel schedules of everyone who would be coming to their house for Thanksgiving. Charlotte arranged for Derek and Laura to stay in one of the bedrooms in the newly decorated guesthouse; Garrett would stay in the other bedroom. His sisters would stay in one of the guest bedrooms in the house, and Caroline would sleep in her old room. Caroline planned get back to her own place on Saturday when everyone was leaving. How she and Garrett would coordinate time alone was yet to be determined. But one thing she knew—it would happen.

Garrett came up the Jetway anticipating seeing Caroline. When he came through the door, she was waiting for him with the biggest smile he had ever seen. He dropped his suitcase, put his arms around her, and kissed her for what seemed like two minutes.

"Let's get back to my house, Garrett," Caroline said.

"I was hoping you would say that," he said, picking up his bag and heading for the terminal. As they drove to her house in Decatur, she told him that she had started taking birth control pills.

"I'm glad you thought about that. I don't know much about women's issues," Garrett admitted.

"I really haven't shared that information with anyone at this point, Garrett. I don't think it's anyone's business except ours," Caroline said emphatically.

"We're on the same page with that," Garrett said amiably.

When they arrived at Caroline's house, the two of them could not get into the house and into the bedroom fast enough. Within a minute, they were naked and in Caroline's bed. After they settled down from their passion, Caroline said, "I think I'll tell my mother that you won't be here until early in the morning."

"Sounds good to me," Garrett said. And they started over again, this time taking longer to enjoy one another.

The following morning, Garrett and Caroline woke up in each other's arms. "It's so good to wake up next to you, Caroline," Garrett said softly, touching her face and kissing her gently. "I love you so much," he said.

"I love you, Garrett," Caroline said. "I'll make coffee," she said as she reached for her robe. Garrett got out of bed, put on his robe, and went to the kitchen with her. They made coffee and enjoyed talking and drinking coffee until nine o'clock. They decided to tell everyone that Garrett's plane had been delayed and would not arrive until Wednesday afternoon. Their time together was filled with talking, planning, and a lot of love making.

The Winthrop family arrived in Roswell late Wednesday afternoon. Robert was on hand to help with the bags and any errands that Charlotte needed. She welcomed them to her home and explained that Garrett's airplane had just landed and that he and Caroline would be there within an hour or so. Ellie, the woman Charlotte had hired to help with cooking, was already involved in the preparation for the Thanksgiving dinner. Charlotte, in her usual style, had arranged for Garrett's sisters to go to the movies in Roswell on Wednesday evening, sparing them boredom with the adults. They saw *Love Story* with Ali MacGraw and Ryan O'Neal. By the time Charlotte picked them up from the movies, it was nine o'clock. They were both very agreeable to visit with the adults for one hour before bed. Allison was a junior at the University of South Carolina and Emily a freshman at the University of North Carolina at Chapel Hill. Both girls were amenable to come to Atlanta for Thanksgiving. They were glad for a change from the usual boring Thanksgiving in Charleston.

Laura and Derek were very cordial, but Charlotte could feel the tension. While the girls were at the movies, she broached the subject of the New Year's situation. "Derek," she began, "I know that the things that happened after Caroline's New Year's visit in 1967 were terrible for you and your family. It was never her intention nor mine to cause you or anyone any harm. I hope you know that. My daughter is a very private person. She guards her privacy quite aggressively. The weekend she spent with you she thought was wonderful up to the time that she was questioned rather directly about her family."

Laura responded to Charlotte. "Charlotte, Derek and I both know that the things that happened were not Caroline's fault in any way.

We are both very happy that they are engaged. I haven't seen Garrett so happy in a long time."

"I'm glad to hear you say that, Laura. Caroline is the happiest I have seen her in a long time too. I think they just had to grow up and figure out they loved each other," Charlotte said, affirming Laura's comments. Derek remained silent.

Charlotte decided to settle the issue with Derek. "Derek," she began, "we have been talking and haven't let you get a word in." Both women turned their attention to Derek.

"I have to admit that Garrett sure seems happy. You know what they say," he continued. "You're about as happy as your unhappiest child."

Charlotte sat back in her chair and looked at him. "Derek, that is the truth if I ever heard it!" she exclaimed.

After that, everyone was friendly and open and Derek seemed to accept that his son would marry Caroline. When they went to bed, Laura said, "She handled you better than anyone I have ever seen."

"Handled me?" he retorted.

"Yes, Derek, she handled you," Laura said. "Go to sleep, honey." Derek laid his head on the pillow realizing that he had been outwitted.

That evening at eleven o'clock, the lovebirds appeared at the back door of Caroline's home in Roswell. Garrett went to the cottage and Caroline went to her room.

The following morning, Charlotte and Laura were in the kitchen with Ellie helping with last-minute preparation. Garrett walked straight to his mother and gave her a hug. "Happy Thanksgiving, Mom," he said.

"Garrett, I'm so glad to see you," Laura gushed as she hugged her son. "I heard you come in, but we were so tired I couldn't get up."

"Good morning, Mrs. Wellington," Garrett said as he gave her a hug too.

"I hope you were comfortable last night, Garrett," Charlotte said, returning the hug.

"Very comfortable, thank you."

"We didn't want to wake anybody up when we got here," Garrett said. walking into the family room to watch TV with his dad. Derek stood to hug Garrett. "Dad, it's good to see you," Garrett said as his father put his arms around him. "Good to see you too," Derek replied sheepishly.

"Mama," Caroline began, "Granddaddy insisted on driving here today by himself."

"Well, Caroline, if it gets too late when they leave, one of you will have to drive them home," Charlotte instructed.

"I don't imagine that will happen, Mama," Caroline offered. "Grandmother can't stay up for any long period of time. Granddaddy will probably bring her about noon and they will leave by two o'clock."

"It will be good to have everyone together," Charlotte said. Caroline went into the family room, where she found Garrett and Derek watching the Macy's parade. Derek turned to Caroline and gave her a fatherly hug. "It's very good to see you, Mr. Winthrop," Caroline said.

"Congratulations, you two," Derek said jovially.

"Thanks, Dad," Garrett said, putting his arm around Caroline. "We are very happy."

Caroline went back to the kitchen to help with the finishing details. Emily and Allison walked down to the old Roswell Mill and explored "The Bricks" apartments that were built before the Civil War for the mill workers. They seemed preoccupied, talking about old friends and college. As they were walking back in the front door, Charlotte asked Caroline to go and get Mama Rene.

Caroline scooted out the door and drove the two blocks to Mama Rene's house. When she walked in, Mama Rene was getting her purse and putting on her coat. "I saw you pull up out there, honey," Irene said. Caroline walked to her grandmother and gave her a very long hug.

"I love you so much, Mama Rene," Caroline said.

"You are my sunshine, Caroline," Irene replied. "You always have been."

Caroline kissed Irene on the cheek. "Let's get down to the house. Granddaddy and Grandmother will be there before long," Caroline said, directing Irene to the door. "Mama Rene, you really look great. What's your secret for staying young at eighty?"

"Hard liquor, two packs of Camels a day, and Pond's cold cream," Irene said with a smile curling around the edge of her mouth.

"That's what I get for asking you a serious question," Caroline said, laughing. "C'mon, let's go."

They arrived at the back door, and the introductions proceeded until everyone had met everyone else. Irene went into the living room with a glass of sweet tea. She sat down to wait for Grant and Elizabeth to arrive. "I'm glad I'm not going to be the only golden oldie here today," Irene said so Allison and Emily could hear her. They both giggled and went upstairs.

Irene watched as Grant pulled his car into the driveway. He got out and went to the other side of the car to open the door for Elizabeth to help her into the house. He was very gentle with her and held her like a porcelain doll. Elizabeth was very slow coming up the steps to the front door. Caroline greeted them with hugs and brought them into the living room. Irene stood and gave both of them a hug. She thought Elizabeth looked very pale, but she was dressed beautifully, with perfect hair, makeup, and lipstick. *What a lady,* Irene thought. Grant looked tired, but he was smiling from ear to ear when Caroline hugged him. "Aren't we all so proud of her?" Irene asked rhetorically.

"She is quite a girl," Grant said proudly.

"She is the best of her mother and her father," Elizabeth chimed in.

Charlotte appeared and welcomed Grant and Elizabeth. "Dinner will be served in about twenty minutes," she announced.

"Everything looks beautiful, Charlotte," Elizabeth complimented her.

"Thank you. I'm very glad that we are all together this year," Charlotte said to all three of them. "Before we begin, I want to introduce all of you to Garrett's parents and sisters," Charlotte said, preparing them to meet Caroline's fiancée's family. Within ten minutes all the introductions were done and Charlotte was inviting everyone to come to the table. The ten of them enjoyed a traditional Thanksgiving dinner with turkey and cornbread dressing, fresh green beans, squash casserole, creamed potatoes, and giblet gravy. Banana pudding and homemade pound cake with strawberries and whipped cream were choices for dessert. Charlotte was very glad to see Grant and Elizabeth participating in the conversation during dinner. When everyone had eaten all they could possibly hold, Ellie brought coffee into the living room for Grant, Elizabeth, Irene, and Laura. Garrett and Derek excused themselves to the television for the football games. Charlotte helped Ellie clear the table and organize the kitchen to get everything cleaned. When she finished that, she joined her guests in the living room.

"Charlotte, that was just a lovely dinner," Elizabeth said softly.

"I'm so glad you were able to be here today. It's great that we're celebrating Caroline's engagement too," Charlotte said.

"She brought her young man to meet us a few weeks ago," Elizabeth said. "Her granddaddy and I really like him."

"Garrett is a fine young man, and I'm glad they finally figured out that they were right for each other," Charlotte said, letting Elizabeth know she approved.

Caroline went upstairs to talk with Allison and Emily. She really didn't know them very well, and if they were going to be family, she thought she should take the first step in getting to know them. The girls told her stories about Garrett when they were growing up. "I bet I will be able to use this information to my advantage. Thanks for sharing," Caroline said to them, making mental notes of the stories that were bound to be really fun to tease Garrett with.

"Caroline," Charlotte called up the stairs.

"Yes, Mama." Caroline came into the upstairs foyer.

"Grandmother and Granddaddy have to leave now," Charlotte said.

Caroline ran down the stairs and helped Elizabeth with her coat. "Thank you for coming today," Caroline said as she hugged her grandmother. "I want you to know that you will always be my example of what love and commitment in marriage is all about."

"Thank you, Caroline," Elizabeth said softly. "I'm very lucky to have shared my life with your granddaddy. It wasn't all perfect, but there were sure some perfect parts." Caroline saw a twinkle in Elizabeth's eye.

She hugged Grant and said, "Now Granddaddy, you know my house is not very far from you. If you need my help with anything, just call me."

"Thank you, sweetheart," Grant said, knowing that he would never call her for help.

Charlotte, Irene, and Caroline joined the men watching football in the den. At five o'clock, Caroline suggested that they all go downtown to Rich's Department Store for the "Lighting of the Great Tree." It had been an Atlanta tradition since 1948. Thousands of people flocked there every Thanksgiving to watch the seventy-five to eighty foot live Christmas tree light up with thousands of colored lights ushering in the Christmas season. Charlotte and John had taken Caroline to the "Lighting of the Great Tree" almost every year since she was three years old. It was tradition. Irene declined the invitation, and Caroline took her home. Caroline walked with her to her door and gave her another very long hug. She felt tears coming at the thought of losing her precious Mama Rene someday.

The seven of them piled into two cars and headed downtown. Garrett was able to show his parents the office building where he worked for Senator Russell when he was in Atlanta. It was a beautiful white Georgia marble building completed in 1908 and occupied in 1909. It was the first US Senate office building and was constructed in the beaux-arts style on Constitution Avenue. Derek and Laura were duly impressed with the beautiful building and their son's employment with one of the most influential US senators in history.

They saw the Henry Grady statue at the intersection of Marietta and Forsyth Streets in downtown Atlanta. "Henry Grady was one of the earliest editors of the *Atlanta Constitution* in 1880. He died in 1889, and the statue was unveiled in 1891. He was one of the biggest boosters of 'the New South' after the Civil War," Garrett said, providing a short history of Atlanta to his parents.

"Wow!" Laura exclaimed. "It didn't take you long to get right into Atlanta, Son."

Although in two cars, the group managed to park close to each other. They walked the short distance for the best vantage point to see the tree on top of Rich's Department Store. The temperature dropped to the midforties after the sun went down. There was a breeze, and it was a very chilly Thanksgiving night. Caroline and Garrett did not feel the chill walking arm in arm to the first of many Thanksgiving-night celebrations.

"What a great way to start the Christmas season!" Laura said to Charlotte.

"It really is, isn't it?" Charlotte said. "John and I used to bring Caroline down here every Thanksgiving. It was a tradition for us. I'm glad we're continuing the tradition."

"Traditions are so important for children," Laura said.

"You're right, Laura," Charlotte said. "Caroline and I had to make some new traditions with all the changes in our lives over the last several years."

"I know your husband's death has been very hard on both of you," Laura sympathized with Charlotte.

"Yes, it has been," Charlotte agreed. "But I have to tell you that Caroline is a very strong girl. When she makes up her mind about something, she is focused and determined. She did not let her father's death affect her in college."

"She graduated near the top of her class, didn't she?" Laura asked.

"Yes, she did, Laura," Charlotte said proudly. "She amazes me sometimes. You know, I think she and Garrett are really perfect for each other."

"I think so too," Laura agreed.

Charlotte was glad to have a chance to get to know Laura. She saw kindness and love in her and felt very good about Laura being Caroline's mother-in-law. She hoped Laura felt the same way about her.

As always, "The Lighting of the Great Tree" was a beautiful sight. On the highest note in "O Holy Night," thousands of colored lights all came on at the same time. It was magical, and for Atlanta, it signaled the beginning of the Christmas season in 1971.

When they arrived back in Roswell, the group walked in to a roaring fire and hot chocolate and coffee in the kitchen. Robert had stayed to be sure everything was perfect at the Wellington home. He had just finished lighting the fire when the group returned to Roswell. Ellie went home, but she would be back at five o'clock the following morning to manage breakfast for the household. She had completed the household chores after they left to be sure Charlotte's guests were comfortable. When Charlotte hired her, she gave her Belle's car to drive. She lived only a few miles away and was very glad to be working for Charlotte.

The following morning after breakfast, the Winthrop family, minus Garrett, packed up and left for the six-hour drive back to Charleston. "Charlotte, thank you very much for having us to Thanksgiving," Laura said genuinely. "We have all had a wonderful visit."

"Thank you for driving down to be with us, Laura," Charlotte said giving Laura a hug. Charlotte turned to Derek, "I'm glad you and Garrett got to spend some quality football time together," she joked.

"Can't have too much quality football time," Derek said, returning Charlotte's wit.

"Call me when you get home," Garrett requested.

"We will," Laura said.

"Hey, Garrett," Allison said, "I want to visit you in Washington after Christmas, okay?"

"I'll set it up," Garrett said.

"I want to be included on that visit," Emily chimed in.

"Well, I don't know if I can take two Winthrop women at once or not," Garrett said, laughing and hugging his sisters. "I would love for both of you to come. Let me see what my schedule looks like and I'll try to get y'all up there in March or April. You don't want to come in January or February. It's way too cold," he continued.

Charlotte, Caroline, and Garrett stood on the front porch and waved to the Winthrop family until they were out of sight.

Caroline and Garrett spent the rest of the day with Charlotte working on wedding plans. Charlotte decided to have a small group of twenty or thirty friends for an engagement party. She would host the engagement party in mid-January at her home. Caroline and Garrett liked the idea and left the plans totally up to Charlotte.

Ellie was busy washing bed linens and towels and working to restore the Wellington home to its previous quiet order. Garrett wanted to go back to Caroline's house for the night. "Garrett, my mother will know we stayed together at my house if we do that. Let's just go in the morning. Your flight is not until Sunday afternoon. We'll have all day tomorrow and part of Sunday together." Garrett relented, and they spent a quiet evening with Charlotte.

After Caroline and Garrett left on Saturday morning, Charlotte went down to check on her mother. When she walked in the front door, Irene was sitting in her reclining chair by the window crocheting beautiful lacy fringe for pillowcases and sheets for Caroline and Garrett as a wedding gift. "Mother, that is beautiful work!" Charlotte exclaimed.

"I'm glad you like it," Irene said not looking up from her work. "One of these days, she will pass it on to her children."

Charlotte thought what a wonderful sentiment that was as she bent down and kissed her mother on the forehead. "Ellie's coming down to help you with a few things around here in about an hour. Please make her a list," Charlotte requested.

"Will do," Irene replied and returned to her concentration on crocheting.

Charlotte stayed with her mother until Ellie arrived. She had a lot to do to prepare for a party and a wedding. She went to Lenox Square to Rich's to have invitations printed and to set up the wedding gift registry for Caroline and Garrett. They promised her that they would get down there to choose their china, silver, and crystal as soon as they could. With Garrett's schedule in Atlanta, it was likely that he would be back within a couple of weeks.

Garrett and Caroline enjoyed their Saturday and Sunday together. They had time to talk and plan. After their marriage, Caroline would finish law school at Emory. Garrett could move into her little rental house with her until they could find a larger house. They expected their schedules to work out pretty well most of the time. After graduating from law school, Caroline told Garrett that she would go wherever she needed to go to allow him to pursue his career with Senator Russell. She wondered what would happen when Senator Russell retired or died. She hoped his successor would find Garrett's work useful.

On Sunday afternoon, Garrett was at the Atlanta airport ready to fly back to Washington with a tearful Caroline in his arms. "I don't know what's the matter with me," she said as they stood with their arms around each other.

"We'll talk during the week, Caroline," Garrett said, comforting her. "You know, this week was just amazing with my family here with your family," he said. "It just seems like we have all been together forever."

"I think everyone enjoyed Thanksgiving," Caroline said, smiling at him. "It's our southern culture."

"Probably so," Garrett agreed. "Nothin' like it!" He kissed her and disappeared down the Jetway.

Caroline's thoughts returned to her schoolwork. She went back to her small house and studied until midnight.

On January 21, 1972, Garrett called Caroline to say that Senator Russell passed away. At that moment, his career was up in the air. Garrett had grown to like and highly respect Senator Russell, and it was a personal loss for him as well. On February 1, Garrett learned that President Carter had appointed David Gabriel to succeed Senator Russell. Mr. Gabriel had been a partner at King and Spalding before his appointment. Caroline called Lawrence Harris at King and Spalding to tell him about her engagement to Garrett and their connection through King and Spalding. Caroline had learned to navigate the shark-infested political waters with some finesse, and this was one of those times when it came in handy. Mr. Harris was gracious and let Caroline know that they were looking forward to her internship in July. She did not know whether the telephone call produced anything favorable for Garrett or not. But the following week, Garrett learned that Mr. Gabriel would be retaining him in the position he had occupied for Senator Russell. Garrett called Caroline as soon as he found out. "Hi, beautiful," he said when she answered.

"Well, hi yourself," she said playfully.

"I have good news," he said.

"Oh yea?" Caroline replied, hoping the news would be good about his job.

"Senator Gabriel will be keeping me in the same position," he said, relieved that he would not have to be searching for a job in the middle of wedding plans. "It's all about who you know, isn't it?" Garrett asked.

"It always will be," Caroline replied pragmatically.

"Thanks for doing that, Caroline," Garrett said. "I'm not sure if the position would still be available if you had not called Mr. Harris."

"Don't sell yourself short, Mr. Winthrop," Caroline scolded him. "You are smart and very capable. They are lucky to have you."

"Thanks for the vote of confidence," he said rather meekly. "I love you, Caroline," he said.

"Well, it's pretty obvious that I love you too, Garrett," Caroline said, trying to lighten the conversation.

Garrett wound up busier than ever. He became a trusted aide to Senator Gabriel and was able to participate in many of the committee meetings in Washington. His negotiation skills were improving every day, and he was managing to hold his own and actually earn the respect of his colleagues on the hill.

CHAPTER 33

O N JANUARY 29, 1972, THIRTY friends and family gathered at Charlotte's home for Caroline and Garrett's engagement party. Caroline was so glad to see many of her parents' long-time friends. Geoff Robinson and his children were there, and Caroline wanted Garrett to meet her father's best friend. The evening was warm, and everyone thought that Garrett was just perfect for Caroline. Ellie and Robert were on hand to help with serving and clean up. As always, Charlotte was a most gracious hostess. A chamber orchestra provided the music, and the evening was lovely as friends wished the happy couple congratulations. Caroline noticed that Geoff seemed to be talking with her mother and staying near her during the evening. She wondered if a relationship might be blossoming. There was so much going on that Caroline forgot to ask her mother about it. Irene was on hand and enjoyed every minute of it. Grant and Elizabeth were unable to attend, but they insisted on paying for the catering and flowers for the event. The evening was perfect.

Caroline and Garrett had not had very much time together since Christmas. Caroline figured it would make their honeymoon just that much better. Garrett surprised her during the party and told her he would be taking her to Maui for ten days for their honeymoon. They would stay in the Hyatt Regency Maui in the Regency Suite. It had a living room, dining room, bedroom, one and a half bathrooms, and three lanais. It was on the twenty-first floor with a view of the ocean and the mountains. Caroline was so excited that she could hardly wait. She was thankful that she would have finished her first year of law school before the wedding. After the honeymoon, she would return to Atlanta for another internship with King and Spalding.

The weeks and months just flew by. Soon it was May, and Caroline was being fitted for her wedding gown. Jackie would be her maid of honor and Emily and Allison her bridesmaids. Regenstein's was an exclusive clothing and accessories store in Atlanta. Charlotte was friendly with Suzanne Regenstein, and it was just a forgone conclusion that Caroline would choose her wedding gown and bridesmaids' gowns from her store. Caroline chose a Badgley Mischka gown called the MacKenzie. It was white silk overlaid with white silk organza. It was fitted at the waist, strapless, with a gathered sheered bodice. Below the hip, the dress flared slightly and had vertical rows of inset silk organza ruffles. In the center of the bodice just above the waist was a stunning marquis-shaped broach with pearls and rhinestones. Caroline looked positively gorgeous in the gown. She chose a veil that did not cover her face but was gathered near the top of her head and flowed to the floor. Her bridesmaids would wear black strapless gowns by Badgley Mischka. With a sweetheart-shaped bodice of black silk, the dresses were fitted at the waist with a small gathered black silk belt. The dresses flared slightly at the knee and had horizontal rows of black silk ruffles to the floor. Jackie, Allison and Emily all loved the dresses, and Caroline thought that each one of them looked quite beautiful.

They had a girl's weekend on May 5, 6, and 7. With the wedding scheduled for June 24, they were having a final fitting. They lunched at Pitty Pat's Porch in downtown Atlanta afterward and enjoyed shopping in Buckhead. Caroline insisted on buying everyone's wedding attire right down to the shoes and earrings. She paid for the girls to fly into Atlanta two previous weekends for fittings and showers. She coordinated fittings for them with showers so they would not have to make too many trips. The four of them had grown close over the past few months, and Caroline was glad to be sharing this time with Emily and Allison. Jackie was in law school at Harvard but managed to get away to Atlanta for the showers and fittings. Caroline and Jackie remained very close friends, and Caroline was grateful for that. She was unique and smart, and she kept Caroline from being too serious most of the time.

Garrett's dad would be his best man. Two of his boyhood friends whom he had known since high school who would be his groomsmen. David Otwell and Mark Simmons both attended the University of South Carolina, but the three of them had stayed in touch over the years. Although he had many close friendships from college, his buddies from Charleston were the men with whom he wanted to share his wedding.

The engagement party in Charleston was a blast. It was at the Charleston Country Club in the formal dining room. The views of the intercoastal waterway were stunning. More than a hundred people attended. Charlotte loved Charleston and enjoyed meeting Garrett's extended family and lifetime friends. It gave her a chance to spend some time with Laura and Derek and meet many of their friends. The orchestra played during dinner and afterward for dancing. The liquor, wine, and champagne flowed freely as everyone danced the night away in honor of Caroline and Garrett. Since Garrett's family hosted the party, Caroline did not voice any opposition to the alcohol that was served. She enjoyed the punch and soft drinks.

Neither of them could remember being happier in their entire lives. It was like a fairy tale in real life.

The wedding would be at Primrose Cottage in Roswell directly across the street from her mother's home on Mimosa Boulevard. Primrose

Cottage was an antebellum mansion built in 1839. Its conversion to a wedding and event facility with a ballroom and terraced gardens made it their first choice for the wedding and reception. It was the perfect size for the 150 guests expected to attend.

For the wedding gallery, Caroline chose white roses and white hydrangeas with black-and-white ribbons and bows at each row. The altar would have two large arrangements of white roses and white hydrangeas on pedestals with large ferns in black pots below. The wedding was to be at seven o'clock and very formal. White candles would be on each side of the floral arrangements and in the center behind the minister. On a separate pedestal, Caroline wanted a vase of fifty-three red roses in memory of her father. On May 12, 1972, invitations were mailed to family and friends from Atlanta, Charleston, Kennebunkport, and Washington, DC. The invitee list was as small as they could make it with the family and friends on both sides of the families.

Mrs. John Andrew Wellington

requests the honor of your presence

at the marriage of her daughter

Miss Caroline Elizabeth Wellington

to

Mr. Garrett Russell Winthrop

On the twenty-fourth day of June, nineteen

hundred and seventy-two

at seven o'clock in the evening

Primrose Cottage

Roswell, Georgia

And afterward for the reception

It was real now. They were getting married!

CHAPTER 34

*G*ARRETT WAS SO BUSY WITH Senator Gabriel that he barely had time to catch his breath for the wedding parties. Although he missed the showers in Atlanta and only made one of the showers in Charleston, Caroline understood, and he was thankful. He had traveled from coast to coast during the last year and believed he was acquiring exceptional diplomatic skills. Senator Gabriel had been too busy to give Garrett any feedback on his performance. He hoped that his work would be recognized.

Caroline was busy with work to finish her first year of law school. She had not been able to focus to the extent that she preferred but worked twice as hard when she could. On Thursday afternoon, May 18, 1972, she just finished arranging for her internship with King and Spalding in July when the telephone rang.

"Caroline," came the voice of her grandfather, "it's Granddaddy."

"Granddaddy," Caroline said, "are you okay?" Caroline detected stress in her grandfather's voice.

"I'm afraid that Grandmother is in the hospital, and it doesn't look like she will make it through the night, Caroline," Grant said as he began to cry.

"I'll be right there, Granddaddy," Caroline said. "Are you at Emory?" she asked hurriedly.

"Yes, honey, we are."

"Hang in there, Granddaddy," Caroline said, crying as she hung up the telephone. She called her mother.

"Hello," Charlotte answered in her usual pleasant voice.

"Mama, it's Grandmother. She's at Emory, and Granddaddy said she's not going to live through the night," Caroline blurted. "I'm headed over there now to be with him and to see her before she leaves us."

"Caroline, I'll be there as soon as I can, honey," Charlotte said. "Be careful going over there. I know you are upset, but just be safe, okay?"

"I will, Mama," Caroline replied with her voice cracking. "You be safe too." Caroline hung up the telephone, grabbed her purse, and went out the door.

She drove to Emory University Hospital and arrived within twenty minutes of her conversation with her grandfather. Elizabeth was in intensive care, but they let Caroline go back with Grant. She walked into the room and put her arms around her grandfather. "I know she is the love of your life, Granddaddy. You have taken such good care of her for so long. You have had a fifty-year love affair," Caroline whispered into her grandfather's ear as she hugged him. Grant wiped his eyes with his handkerchief. Caroline walked over to Elizabeth's bed and found her barely breathing and unconscious. Caroline thought how peaceful she looked.

"They're keeping her comfortable until she passes away," Grant said. "It is so hard to not ask them to do something more for her to make her live longer. I have tried to take care of her to extend her life. But I love her so much I can't prolong her death."

"I know this is so hard for you, Granddaddy," Caroline sympathized. "If it helps you at all, she looks very peaceful to me."

"You know your grandmother can hear you, Caroline," Grant said.

Caroline turned and walked closer to her bedside. "Grandmother," she began as she gently took her hand, "it's me, Caroline. I know you will be leaving us soon. I have a favor to ask of you. Would you please tell Daddy that I still love him very much and that I hope he is near when Garrett and I get married? I know he will be waiting for you, Grandmother. I would give anything to see him and talk with him again. Would you give him that message? I love you very much. You and Granddaddy will always be my examples. It's okay for you to rest. Mama and I will take care of Granddaddy now." Caroline sat down in a chair and cried so hard she almost got nauseated. "Losing people we love is so hard, Granddaddy," Caroline said as she stood and put her arms around him again.

"I know it is, honey," Grant said as he tried to comfort Caroline. "But our lives must go on. We have to find something good every day in our lives."

"There are good things," Caroline said, "but times like this are so difficult."

Within an hour, the intensive care nurse came into the room and said that Caroline's mother was waiting. "We usually don't allow more than two people at a time in the room, Mr. Wellington," the nurse said sternly.

"Could you make an exception today?" Grant asked almost timidly.

"Under the circumstances, I will make the exception now, but three is the most I can allow without my supervisor calling me in," she replied matter-of-factly.

"Thank you very much," Grant said, relieved that Charlotte would be with them.

Charlotte came into the small room with two chairs and the bed with Elizabeth's withered body. She saw all the equipment monitoring her respiration and heartbeat. Elizabeth's blood pressure was dropping, and the last reading was 60/40.

Charlotte walked to Grant and put her arms around him. "It's so hard to lose your life partner," she sympathized.

Grant shook his head, unable to speak. He wiped tears with his handkerchief again.

Charlotte hugged Caroline and then walked over to Elizabeth's bed. "She looks very peaceful," she commented.

Grant, Caroline, and Charlotte sat together in Elizabeth's room talking about the memories they all had shared. At ten forty-five that evening, the three of them were standing around Elizabeth's bed. Her heart rate and respiration were so low they knew she would not be with them much longer. As they stood together, Elizabeth opened her eyes and looked around at all of them as if to say good-bye. She looked down at the foot of her bed and said, "John!" She quietly closed her eyes, and her breathing and heartbeat stopped. The Wellington family was almost beyond comforting. Elizabeth was gone, and John had come to get her. He was there with all of them at the moment she died.

The nurse came into the room having seen the monitors. "Mr. Wellington, Mrs. Wellington has passed away," she said quietly.

Grant could not speak. Charlotte spoke for him. "We know that she passed away. We would like to stay until Patterson's comes to take her."

"That will be fine," the nurse replied and began unhooking the monitors and removing the IVs.

Grant went to the telephone and dialed Patterson's Springhill Funeral Home. He had put them on notice to be expecting a call from him. Within an hour, two gentlemen dressed in dark suits came to the room. "Please be very gentle with her. She has been sick for a long time," Grant requested.

"We will, Mr. Wellington. We are very sorry that you have lost Mrs. Wellington," the elder gentleman offered his sympathy. They gently moved Elizabeth's body to the bed that would take her to the funeral home.

"Dad," Charlotte said, "why don't you come home with me tonight? I'll take you home first thing tomorrow and help you with the arrangements."

"Thank you, Charlotte," Grant replied, and he willingly went with Charlotte to Roswell. Caroline followed them in her car, and the three of them spent the night there.

The following morning, Charlotte made breakfast. "Caroline, you go on to your classes today, honey," Charlotte instructed. "I'll take care of things with Granddaddy. Call me tonight, and I'll let you know what is going on."

"Are you sure, Mama?" Caroline said, hesitating to leave her mother to take care of everything.

"I'm sure, honey," Charlotte replied, trying to reassure her.

Caroline was tired, but she drove to her small house and quickly showered and gathered what she needed for her classes. She did not have time to call Garrett to tell him, but she would when her classes were over at two o'clock.

Caroline found it very difficult to focus on her classes. She was exhausted physically and emotionally. After classes, she walked back to her car and drove the short distance to her house. *I wonder if Garrett is in his office in DC*, she thought. She dialed the number.

"Senator Gabriel's office," Garrett answered professionally.

"Garrett," Caroline began, "it's me."

"Hi, sweetheart," Garrett said. "Are you okay?"

"Garrett, Grandmother died last night," Caroline said, trying not to cry.

"Oh, Caroline, I am so sorry," Garrett said ardently. "How is your grandfather?"

"Doing the best he can. He lost the love of his life, Garrett," Caroline said tearfully.

"Your mother can sympathize with him, Caroline," Garrett said softly.

"I know," Caroline said, still tearful. "Listen, I just wanted you to know. There's no need for you to come to Atlanta. I know you are so busy."

"As it turns out, I will be in Atlanta tomorrow anyway. I have to be in meetings in Senator Gabriel's office there for the next three days. I will explain the circumstances and see if I can at least get to the visitation," Garrett said sincerely.

"I'll be very glad to have you here," Caroline said. "I'd better go. I have to call Mama and see what's going on that needs my help. Would you call me when you get here?"

"Sure. Hang in there, honey," Garrett said. "I love you so much."

"I love you too, Garrett," Caroline replied and hung up the telephone.

Caroline finally reached her mother at her grandparents' house. "Mama, I can be over there in ten or fifteen minutes. I'll be glad to help," Caroline offered.

"It would do your grandfather good to see you, sugar," Charlotte said. "Why don't you come on over?"

"Be right there," Caroline said and hung up the telephone. She grabbed her purse and left for Inman Park.

When she arrived, Charlotte and Grant were working together to get Elizabeth's funeral plans completed. They would go to the funeral home tomorrow to finalize everything. The visitation would be on May 21, and the funeral would be on May 22. Grant had her clothes all together with her jewelry and makeup. Elizabeth's hairdresser would fix her hair for the last time tomorrow afternoon. There was an emptiness in the house that was real. It felt hollow to Caroline. Caroline walked slowly through the house and found pictures of herself from when she was a baby all the way through college. They were in the guest bedrooms, down the hallway, and in Grant and Elizabeth's room. Caroline had never noticed all the photographs. So many of them were of her and her father, and some of the photographs she had never seen before. She wanted to ask Grant to give her some of them, but today was not the right time. She found him in the den sitting with a legal pad making notes for the meeting at the funeral home the next day.

"Granddaddy," Caroline began, "what can I do to help you?"

"You help me by being here, Caroline," Grant said, looking up from his pad and smiling at her. "You really are such a light."

"Granddaddy," Caroline replied, "surely I can do more than just be here."

"Caroline, do you know how important 'being there' is at a time like this?" Grant asked, not expecting an answer. "The gift of your time and love is more special to me than anything you could do."

"That is so sweet," Caroline said as she bent down to give her grandfather a kiss on the cheek.

Ida fixed vegetable soup, and they sat together in the breakfast room and ate. While they were eating, Charlotte said, "Caroline, I'm going to stay here with Granddaddy tonight. I'll go with him tomorrow to Patterson's and then he will come back home with me. I want you to get some rest and go to your classes tomorrow."

"Okay, Mama," Caroline said, truly thankful that she would be able to finish her classes that week. "I should be finished around three o'clock tomorrow. I'll call you as soon as I get back to my house."

"Okay, honey," Charlotte replied, and Caroline could tell that her mother was very tired.

"By the way," Caroline continued the conversation, "Garrett will be here tomorrow on business. He hopes to get to the visitation at the very least. He is not sure where his meetings will be yet."

"It's good that he will be here for you, Caroline," Charlotte said, smiling. She was very happy that Caroline and Garrett were so in love and so devoted to each other.

"Caroline," Grant spoke, "you know that your grandmother and I didn't have much of anything when we got married. After I graduated, I went to work for the post office in Athens to wait for her to graduate. We got married in 1910 and moved to Atlanta. Your daddy came along three years later. I didn't want her to work, so she took in sewing to help pay for groceries. It was not too long before you were born that Georgia Life really started making money for us."

"Daddy has told me the story of your life so many times, Granddaddy," Caroline said sweetly. "He really admired you starting with nothing and being so successful. I think that's why he decided to come to work for Georgia Life."

"Well, that might have been part of the reason," Grant said, chuckling, "but mostly it was your mother. He couldn't take his eyes off of her."

"Oh, Dad," Charlotte said, laughing.

"It's true," Grant said, smiling at her. "I couldn't get any work out of him until after he married you."

"He had it bad, Mama," Caroline said, teasing her mother.

"Those were good days," Charlotte said, her voice trailing off. "We made some really special memories."

"I'm glad I was there for some of them, Mama," Caroline said sweetly.

"Hey, you'd better get home before it gets too late," Charlotte instructed her grown daughter.

"Yes, ma'am, Mama," Caroline said obediently. After hugs and kisses, Caroline headed home to her small house.

The following morning, Grant and Charlotte went to Patterson's to deliver Elizabeth's clothes, jewelry, and makeup. Flowers had already been delivered, and they moved the room she was going to be in to a larger room. After the meeting, Charlotte took Grant to Roswell. When they arrived, Irene was there. Ellie was cooking and had prepared the guest room for Grant.

Irene walked to Grant and took his hands, "Grant, I am so sorry that you have lost Elizabeth," she said with genuine sympathy.

"Thank you, Irene," Grant replied weakly. "It is very hard to lose her."

"You took such good care of her, Grant," Irene said, trying to lend her support. Irene led Grant into the family room, wanting to give Charlotte a chance to have some time to herself. Charlotte took advantage of it and went straight for a hot bath and then changed into Bermuda shorts and a cotton blouse.

Lunch was ready when she reappeared in the family room. The three of them had homemade chicken salad and cantaloupe with water rolls and iced tea. After lunch, Grant wanted to sit on the front porch. It was a beautiful spring day, and the trees in Charlotte's front yard had bright green new leaves. The dogwoods were blooming, and the azaleas were bright red. Grant could smell the tea olive bush growing in the yard behind the porch swing. Irene joined him on the porch, and Ellie brought fresh coffee.

They had been sitting on the porch for about an hour when the telephone rang. Ellie came to the door and said, "Mr. Wellington, Senator Gabriel's office is on the phone for you. Would you like to take it in the den?"

"Yes, Ellie," Grant replied as he rose. "That will be fine."

"Hello," Grant spoke into the phone.

"Mr. Wellington, this is Claire Everett. I am Senator Gabriel's assistant in Atlanta. The senator knows that you and Senator Russell were very good friends. He wishes to pay his respects and would like to see you briefly tomorrow evening at Patterson's, if that meets with your approval."

"Of course, Ms. Everett," Grant replied formally. "Please tell Senator Gabriel that I look forward to seeing him." Grant hung up the phone and wondered what that was about. He was not expecting a US senator to come to Elizabeth's visitation.

When Grant returned to the front porch, Irene looked at him expectantly. "Don't know what that was about, but I guess I will have to wear my best suit tomorrow evening. Senator Gabriel will be at Elizabeth's visitation," Grant said, sounding somewhat puzzled.

"Grant, he will be there along with half of the rest of old Atlanta," Irene said to him. She was surprised that he did not already know that Elizabeth's funeral would be attended by the old Atlanta elite, including all the people who were still alive and able to get around who were the movers and shakers in Atlanta in the forties and fifties. She thought that Grant could not possibly be so naïve, but she reserved her opinion and kept it to herself.

Grant learned that Ida had been receiving calls all day and had simply said that Mr. Wellington was unavailable. The doorbell rang about six times with members of their church bringing casseroles, ham, salads, and desserts. They were members of Druid Hills Presbyterian Church and had been for over thirty years. Grant had asked to use the fellowship hall at church to receive visitors after Elizabeth's funeral and burial at Arlington Cemetery. Grant instructed her to keep the food fresh and have it ready to go to the church on Monday morning. Several women from the church would be on hand to organize everything. Ellie volunteered to go to help also, and Grant accepted her offer. Later he learned that Charlotte had made all the arrangements at the church and enlisted many of its members to set up, serve, and clean up the fellowship hall.

It was no secret in those circles that Grant was independently wealthy and still owned a great number of shares of Georgia Life stock. His investments and trust were handled by Trust Company of Georgia, and Bob Strickland, the chairman, was very well acquainted with Grant. Grant guarded his privacy very carefully, but when that kind of wealth was held by one individual, it was difficult to preserve privacy.

After dinner, Irene went home. Charlotte was on the telephone most of the day taking care of arrangements. It seemed that the list of people attending the funeral was growing by the hour. Charlotte and Grant talked for over an hour about the plans. He was very grateful for her help and told her so. "Charlotte, I don't know what I would have done without you," he said genuinely.

"Dad, I'm glad to help," she replied as if it were no trouble. "You and I are both exhausted. Let's get some sleep. We have a lot to do tomorrow, and I have to get you home pretty early."

"You won't have to ask me twice," Grant said with the keen wit that he didn't always share.

Caroline stayed at her house studying and getting prepared for Garrett's arrival. The next several days would be really crazy for their small family. When she talked with Garrett, he said that his plane would land about noon. He needed to rent a car so he would drive to her house. Caroline was relieved, because she had classes until one o'clock. He told her that his parents would not be able to fly down but had sent flowers. Caroline was actually thankful that her mother would not have one more thing to deal with.

The following day, Charlotte was packed and prepared for the visitation. She took Grant home at ten o'clock to get ready to go to the funeral home. He was scheduled to see Elizabeth at three o'clock.

The visitation would be from five to eight. Charlotte planned to be with him throughout the day and that night. Ellie would drive Irene to the funeral home downtown. Charlotte did not like Irene to drive anywhere except right around Roswell where she was familiar with everything. Charlotte's planning paid off, and the day went as well as a day like this could go.

Caroline pulled into the driveway of her house. Before she could open the door, Garrett pulled in behind her. She went inside, put her books and purse down, and came back out to greet him. They stood with their arms around each other, and Caroline felt comforted. "Come on in," she said as she opened the screened door.

"I'm sorry I couldn't get here sooner, Caroline," Garrett said apologetically. "It has been so busy in Senator Gabriel's office, and I haven't had a minute. I have been working fourteen-hour days for the last two weeks."

"Good heavens, Garrett!" Caroline exclaimed. "You must be exhausted."

"Not really," he replied. "I actually enjoy the energy up there. I guess we need to get ready to go to the visitation tonight."

"We do, but first . . ." Caroline put her arms around Garrett and kissed him.

"Do you think we have time?" Garrett asked sheepishly.

"I bet we can make time," Caroline said as she took his hand and led him into the bedroom.

In less than a minute, they were both naked and making love. Within a few minutes, the lovebirds were satiated for the moment.

They both showered and changed into church clothes. Caroline wore a black silk A-line dress with a fitted bodice and a small leather belt and black lizard pumps. As always, she wore the necklace that her father gave her when she was two. Garrett wore a dark blue pinstripe Hart Shaffner Marx suit with a dark blue and burgundy British regimental Robert Talbot tie and his black wingtip shoes. They both looked like they had stepped out of a magazine.

As he opened the door for her to get into his rental car, he said, "By the way, Senator Gabriel will be at the visitation tonight, and he has insisted that I be there and with you at the funeral tomorrow."

"Really? Why?" Caroline asked honestly.

"He knows that your grandfather and Senator Russell were close friends. He is being respectful," Garrett said, knowing that Senator Gabriel knew that half of old Atlanta money would be at the funeral home tonight.

"That's awfully nice of him, Garrett," Caroline said.

"Yes, it is," Garrett replied and then dropped the subject.

Caroline and Garrett arrived at Patterson's Spring Hill Funeral Home at three thirty. The last time Caroline was here was at her father's funeral. She suddenly felt as if the weight of the world were on her shoulders. *I hope I can get through this,* she thought. Garrett helped her out of the car, took her hand, and led her through the front door.

"Miss Wellington." A gentleman working at the front door spoke.

Caroline looked up. "Yes," she said.

"I will take you to your mother and grandfather," he said quietly and then led them down a hall with beautiful black-and-white floor tiles lined with Queen Anne chairs, tables, and lamps that looked like they were from the 1940s. Caroline felt a shiver go up her spine.

Grant and Charlotte had arrived at three o'clock, and when Caroline came in Grant was still trying to compose himself. She walked over and put her arms around him.

"Caroline, she looks so beautiful," Grant said, sobbing. They stood together at Elizabeth's casket.

"She is beautiful, Granddaddy. You helped her stay beautiful," Caroline said, trying to comfort him. Caroline looked around the room and gasped when she saw all the flowers.

Garrett walked over to give Charlotte a hug and talk with her while Caroline was talking with Grant. When he saw that their personal moment had ended, he walked over to Grant and shook his hand. "Mr. Wellington, I am so sorry that you lost Mrs. Wellington. I am glad that I had the privilege of meeting her. Caroline has told me so much about your life together and how devoted you were to each other."

"I'm glad the two of you met too, Garrett," Grant said, looking back at Elizabeth. "She will be watching over you two, I'm sure."

Having sex with Caroline a few hours earlier flashed into Garrett's mind, and he hoped that Elizabeth Wellington had not witnessed it. He quickly dismissed the thought.

At five o'clock, the throngs of people paying their respects to the Wellington family began. As with John's funeral, there were dignitaries old and young. At seven o'clock, Senator Gabriel entered the room. It was obvious that most of the people recognized him, because the chatter got very quiet. He walked directly to Grant, introduced himself, and shook his hand. "Mr. Wellington, I am very sorry about your loss," the senator said.

"Thank you, Senator," Grant said returning his handshake.

"Your granddaughter has a fine young man there, Mr. Wellington. We are very glad to have him on our team," the senator said, trying to gently offer some familiarity between the two of them.

"We are looking forward to having him in our family, Senator," Grant replied cordially. "Thank you very much for coming. I know your schedule must be hectic."

"It is important to take time to support each other during difficult times," he responded. The senator moved on to meet Charlotte. "Mrs. Wellington," he began, "I am very sorry for your loss."

"Thank you, Senator," Charlotte replied. She already suspected the ulterior motive for the senator's presence. He continued his compliments about Garrett.

When he approached Caroline, Garrett stepped up for the introduction. "Senator Gabriel, I would like you to meet my fiancée, Caroline Wellington. Caroline, please meet Senator Gabriel." Garrett's formality and manners were notably excellent.

"Miss Wellington," the senator began, "I am very sorry you have lost your grandmother. I know this is a difficult time for your family."

"Thank you for taking the time to come, Senator," Caroline said cordially.

"May I offer my congratulations on your upcoming marriage," the senator continued.

"Thank you, sir," Caroline replied, smiling.

"Garrett, you are a very lucky man," the senator said as he winked at Garrett. Then he walked around the room "working the crowd." The representation of money and power in Atlanta was truly concentrated that evening at Patterson's.

At eight thirty, after everyone had gone, Charlotte and Grant stood beside Elizabeth. He wanted to tell her good night. Charlotte's heart broke for him as he stood there looking at his lifetime love in her casket. "Come on, Dad," Charlotte urged him. "Let's get some rest." Reluctantly, Grant went with her. Ida had prepared a light dinner for them of chicken soup and ham sandwiches. Grant was grateful, and he and Charlotte ate and went to bed.

Garrett took Caroline to dinner at the revolving restaurant at the top of the Regency Hotel. As they sat by the window looking at the lights of the city, Caroline's emotions came spilling out. "Oh, Caroline, I am so sorry, honey," Garrett said. "I should not have taken you out tonight."

"That's not it, Garrett," Caroline said, wiping her eyes. "It's like there is so much sadness and so much joy at the same time. I miss my daddy more than I can ever tell you. My grandmother is dead. But I am going to marry you in a month, and I have never been happier about anything in my life. It is like all the emotion has just been bottled up and is coming out whether I like it or not."

Garrett took her hand across the table. "I love you so much, Caroline," he said sweetly. "I don't know how I got so lucky to have the chance to spend my life with you. The more I know you the more I love you."

"I feel the same way about you, Garrett," Caroline said, smiling at him. Caroline joined him in a glass of Cabernet Sauvignon, a rare occurrence for her. They toasted to their future.

After dinner, they returned to her house and picked up right where they left off. This time they took it slow, and an hour later they were both exhausted. They fell asleep in each other's arms.

The following day, the funeral was at the Druid Hills Presbyterian Church. It was a beautiful spring day in Atlanta. Dr. Mitchell had been the elder Wellingtons' pastor for the last ten years. In the eulogy, he included the passages from Ecclesiastes 3. Caroline would remember these passages for the rest of her life.

Ecclesiastes 3

[1]To everything there is a season, and a time to every purpose under the heaven:

[2]A time to be born, and a time to die; a time to plant, and a time to pluck up that which is planted;

[3]A time to kill, and a time to heal; a time to break down, and a time to build up;

[4]A time to weep, and a time to laugh; a time to mourn, and a time to dance;

[5]A time to cast away stones, and a time to gather stones together; a time to embrace, and a time to refrain from embracing;

[6]A time to get, and a time to lose; a time to keep, and a time to cast away;

[7]A time to rend, and a time to sew; a time to keep silence, and a time to speak;

[8]A time to love, and a time to hate; a time of war, and a time of peace.

[9]What profit hath he that worketh in that wherein he laboureth?

[10]I have seen the travail, which God hath given to the sons of men to be exercised in it.

[11]He hath made everything beautiful in his time: also he hath set the world in their heart, so that no man can find out the work that God maketh from the beginning to the end.

[12]I know that there is no good in them, but for a man to rejoice, and to do good in his life.

[13]And also that every man should eat and drink, and enjoy the good of all his labor, it is the gift of God.

She took these passages as her instruction to lighten up in her life. *Enjoy yourself,* she thought. *Stop being so focused and serious that you forget to have fun and make good memories. Life is pretty short, after all.* Caroline realized that her life, especially since her father's death, had been ordered and focused on her goals. She had put blinders on and just filtered out almost every distraction. At least she did before she and Garrett were engaged. *Maybe this is my grandmother giving me permission to have fun and love and live,* Caroline thought to herself. *Yep, that's it.* She was convinced that it was instruction from her grandmother, who could see things from a different perspective now. And so she would do just that. *Indeed, to everything there is a season,* she thought. *This is our season for living.*

The burial at Arlington Cemetery near John's grave was sad and sweet at the same time. Grant put a single pink rose on top of Elizabeth's casket and said good-bye to her for the last time. The ride in the limousine back to the church was quiet and solemn. When they arrived back at the church, Grant was surprised to see the fellowship hall filled with people from all across his life. He realized, maybe for the first time, the importance of friends, family, and people who love you in your life. He would need them if he planned to enjoy the years he had left.

CHAPTER 35

O N May 26, Caroline completed her first year of law school
at Emory. Her record was excellent, as always. She was glad to
be finished and have the time to focus on the wedding. One
more business item to take care of before the wedding was a meeting
with Lawrence Harris at King and Spalding to finalize her internship
plans. He agreed that her internship would begin on July 10 and
end on September 15, just before she returned for her second year
of law school. He was impressed but not surprised by her first-year
performance at Emory. "Miss Wellington," Lawrence Harris began,
"you had a very good year at Emory. Congratulations."

"Thank you, Mr. Harris," Caroline replied, not sharing all the events
during the last year that provided considerable distractions.

"Please accept my condolences for your grandmother's death," he
continued.

"Thank you, sir," Caroline replied.

"I would like you to work with Franklin Delaney in the wills and
estates area of the practice."

"Thank you, Mr. Harris," Caroline said. "I believe that will be a very good area of the practice for me to have exposure. I appreciate the thought that you put into this decision." After meeting Mr. Delaney, Caroline left the downtown Atlanta office and headed to Roswell. Her focus would now be totally on the wedding and the honeymoon.

When Caroline got to Roswell, she found her mother talking with Laura about the rehearsal dinner location. The final choice was Van Gogh's in Roswell. Caroline was thrilled, since it was a wonderful French restaurant with simple elegance and dining rooms large and private enough to accommodate their wedding party. Caroline invited Virginia Adams and Susan Spencer, her sorority sisters, to the wedding and the rehearsal dinner. She had seen Jackie a number of times since graduation, but not Virginia or Susan. They wrote to each other often. Besides Jackie, who was her best friend, Caroline, Virginia, and Susan had become very close friends in their last two years at UVA.

After Charlotte got off the telephone with Laura and explained the decision regarding the location of the rehearsal dinner, she changed the subject.

"Caroline," Charlotte began, "I hope it will be all right with you if Geoff Robinson sits with me at the wedding."

"Mama," Caroline asked, "do you have something you need to tell me about Geoff and you?"

"Not really," Charlotte said hesitantly. "I'm not sure what to make of our relationship, to tell you the truth." Caroline sensed that her mother was looking for some kind of approval from her before she shared any more information.

"Mama," Caroline began, sounding pragmatic, "I hope you know that I love you so much and I want you to be happy and have a wonderful life. If that means you get married again, I'm fine with that."

"You are?" Charlotte asked.

"Of course," Caroline replied. "Daddy has been gone for seven years. You deserve to be happy."

"Caroline," Charlotte began, "I really don't get involved in too many organizations, but Geoff and I are both members of the Alliance Theater and the Atlanta Symphony, and we have run into each other numerous times at those events. Your daddy and Geoff were best friends for so many years. He has had such a hard time since Camilla's death. His children are grown up and out of the house now, and I think, he is ready to find someone to share his life with."

"Mama," Caroline said, looking at her mother, "if this is what you want, go for it. It's time for us to live." Caroline wanted her mother to see that she was committed to enjoying life.

Charlotte sat down in one of the chairs in the breakfast room and cried. Caroline sat down beside her and held her hands and cried with her. "It just seems like our lives have been one struggle after another," Charlotte said through her tears. "Losing your daddy was so devastating to me, especially since he had not been able to stop drinking and really enjoy his life with us. I will always be sad about that."

"Me too," Caroline said as they sat crying together. "But we have today," Caroline continued. "We can't fix the past. We just have to not let it keep us from enjoying the rest of our lives."

"You're right, Caroline," Charlotte said, composing herself. "You know, you amaze me sometimes. You are so wise for one so young."

"We had these lessons whether we wanted them or not," Caroline replied, wiping her tears. "I'm going to marry a man I love more than I can explain to you. He and I should enjoy our lives and not take everything so seriously. I'm working on trying to lighten up, look around, and enjoy myself instead of being so focused and serious about everything. I have realized recently that I am allowing life to pass me by without enjoying it."

"I guess we both have, Caroline," Charlotte confessed.

"Geoff is a really nice person, Mama," Caroline said. "He likes to travel, and I think he knows how to enjoy life. He will be good for you."

"I think so too," Charlotte said and hugged her daughter. "We really are so lucky, Caroline."

The telephone rang. When Charlotte answered, Caroline could tell she was talking with her grandfather. "She's here now. Would you like to speak with her?" Charlotte asked him. She handed the telephone to Caroline.

"Hi, Granddaddy," Caroline said. "What's up?"

"Caroline, can you meet me at Harvey Bernstein's office on Tuesday next week?" he asked.

"Sure, what time?" Caroline asked him.

"Ten o'clock. I'd like your mother to come with you, if she can," Grant said.

"I'll ask her now," Caroline said. She turned to her mother, putting her hand over the mouthpiece. "Mama, Granddaddy wants us to come to Harvey's office on Tuesday next week at ten o'clock. I think it is about the prenup. Can you go with me?"

"Sure," Charlotte replied.

"We'll be there, Granddaddy," Caroline said, returning to her conversation with him. "Is this about the prenuptial agreement?"

"Yes," Grant replied. "I wanted you and your mother to see it before we talk with Garrett about it."

"That's what I thought," Caroline said. "We'll be there." She hung up the telephone.

On Tuesday of the following week, Grant, Charlotte, and Caroline met in Harvey Bernstein's office. He presented them with a twelve-page document. They would learn that Elizabeth owned one-half of the $50 million estate. She had left one-quarter of it to Charlotte and one-quarter to Caroline, and half of it went into a trust that would be divided equally between or among Caroline's children when they became twenty-five years old. The trust would provide income for Charlotte and Caroline until that time. The prenuptial agreement provided for Garrett only in the event that Caroline predeceased him and then only for the benefit of their children as long as they remained married. Should they have no children, one-quarter of the remaining trust would go to Garrett and one-quarter would be divided equally between Druid Hills Presbyterian Church and the Atlanta Symphony. Caroline and Charlotte would each receive $6.25 million. The other $12.5 million would be handled by the Trust Company Bank's trust department. Nancy Reed was a trust advisor in that department but was not allowed to handle any of the Wellington family money because she was a relative. Caroline knew she could get advice and direction from her and was thankful to have an "insider."

Grant provided a copy of his will to Caroline. It placed his entire estate in a trust for Caroline's benefit providing her with $250,000 in annual income with the remaining balance of the trust given in total to her on her thirtieth birthday. The prenuptial agreement included all of the money that Caroline currently had, the money that Elizabeth had left her, and the money that Grant would leave her.

"Caroline," Harvey Bernstein said, "your grandfather and I discussed this at length, and we believe that this is fair and right for you and your mother." Charlotte was in shock that Elizabeth had left her anything. "You know that Garrett will be required to sign this document also."

"Of course, Mr. Bernstein," Caroline replied. "Do you mind if my mother and I have a few minutes to talk about this?"

"Of course not," Harvey said. "Grant, can I buy you a cup of coffee down the hall?" Harvey and Grant stood and left the office.

"Mama, I think this is fair, don't you?" Caroline asked.

"I am still in shock that your grandmother left me six and a quarter million dollars," Charlotte said. "But aside from that, I think it is fair to Garrett too. You will have access to most of the money all of your life."

"Okay, we agree," Caroline said, relieved that her mother was okay with it. "Let's get the boys back in here, shall we?" Caroline walked down the hall and found Harvey and Grant drinking coffee and talking in a large conference room. "We're ready," Caroline said.

"That was fast," Grant replied, standing and following Caroline and Harvey back to his office. They all signed the agreement.

"Granddaddy, I think you did a good job of being fair. Thank you for doing that," Caroline said as she hugged her grandfather. Grant's eyes twinkled, and he put his arms around her and kissed her on the cheek. "You're going to be so handsome when you walk me down the aisle, Granddaddy," Caroline whispered to him. He chuckled and squeezed her hand. They said their good-byes to Harvey and rode the elevator down to the parking garage.

"Dad," Charlotte said to Grant, "I've been thinking about it, and I would like you to move to the cottage behind my house as soon as you feel comfortable doing that."

Grant looked at Charlotte, surprised by the invitation. "Well, honey," he began, "I want to be independent as long as I can, but I really appreciate that more than I can tell you. I'm relieved that I won't have to be in an old folk's home."

"Dad, don't be silly. We would never let you do that!" Charlotte exclaimed, smiling at his comment. "Call me if I can help you, okay?" Charlotte asked him.

"I will," he said as he got into his car.

"Ida is there with him, Mama," Caroline reminded Charlotte.

"I know she is, but I wanted him to know that he has a place to go if he needs us," Charlotte replied.

"I would be surprised if he ever leaves Inman Park," Caroline said. "He and grandmother bought that house in 1930. Forty-two years is a long time to live in one house."

"It sure is," Charlotte said.

The prenuptial agreement was sent to Garrett, and he signed it and returned it to the law office for recording with no fanfare or questions whatsoever. Caroline had told him to expect it, but they never discussed it after that. He really didn't want it to have any effect on them at all. It just was what it was and he was okay with that. The dollar amounts in the document shocked him. He knew that Caroline was wealthy, but until he saw the prenuptial agreement, he didn't know how wealthy.

Garrett was finding the political landscape interesting and challenging. There were very few people that he could really trust in Atlanta and even fewer in Washington. Senator Gabriel was in the middle of an election campaign and had pulled out all the stops to get re-elected. Garrett traveled with him frequently, and on one of their trips to Savannah, Jerry Rowland, one of the junior staff members, asked Garrett to if he could get copies of two of his speeches ahead of time. He had heard there was a sensational revelation in the speech that the senator would deliver to his constituents in Savannah. Jerry found a way to make extra money by selling information to the press. A "scoop" was very valuable to the press corps, and Jerry used his influence to get information to them in the past. In exchange, he had made more than $50,000 over the past two years in "under-the-table" payments from Martin Murray at the *Washington Post*. Garrett knew that this type of activity was going on, but this was the first time he had been approached to participate.

"I can make it worth your time," Jerry said to Garrett, trying to persuade him to leak information. Garrett knew that Jerry was not the most trustworthy person he had ever met.

"Jerry, you are putting me in a very bad spot," Garrett said, trying to put him off. "Besides, I don't have access to his speeches or any other information on a regular basis."

"But he trusts you, Garrett," Jerry continued, coaxing Garrett to comply.

"Trust is a great value to have, Jerry," Garrett said, admonishing Jerry.

"You want to get ahead in this game, you need to play, Garrett," Jerry said, still trying to convince Garrett to betray his boss's confidence. "You can make some really good money with these press boys."

Garrett thought about how disappointed Caroline would be if he got involved with Jerry like this. It also occurred to him that it was funny that Jerry thought he needed to make more money. Garrett's mind leapt into the future when Jerry would learn that he had married into one of the wealthiest families in Georgia.

"Jerry, it's a great offer, but I can't help you," Garrett said with a finality that left Jerry no choice but to give up.

"Listen, Garrett," Jerry said, as he stood up, realizing that he would not get what he wanted, "you won't say anything about this conversation, will you?"

"Only if I am asked about it, Jerry," Garrett replied, looking Jerry straight in the eye. Jerry left the room quietly and from that day forward bent over backward being nice to Garrett. Word got around about the "straight arrow" working for Senator Gabriel. Garrett knew that he would never get into politics himself. He was satisfied to stay on the periphery. He noticed that most of the staffers steered clear of him after that. He began to be more aware of the corruption and collusion that seemed to be business as usual in Washington. Cronyism and quid pro quo were everyday occurrences. Garrett wondered if he needed to change professions. How could he have been so naïve? This was part of his education and experience that he could do without. The wedding was around the corner, and he decided to focus on his job and forget the politics of corruption. And that is what he did.

Caroline was very busy with the logistics of the next few weeks. She decided to stay in Roswell until after the wedding. She and Garrett would fly to Hawaii on Monday morning. Charlotte planned a brunch at her house on Sunday for the out-of-town guests who would still be in town. Caroline and Garrett would be the guests of honor at the brunch.

Caroline had arranged to give up her rental house when her lease expired in September. She and Garrett would find a larger house to rent near the Emory campus until she could graduate from law school. Caroline wanted them to do that together.

On Tuesday, June 20, Jackie flew to Atlanta, where she would stay with Caroline and Charlotte until the Monday after the wedding. Jackie would stay in one of the guest rooms, and Virginia and Susan would stay in the cottage. They planned to fly in on Thursday. Virginia was working in New York City for an investment firm on Wall Street, and Susan was in graduate school at the University of North Carolina. Caroline was thrilled to have time to spend with them.

Garrett was still working and would be in Washington until Thursday. He would fly to Charleston, and he, Derek, Laura, Allison, and Emily would drive down on Thursday afternoon. Charlotte had friends who lived in Roswell and would be in Europe for the summer. They offered their home to the Winthrop family for the week of the wedding. Charlotte was thankful that they would not have to stay in a hotel. The home was large enough to accommodate the Winthrop's and Garrett's friends who were in the wedding. The other out-of-town guests would stay at the Doubletree Hotel. It was a beautiful hotel on a pinnacle in Roswell with beautiful views. Everything was falling into place.

Jackie and Caroline spent Wednesday picking up dresses, shoes, and gifts for the bridesmaids. Caroline gave Jackie a beautiful pearl bracelet with a diamond clasp as her maid-of-honor gift in addition to the earrings, dress, and shoes. She planned to give Emily and Allison gold bracelets along with their earrings, dresses, and shoes. They had a ball running around Buckhead shopping and having lunch at the Ritz. Charlotte was busy with the last-minute reception details for the cocktail party and dinner that would happen after the wedding. A small orchestra would provide the music for the cocktail party and dinner. Afterward a DJ would play sixties and seventies music. Garrett told Caroline that their first dance music would be a surprise for her. She had no idea what he was planning, but she decided to leave that to him.

Ellie was as busy as she ever had been at the Wellington home. Robert had come the previous week and brought a crew of people to plant flowers in Charlotte's yard. There were beautiful pots of impatiens, begonias, and ivy on the front porch. The hydrangeas were blooming, and the yard and porch was beautiful with hanging ferns and pots of flowers. Robert had arranged for a crew of men he trusted to provide the valet services for the guests' cars. The Baptist church next door graciously offered their parking lot to accommodate them. Robert, Karen, and Samantha Belle were wedding guests, and Robert would not be working that evening.

On Friday morning, the doorbell rang at nine o'clock. Ellie went to the door to find Garrett standing on the porch with a bouquet of pink roses for Caroline. "Miss Caroline," Ellie called up the stairs, "if you are decent, you need to come downstairs."

Caroline came to the top of the stairs and saw Garrett standing at the door with roses. She flew down the stairs and into his arms. They had not seen each other for over a month. He came into the house and said, "I can't stay long, honey, but I had to see you. I have missed you so much."

"I have missed you too," Caroline said. "C'mon, let's get those in some water. They are gorgeous!"

"Glad you like them," Garrett said, smiling and giving her a quick kiss.

Caroline found a beautiful faceted glass vase and arranged the roses. She put them on the dining table. "Thank you very much," she said to him.

"Tomorrow night you will be Mrs. Winthrop," Garrett said sweetly.

"Yes, I will, and I can't wait," she replied.

"Gotta go. I am assigned to take my family to Lenox Square shopping. There are always those last-minute things. I'll see you tonight at rehearsal at six o'clock," Garrett said as he turned to leave.

"Looking forward to it," Caroline replied as she walked him to the door. He kissed her for a long time and then took off down the stairs and back toward the car. "Have your sisters back here by one o'clock for the bridesmaid's luncheon, okay?" Caroline said.

"Will do," he said as he pulled out of the driveway.

At one o'clock, the girls all gathered at Caroline's house in Roswell. Caroline had invited Virginia and Susan to join them for lunch. Just as they were about to leave for the Public House, Irene walked in the back door. "I do declare," she announced in her southern drawl, "that the gnats out there are thicker than fleas on a hound dog in August." All of the girls howled with laughter. "Where's your mama, honey?" Irene said to Caroline.

"She's upstairs," Caroline said as the group went out the back door, still laughing.

They walked to the Public House and enjoyed brunch in a private room upstairs overlooking the square in Roswell. By two thirty, they were back at Caroline's house.

Garrett's father picked up Emily and Allison, and they went to get ready for the rehearsal. At three o'clock, Grant arrived with Ida. Charlotte had arranged for Ida to stay with Ellie for two days to help with the preparation and the brunch on Sunday. Grant would stay in the second guest bedroom on the second level. Charlotte hoped he could climb and descend the stairs without too much trouble. Ellie met them at the door. "Mr. Wellington, Miss Charlotte is in the kitchen." Grant went to the kitchen, and Ida took his suitcase and the bag with his clothes for that evening and his tuxedo for the wedding upstairs.

Grant found Charlotte sitting at the breakfast table making a last-minute list for Ellie and Ida. "Well, there you are!" Charlotte exclaimed as she stood to give him a hug.

"I thought we had better get on over here. I'm not as fast as I used to be," Grant said, chuckling.

"None of us is, Dad," Charlotte said, laughing with him.

Ellie came into the kitchen. "Miss Charlotte, I'm going to help Miss Irene get ready. Is that all right?" she asked.

"Perfect, Ellie," Charlotte replied. Ellie went upstairs to find Irene.

At six o'clock, everyone was at Primrose Cottage for the rehearsal. Dr. George Patterson, Irene's pastor at First Baptist of Roswell, would be officiating. He was a veteran, and he took charge of the rehearsal along with the wedding planner from Primrose Cottage. At seven thirty, everyone felt comfortable with his or her part in the ceremony. The wedding planner spoke with the wedding party about the reception and their parts at the beginning before the bride and groom made their appearance.

By seven forty-five, the group was seated at Van Gogh's and drinks were being served. The guests had specially printed menus for this occasion. Their choices were lamb, filet mignon, or chicken. By the end of the meal, the champagne was being passed for the evening toasts. Derek stood first. "Thank you all for coming to celebrate Caroline and Garrett's marriage. Garrett has always been a very inquisitive boy. When he was about five, he wanted to know how airplanes flew. I could explain aerodynamics to him. When he was seven, he wanted to know how the moon knew when it was supposed to be full. I had answers for him then. I think that now he can answer my questions better than I can answer his. He has made me proud for so many reasons. His mother and I are happy that he and Caroline are getting married tomorrow. His choice for a life partner is a perfect example of the ways he makes us proud." Derek raised his glass. "So here's to the bride and groom with wishes and prayers for a happy and fulfilling life."

"Here, here!" rose the voices of the people attending the dinner.

Grant stood next and spoke. "Good evening. I, too, would like to thank all of you for sharing in this very special time for our families. I stand here tonight in the place of my son, John Andrew Wellington. He was a brilliant lawyer, but he was brilliant in many other ways. He was brilliant to choose Charlotte to be his wife. He was brilliant to decide to give my wife and me a granddaughter. There were giggles in the audience. "His brilliance is shining tonight in the face of my beautiful granddaughter, Caroline Elizabeth Wellington. She is amazing and is a wonderful light in my life. My precious Caroline and Garrett, I wish you blessings throughout your lives. Please remember that every moment is a treasure to be enjoyed and lived." Grant raised his glass. "Here's to Caroline and Garrett and my wish for blessings of love as they enjoy their lives together."

Once again, "Here, here" rose from the guests.

Caroline stood and walked to her grandfather and embraced him. "Granddaddy, you are so wonderful. I love you," she said as she put her arms around him.

"I love you too, baby girl," Grant replied. Caroline stood back and looked at him. He knew why. "I wanted you to know that I believe your father and grandmother are with us tonight," he said.

"I think they are too," Caroline said as she gave him one last hug and went back to her chair.

Irene had a wonderful time, and Charlotte thought she might have had too much champagne. But she was happy to see her enjoying herself. She was eighty but still pretty spry. So often, she had a look on her face like the cat that swallowed the canary. Charlotte sometimes wondered what she was up to. Tonight was no exception.

As is southern tradition, the groom must not see the bride on the day of the wedding before the ceremony. So Caroline had to be sure that she and Garrett would not be together after midnight. Caroline thanked Derek and Laura for a wonderful evening. Charlotte heaped compliments on both of them for the wonderful dinner and perfect location. The evening ended at ten forty-five when everyone went to their respective homes and hotels.

The following morning, Caroline woke up at six thirty. As soon as she opened her eyes, she thought, *Today I am marrying Garrett.* She started thinking about all the things she had to do, and she got out of bed, got dressed, and went down for coffee. Ellie was in the kitchen with a fresh pot of coffee ready. Ellie was making bacon and eggs with toast for the household.

Charlotte appeared at the kitchen door. "Well, well," she said when she saw Caroline in the kitchen. "You're up bright and early."

"I woke up thinking about everything I have to do today and I couldn't sleep anymore," Caroline said sleepily. Caroline, Jackie, Emily, and Allison had hair appointments at noon in Buckhead. They would have their nails done at the salon and then head back home to do makeup and clothes. Caroline quickly drank her coffee, ate her bacon and eggs, and went back upstairs to shower. Within an hour, Jackie, Virginia, and Susan were in the kitchen with Charlotte drinking coffee and eating breakfast. By ten o'clock, everyone was dressed and ready to go to Buckhead. Caroline took her mother's car because hers was too small to hold everyone.

At ten fifteen, Derek brought Emily and Allison to the house for the trip to the salon. The house was filled with laughter and chatter. Charlotte enjoyed the wonderful atmosphere and loved having the girls there. Everyone was excited, and Caroline was trying to keep everyone organized and on time. They arrived at the salon at Lenox Square at eleven forty-five. They were quite a group, and the salon fell silent when the six of them walked in. Fortunately, the receptionist was expecting them and showed them to their respective stylists. Virginia and Susan were not getting their hair done, so they went shopping while the wedding party got their salon services. By two thirty, everyone was coiffed and polished. The front of Caroline's hair was pulled back into a beautiful twist at the top of her crown. The back of her hair was down with soft curls. She would anchor the floor-length veil at the front of the twist for the ceremony and remove it for the reception.

The girls returned home to find a light lunch of pimento cheese sandwiches, turkey sandwiches, and iced tea. Jackie and Virginia did not know what to make of the pimento cheese, so they chose turkey. Emily, Allison, and Susan enjoyed the pimento cheese sandwiches along with Caroline. It wasn't quite as good as Belle's, but it tasted pretty good to Caroline. It was time for makeup and getting organized to move their dresses and shoes to the bride's room at Primrose Cottage. They would all get dressed there.

Fortunately, the weather was beautiful. There was hardly a cloud in the sky, and the high temperature was expected to be eighty-five degrees. Anything below ninety degrees was good in late June.

At five o'clock, Primrose Cottage came alive with girls getting dressed, the photographer taking pre-wedding photographs, and the groom and his party arriving. Garrett would remain in the groom's quarters until the minister escorted him into the wedding gallery. David and Mark would be at the front of the wedding gallery ready to escort the guests to their seats. Virginia and Susan made sure the wedding party had plenty of water and snacks. At six thirty, Jackie, Emily, and Allison left the bride's room to meet with the wedding planner to get to their places. Caroline was alone in the room when Grant knocked on the door. When he entered the room, he saw Caroline standing near the palladium window.

"My God, Caroline!" Grant gasped. "You are stunning. I have never seen a more beautiful bride!"

"Thank you, Granddaddy," Caroline said as she hugged him. "You're quite handsome yourself."

"Haven't had my tux on for quite a while," he said reflectively. "I used to wear it a couple of times a month at least."

The photographer knocked on the door and took pictures of Caroline and her grandfather. Charlotte and Irene came in just as he was finishing, and he took individual pictures and group pictures of their family. When he was finished, he said he was going to the groom's room for their photographs. Caroline liked this photographer because he tried to get as many photographs taken before the wedding as possible.

In the groom's room, things were pretty boisterous. Someone had brought a radio, and rock 'n' roll music was blaring. The guys were laughing, talking, and having a great time teasing Garrett. The photographer got some great candid shots of the scene. Derek and Laura were in the room with the boys, and their photographs were done within fifteen minutes. Laura left and met Charlotte and Irene in the hall on the way to the front of the wedding gallery for last-minute instructions from the wedding planner.

The white wedding programs were beautiful, printed in black script tied at the fold with a black bow. They were made of cotton and were very elegant. On the inside of the first page was a wonderful verse from 1 Corinthians 13.

> ### The Way of Love
>
> Love is patient and kind. Love is not jealous,
> boastful, proud, or rude.
> Love does not demand its own way.
> It is not irritable, and it keeps no record of when it
> has been wronged.
> Love is never glad about injustice but rejoices
> whenever the truth wins out.
> Love never gives up, never loses faith, is always
> hopeful and endures through every circumstance.
> There are three things that will endure –
> Faith, Hope, and Love.
> But the greatest of these is Love.
> Love lasts forever.

As Caroline wanted, there was a dedication in the program to the memory of her father and grandmother. None of Garrett's grandparents could attend. A dedication in their honor was also in the program.

By six forty-five, the wedding gallery was filled. A couple of stragglers rushed in to be seated before the wedding began.

At seven o'clock, the minister walked to the front of the wedding gallery with Garrett, who was so handsome and very nervous. A choir member from Irene's church, Ray Lassiter, sang the theme song from *Love Story* in a beautiful tenor voice. It was Garrett's love song to Caroline.

The doors to the back of the gallery opened, and the organ and harp began to play Vivaldi's "Spring." Irene was the first to be seated. She wore a light blue two-piece beaded chiffon gown. Her silver hair was fixed perfectly, and she wore small diamond earrings. She was beaming as she walked down the aisle. Laura followed her down the aisle wearing a periwinkle two-piece taffeta gown with a wrap top and a portrait collar. She looked wonderful with her dark hair and her blue eyes sparkling. Charlotte followed Laura wearing a Tadashi Shoji chiffon-overlay gown in bright pink with beading on the fitted crisscross textured bodice. She was gorgeous with her salt-and-pepper hair. Charlotte was wearing the necklace that John had given Caroline when she was two. She was seated next to Geoff Robinson.

The organ and the harp began to play "Canon in D." Emily was the first down the aisle. The bouquet of red roses and babies' breath was beautiful with her black gown. Allison was next down the aisle. She walked to the front of the gallery and stood next to her sister. Jackie walked down the aisle followed by the flower girl, who was David Otwell's five-year-old daughter, Meghan. She was precious in a white organza floor-length gown with babies' breath and orange blossoms in her hair. Her six-year-old brother, Ryan, followed the with the ring pillow. He was adorable in his mini-tuxedo.

After the ring bearer reached the front of the church. The doors to the wedding gallery were closed. The organ chimed the hour—seven chimes. The trumpet player stood and began playing "Trumpet Voluntary" with the organ and harp. At the first note, the doors opened, Charlotte stood along with the guests, and Caroline started down the aisle with her grandfather. She was a vision in her gown. She wore small pearl-and-diamond earrings. The bridal bouquet was white roses, white hydrangeas, and Queen's Anne's lace tied with candlelight ribbon. Grant was smiling from ear to ear. When

Caroline saw Garrett, she smiled sweetly. A tear rolled down her cheek. Garrett could not take his eyes off her. When they arrived at the altar, the minister asked, "Who gives this woman in marriage?"

Grant said, "Her mother and father and I do." And, he stepped back and took his seat next to Charlotte.

Caroline handed her bouquet to Jackie, and she and Garrett faced each other, holding hands. The minister took them through their vows. After their vows, Glenda Wilson, a woman who attended church with Irene, sang "The Wedding Song" by Paul Stookey. The minister performed the ring ceremony. Caroline still couldn't believe she was getting married. After the ring ceremony, Glenda sang the Lord's Prayer. Then minister then said, "Caroline and Garrett, inasmuch as you have made your journey to this holy pledge to one another and have witness of this commitment before God and your family and friends, it is my privilege to pronounce that you are husband and wife. Garrett, you may kiss your bride."

Garrett gently took Caroline in his arms and passionately kissed her. They turned to face the guests and slowly walked back down the aisle to the organ playing "The Halleluiah Chorus" from Handel's *Messiah* (Garrett's idea). When the remainder of the wedding party was escorted back down the aisle, the guests made their way to the reception hall on the lower level. The tables were set with white tablecloths and black napkins. The chairs were draped with sheer white fabric and tied at the back with a black ribbon. Each table had a different floral arrangement. Some were red roses, some were blue hydrangeas, and some were white and pink peonies. There were fourteen tables, each seating ten guests. The ceiling-to-floor windows looked out on the rear garden, which was lighted with thousands of tiny white lights. There would be champagne punch and hors d'oeuvres now and dinner after the wedding party arrived. The serving tables were set with elegant floral arrangements that included red and white roses, hydrangeas, and Queen Anne's lace.

Everyone was enjoying the orchestra music, hors d'oeuvres, and punch. Charlotte and Laura were busy with introductions to each other's families and friends. Geoff stayed beside Charlotte during most of the evening. Laura had fallen in love with Irene and talked with her every chance she got. Derek was talking with David's and Mark's parents, who had come from Charleston. Anne and her husband and Nancy and her date were enjoying visiting with friends. Within twenty minutes, the orchestra director announced the wedding party.

Caroline and Garrett went to the dance floor for their first dance as husband and wife. The orchestra began to play the first notes of "The Way You Look Tonight." Caroline put her hand over her mouth, trying not to cry. Garrett took her in his arms and waltzed with her around the room, singing the words as they danced. The orchestra director sang the song, and it sounded just like it did the night of Caroline's cotillion. Not many people knew the significance of the song, but Charlotte, Irene, and Grant did. It was a very special moment for them all.

At the end of the dance, she put her arms around him and said, "Thank you. That will be one of the most precious memories of my life." And, she kissed him.

Caroline and Garrett spent the next hour greeting guests. At eighty thirty, dinner began. The orchestra played wonderful classical music. At nine fifteen, the party started. The music changed to a disc jockey playing rock 'n' roll from the sixties and seventies. The Beatles, Earth, Wind and Fire, Elton John, the Eagles, Stevie Wonder, Fleetwood Mac, and the Jackson Five were among the artists whose hits were played by the DJ. The dance floor was filled to capacity, and everyone was having a ball. The champagne punch flowed freely, and they rocked the rafters. Charlotte, Geoff, Laura, and Derek were dancing the night away too. Caroline loved watching Robert and Karen dancing. Robert waltzed around the dance floor with Samantha squealing with delight. Irene took every chance she could get to watch Miss Samantha Belle while they enjoyed dancing and eating. There was laughter and singing throughout the room.

By eleven o'clock, when the cakes had been cut and the bouquet and the garter had been thrown, it was time for the newlyweds to leave. The guests were given rose petals to shower the couple as they left. Right on cue, the Bentley was waiting at the front of the circular pebble driveway. Caroline stopped to give her mother a long hug. "Mother, this has been the most wonderful night of my life, and you made it happen. Thank you very much," she said to her.

Charlotte had tears spilling over and rolling down her cheeks. "You, my dear, have made my life the most wonderful life anyone could hope to have. It has been a joy to do this for you. I love you very much, Caroline," Charlotte stopped speaking while she was trying to get composed.

Irene was next. "Mama Rene," Caroline said, "you are just the best grandmother in the world. Thank you for sharing so much of your life with me."

"It is I who am thankful, Caroline," Irene said. "Thank you for sharing *your* life with *me*." Caroline kissed her grandmother on the cheek.

She turned and put her arms around Grant. "Granddaddy, I love you very much. Thank you for everything you have done for me."

"Caroline, it makes me happy to see you so happy," he said as he hugged her. She kissed him on the cheek.

Garrett was saying his good-byes to his mother, father, Emily, and Allison and getting high-fives from his buddies from Charleston. They would all be together again in the morning for brunch, but this was a special end to a perfect wedding.

The Bentley slowly pulled out of the driveway and headed to the Ritz Carlton in Buckhead. Garrett and Caroline drank champagne and kissed each other the entire way there. "Mrs. Winthrop," Garrett said, as they were pulling into the hotel entrance, "will you sleep with me tonight?"

"You betcha," Caroline replied. They were escorted to the Buckhead Suite. It was a seven-hundred-square-foot suite with a king-sized bed, a living room, and a small dining room. There were two dozen red roses on the dining table when they arrived, with a note of congratulations from the hotel manager. There were fresh strawberries, grapes, gourmet cheeses, and more champagne. When they arrived at the room, the bellhop unlocked the door and proceeded inside with their bags. Garrett picked Caroline up in his arms and carried her across the threshold into the hotel room. He tipped the bellhop and closed the door.

"All day I have wanted to pinch myself to be sure this was real," Garrett said as he stood looking as his new wife. "You are so beautiful. I am so happy, and I am very proud that you are my wife."

"Garrett, I love you so much. Your love has changed my life. You have made me realize that I need to wake up and live. Thank you for believing that we could be together," she said as she put her arms around him and kissed him. As she stood back, Garrett began unbuttoning her wedding gown in the back. When the last button had been pulled through its silk fabric loop, Caroline's dress fell to the floor, revealing a white lace strapless bra and lace bikini panties to match.

"Ooooh!" Garrett exclaimed. "Just a few buttons and I can see this?" He unfastened her bra, and her breasts were exposed.

Caroline walked closer to him and began removing his jacket. She unbuckled his belt and began unbuttoning his shirt. "It's only fair," she said in a pouty, sexy voice.

"Well, I want to be fair," Garrett said, fully cooperating. When his shoes and trousers were off, Caroline could see the bulge in his briefs. She put her hands on both sides of his pants and pulled them to the floor. He easily stepped out of them. He removed her panties and turned back the covers on the bed. He gently picked her up, laid her down in the bed, and climbed in beside her. They kissed passionately and consummated their marriage. "I love you, Caroline," Garrett said, smiling down at her.

"I love you, Garrett," she whispered back. "I did not know I could be this totally happy, but I am."

"I'm so glad, sweetheart," Garrett said as he rolled off to one side, "because I am too." They got out of bed. Caroline put on her nightgown and Garrett put on his shorts and they went into the living room of the suite and ate strawberries, drank champagne, and laughed and talked until two o'clock. They crawled back into bed, exhausted, wrapped their legs together, and fell asleep.

Garrett woke up first at eight o'clock. *Six hours of sleep is not enough,* he thought. As he sat up on the side of the bed, Caroline opened her eyes.

"Good morning, handsome," she said.

"Good morning," he replied.

"You know, sex is really great," Caroline said spontaneously.

"I couldn't agree more," Garrett said laughing at her again. And they had sex again.

After showers and packing the wedding clothes, the limousine was at the Ritz to take them back to Roswell. Caroline was wearing a pink linen sheath dress with pearls. Garrett wore khaki trousers and a light-blue oxford cloth shirt. They truly were a beautiful couple.

They arrived in Roswell at ten forty-five to a houseful of family and friends. Jackie, Virginia and Susan were sitting on the front porch drinking Mimosas. "Just in time," Jackie shouted, holding up her glass as they exited the limousine. Garrett tipped the driver and he left.

"Looks like you have a head start," Garrett said.

Caroline walked onto the porch and gave each of the girls a hug. "All of you were wonderful during this whole time. I don't know how I could have done it all without you."

"We have had a blast," Virginia said, raising her glass.

"Caroline, your mother is just the best!" Susan exclaimed.

"She really is. Y'all enjoy," Caroline said as she walked in the screened door with Garrett following her.

Laura came from the kitchen into the foyer to give them hugs. "Good morning, newlyweds," she said.

"Mom," Garrett said, "this has been the most wonderful wedding in modern history. You and Dad have been so great. Thank you for everything you did."

"We love you both very much. It's great to see you happy," Laura said as she hugged her new daughter-in-law.

"Garrett is right," Caroline said. "It really was the perfect wedding."

"I think so too, Caroline," Laura said, "But you know your mother had a whole lot to do with it."

"I know," Caroline said. "She is the master of event planning. I watched her when I was growing up entertain hundreds of people and make it look easy. She learned the fine art of delegating." Laura laughed.

Irene appeared from the kitchen. "There's my girl," she said as she hugged Caroline. "Never thought we'd have a boy in our family, but we do now," Irene said, laughing. She gave Garrett a hug and went to the porch to drink her coffee and sit with Laura and the girls. The ceiling fans were creating a nice breeze, and the group enjoyed their coffee and Mimosas.

Derek walked into the foyer from the family room. "Good morning, Son," he said. "Good morning, Caroline. I hope you had a good evening." He winked at Garrett.

"It was perfect, Dad," Garrett replied.

"Good morning," Caroline said and blushed as she walked into the kitchen. "Mama, where's Geoff?" she said as she put her arms around her mother.

Charlotte was helping with last-minute details for the brunch. With Ellie and Ida working together, she knew that everything would be handled well. "He couldn't come today, honey," Charlotte said. "His son is home from college, and they had some things to take care of."

From the family room, Grant saw Caroline walk into the kitchen. He rose slowly. Caroline walked into the family room. "Don't get up, Granddaddy," she said as she gave him a hug.

"I need to stir around a little bit, honey," he said returning the hug. He walked into the kitchen, and Ida gave him a large glass of orange juice, which he accepted gratefully. He walked back into the family room and continued reading the *Wall Street Journal.*

Emily and Allison came back into the house from a walk down to see Bulloch Hall. "Did you know that Mittie Bulloch married Teddy Roosevelt in the dining room of that house?" Allison asked Caroline as she walked in the front door with Emily.

"Yes, I did. My grandmother remembers it," Caroline said. "There's lots more history in Roswell. When y'all come back, we can do the walking tour sometime." There were so many historical sites within walking distance of Charlotte's house.

A large party tent was in the back yard with a buffet and tables set for fifty guests. At eleven o'clock, the brunch guests began to arrive. Once again, there was laughter and music celebrating the wedding. Charlotte had hired a photographer to chronicle this event too. Mostly, there were candid shots of each guest arriving and greeting the newlyweds. Many of the out-of-town guests had airplanes to catch or had to leave to drive home. By three o'clock, everyone but the core group of friends and family were gone. By five o'clock, most of the evidence of the outdoor buffet was cleared out. There were plenty of leftovers and lots of cold cuts and desserts. Charlotte notified everyone to help themselves to anything they wanted to eat. At six o'clock, she sent Ellie and Ida home to rest.

Caroline and Garrett spent the night at the Doubletree Hotel in Roswell.

On Monday, Garrett's family would drive back to Charleston, Jackie, Virginia, and Susan would fly to their respective homes, and Caroline and Garrett would fly to Maui.

When Monday arrived, Ellie and Ida were at Charlotte's house by five thirty. They were organizing a small breakfast for the remaining family and friends. At eight o'clock, Caroline and Garrett arrived packed and ready for the limousine to pick them up to take them to the airport. After breakfast, there were tearful and joyful good-byes when the limousine arrived at nine o'clock. Charlotte waved until she could not see them anymore. Robert drove Jackie, Virginia, and Susan to the airport. Ida packed Grant's things, and they left for Inman Park. Derek, Laura, Allison, and Emily pulled out of the driveway headed home to Charleston at ten o'clock.

By ten thirty, Charlotte, Irene, and Ellie were alone in the house. It seemed strangely quiet after all of the commotion over the last week. "Mother, do you want to take a walk around the square with me?" Charlotte asked, knowing she would need to walk at Irene's pace.

"I sure do, honey," Irene said as she stood to open the back door. The two of them walked, talked, and reflected on their lives. It was a touching and loving experience for both of them.

CHAPTER 36

THE ELEVEN-HOUR FLIGHT TO MAUI, changing airplanes in Los Angeles, was exhausting. But, stepping off the plane into paradise was worth it. Caroline and Garrett were greeted with flower leis and escorted to the limousine provided by the hotel. Upon arrival, they entered a fabulous hotel with more than eight hundred guest rooms. They were taken to check-in, where they each received another flower lei. A small open tram waited to take them to the elevator that would take them to the Regency Suite. It was over 1,300 square feet of gorgeous furniture, including a living room, dining room, bedroom with a king-sized bed, one and one-half bathrooms, and three lanais. Their view of the ocean and the mountains from the private balcony was spectacular. Although to them it was midnight, it was only six o'clock in the evening in Maui. After they unpacked, they took a shower together, which was a rather sensual experience. Then they dressed and went to have dinner at the 'Umalu Restaurant. They enjoyed a dinner of local fish and white wine poolside with lively entertainment. After dinner, they went to the concierge desk to get information on local sites and attractions. The concierge suggested that they get up early in the morning before they adjusted to the time and drive to the top of Haleakala, the world's largest dormant volcano, to watch the sun come up. He arranged for their transportation up the ten thousand foot mountain to the top where they would have bicycles to ride back down after sunrise. That sounded like a fabulous adventure to them.

The next morning, they both were awake by four o'clock. The van would leave at five o'clock to take them to the top of the mountain. The concierge had warned them that it would be very chilly at the top, so they both took sweaters. The ride to the top was unnerving. They drove through clouds and fog for almost an hour on a narrow road that often had no guardrails. Caroline, especially, was glad to be at the top. It was worth every second of the ride when they stood at the top of the mountain and watched the sun peek over the horizon. They felt as if they were on the top of the world. Garrett took photographs and had the guide delivering the bicycles take pictures of them before they began their bike ride down the ten thousand foot mountain. They pedaled back to the hotel, returned the bicycles and walked to Swan Court to have a continental breakfast.

And so began the first day of their honeymoon. The concierge arranged for a jeep tour on the "Road to Hana" for the second day. They would travel on fifty-three one-lane bridges and over six hundred curves.

When the jeep tour began, Garrett was glad he wasn't driving. They were able to see and photograph spectacular waterfalls and amazing black sand beaches. They had lunch at Paia Plantation. It had been a thriving sugar plantation in the 1800s. Today, it was a quaint little town with charming restaurants and homes that were rented to tourists.

On Wednesday, they went on a catamaran snorkeling cruise. They lunched on the catamaran after snorkeling in the morning. Every afternoon after their activities, they went for a swim in the Lahaina pool. On Thursday morning, the concierge arranged for Garrett to have a foursome golf outing at Ka'anapali Golf Resort. Caroline would enjoy a complete day at the Moana Spa with a facial, massage, manicure, and pedicure. That evening they enjoyed a **Lu'au at the hotel on the Sunset Terrace on** Ka'anapali Beach. They received shell leis and enjoyed mai tais before the dinner and show. They loved the show, which depicted Polynesian history with the sound of the conch, the drums, and the traditional Hawaiian chants. The evening included an imu ceremony, and they were treated to exotic Hawaiian cuisine.

On Friday, they decided to stay in their room for most of the day. They enjoyed the passion in their marriage every day. But, Friday was a special day where they enjoyed making love and talking and laughing. They each called home to talk with their families. Charlotte was thrilled to hear that they were having such a wonderful time. Laura could hardly wait to tell Derek and the girls about the telephone call.

Maui was truly a paradise. Caroline and Garrett felt as if they were in an impenetrable bubble that they wanted to last forever. On Friday evening, they dined oceanside at the hotel. They were served by candlelight under an oceanfront canopy just as the sun started to set. It began with a champagne toast followed by dinner service by their personal attendant. The Ka'anapali seafood trio included grilled lobster tails, Hawaiian snapper, and scallops. The romantic dinner ended with rich Tahitian vanilla crème brulée. After dinner, they walked on the beach and talked about their plans when they returned to reality.

Saturday, they took a trip into town to do some souvenir shopping. They enjoyed walking through the beautiful town and in and out of the shops. They bought gifts for their family and friends who had been in the wedding. They decided to have an early dinner at four o'clock. They walked into a little oceanside restaurant, ate salmon and shrimp, and listened to a two-man band for three hours. At seven, they took a taxi back to the hotel and made love until they fell asleep in each other's arms.

On Sunday, they slept in and enjoyed a late Sunday brunch in the hotel. The concierge arranged for a private helicopter tour of the island. They flew over the Haleakala Crater, the Hana rainforest, the Seven Sacred Pools, and the waterfalls, which were even more amazing from the air. Caroline and Garrett saw a rainbow that was so large that the helicopter flew into it. The colors were breathtaking. They flew over the island of Molokai and saw the spectacular waterfalls that lined the world's tallest sea cliffs. The three-hour tour was a highlight of their trip.

They went horseback riding for four hours on Monday through some of the most scenic trails either of them had ever seen. After four hours on horseback, neither of them could sit down comfortably. "Oooh!" Caroline exclaimed. "What were we thinking? My butt hurts like hell!"

"Mine too," Garrett lamented. "It feels like my butt is bruised!" They went back to the hotel, changed into their bathing suits, and went to the hot tub to soothe their aching bottoms.

On Tuesday, their last day in Maui, they went to the Old Lahaina Book Emporium. They enjoyed the funky bookstore and bought a coffee table book on Maui. It seemed like the best way to share the island with their family and friends.

Wednesday at noon, they boarded their airplane back to Los Angeles and then back to Atlanta. By the time they got back to Atlanta, they were both glad that they did not have to report to work until the following Monday.

Charlotte picked them up at the airport and drove them to Caroline's rental house. They were both chattering about the wonderful vacation and honeymoon. "Mama!" Caroline exclaimed, "We have to go back, and you and Garrett's parents have to go with us. Maybe Geoff could go too!"

"I can't wait to see the pictures and hear all about it," Charlotte said genuinely.

"We have a lot to do before we go to work next week," Garrett said to both Caroline and Charlotte.

"Garrett and I would like to come to your house on Saturday and talk with you about where we are considering moving," Caroline said to Charlotte.

"That's great, honey," Charlotte replied as she pulled into their driveway. "Y'all just give me a call when you are on your way."

"Thank you for picking us up, Mrs. Wellington," Garrett said as he gave his mother-in-law a hug.

"Thanks, Mama," Caroline said, kissing Charlotte on the cheek. They disappeared with their luggage into the small rental house that would be home for the next couple of months.

CHAPTER 37

*C*AROLINE AND GARRETT SPENT THURSDAY and Friday trying to get organized in their new household. They still enjoyed sitting on the screened porch in the evenings drinking coffee after dinner. They were so in love that they felt as if the outside world was impervious to them.

They identified a home that was for sale in Druid Hills. Caroline decided that it was best to purchase the home instead of renting again. It was a wonderful house built in 1920 with three bedrooms and three and one-half bathrooms that was in the budget that Caroline had allocated for their home purchase. It had a red tile roof and was on more than an acre of land. It was big enough for entertaining when they needed to do so. There was a flagstone patio with a barbeque grill and picnic table at the back of the property along a natural stone path. The heating system was still radiant heat, but they could deal with that. It was well priced at $125,000. Caroline thought Charlotte's real estate agent could work with them and get it for less.

On Saturday morning, Caroline called her mother at nine o'clock. "I hope I'm not calling too early, Mama," Caroline said when Charlotte answered the phone.

"Of course not, Caroline," Charlotte replied. "Your call is always welcomed."

"Garrett and I would like to come over around two o'clock to talk with you about the house we're considering buying," Caroline said, almost as a question.

"That will be fine, honey. I have asked Cathy Bishop to join us. I hope that is all right," Charlotte said.

"Great idea, Mama," Caroline said. "I was hoping she could help us. We will see you at two o'clock." She hung up the phone and told Garrett about the conversation. Garrett was thankful for being in a family that was well connected.

Their meeting with Charlotte and Cathy wound up being very productive, and the following Monday they asked Cathy to submit an offer of $115,000. She did, and it was accepted. Neither of them could believe that that were purchasing their own home.

Garrett returned to work with a re-election campaign in full throttle. The preliminary election was coming up, and Mr. Gabriel was running against a relatively unknown candidate named Sam Nance. Garrett was enlisted to be on the campaign trail with Senator Gabriel and was out of town at least three days of every week. Caroline was left to participate in her internship at King and Spalding and take care of purchasing their new home on her own. She knew that Garrett had no choice except to be where the senator needed him, but she missed him and wished he didn't have a job that took him out of town for so many days each week. He apologized very often and told Caroline that he would work toward having a job that did not require that he be gone so often. Caroline knew he was sincere, and they worked together to accomplish their mutual goals.

On September 8, they closed on the purchase of their new home on Oakdale Road in Druid Hills. Caroline especially loved the red tile roof and the sunroom with black-and-white Italian marble floors. So much of the original home was still in place. It had beautiful Corinthian columns, and the three bedrooms and three and one-half bathrooms gave them the additional space they needed. Garrett loved the barbeque grill on a secluded patio in the backyard. Because the lot was over an acre and since Garrett was out of town so often for his job, Caroline knew she would have to hire a gardener. When they moved into the house, Charlotte gave them some of the furniture from the Peacock House that would not fit into her home in Roswell. They purchased a new king-sized bed for the master bedroom. Garrett lovingly referred to it as "their playground." The home would serve them well until Caroline graduated from law school.

In November of that year, Senator Gabriel lost his bid for another term in the Senate. Sam Nance won the seat. Garrett was unsure if he would continue to have a position, since staffers were usually replaced. In December, Senator Nance interviewed him and decided to keep him on his staff. He recognized Garrett's extraordinary interpersonal and diplomatic skills. He had also heard about his trustworthiness. Garrett was assigned to Senator Nance's Atlanta office as his constituent liaison. It was a perfect job for him. He still traveled to Washington about once a month, but he was home almost every evening. They enjoyed entertaining, finding new restaurants to enjoy alone or with friends, meeting friends and family in Hilton Head a couple of times, and taking romantic trips to the mountains. Caroline was more outgoing and social than she ever before in her life. In her quiet moments, she thought of her life as a metamorphosis. She had been in a cocoon for most of her life. Now she was enjoying being a butterfly.

In May of 1973, Caroline graduated "with distinction" from Emory Law School. She received an appointment to clerk for a judge in the Eleventh Circuit Court of Appeals in Georgia. She gladly accepted the appointment, and in June she began clerking.

Garrett was still very busy working with Senator Nance. But neither of them was too busy to celebrate their first wedding anniversary in Destin. They rented a small cottage on the beach with beautiful views. Every evening they sat on the porch and watched the tide come in, drinking champagne and eating seafood. Although they were only able to get away for four days, it was a very relaxing time for them and a time to remember their wedding and honeymoon. They were happy and very devoted to each other.

In the spring of 1975 Caroline's clerk appointment was ending. She was asked to join King and Spalding as an associate, and she gladly accepted. Although she was interested in corporate law, she chose to work with Chris Wright, who was a partner in the government investigations practice group. Her job took her to Washington at least twice a month and to New York several times a year.

She and Garrett were settling in to their very busy lives. They got lucky once in a while and were in Washington at the same time. They enjoyed meeting one another's colleagues and friends in the evening and on weekends. Alexandria was one of their favorite spots, and they toured and dined in Olde Town as often as they could. Both their spheres of influence were expanding very quickly. Occasionally, they flew to New York on the weekend and took in a Broadway show.

Caroline's work with the firm was recognized, and she believed that she was on a fast track to becoming a partner. Typically, an associate would be with King and Spalding for ten years before being considered to become a partner. Caroline hoped her opportunity would come within five to seven years.

One Friday evening in July, they were sitting in their small den talking about the week. Garrett said, "Caroline, I have been approached to join a group in Washington that lobbies for the legal industry. That means that I would be there at least four days every week and sometimes over the weekend. The job is very interesting to me and would definitely expand my skills, and I would have the opportunity to meet a lot of powerful people who could help me advance my career."

"Garrett," Caroline said with an objective note in her voice, "have you really thought this through?"

"I'm starting to do that by talking with you," he said, hoping she knew that he wanted her to be involved in the decision.

"It's very important to me that we spend time together," Caroline said as she began working through the pros and cons of his decision. "We really have a pretty good set-up right now."

"I know we do, honey," Garrett said, almost sad that he had this opportunity. "I'm trying to weigh the future with the present. Caroline, I do not ever want you to think that I would sit back and allow you to support us. I really am ambitious, and I need to move forward when I have an opportunity."

"I know you are, and I really love that about you," Caroline said as she moved close to sit next to him on the sofa. "It's just that what we have right now is so wonderful that I really don't want to give it up."

"Me either, really," Garrett said, realizing that he would probably turn down the job.

"I'll tell you what," Caroline said, "Let me get at least one year with King and Spalding under my belt, and then if you have an opportunity like this, I will request a transfer to Washington and we can move."

"That's fair," Garrett said. "Thanks for helping me talk through this. I really like Senator Nance, and I'm still involved with some of the most powerful people on Capitol Hill."

"Thank you, Garrett," Caroline said, kissing him on the mouth. "I love you more every day."

"You know, you are pretty amazing, Caroline," Garrett said. "I have to tell you that I feel like I am married to my best friend and the love of my life all rolled into one."

"Me too," Caroline said. "It doesn't get any better than this."

Neither Caroline nor Garrett saw their families very much. There were lots of telephone calls, but not many visits. Caroline missed her mother and Mama Rene and sometimes longed to sit on the front porch of her mother's house with both of them. It just seemed like the world was going faster and faster every day. Her life with Garrett fulfilled so much in her and her job kept her so busy that there was rarely any time to think about that.

Before they knew it, they were ringing in the New Year in 1976. Neither of them could believe that they had been married for two and a half years. In that time, they had a few spats, but typically one or the other of them or both apologized within an hour and all was well again.

Caroline was enjoying practicing law, and Garrett still loved the work he did with the senator. On New Year's Day, they had a rare opportunity to visit Charlotte. Irene was on hand for a traditional southern New Year's day dinner with ham, black-eyed peas, and turnip greens. Garrett surprised everyone when he announced that he would take Caroline to London and Paris for their third anniversary in June. They enjoyed the day with Charlotte and Irene. Caroline thought Irene looked more feeble than she remembered. She had faced so much death to be so young, and she knew she would have to brace for Mama Rene's death. She promised herself that she would come to Roswell more often and have her mother and grandmother visit them more often. Caroline managed to get to Roswell once in

February and once in March. In April, Charlotte and Irene came to spend a weekend with them in their Druid Hills home.

Before she knew it, their fourth anniversary arrived and they left on a Friday afternoon for Paris. They would be in Paris for four days and London for four days. The last time Caroline was in Europe was with her mother before she started law school. She was pretty young when she was there with both her parents. But eight years of French in high school and college came in very handy. They stayed at the Ritz in Paris and loved the luxury. They walked up and down the Champs Élysée and rode the Metro all through Paris, taking in as many of the amazing sights as possible. They both agreed that Notre Dame and the Louvre were their favorite places in Paris. All but one of the evenings, they dined at L'Espadon, the fabulous restaurant in the hotel. Their time in Paris was romantic and exciting.

In London, the Ritz was different but equally as exquisite as the Paris hotel. The couple enjoyed afternoon tea in the hotel after a day of sightseeing. They had dinner at the Ritz restaurant with dancing after dinner. Being together was more special to them than ever.

When they returned, Caroline got her photographs developed and made an album that they could share with their families. Caroline loved the seven bridges in Paris, and Garrett loved Westminster Abbey in London. They vowed to return to Europe for another anniversary celebration.

CHAPTER 38

*T*HEY WERE BACK TO WORK and as busy as ever. It was late August and hot, as usual, in Atlanta. They were having dinner on Friday evening at home when Caroline said, "Garrett, I think I have the flu."

"Honey, I am so sorry," Garrett said. "Do you think you need to go to the doctor?"

"It will probably pass by tomorrow," she said. But it didn't pass. Caroline woke up on Saturday and Sunday throwing up. She stayed in bed and slept almost the whole weekend. Charlotte called to check on her, and when she heard the symptoms, she knew right away that Caroline was expecting a baby.

"But how could I be pregnant, Mama?" Caroline asked. "I have been taking birth control pills."

"They don't always work perfectly, Caroline," Charlotte said.

"Oh, I know it's just a stomach bug," Caroline said dismissively.

"Honey, why don't you go to see your doctor one day next week?" Charlotte instructed her. "You can find out for sure what this is."

"If I don't feel better by Wednesday, I will make an appointment," Caroline said. Garrett was not privy to that conversation, and Caroline decided not to mention it until she knew one way or the other.

The following week, it was all she could do to stay at work. She was so ill on Monday morning that she had to leave her desk at least five times. She felt as if she could fall asleep standing up. She phoned her physician on Tuesday afternoon and made an appointment for Wednesday afternoon. If she had a bug, he could give her something to stop the awful nausea. If not, she wasn't sure what she would do.

At four o'clock on Wednesday, Caroline waited for the urine test results. Dr. Meade had checked her from head to toe and could not find anything wrong. At four thirty, Dr. Meade's nurse came to the waiting room and said, "Caroline, Dr. Meade would like to see you in his office." Caroline walked into Dr. Meade's office and sat in the chair next to his desk.

"Caroline, it looks like you do not have the flu. But you are expecting a baby. With the information I have right now, I would say that you could expect to deliver around March 7 of next year."

Caroline could hardly speak. "Are you sure?" she asked.

"I've been doing this for twenty years, Caroline," he said, chuckling. "Yes, I'm pretty sure that you are pregnant."

"But I've been taking birth control pills," she said, obviously shocked with the news.

"There are times when the pill just doesn't work like it should," he replied. "It's usually about 95 percent safe, but it looks like you fell into that 5 percent. I'm going to write you a prescription for nausea medication and for prenatal vitamins. Please begin both of these medications as soon as possible." He was writing the prescriptions but continued talking with her. "If you do not have an obstetrician, I would recommend that you contact Dr. Gerald Sheffield. He is one of the best, and he delivers at Northside Hospital. I think you will like him and like the hospital. They are very well known for their labor-and-delivery area."

Caroline took the prescriptions and drove to the drugstore to have them filled. She was still in shock. When she got home, Garrett was already there. "What did the doctor say, honey?" he asked. "Do you have the flu?"

"No, Garrett," Caroline said. "It's not the flu."

"What's the matter, Caroline? Are you all right?" Garrett seemed a little panicked.

"Oh yes, I'm fine," she said. "I'm pregnant."

Garrett looked up at her and said, "Really?"

"Yes, really," she said.

He walked over to her and gathered her in his arms. "Caroline, that is wonderful. I know we weren't planning on it right now, but it is wonderful!" he said. "I love you so much."

"I love you too, Garrett," Caroline said. "I have to get used to the idea of being a mother. The doctor said the baby was due around March 7 next year." Garrett did a happy dance in the small den.

"I'm so tired, I just have to go to bed," Caroline said.

"Not before you eat something," Garrett said. "You sit down right here and I will have some soup for you in about ten minutes." She ate the soup with saltine crackers, which is what the doctor recommended to help with the nausea, and went to bed.

The following morning at eight o'clock, Caroline was up and throwing up again. She wondered how in the world women sustained pregnancies when they were as sick as she was. By ten o'clock, she was feeling better. "Garrett," Caroline said, "Don't you think we should call our parents?"

"Absolutely," Garrett replied. "I was waiting until you felt like talking."

"I do feel better now," Caroline said weakly.

"Who do you want to call first?" Garrett asked.

"You decide," Caroline said.

"Okay, we'll call your mother first," he said. Garrett dialed Caroline's mother's telephone number.

"Hello," Charlotte said.

"Mrs. Wellington," Garrett began, "this is Garrett."

"Yes, Garrett, I recognize your voice," Charlotte responded. "How is Caroline feeling?"

"She's a little better this morning," Garrett said tentatively. "She wants to talk with you." And he handed the telephone to Caroline.

"Mama, you were right, as usual," Caroline said.

"Really!" Charlotte exclaimed, not trying to hide her excitement. "That's wonderful, Caroline. Congratulations to you and Garrett, honey!"

"Thanks, Mama," Caroline said, halfheartedly. "I'm still so sick that I can't be too excited yet."

"I understand, honey," Charlotte said sympathetically.

"Were you this sick when you were first expecting me?" Caroline asked.

"I'm afraid so," Charlotte said. "I was probably in bed for about three weeks."

"I hope I can go back to work on Monday," Caroline said.

"The most important thing is that you take care of yourself, Caroline," Charlotte said sternly. "There is only one of *you*."

"I know, Mama," Caroline said. "You're right. Garrett is taking great care of me."

"I'm sure he is, sweetheart. If you need me, call me. Is it okay if I tell Mama Rene?" Charlotte said.

"Sure, Mama," Caroline said. "Tell her I love her, will you?" Caroline asked.

"Yes, I will, honey," Charlotte said. And they hung up.

Garrett dialed his parents' home telephone number. "Hello," Laura answered.

"Hi, Mom," Garrett said.

"Well, good morning, sweetheart" came Laura's happy voice. "How are you two doing?"

"We're great!" Garrett said. "Well, Caroline is pretty sick right now."

"Really?" Laura asked with concern in her voice. "What's wrong?"

"We're expecting a baby!" Garrett said excitedly, listening for his mother's reaction.

"Oh my gosh!" Laura screamed into the telephone. "That is fabulous, Garrett! Let me talk to Caroline."

Garrett handed the phone to her. "Mom wants to speak with you," he said.

"Hello" came Caroline's weak voice.

"Caroline, honey, I am so happy for y'all! Has the doctor told you when the baby is due?" Laura asked.

"He said probably around March seventh," Caroline answered. "I have to make my initial appointment with the obstetrician next week."

"I know you probably don't feel very well right now, but it will get better soon," Laura offered as comfort to Caroline.

"I hope so," Caroline said. "I've been pretty sick for the last few days."

"Usually, after the first two or three months, you feel better. Being pregnant is a very big adjustment for your body, you know," Laura said.

"So I am finding out," Caroline said, laughing. "Garrett wants to talk with you again."

Caroline handed the phone back to Garrett. "Mom, would you tell Dad and my sisters?"

"I will be very glad to share this happy news!" Laura said excitedly. "Listen, when Caroline feels better, Dad and I would like to come to Atlanta to visit you for a few days."

"That would be great, Mom," Garrett said. "Just give us notice so we can be sure our work schedules can be arranged so we can spend time with you."

"We will, honey," Laura said. "Take care of your wife, Garrett."

"You know I will," he said, and he hung up the phone.

Caroline decided that weekend to wait to tell her boss about the pregnancy. In fact, she planned to tell Lawrence Harris first. The nausea medication the doctor gave her worked wonderfully. She managed to perform well at work except for being extremely tired. She and Garrett went together to her first appointment with Dr. Sheffield. They really liked him and felt comfortable that he would take great care of her and their baby.

By the middle of October, there was no choice but to tell Mr. Harris about the pregnancy. Her clothes were tight, and she wore jackets and sweaters to hide the growing bulge. She made an appointment with him for Friday, October 17, at four o'clock. "Caroline," Lawrence Harris said as he stood when she walked into his office, "I hope everything is all right."

"Mr. Harris, everything is great. I love the area that I am working in, and Chris has been fabulous!"

"He has been very complimentary of you, Caroline. To what do I owe this visit?" he requested.

"Mr. Harris, I wanted you to be the first in the firm to know that Garrett and I are expecting a baby," she said, waiting for his reaction.

"Caroline, congratulations!" he said. "I know your families must be very happy."

"Yes, everyone is excited," she replied. "I need to know what the policies of the firm are with regard to how long I can stay in my position before maternity leave begins."

"Caroline, I'm going to put you in touch with our human resources director for that answer," he said. "But I believe that the firm requires that you stop work at seven months. I will have Kathy Malone call you next week and give you the information."

"Thank you, Mr. Harris," Caroline said as she stood to leave his office.

"I hope you're feeling well," he said.

"It was pretty rough at the beginning, but I feel great now," she said.

"Well, you didn't let anyone know you were not feeling well," he observed.

"We thought it best to get past the first trimester before we announced it," Caroline said.

Lawrence Harris sat back in his chair, thinking that Caroline had a glow about her that he had not seen before. "You look wonderful, Caroline," he said, surprising her with his personal compliment.

"Well, thank you, Mr. Harris," Caroline said, blushing. She rose to leave his office and return to hers on a lower floor.

"If I can help you in any way, please just call me," he said. Caroline thought he sounded rather fatherly.

"I appreciate that very much, Mr. Harris," Caroline replied as she turned to look at him. She observed a sadness in his eyes that she had never noticed before. Being too personal with him was not something she ever considered. She was tempted to ask him about his family. Instead, she left his office.

When she arrived back at her office, she thought it best to let Chris know too. He was on the telephone and looked up to his ears in paper. That was typical for a lawyer. When Caroline heard him end the conversation, she walked to his office. "Chris," she said as she stood in the doorway.

"Come on in, Caroline," he said. "I don't know about you, but I'm glad it's Friday. I am going to go home and collapse."

"Sounds like a great idea to me," Caroline replied. "Hey, Chris," she began again, "I need to let you know about something."

"Okay, shoot," he said.

"Garrett and I are expecting a baby," she said, smiling at him. Caroline was very fond of Chris and felt that they had a good working and personal relationship. Chris knew Garrett, since they had entertained clients in Washington several times during the past year.

"Caroline, congratulations to you both!" he said as he stood to walk to give her a hug. "I know your families must be thrilled."

"Yes, we are all pretty excited," Caroline said as she accepted his hug and returned it.

"Does Larry know?" he asked.

"Yes, I thought it best to tell him first since he hired me," she answered.

"You let me know if you need anything," Chris said genuinely.

"Thank you, Chris," Caroline replied. "I really appreciate that."

Caroline returned to her office to finish some paper work before she left for the weekend.

On Saturday, Caroline and Garrett went maternity clothes shopping. Caroline insisted that they buy professional clothes for her to finish her time at the firm. She would continue until they made her quit. By Saturday afternoon, her closet was filled with all things maternity.

They enjoyed the Thanksgiving and Christmas holidays with their parents. Charlotte and Irene flew to Charleston with Caroline, and Garrett for Thanksgiving and the Winthrop family came to Roswell for Christmas. Everyone was thrilled about the baby. Caroline got tired of everyone asking her if she was okay. She felt as if they thought she was ill instead of expecting a baby. Her aversion to being in the limelight was as evident as ever.

Dr. Sheffield revised the expected due date to March 15, and her last day practicing law at King and Spalding was January 15 due to the policies of the firm. She spent the time organizing their home and the nursery. She understood, for the first time, the concept of "nesting." Caroline drove to Roswell at least once a week to spend the day with her mother and Mama Rene. Mama Rene told her one story after another of her childhood in Roswell and about the birth of her mother and her aunts. Caroline loved hearing the stories about her family.

She made it a point to visit Grant every couple of weeks also. During her visits, she asked him to tell her about his childhood and Elizabeth's. As he strung the stories together, Caroline realized how fortunate she actually was. Her grandparents on both sides had worked hard and were poor during some portion of their lives. Even her mother and father had not understood what it was to be wealthy until they were adults. She, on the other hand, had been born into wealth. She made a commitment to herself to keep her child grounded in reality and not overindulge him or her.

Garrett did not grow up with the privilege and prestige that she had. They had long conversations about the importance of raising a child in reality. Character, responsibility, honor, and integrity were of the utmost importance to both of them. Caroline knew they would have philosophical differences, but on those issues, they were in perfect sync.

Valentine's Day was on a Saturday in 1977, and Caroline and Garrett drove to Hilton Head on the Friday morning before Valentine's for a long weekend. They rented a small house on the beach in Sea Pines, and although it was cold, they enjoyed the fire and listening to the ocean. Their lovemaking never slowed down except for the first few weeks when Caroline was so ill. Garrett told her every day how beautiful she was. He loved putting his head on her bare stomach and feeling the baby kick. They shared quiet, intimate moments leading up to the birth of their child. They were more in love than ever.

By the end of February, the nursery at their Druid Hills home was done. They chose green and yellow for the nursery colors since they did not know if they would have a boy or a girl. They painted one wall a light yellow and the other walls a soft green. They chose a nursery ensemble called "Little Tree." The ensemble was an outdoor theme with birds, trees, and leaves in beautiful soft blue, green, yellow, and light brown. Charlotte gave them Irene's mother's rocking chair, which had been in Caroline's nursery. Laura gave them a small chest that had been in Garrett's nursery. They chose a crib and a dresser that was also a changing table in an arts and crafts style in a rich dark cherry. It looked wonderful with the bedding set.

Caroline had one baby shower at work, one in Roswell, and one in Charleston. They were set for the arrival of their baby.

"You know, Caroline," Charlotte said to her during one of their visits, "your child will learn far more by what you do than what you say. Children are little sponges, and they rapidly absorb the personality and character of their parents."

"I can see that," Caroline replied. "I watched you and Daddy, and I remember trying to be like you. I thought you were the most wonderful and beautiful person in the whole world. And I thought Daddy was a super hero who could do anything. I knew I was loved, Mama."

Charlotte felt overwhelming sadness for the abuse Caroline had witnessed during her life. She could only hope that the good outweighed the bad. John had been dead for ten years. It was difficult to believe so much time had passed, but Charlotte observed that time healed the open wounds and left mostly good memories. She hoped the good memories were the ones Caroline kept too.

Caroline spent time looking through photograph albums of her childhood and of Garrett's. Garrett was an adorable little boy with dark curly hair and beautiful green eyes. She decided to take photographs of him and herself when they were two years old and have them framed and put into the living room. She would add the baby's photograph to the group when he or she was two. In almost all of the photographs of her, she was wearing the necklace that her father gave her on her second birthday. In fact, she was wearing it right then. She touched it and closed her eyes, trying to remember her father. She had forgotten what his voice sounded like, but she could see him as clearly as she did when he was alive. "I love you, Daddy," she whispered to herself. A tear rolled down her cheek as she struggled to see him in her memory. She had not realized how handsome he was until she was an adult.

CHAPTER 39

*I*T WAS EARLY MARCH, AND Garrett was very attentive to Caroline. Although she rarely asked him for help doing things around the house, he always volunteered and took over some of the things Caroline had been doing. They hired a housekeeper to come in two days a week. She was Ida's friend, and the family she worked for moved to Florida and she was looking for a new family. Josie Williams was forty-eight years old and had worked for wealthy Atlanta families most of her life. She was the soul of kindness, and Caroline was grateful for the help. Charlotte helped Caroline hire a nurse to come to stay with them until the baby was a few months old. Caroline planned to breast feed, but she knew she would need help for a while. Carol Morrison was a baby nurse who had worked for fifteen years for families with new babies. She came to the Winthrop's home to meet Caroline and Garrett. Charlotte was on hand and was obviously in charge of the decision. Charlotte liked her, and they were glad to have that decision behind them.

After Carol left the house, Caroline said to Charlotte, "I miss Belle, Mama. There will never be another Belle."

"No, there will never be another Belle," Charlotte said. "I miss her every day."

"Me too," Caroline said.

On March 10, Garrett went with Caroline to her doctor's appointment. When the doctor checked for any sign of dilation, he told them that Caroline was showing signs of beginning labor. The baby's head was in position, and it looked like she would be delivering within a week or so. Caroline was particularly thrilled to hear that since she was very uncomfortable. They decided that Caroline would have an epidural to allow her to be awake when the baby was born. Garrett would stay with her in a suite at Northside Hospital where she would labor and deliver the baby.

The following Sunday, March 14, Caroline and Garrett were sitting in their den talking about last-minute logistics. Caroline wanted a glass of tea and got up to walk to the kitchen. On the way, she felt a twinge in her back. She didn't mention it to Garrett, thinking it was nothing. When she sat back down, she felt her stomach tighten like a strong flexing muscle, and the twinge was there again. "Garrett," she said, "this may be nothing, but when I have this contraction again, I want you to put your hands on my stomach."

"Okay, honey," Garrett said, and he moved to sit close to her. Within a couple of minutes, the contraction started again. He put both his hands across her stomach. "Wow!" he exclaimed. "That feels like what they told us a contraction would feel like in our birthing classes. I'll start timing them." For the next half hour, they wrote down the timing between the contractions and the duration of them. "Honey, this may be it," Garrett said.

"I don't want to go to the hospital for a false alarm," Caroline said. "Let's just wait a while and see what happens."

"Hey, this is your call, Caroline," Garrett said, supporting her decision to wait to call the doctor.

They were both still awake at midnight. The contractions were about three minutes apart and were lasting about forty-five seconds. "I think we'd better go on to the hospital, Caroline," Garrett suggested.

Caroline was beginning to feel pressure, and she agreed to go. Garrett got her bag and gently helped her to the car. It was a twenty-minute drive to the hospital. When they arrived, Caroline's contractions were two minutes apart and were lasting longer. They were preregistered and after showing identification were taken back to a birthing room. The room was bright and comfortable, with a sofa and chairs and cheerful art. They got her set up, and the labor-and-delivery nurse checked her for dilation. "You are seven centimeters dilated," she said. "The anesthesiologist will be here within five minutes to give you an epidural."

Caroline was uncomfortable but not in horrible pain. Each contraction seemed to get worse, though. After the epidural was administered, she felt herself relaxing. Dr. Sheffield walked into the room. "Well, I see we're having a baby tonight," he said as he patted Caroline on her arm. He shook Garrett's hand and said, "I'm going to need you to help coach her."

"I have been highly trained," Garrett joked. "I paid close attention in our birthing classes."

"Good for you," Dr. Sheffield said. Garrett was holding Caroline's hand and telling her how great she was doing. Caroline was hooked up to a fetal monitor for the baby and to oxygen and a heart monitor for her.

At 4:47, a beautiful baby boy was born. When Dr. Sheffield held him up for Caroline to see before cutting the cord, Caroline said, "Oh my God, he is perfect!"

Garrett kissed her and said, "I love you, beautiful. You are amazing." And he walked to the foot of the bed where the doctor allowed him to cut the umbilical cord.

Garrett was amazed at this tiny little person that their love had created. John Garrett Winthrop was making a noisy entrance. The nurse cleaned him up, put a diaper on him, wrapped him tightly in a blanket, and handed him to Caroline. He was struggling to look at her, and her heart melted the moment she held him. Before they left the delivery room, Caroline was nursing him. He seemed to know exactly what to do, and she didn't have to coax him very much. Garrett walked beside the bed as it was rolled up to their private room in the maternity ward.

By now, it was six thirty. As soon as they reached the room, Garrett called Charlotte to tell her that they had a baby boy. "I'll be there as soon as I can," Charlotte said. She called Irene, who wanted to go with her to the hospital. Garrett called his parents, who said they would be there by seven o'clock that evening. Garrett telephoned his office at eight o'clock to say he would not be in. Senator Nance called to congratulate him and gave him the week off to be with Caroline and the baby.

Charlotte remembered how her mother's presence had comforted her when Caroline was born. When she arrived at the hospital at eight o'clock, she told Garrett to go home and get some rest. He put up a mild argument but gladly went home to sleep for a few hours before his parents arrived. By eight o'clock that evening, Caroline's hospital room was filled with family ooohing and aaahhhing over baby John. He had dark hair and fair skin. No one could really tell who he looked like yet.

By the following morning, Caroline's room was filled with flowers. Jackie called, very excited to hear the news. Derek and Laura stayed at Caroline and Garrett's house. Derek would drive back home on Tuesday, and Laura would stay until the Saturday and then fly home. Charlotte planned to be at their house for the first couple of days and then return on Saturday when Laura went home to help Caroline the following week.

Caroline had read as much as she could get her hands on to understand everything she needed to know about caring for her baby. She was organized and very calm. John seemed to feel that and was a very good baby. He mostly cried when he was hungry or needed a diaper change.

The young Winthrop family was doing well and working together like a hand in glove. Garrett was involved in John's everyday life when he was home. He gladly gave Caroline a break every evening that he was in town. His son was the light of his life.

By the time John was three months old, Caroline realized that she could not leave him to go back to work. She wrestled with the decision to stay home with him, trying to justify the years she spent getting a good education and a law degree. Garrett was supportive of her and really wanted her to stay home with John. He was prepared for whatever decision she made. She would be giving up one of the best jobs she would ever find with King and Spalding, and working with Chris was a dream. But the maternal pull to stay with her son won.

She called Larry Harris a month before she was to return to work and told him she just could not leave her baby. "I was half expecting you to make this decision, Caroline," he offered kindly.

"Thank you so much for understanding and for the opportunities I have had with the firm. I really like Chris, and it has been a very difficult decision for me. I hope to have the opportunity to work with you again, if there is a place for me," Caroline said, thankful that he was so kind.

Chris was equally as kind, and Caroline was relieved to have that decision made. She turned her focus to Garrett, John, and their home.

CHAPTER 40

AROL MORRISON STAYED UNTIL JOHN was three months old, and Caroline was grateful for the help. After she left, Caroline began thinking about hiring a nanny. That quest took her to the realization that their current home would be too small for a live-in nanny and a housekeeper. She began looking for a larger home. Garrett was satisfied to allow her to handle the search. They discussed John's attending Westminster, as she had. The quality of education he would receive was unquestioned, and Garrett was all for it. Although John was still a baby, they wanted to move to Buckhead to be closer to the school. Their goal was to not affect Garrett's commute to work to any great degree and have reasonable proximity to their doctors, shopping, and the airport.

Their search took them to the charming community of Vinings. Its proximity to Buckhead and the fact that it was not inside the Atlanta city limits or Fulton County was attractive to the young couple. Caroline had become disgusted with the current mayor and the way the city was being run. Garrett had enough inside information through the senator's office to affirm her opinions and fuel her decision to move to the metro Atlanta suburb. The Westminster School was about two miles from their home, and that made the area perfect.

On September 30, 1977, Garrett and Caroline purchased their dream home on Polo Lane in Vinings. The home was a six thousand square foot six-bedroom, six-bathroom home with two half baths on two acres. The rear of the property sloped down to the Chattahoochee River. The brick sidewalk and steps led to the white wood structure with a round Georgian-columned entry. There were five dormer windows in the main part of the house and two in each of the symmetrical offsets on each side of the house. There were four fireplaces, one each in the living room, the den, the dining room, and the master bedroom. Caroline loved the symmetry of the house. Out back, there was a slate patio with a fifth fireplace on a beautiful covered porch. It would be perfect for entertaining. There was a detached cottage with a small living room, kitchen, bedroom, and bathroom. It would be the living quarters for their housekeeper. Two bedrooms were joined by a "Jack 'n' Jill" bathroom that would good for John's nursery and a nanny.

Charlotte called Katy Rucker for a recommendation for a nanny for John. After she stopped working for the Wellingtons, Katy had returned to teaching. She had a friend whose daughter was a young woman teaching in the Atlanta public school system. She hated her teaching job and wanted out. Charlotte arranged for an interview, and after checking references, Caroline hired twenty-two-year-old Gail Pryor to be John's nanny. At the same time, she hired a housekeeper who came recommended by Belle's brother and sister-in-law. Rachel Watkins was very glad to get out of her current job at the Atlanta airport. She hated the bureaucracy and was happy with the offer from the Winthrop's. With her living quarters provided, and a good salary to boot, she readily accepted the position. Caroline was quickly recreating her childhood for her son.

As Caroline expected, John was very precocious. She spent a lot of time with him. Gail's teaching experience was very valuable, and Caroline was glad have her there to help care for him.

Caroline had been so busy and distracted with the purchase of their home and hiring a housekeeper and a nanny that she and Garrett had not spent as much time alone as they wanted to. It was Friday, November 12, and the two of them were just starting to look at their Thanksgiving and Christmas schedules. John was just eight months old, and both Charlotte and Laura and Derek wanted as much time as possible with him. Caroline had taken him to stay with Charlotte a couple of times after he was six months old, so she and Garrett decided to have Thanksgiving in Charleston. Naturally, Charlotte and Irene were invited. Caroline made sure that Grant had an invitation to Charleston too. Charlotte talked him into going, and on Wednesday, November 24, the three of them flew to Charleston. The elder Winthrop's did not have the space to accommodate them, but they arranged for a hotel for them close by. Charlotte and Irene stayed together, and Grant stayed in an adjoining room. Everyone enjoyed being together, and John got even more attention than usual. Rachel and Gail were given the week off to spend with their families, for which they were grateful.

Christmas that year was in Atlanta, with all family members coming to the young Winthrop's home in Vinings. John was crawling everywhere and standing, and he kept the whole group busy.

Charlotte spent hours with him when she could, holding his hands and allowing him to walk safely. Joy was inadequate to explain how she felt when she was with him. Irene understood perfectly how she felt about John. Caroline refocused her time to include Garrett. After Christmas and the New Year, she and Garrett spent more time traveling together. When he was working, often she would go to Washington with him and they would have a romantic weekend together in Georgetown and Alexandria. They both enjoyed their time alone, and their schedules were adjusted whenever possible to accommodate that. But Caroline was restless and needed intellectual stimulation. She would find it the following year.

CHAPTER 41

*C*AROLINE GOT INVOLVED IN SEVERAL nonprofit foundations, but one that was in her heart more than the others was a foundation that offered shelter to mothers and children who were been in abusive situations. She gravitated to the foundation and offered her personal help as often as she could. During one of her volunteer sessions, she was introduced to young mothers who had been beaten and abused by their husbands or boyfriends and did not have family or friends to provide a safe place for them. Caroline's heart broke for these women and especially for the innocent children who were affected. When she volunteered with the foundation, she saw so many ways to improve the quality of life for these women and children, but it seemed that the only thing these shelters were doing were providing a temporary bed and food. Caroline saw the opportunity to provide so much more. Her organizational, project, and legal skills went into overdrive.

As she was trying to make the decision to dive head first into the project, she thought she should tell Garrett why this particular situation was so near and dear to her heart. On a Saturday evening when they were having dinner at home alone, she told Garrett about her childhood. Garrett could not believe what she was telling him. He had no idea that Caroline and her mother had such a difficult life.

Caroline apologized to him for not telling him sooner and simply told him that her privacy was the driving factor in not sharing the truth with him earlier. It also helped him understand her aversion to drinking alcoholic beverages. Garrett told her that he loved her more than ever and that his admiration for her was off the charts. With his support and love, Caroline felt unstoppable.

After John's first birthday, she began her campaign for donations from large companies to start a program for women and children that would give them more than a place to sleep and a meal. She created a business plan that outlined the structure of the organization, the scope of the services it would provide, and the plan to put it all in place. She covered the legal and regulatory aspects of the project and the funding it would take to get it all up and running. She created a pro forma that outlined the ongoing financial requirements to sustain the organization and services. She organized the New Beginnings nonprofit foundation for abused women and children.

She began presenting her project to potential contributors. Her contacts easily opened doors for her in Atlanta. The program included housing and education for mothers as well as their children. The education for mothers would include life skills that showed the women how to dress for business and advice on hair and makeup and manners in personal and business settings as well as academic classes. The women also would be given an interest inventory test, and an educational program would be developed that allowed them to pursue gainful employment in an area they liked that would also be useful in business.

The school-age children would be placed in public schools in the area. Babies would be cared for by their own mothers, under the supervision of life coaches, except when the mothers were in classes. Caregivers were available for babies and for school-age children after school. The residents would be responsible for keeping their own areas clean and neat with instruction and inspections.

On August 31, 1978, the doors opened to the New Beginnings Home for Abused Women and Children. It started small, with two women and three children, and grew so fast that Caroline found herself with a full-time job trying to accommodate all of the referrals she received from social agencies, schools, the court system, and God only knew where else. The goal of the program was to have the women graduate to live independently and self-supporting within one year.

The facility was located in Smyrna in Cobb County, west of the city of Atlanta, about eight miles from Caroline and Garrett's home. It could house fifteen women and twenty-five children. Caroline received funds from many of the law firms in Atlanta and surrounding areas that she lobbied and from local businesses. She invested over $350,000 of her own money in the project. It was comprehensive and allowed the women to progress at their own pace.

Initially, Caroline oversaw the operation. She was skilled at hiring great talent to provide the services needed for the women and children. Every morning, the mothers living in the facility would get up and get their child or children ready for school. That meant preparing a good breakfast for them and being sure that their clothes were clean and that they had everything they needed for the day at school. All of this was done under the supervision of the life coaches. Then, depending on where they were in their progress, some women would attend classes in basic academic skills and others would attend more advanced classes. Classes in child rearing were an important centerpiece of the curriculum. In the afternoons, they would work with their children on homework and help prepare their evening meal. After dinner and after they put their children to bed, each woman was required to attend a class in manners and etiquette for personal and business applications along with advice on hair and makeup and dressing for success. Many department stores offered their services and merchandise at a deep discount to provide the women with appropriate clothing and accessories.

Adult and child psychologists offered their time the first and third Thursday each month providing individual and group therapy. When the women had been in the program for six months, they graduated and, if they qualified, moved to an apartment in the area where life instructors would be available on a weekly basis to monitor their activities and progress. Most of the women found jobs and began the process toward safe, independent living.

Caroline enlisted doctors, pediatricians, and dentists to volunteer their services to the women and children. Many of them had never received vaccinations and had never been to the dentist. The services and education were life changing for the residents, many of whom were homeless before coming to New Beginnings.

Caroline realized that some of the real estate in the area where the facility was built was for sale at a great price. The economy wasn't good during that time, and real estate values were depressed. Her sense of timing to purchase 165 acres adjacent to the property for the facility was a stroke of luck and brilliance at the same time. Within seven years, she would more than quadruple her $1,100,000 investment.

By February 1979, Caroline was very proud that 80 percent of the women who participated in the program were leading productive lives and providing good homes for their children. They managed to stay out of abusive relationships. Most of them performed well in their jobs and were considered an asset to the company that hired them. New Beginnings was more successful than the judicial system, which rehabilitated only 35 percent of its people. Caroline had a sense of satisfaction and success that she could not explain.

Charlotte was amazed that Caroline had turned a portion of her life that was so sad and so hard to deal with into a joyful endeavor where she helped women and children who had nowhere to turn in abusive and homeless situations.

Garrett's Washington connections, because of his lobbying efforts, soon were aware of Caroline's organization, and she was asked to come to Washington to meet with thirty-five governors to provide information on the details of the operation of the facility and the foundation. Caroline presented her business plan and operation details to a group of very interested governors. Within two years, there was funding in twenty-five states for facilities in inner cities around the country. Caroline engaged an attorney with King and Spalding to draft all of the documents necessary to put such facilities in place and have them run according to her model. She set up training facilities for the people who would run the New Beginnings homes, and reports and inspections were coordinated monthly. The foundation took on a life of its own. Caroline often wondered how she could turn the reins over to a new chairman and become the retired founding chairman.

John was three and a half, and Caroline wanted to spend more time with him and with Garrett. In October 1980, Caroline learned that she was expecting another baby. That was the catalyst she needed to justify stepping aside. A friend of her mother's, who chaired a number of nonprofit foundations in Atlanta, stepped up to take the reins. Caroline would continue in an advisory capacity and would visit the home and be involved in changes to curriculum and operations, but the day-to-day work would be the responsibility of Catherine Winfield Mitchell. Catherine was a forty-six-year-old widow who was independently wealthy and had no children. It was a perfect situation for Caroline and a perfect job for Catherine.

Caroline enjoyed spending more time with John and Garrett. They took trips to Hilton Head, and Caroline and John went with Garrett to Washington several times.

She spent a lot of time in Roswell visiting her mother and Mama Rene with John, and she flew with him to Charleston as often as she could. With the baby due in June, Caroline was busy preparing a nursery.

On a beautiful spring morning in April, Caroline was busy with an interior designer who was helping her with the nursery. They were sitting at her breakfast room table when Charlotte appeared at the back door. When Caroline stood up to greet her mother, she knew immediately when she looked at her that something happened to Mama Rene. "Mama!" Caroline screamed. "Is it Mama Rene?"

"Yes, honey," Charlotte said, and she broke down crying. "She went home during the night. I found her this morning. She was in her bed. She must have died peacefully."

"Oh my God," Caroline cried and sobbed. "My precious Mama Rene. I knew this day would come, and I have been dreading it."

"I know, sweetheart. Me too," Charlotte said, trying to comfort her daughter.

Caroline asked the designer to reschedule their meeting for two weeks from then. She was very sympathetic and left the family alone. Caroline called Garrett at his office. "Garrett," Caroline began.

Garrett could hear in her voice that something was wrong. "What's wrong, Caroline?" he asked quickly, fearing that something was wrong with John.

"It's Mama Rene. She died during the night last night," Caroline said, still sobbing.

"I'll be there within an hour, honey. I am so sorry. I love you," he said.

"I'm going to Roswell with Mama." Caroline hung up the telephone. "Where is she, Mama?" Caroline asked.

"She's at the Roswell Funeral Home, honey," Charlotte said.

Caroline stood, took John to Gail, and told her what happened. Caroline went with Charlotte to Roswell, where she went straight to the funeral home. She walked through the front door and was greeted by an older woman who had worked there for twenty-five years. "Mrs. Winthrop," Gladys Rucker said, "I am very sorry about your grandmother. Everyone loved her so much."

"Thank you, Mrs. Rucker," Caroline said. "I want to see her now."

"Mrs. Winthrop, she only just arrived and is not ready for viewing," Mrs. Rucker said urgently.

"I don't care," Caroline said. "I have to see her now." Mrs. Rucker disappeared behind a door to the left of her desk. She reappeared within a minute with one of the undertakers.

"Mrs. Winthrop," he began, "typically we advise family members to wait until their loved one has been properly dressed before they see them."

"I understand that, and I appreciate your advice, but I want to see my grandmother now," Caroline said, starting to sob.

Charlotte touched Caroline's arm. "Do you want to do this?" she asked.

"Yes," Caroline answered emphatically. She turned back to the undertaker and said, "Take me to her." Her tone was demanding, and to avoid a scene, the gentleman acquiesced to her request. Caroline walked into the preparation room. Irene was lying on a table covered up to her neck. Caroline walked over to her and kissed her. She stroked her hair and cried. "Mama Rene," she said, "I love you so much. It is so hard for me to say good-bye to you. You taught me so much about life. Thank you for sharing so much of your time with me. I can't measure the joy you have given me. One day we will climb trees together again. I hope you will see my daddy and my grandmother. Tell them I love them and I miss them too. Make sure Belle knows how much I miss her. You will always be my angel. Now fly away, my precious Mama Rene." Charlotte was standing beside Caroline sobbing. The undertaker stood behind her and caught her as her knees buckled. Caroline looked at Charlotte and said, "I have never had to live without Mama Rene."

"Me either, honey," Charlotte said as she and the undertaker escorted Caroline out of the room. "I want to go to her house, Mama," Caroline said. Charlotte did not talk but drove straight to the small neat house on Mimosa Boulevard. Caroline walked through the house touching the furniture that she spent so much time on with her grandmother. She walked to the sleeping porch and lay down on the bed where she had taken so many naps with Mama Rene.

She cried for twenty minutes. Charlotte was comforting her to the best of her ability, and Caroline realized that her mother needed comforting too. She got a hold of her emotions and knew she had to work with her mother to prepare for Mama Rene's funeral. Just as they arrived back at Charlotte's house, Garrett pulled in behind them. He got out of his car, walked to Caroline, and engulfed her in his arms. She broke down again. Garrett helped her into the house and then put his arms around Charlotte. "I am so sorry," he said to her. "There is no easy way to get through this."

"No there isn't," Charlotte said. "We just have to face it." Garrett helped them with telephone calls and arrangements. By five o'clock, everything that could be done was done. Garrett asked Charlotte to come home with them for the night. She gladly packed her bag and followed them home.

Charlotte called Ida to tell her to have Grant call her at Caroline's. Grant no longer left the house except for doctor's appointments. He was ninety-one, and his health was steadily failing. He was unable to attend the funeral, but he sent flowers. Caroline knew she would have to face his death soon. She prayed, "Please, not now, Lord." She hoped that He heard her and would not take Grant yet.

Irene's doctor called Charlotte to say that it appeared that her mother had a stroke during the night. He believed that she never felt any pain but just died instantly and peacefully. Charlotte was comforted by that. *Lord knows,* she thought, *Mother had enough physical and emotional pain in her life. Thank God she didn't have any pain when she went home.* Irene was laid to rest in Arlington Cemetery near John's grave.

Geoff was with Charlotte over the next few days, and Caroline observed that he seemed to bring her comfort and made her smile. She was glad that her mother had someone who she enjoyed spending time with. Charlotte was sixty-seven years old, still beautiful and still very engaged in life.

After the funeral, Caroline talked with Garrett about taking John and her mother to Hilton Head. He was very busy in the senator's office and could not take time off. Caroline knew that Charlotte would have plenty to take care of with Mama Rene's house and personal things when they returned. Three days after the funeral, they drove to Hilton Head to a beautiful house on the ocean at Sea Pines. The change of scenery and spending time with John did Charlotte a world of good. They spent four days at the beach. When they returned, Caroline felt better about leaving her mother in Roswell.

Charlotte's attorney helped her probate her mother's will. Irene left everything to Charlotte, Anne, and Nancy equally. Although her estate was small, Charlotte took great care to allow Anne and Nancy to retrieve memories of their mother from her home. It seemed that each one of them wanted a different keepsake, and her small estate was divided and settled with no objections. Charlotte and her sisters decided to keep the house. They couldn't bear to sell it. Caroline had many photographs of Mama Rene, and she framed several of them and put in them in their family room and bedroom.

Memories of her grandmother always made her smile every time she looked at one of the photographs. Nevertheless, she could not shake an emptiness inside. Caroline clung to her mother more than ever.

Love comes at a big emotional price sometimes, Caroline thought to herself. *You put your love and your life into your family and friends, and when they leave, it is so painful to adjust to life without them.* She sometimes wondered if loving to the extent that she did, loving the way her mother and father taught her to love was worth the cost. She loved John so much that there were no words to explain it. She began to worry about losing him.

Caroline went to talk with her pastor at Peachtree Presbyterian Church. She had known Dr. Hansen since she was a little girl attending church with her parents. "Caroline, the emotions you are having now are not unusual for someone who has had so much personal loss at so young an age," he counseled her. "I know you are a Christian and you believe that God has you and your family in His hand. You must also realize that, if you allow Him to, he will help you face anything that life throws your way. You will never be alone as long as He is walking beside you. Take your strength from that. I would like you to read the Sermon on the Mount in Matthew 5, 6, and 7. Also, Jesus made you a promise in Matthew 11:28, 29, and 30. It says, 'Come to Me, all who are weary and heavy-laden, and I will give you rest. Take My yoke upon you and learn from Me, for I am gentle and humble in heart, and you will find rest for your souls. For My yoke is easy and My burden is light.'

"Let Him help you carry this burden. He keeps His promises. You will be glad you let Him help you carry it. So live your life loving everyone the way you do knowing that He is walking every step with you. Caroline, you are never alone."

Caroline cried in her pastor's office and got the comfort and guidance she needed. Dr. Hansen was a wonderful pastor and a fabulous preacher. His impact on her continued. She believed that her grandmother wanted her to love her family and her life as she loved her.

As she reflected on Mama Rene's life, it occurred to her that she never heard her complain about anything. She always tried to bring laughter into any conversation. She had never lived outside of Roswell, but she had a very positive impact on the people she knew and loved. She skillfully guided the people she loved without interfering in their decisions. Caroline decided that day that she would pass that gift on to her children. *Why do we see things more clearly when we lose people we love?* she wondered.

Over the next few weeks, she felt relieved and strong, and her grief turned to joy. Of all people in the world, in spite of the sadness and loss, she was a very lucky person.

CHAPTER 42

ARRETT'S TRAVEL SCHEDULE WAS HECTIC, and he was between Atlanta and Washington quite often during the month of May. He was tying up loose ends getting ready for the birth of their second child. Caroline was working with Catherine Mitchell to get her oriented as she was taking the helm of New Beginnings. Caroline would continue in an advisory capacity, but for now, her family had to come first.

On June 18, 1980, Caroline delivered a beautiful baby girl at Northside Hospital. Garrett was beaming. She had dark hair like her brother. Caroline thought she looked like Garrett. There were no complications, and the baby was perfectly healthy. They agreed to name their daughter Laura Katharine Winthrop. Charlotte's middle name was Katharine. They would call her Katie. Little Katie was noisy and demanding—John had been an easy baby by comparison. There was little sleep for Caroline and Gail for the first three months of Katie's life, but sometime at the beginning of October she seemed to adjust and everyone enjoyed her. John was so proud of his baby sister and tried to help his mother and Gail care for her. He was precious and sweet and very gentle with her. Caroline's heart melted when she saw him loving her the way he did. She knew he would take care of his little sister throughout his life.

Garrett and Caroline decided when Katie was nine months old that they had their family. Garrett had a vasectomy, and they were both glad to be enjoying their sex lives again without thinking about pregnancy. Caroline began traveling to Washington with Garrett again after Katie's first birthday. Many times, Charlotte would come to their home in Vinings to stay with Gail while they were away. Although the children wore her out, she felt young again when she was with them. John and Katie loved their "Grammy." Charlotte told them stories about their grandfather John so he would be real to them.

Laura came to Atlanta as often as she could to visit and help with the children too. Caroline and Garrett had peace of mind when they were away knowing that the children's "Grammy" or "Nana" was on hand to care for them along with Gail. Life was good, and Caroline and Garrett were more in love than ever.

On January 19, 1981, word came from Ida that Grant was in Emory Hospital. His heart muscle just could not pump well enough anymore to sustain his life. Caroline and Charlotte arrived at the hospital two hours before he passed away. He was buried next to Elizabeth in Arlington Cemetery in Sandy Springs. Caroline was sad but relieved that he did not have a long and painful illness. He died with dignity, as he had lived.

Grant left his house to Caroline, and the estate was divided as he told her it would be before she and Garrett got married. Caroline allowed Ida to retire comfortably and saw to it that she was able to purchase a small condominium where she could live her life out worry-free. She had been very loyal to the Wellingtons, and Caroline wanted to care for her. In addition to her Social Security payments, Caroline gave her an annual income of $30,000. With no housing expense, she was happy and had everything she needed. Ida was sixty-eight years old and was still very active. She would live out the rest of her life in comfort.

Caroline began having monthly meetings with her investment advisor at Trust Company and became involved in directing the investments. She did a lot of research and had a very good sense about making profitable investments. Her investment portfolio grew and increased in value in spite of the monthly living expense payments that Caroline withdrew.

The following July, Caroline learned that Charlotte and Geoff would be getting married. He sold his house and planned to move to Roswell with Charlotte. Caroline was thrilled that her mother would have another chance to love and share her life with someone. John had been gone for fifteen years, and Camilla had been gone for thirteen years. Geoff's children were equally thrilled about their father's marriage to Charlotte. Garrett and Caroline thought Charlotte and Geoff were so cute, and they really seemed to enjoy being together. On July 10, 1981, they were married in Charlotte's living room. They went to London for a month for their honeymoon, taking side trips to Paris and Rome. When they returned, they amicably merged their households. A master bedroom suite was added to the lower level of her home. The bedroom had access to the front porch through French doors. It had a fireplace, a sitting room, and a large master bathroom with a separate spa bathtub and shower. The addition was done beautifully and maintained the architectural integrity of the old house.

Charlotte and Geoff enjoyed traveling and being involved in the art community in Atlanta. Between their children and grandchildren and their activities, they stayed busy and were very happy together.

CHAPTER 43

$\mathcal{I}$N DECEMBER 1985, CAROLINE AND Garrett sold the 165 acres they had purchased seven years earlier in Smyrna to a commercial developer for $4.5 million. Rather than pay income tax on the sale, they chose to use an IRS loophole to delay paying taxes on the gain by doing a 1031 tax-free exchange. They bought a six-bedroom home at Seaside, Florida and a six-bedroom home in Highlands, North Carolina. Caroline bought Mama Rene's house too and had a ball decorating the homes.

Seaside was a family-oriented second-home community on the gulf coast of Florida near Destin. The community quickly grew with many Atlanta families purchasing second homes. Many of the parents of John and Katy's friends at Westminster owned homes there, and the children loved to go to the beach and play with their friends from school.

In Highlands, Caroline and Garrett took their children on long hikes, and they went fishing and loved shopping in the small mountain town. The mountains in the summer were a great respite from the Atlanta heat. The Winthrop's and the Wellington's enjoyed Thanksgiving in the mountains and Christmas at the beach almost every year.

New Beginnings continued to do very well. Caroline became the fundraising chairperson of the foundation and managed to raise enough funds to sustain the operations of the home and expand the services for women and children. The success of the program continued to justify the operation and the expense. Most of the women became productive citizens and raised children who were on track to graduate from high school and go on to college.

Foundations continued to be opened up in large cities all over the country based on Caroline's model. She traveled across the United States several times a year speaking to groups of people about the program and working with them to establish the facilities, obtain donors, and attract talented people to work in the facilities. Garrett was her biggest fan, and he lobbied in Washington to his colleagues working in other states for the foundation's benefit.

In 1990, the governor of the state of Georgia approached Caroline about her foundation becoming a state agency. Caroline was hesitant to turn her successful foundation over to a bureaucratic agency. After consulting with her, her attorneys agreed to draw documents that would, for all intents and purposes, circumvent bureaucratic red tape for the women and children applying to get into the program. At the same time, Caroline set up "safe houses" throughout metro Atlanta. She worked through local churches and with members of their congregations to provide temporary housing and food to women and children in crisis who were waiting for a place in the program. The safe-house program became incorporated into the New Beginnings program. Caroline was satisfied that it would be run well, and the governor agreed that she should remain a member of the board of directors of the foundation.

Catherine Mitchell continued as head of the state agency. She loved the work and often travelled with Caroline and by herself to present the model in large cities across the United States.

Caroline could hardly fathom that an idea that came from so many difficult experiences in her life could have been this successful. She thanked God every day for the chance to make a difference in the lives of the women and children that the program touched.

Their lives were hectic, but they managed to spend time alone and time with their children. They took a three-week trip to Europe when Katie was ten and John was thirteen. Both children were thriving at Westminster, and Caroline's life took on a whole new level of busy with their activities. John was a very handsome boy with dark walnut brown hair and crystal blue eyes like his mother. At thirteen he was almost as tall as his father. Katie was a stunning young lady with dark auburn hair and green eyes like her father. Caroline thought she would be taller than she was. John looked so much like Caroline, and Katie was the spitting image of Garrett.

In 1992, Caroline and Garrett celebrated their twentieth wedding anniversary by going back to Maui. They stayed in the same hotel and in the same room where they had spent their ten-day honeymoon. They had time to reflect to the past twenty years, and in spite of the losses and difficulties, they both felt wonderfully blessed.

CHAPTER 44

*C*AROLINE AND GARRETT WERE VERY involved in their children's lives. Sometimes Caroline thought they were too involved, and she remembered her promise to herself to pass along Mama Rene's gift. This gift became very evident when Garrett began trying to persuade John to attend the University of Virginia. John was thoughtful but opinionated. Caroline encouraged Garrett to allow John to make his own decision. Garrett found his son to be a formidable debate opponent and relented when John insisted that he wanted to attend Georgetown University in Washington. Caroline hoped that one of their children would go to UVA, but she knew better than to push them in a direction that suited her more than it did them.

In 1995, John graduated from Westminster and left for Georgetown University. He had traveled to Washington with his father often during his life. Garrett thought it was important to allow him to see and experience what he did and get a taste of life in the seat of power for the greatest country in the world. John had an interest in politics that went far beyond his father's. Because of that exposure, John decided to become a lawyer. He believed it was never too soon to make contacts to help you in the future. His ultimate goal was to be in the US Senate. Garrett and Caroline agreed that he would be a great senator, and they encouraged his decision.

In 1998, Katie graduated from Westminster and went to Duke University in Durham, North Carolina. Caroline felt good about her children's decisions and the fact that she supported them and had not made the decision for them. Katie was kind-hearted but was a force to be reckoned with when she became determined about something. Caroline believed that Katie was exactly like her mother. Her mother's gift to Katie was like Mama Rene's gift to her, in a different way.

Katie had very different interests than John's. Their personalities were as opposite as they could be. John was serious, but Katie was social and personable. She had an aptitude for science and biology and told her parents that she wanted to be a pediatrician. Her parents thought she would be a wonderful pediatrician, and Duke had a fabulous school of medicine.

It was hard to believe that both their children were grown up and off to college. *Where in the world did the years go?* Caroline often thought.

Once again, Caroline and Garrett were home alone. Garrett was still working in Atlanta, but now he was a lobbyist for the legal industry. Caroline traveled with him often, and they managed to see their children at college frequently as they made their rounds in Washington and North Carolina.

In 2000, Caroline began writing her memoirs. In the process, she realized that everything that had happened to her during her life, even the tragedies and sadness, had molded her into the person she became. She forgave her father posthumously for his alcoholism and for being abusive to mother. That process was painful and joyful at the same time. The part of her that needed to be the founder of New Beginnings, which helped so many people, came from that part of her life. Her father had done amazing work at Georgia Life that, in part, created the wealth that she and her mother enjoyed during their lives and after his death. Over the years, she believed that she felt his loving and guiding hand in her decisions. Garrett's tenacity in pursuing their relationship would always be miraculous to her. She could not imagine her life without him. Through his love, finally, she learned how to enjoy her life. Mama Rene and her mother taught her the joy of unselfish love, and her mother, especially, taught her how to have courage and strength in the face of overwhelming adversity. She showed her by her actions that holding grudges and being angry only hurt you and did nothing to solve the issues. Her grandfather taught her the art of humility and by his example taught her that anyone could change a temperament of greed and hostility into one of generosity and love. She would always give her grandmother credit for those changes in him. And, Belle, precious Belle, taught her the joy and satisfaction of serving others. Belle's loving and generous nature was part of her inspiration for New Beginnings.

She would share her written memories with her children when they were older in the hope that it would give them a perspective about life and love that she wished she had when she was young. The choices to live, enjoy their lives, and feel free to love without fear of loss was foremost in her mind.

Caroline marveled at the changes that had occurred since her birth in 1948. She had experienced five decades of unprecedented change, and now at the millennium she was beginning a new century. She thought how her mother and grandparents felt about the changes they saw during their lives. Electricity became common in homes during her grandparents' lives. Automobiles were invented. Interstate highways were built during her and her parents' childhoods, and computers were developed during her lifetime. Today, almost everyone used cell phones. She wondered what changes would occur by the time her children were her age.

She and Garrett had two positively beautiful and brilliant children who were happy and enjoying their lives. Caroline was very thankful that neither of them had to endure the sadness and tragedy that she had to endure when she was so young. She believed that they taught her at least as much as she taught them.

The couple spent many days in Florida at their Seaside home sitting on the porch overlooking the ocean and continuing to enjoy their love and friendship. They would sit by the fire in the den of their Highlands home drinking coffee and reflecting on the wonderful memories they shared and their plans for the future. They agreed to sell their home in Vinings and bought a three-bedroom condominium in Atlanta near Garrett's office when he was in town. They wanted to have enough room for John and Katy when they came home.

One late spring evening as they sat on the porch at their Seaside home, Caroline said, "Have you ever noticed that no sunset is exactly the same here?"

"I never get tired of seeing them," Garrett replied, obviously relaxed in his lounge chair and enjoying the ocean breeze.

"Life is filled with so many choices," Caroline said, lying back in her lounge chair and looking up at the evening sky.

"Somehow I knew our lives would be wonderful together," Garrett shared philosophically. "You know I almost didn't call you to ask you to dinner that day when I was in Atlanta. There was a nagging voice in the back of my mind that kept prodding me to call you."

"Garrett, you never told me that," Caroline said, faking her irritation. "So why did you call me?"

"You know the answer to that," Garrett said. He leaned over and kissed her.

"I feel so lucky," she said.

Garrett looked at her for more than a minute before he spoke. "I love you, beautiful."

Caroline smiled as a tear ran down her cheek.

Belle's Recipes

Shhhh . . . y'all don't share these with just anybody, ya' hear?
Makes your family *love* comin' home.

❦ *Belle's Biscuits* ❧

2 cups self-rising White Lily flour
Dash of salt
½ teaspoon sugar
3 tablespoons Crisco all-vegetable shortening
½ cup buttermilk
½ cup sweet milk
1 tablespoon water
1 tablespoon melted butter

Sift flour, salt, and sugar together into mixing bowl. Cut in
shortening until mixture is coarse. Add buttermilk, sweet milk, water,
and 1 tablespoon melted butter.
Mix lightly until mixed well. Do not over mix. Pour mixture onto a
lightly floured surface. Knead dough two to three times. With floured
hands, pat out dough to approximately ½ inch thickness. Cut with
floured biscuit cutter. Do not twist cutter. Bake at 475 degrees for
10-12 minutes until golden brown. Brush with melted butter after
removing from oven.

❧ Belle's Homemade Pimento Cheese ❧

Block of Cracker Barrel Gold Label sharp cheddar cheese,
finely grated
Block of Cracker Barrel Gold Label mild cheddar cheese, finely grated
(you can cheat and get the already grated cheese if you want to)
8 oz. jar of pimentos—drain ½ the liquid
8 oz. of real mayonnaise (not low-fat)

Add 1 tablespoon of white pepper, one tablespoon of paprika,
and 1 teaspoon of kosher salt
Mix thoroughly.
Keep leftovers refrigerated

❧ Belle's Fried Chicken ❧

4-6 boneless or bone-in chicken breasts
In a bowl, put ½ cup flour for each chicken breast
Add1 heaping tablespoon salt for each chicken breast
(kosher salt is best)
Add 6 heaping tablespoons paprika
Add 1 tablespoon ground black pepper

Place chicken breasts in a bowl. Cover them with whole sweet milk.
Salt the milk generously. Soak chicken in milk and dredge in
thoroughly combined flour mixture. Put into hot skillet (medium
high heat) with safflower or other vegetable oil so that chicken
is more than half covered by oil. Allow chicken to brown before
turning. Turn frequently after browning on both sides to desired
crispness. Drain on paper towels.

❧ Belle's Creamed Potatoes ❧

(You might call them mashed potatoes.)

5-pound bag of Yukon Gold potatoes, peeled and cubed
In large Dutch oven, cover potatoes in water.
Salt and cook until tender.
Drain potatoes in colander and place in large mixing bowl.
8 oz. heavy cream
2 sticks of real butter
Small container of sour cream
Salt and pepper to taste

With mixer, combine drained, hot, cooked potatoes with 4 oz.
heavy whipping cream
Add 2 sticks of butter—melt slightly before adding
Add container of sour cream
Continue to add heavy cream until potatoes are creamy but not runny.
Keep warm before serving.